I0639296

Heroes

Sylvia Massara

Published by Tudor ENT, 2024.

Published by Tudor Ent
Sydney, Australia
Copyright © 2024 Sylvia Massara
Sylvia Massara asserts the moral right to
be identified as the author of this work.
A catalogue entry for this book is available
from the National Library of Australia.
ISBN: 978-0-9875475-9-0

Titles by Sylvia Massara

Romantic comedy:
Like Casablanca
The Other Boyfriend

Contemporary drama:
The Soul Bearers

Historical fiction/modern fiction/
action romance:
Heroes

Mia Ferrari mystery trilogy:
Playing With the Bad Boys
The Gay Mardi Gras Murders
The South Pacific Murders

Sci-fi apocalyptic romance:
The Stranger

~ In memory of Belinda Woodhouse neé Mainwaring ~
1963 - 2016
~ In memory of Carol Hynson ~
1963 – 2022

"We can be heroes
just for one day..."
~ David Bowie, from his title track of the album "Heroes"
Released in Berlin, Germany, 1977

Chapter 1 - Samantha

<u>4th of July, 1985, Berlin, Germany</u>

Today is the 4th of July, not only American Independence Day, but also the day I might meet with my father.

I look out the window of my room at Pension Fasanen, a surprisingly inexpensive family run hotel on Fasanen Strasse, located just around the corner from the renowned and fashionable Ku-damm or Kurfürstendamm Avenue, to give it its proper name, which is considered to be the Champs-Élysées of Berlin. The streets and avenues around this area are filled with high-end shops, department stores, hotels, bars, restaurants, cafes, and trendy nightclubs.

I love the feel of Berlin, where the present lives alongside the past reminding people of a glorious epoch that ended with the defeat of the Third Reich. Berlin was considered a cultural mecca in bygone days, one often envied by other European cities, but it only took Hitler and WWII to destroy its reputation of pomp and elegance, so when the Allies marched into the city in 1945, Berlin remained silent for a very long time. Despite this, its spirit never left and over the years the city reinvented itself.

I have been coming to this vibrant place for eight years in a row, always during the week surrounding the 4th of July, and all of a sudden a wave of expectation consumes me with thoughts of how my father and I would celebrate this day together.

A knock at the door startles me and I cross the room with my heart beating wildly. "Yes?" I call out expectantly even though I know it is not my father on the other side of the door; I recognise the voice of Herr Groth instead, the owner of Pension Fasanen.

"Fräulein Kelly, *essen Sie heute Abend hier im Hotel?*"

My German is rusty, but I understand Herr Groth is saying something about eating at the hotel this evening. The 4th of July, being a major event for the city, means one has to have dinner reservations due to the major festivities and the thousands of tourists and military personnel descending upon the glittering excitement that is Berlin on this particular night. There probably won't be a single restaurant or café that isn't full of patrons.

I open the door and smile at the rotund little man. "*Danke, Herr Groth, nicht heute Abend.*"

Herr Groth switches to English. "Ah! You have other plans, yes?"

"I'm going to watch the fireworks. Besides, I'm not really hungry."

"You're too skinny, *Fräulein*," Herr Groth remarks with fatherly concern. "But if you change your mind, let me know and I'll arrange a tray for you. The restaurant is open until late this evening."

I smile my thanks. "I appreciate your kindness."

"You are welcome. Have a good evening." He gives me a little bow and walks away.

I close the door and go back to the window wondering what Herr Groth would say if I told him I couldn't afford to eat in the dining room. My funds are depleting quickly, but one way to save money is to buy bread and cold cuts at a local market. I learned this over my many years of living in a major city like London, where I busk with my guitar and work the odd pub gig for a living.

The fireworks and celebrations reign over the city while I walk the streets. The noise is deafening, especially when the Americans fly overhead in a spectacular demonstration of their fighter jets, which adds to the merry atmosphere and excitement of the crowd.

I see exhilarated young girls heading towards pubs and nightclubs followed by a multitude of American GIs and personnel from other military sectors, predominantly the UK and France. The boys are wearing their best uniforms ready for a night of revelry while around them are the local folks of West Berlin plus a horde of tourists, and I cannot help but wonder what the people living in East Berlin think of the merrymaking atmosphere on our side of the Wall.

HEROES

The traffic in the streets is heavy and I'm glad I chose to walk to Potsdamer Platz, which is hosting one of the better firework displays. I suppose I could have taken the U-Bahn and arrived at my destination within minutes, but I love walking through the city absorbing the sights and enjoying the thrill of this very special night.

As I get closer to my destination, I find the crowd is much thicker than I thought and it is difficult for me to walk freely. Instead, I have to push my way through the many revellers that are drinking and dancing all around me, and on a number of occasions I lose my footing and almost trip and fall.

In hindsight, I tell myself, it was not such a great idea to come here after all. I could have chosen a number of other spots from which to view the fireworks, but I keep coming back to Potsdamer Platz because this is where my father told me to meet him.

I remember he used to describe this outdoor area where one could see over the heavily graffitied Wall on the western side of Berlin and peek across the field dividing East from West. This is where the towers with armed guards stand to attention and each side can see the other beyond the Wall, but the distance between the two points, called the death strip, is heavily fortified with guards, barbed and tripwires, and other deadly traps.

No one really knows how many people have died since the Wall was erected in 1961. Some put the number at close to six hundred out of almost one hundred thousand escape attempts so far. However, the exact number of casualties is unknown seeing as guards don't worry too much about numbers plus the fact that they're encouraged to shoot to kill when they see escapees and those who attempt to help them escape.

When I was a child, I once asked my father why he liked this desolate and sad place with such a violent history and he said: *"One day when you're older, I'll tell you everything and I'll take you to Berlin to visit the Wall on the 4th of July."* I had just turned eight years old at the time and I never discovered what he meant because a few months after our conversation he disappeared from my life forever.

Despite the warmth of the evening made worse by the humidity of summer and the legions of people advancing towards the plaza, I push on. Memories of talks with my father haunt me as they do every time I visit this city and I ask myself why I even think I will find him. Perhaps it's because growing up pretty much alone my dream has always been to find the only parent I loved, but after getting no information from my estranged mother regarding my father's whereabouts, I have nothing to go on with. I shake my head in frustration and manage just in time to avoid a collision with another merry group of revellers.

Finally, I arrive at my destination feeling somewhat lightheaded. I should've stopped to buy something to eat and bottled water to slake my thirst, but it's too late now to walk back and look for a sandwich bar. I feel hot and tired and my only thought is to reach the Wall so I can lean against it before I fall into the crowd. My T-shirt sticks to me like a second skin and I curse myself for having worn jeans that make me feel even warmer.

A sudden wave of panic engulfs me and my mind tells me I have to get to the Wall and rest. I push through yet another bunch of merrymakers and then the world starts to spin. I fall backwards and everything goes black.

"Entschuldigen Sie bitte! Entschuldigen Sie bitte!" I hear a man shout 'Excuse me' above the noise of the crowd. I want to open my eyes, but my eyelids seem to have a life of their own and they refuse to open. I feel the gentle sway of whatever is supporting my supine body and I can only guess I'm lying on a stretcher. I hear the fireworks exploding high up in the sky and the oohs and aahs of the delighted crowd: yelling, laughing, and cheering above the din around me.

I want to get away from the noise, but I can't seem to be able to move. My heart is beating rapidly and I'm finding it difficult to breathe. I want to scream for help, but my voice doesn't work and my tongue feels like it's stuck to the roof of my mouth. I'm sure I'm dying, but then I feel the coolness of a wet cloth wiping at my face and lips, and a few drops

4

of water slip into my mouth. I swallow greedily while the same man who was shouting earlier calls out to someone nearby, "Hey! Throw me that bottle of water. She's conscious." The swaying of the stretcher stops for a moment and within seconds I feel the rim of a water bottle at my lips while someone's hand raises my head slightly.

"Take a few small sips and drink slowly, not too fast or the water will go down the wrong way." I manage to nod and do as he instructs, but something about him is strange. "Slowly, slowly," he repeats. "Just a few sips and we'll get you into the ambulance. You're safe and you're going to be okay."

My entire body begins to relax at the reassuring tone in his voice. I'm safe and I'm going to be okay, he says, and I hold on to his promise and drink a few more sips of water until he takes away the bottle like he seems to know I've had enough. My eyes are still not ready to open, but suddenly I know what's strange about the man: he switched from German to fluent English. How does he know I speak English and not German? I feel too tired to try and figure this out. All I want is to get away from the noise around me and when I feel the swaying of the stretcher once again I fully relax to its rhythm.

<hr />

I become aware of the quietness around me, except for low beeps from some kind of monitor and soft footsteps passing to and fro. My eyes open easily and I find myself in a hospital cubicle lying in bed and hooked up to whatever is beeping.

The first thing I see is the attractive face of a man with blue eyes and longish blond hair falling over his brow. He leans towards me with a smile. "Welcome back," he says in English. "How do you feel?"

"Better, thank you, or at least I think so. Are you the doctor?"

He shakes his head. "No. I'm kind of helping out. You fainted and fell against me before you hit the ground with your head. I was nearby and called the ambulance."

"I remember your voice. You're the one who brought me water."

"You were lucky you didn't hit the pavement full on or you could've split your head open. Fortunately, falling in my direction broke the full impact of the fall."

I want to ask him for more details, but my thoughts are jumbled. Hopefully, the doctor will tell me what's going on. "Thank you for helping me," I say. "Is there any water here?"

The man turns to a cabinet near my bed and hands me a container with water and a drinking straw. "I'm not sure I should raise your bedhead before the doctor arrives so I'll check with the nurse first. Can you wait a moment?"

I nod and he disappears through the cubicle curtains, but he's back in a short while. "The nurse says it's okay as long as you don't sit up all the way. The doctor will be along soon to check you out, but you can have a few sips of water." He raises my bedhead a little and I sip some of the refreshing liquid while he sits in the visitor's chair by the bed and watches me drink.

I feel self-conscious, especially when I realise I'm wearing a hospital gown with nothing on underneath, except my knickers. I hope he doesn't see me blushing so in order to distract him, I say, "I've been meaning to ask how you knew I spoke English. I couldn't speak after I bumped my head, but I heard everything you said to me at the time and I'm grateful for your reassurance."

"I found a wallet on you and looked through it so I could pass on any relevant information to the ambulance guys. You have a UK health card."

I nod. "That's right. I live in the UK and I'm only here for a visit."

"Is there someone I can call for you; family, friends?"

"No. I'll be okay. I just wish to thank you yet again for all the trouble you took for me, and your English is perfect by the way."

He smiles as he flicks back the long fringe of hair over his eyes. "Well, that's easy," he replies, "I'm English, too."

"Oh, I see! But it sounds to me like your German's quite fluent."

"I travel to Germany a lot and I also used to live here in Berlin for a number of years." It seems as if he's going to tell me more, but just then the doctor enters the cubicle and goes straight for my chart, which is hanging at the end of the bed. My rescuer stands up.

"Miss Kelly, right?" the doctor reads off the chart. "Samantha Kelly?"

"Yes, doctor."

"I'm Dr Werner." The doctor says in fluent English and then turns to my rescuer, "And you are family?"

"No. I'm the one who called the ambulance. My name's Luke Hart." He shakes hands with the doctor.

"Well done, Mr Hart. It must've been hell out there with that crowd partying this evening."

Luke smiles in accord and the doctor turns back to my chart. "Miss Kelly, you're free to go," he announces. "All tests came back negative and your vital signs are back to normal." He draws a business card out of his pocket and hands it to me. "Any strong headaches, dizziness, double vision, nausea or any other symptom of concern and you come right back to the hospital and ask for me."

"Thank you very much, doctor." I suddenly feel buoyant and my relief knows no bounds. I'm okay after all.

"Your clothes are in the cupboard next to your bed so once you're ready see the ward nurse and she'll sign you off." Dr Werner smiles, shakes my hand, nods at Luke, and he disappears from the cubicle.

"Wow!" I say. "I guess I can sit up then."

"I'll let you get dressed, and please allow me to escort you back to wherever you're staying. The atmosphere's quite wild out there and I want to make sure you're okay."

"Thank you, Luke, but why are you being so nice?" My guard always goes up when someone offers to do something for me without asking for anything in return. I call this the result of having had a rough upbringing.

Luke doesn't seem to notice the tone of caution in my question. "Why? I always try to be nice, that's why. You were injured and while cleared by the doctor you still have to rest. A taxi will cost you a fortune considering the traffic tonight and I'm not in the habit of abandoning anybody to the somewhat murky fate of a late trip on the U-Bahn."

I laugh, feeling secretly relieved. "You're on then. And Luke, thank you once again."

He smiles. "You're welcome. I'll meet you by the nurse's desk."

Chapter 2 - Robert

<u>4th of July, 1945, Berlin, Germany</u>

I put off writing in this journal ever since I arrived in Europe in 1943. My best friend, Ollie, gave me this book as a gift upon our graduation from senior high school. We were both elated to be able to join the war effort immediately so we celebrated the occasion with a small gift.

I gave Ollie a Swiss army knife that I purchased from a pawn shop in New York City and told him it would come in handy for peeling and cooking potatoes over a campfire. I remember we laughed, knowing we were embarking on the biggest adventure of our lives. We were eighteen years old and ready to take on the world—little did I know at the time that my friend's life would come to an abrupt end.

On completion of basic training in the States and only a short three weeks after deployment to Europe, Ollie was killed in action at the Battle of Sicily in July, 1943.

The hardest thing I had to do was write a letter to his parents to let them know their son had died swiftly, with no pain. I imagined my letter would have arrived a long time after the official military telegram sent to families of the dead, and I was sure my little white lie about a painless death would provide some comfort to Ollie's parents; this was better than getting the telegram from the US War Department formally announcing their son's demise.

Despite this, I felt a fraud for sending the letter because I had no idea how Ollie truly died. We were stationed at different strategic attack areas, which were miles apart, so I never even saw his body. I was simply informed of his death by one of Ollie's regiment buddies way after the battle took place, and the guy only knew Ollie was dead because he saw his name on a casualty list. Therefore, I could only pray my best friend had been fatally shot rather than left to suffer the agonies of a slow death.

It was after Ollie's passing that I ripped out and burned the pages of my journal, where I had initially written entries about our experiences in the war, but after the death of my friend I closed the journal, vowing never to write in it again. I only kept the book itself, with its blank pages, for the sake of Ollie's memory and his gift to me.

The war went on and I with it, waiting for an end just like Ollie's, but somehow luck was on my side and I lived to see the defeat of the Nazi devils. VE Day (Victory in Europe Day) came and went on May 8th, 1945, and a short two months later on July 4th, American Independence Day, we took charge of our occupation sector in southwest Berlin.

Our troops marched into an almost obliterated city and I wished that somehow Ollie could have joined in our victory—and perhaps he did. I imagined him looking down on us from a window in the sky, smiling and happy that his death, and that of the millions of people who had lost their lives in this awful war, had not been totally in vain.

With this one journal entry, I ended up breaking my vow about never writing in the journal again because I finally have a reason to start feeling optimistic. The war is over and I can now record whatever is in store for me in the future; hopefully, it will be a good one.

I won't be able to record anything about Ollie because he's gone forever, but in my heart he will always be my very best friend.

Chapter 3 - Samantha

<u>5th July, 1985, Berlin, Germany</u>

I hear the loud sound of an ambulance in my ears, but at the same time I know I'm in my bed at Pension Fasanen. How can this be? I open my eyes to see what's going on and it is then I realise I must've been dreaming. It's not an ambulance but the telephone on my bedside table that's ringing. I glance at the digital clock next to the phone, it's almost eleven and I sit up in surprise. I recall having gone to bed early last night, but I don't remember anything else. I obviously slept right through the night.

The insistent ringing reminds me that someone is waiting to speak with me so I pick up the receiver. "Hello?" My voice is croaky due to a dry throat and I look around the room to try and locate my water bottle, which I see resting on the vanity top in the bathroom. Damn!

"Samantha? It's Luke. Are you ready?"

What the hell is he talking about? And then it dawns on me: last night, when he escorted me back to the hotel, we agreed to meet for a late breakfast at ten. I forgot all about it!

"Samantha, are you okay?" Luke's voice sounds concerned.

"Just hold a moment." I drop the receiver on the bed and rush to the bathroom where I retrieve my water bottle and take a long drink until the croakiness in my throat disappears. I then return to the phone and pick up the receiver, my voice back to normal. "I'm back and I'm so sorry to have kept you waiting. I was exhausted and slept right through. In fact, if you hadn't called I would've kept on sleeping."

"Oh," he sounds contrite, "I should've thought of that. Of course you'd want to rest, but Samantha, you haven't told me how you're feeling this morning."

"Much better, thank you, but quit calling me Samantha because I turn around and think I'm going to be scolded by my mother. Just call me Sam."

There's a tone of laughter in his voice when he replies, "Got that, Sam. As for our breakfast, well, we should've made it lunch to give you more time to rest." He pauses for a moment and I think we've been disconnected, but his voice is back in seconds. "I was just thinking why don't we make it lunch after all? I'm free today."

Free? Does this mean he doesn't work or is it just his day off? And if he works, what does he do for a living? Did he even tell me last night? I can't recall. Anyway, I'll just have to play it by ear. It was very nice of him to take me back to the hotel and it's certainly worth a lunch date; furthermore, I'll insist he lets me pay for it. "Okay," I say to him. "How about we meet in the hotel's foyer at noon?"

"You're on. I'll see you soon." We ring off and I run for the shower. I can't wait to feel the hot water clear away the memories of my accident. I have enough time to wash and dry my hair plus change my clothes from last night, which I didn't even bother to take off when I went to sleep.

At exactly noon, I come down the stairs from my first floor room and I make my way to the small foyer by the hotel's front desk. Luke smiles a greeting from the entrance door and I blush. At the risk of sounding vain, I know I look good in white jeans and a yellow blouse that makes a pleasant contrast with my wavy, shoulder-length red hair, and I'm glad I made the effort to blow-dry it. I normally don't bother with such things as hair and make-up, but this morning I decided to do so and I even added a little mascara and a dash of lipstick.

I figure if I'm going to thank Luke for rescuing me, I have to make an effort to look decent. Normally, I'm a blue jeans and T-shirt girl that uses lip balm to keep her lips from drying. I like the natural look, especially when I go busking. This is important because bare of make-up, I look much younger than my twenty-three years, and people tend to throw coins at the younger buskers. So in my jeans and T-shirt and with a natural look I'm often taken for a teenager.

Thinking about age, I suddenly wonder how old Luke is. He also seems to be a jeans and T-shirt person, and today this is exactly what he's wearing: white T-shirt and blue jeans with black leather ankle boots. He's leaning near the doorway, sunglasses on, and with his slim but toned build he reminds me of a cool character from a Hollywood movie.

I shake my head at the silly notion and try to work out what he does for a living. Hopefully, he's not a rebel without a cause so I try to picture him as some kind of rebel with a real cause, but I come up blank. The guy could be anything, but in his current get-up he fits into several categories like male model, actor, artist or even a musician. Whatever the case, there's definitely an artistic air about him that goes with his devil-may-care looks.

"Hey there," he says when I reach him. "Hungry?"

I nod. "Most definitely. I missed breakfast, remember?"

We laugh and walk out of the hotel. "So where are we going?" I ask.

"Do you like Italian?"

"Yes."

We walk in the direction of the Ku-damm and I start to feel somewhat anxious. The Ku-damm, with many of the best cafes and restaurants in Berlin, means that this is going to be pricey. I mentally start to go through my budget while Luke chats about the city and points out some landmark of interest that I should see. In the meantime, I'm trying to work out how I'm going to pay for this lunch.

Luke suddenly stops walking and I bump into him, tripping over his foot. His hands reach out to steady me. "Are you okay?"

"I'm so sorry," I say, feeling embarrassed. "Sometimes I don't know what planet I'm on. Normally, I'm not this clumsy. Did I hurt your foot?"

"Not at all. Come on, we're here." He takes hold of my forearm and guides me into Gianni's. The place is buzzing with patrons and as soon as we enter the aroma of strong coffee and delicious Italian fare makes my stomach rumble with hunger.

"*Ciao, Luke! Per due?*" A tall and handsome young man calls out from behind a bar counter.

"*Si, grazie, Gianni,*" Luke responds as Gianni beckons him for a moment.

I know some Italian and from his confident demeanour it seems this Gianni guy is the café owner. The fact that he's friendly with Luke, plus the way he gazes my way, makes me think he's also familiar with the many times Luke brings a female guest to lunch. I look towards the bar counter and see Gianni currently engaged in a short but very fast Italian conversation with Luke, so I also learn that Luke is fluent in two languages besides English.

The men catch up with me and Gianni greets me in English and shows us to our table—a corner one with a view of the Ku-damm. We sit and while Gianni goes through the specials I make a mental sum, yet again, of the diminishing limit on my credit card balance, and I pray whatever's left is enough for me to pay my hotel bill.

Luke recommends we have pizza. Apparently, Gianni's is renowned throughout Berlin for its German salami pizza, made locally. We decide to share an extra large pizza topped with fresh local vegetables and the so-called German salami, which is supposedly to die for. We order a couple of coffees and a bottle of mineral water to share.

Gianni takes our order and then says to Luke, "Big crowd for tomorrow night, so I hope you're ready."

"I'll be ready. Don't you worry," Luke assures him.

"Good thing, too, because we're starting to get bookings well in advance now that people know you're a regular." Gianni smiles and walks away.

"The lunch is on me as a thank you for all your help," I say while I'm dying to find out what kind of 'regular' Luke is supposed to be.

"In that case I'll have to take a rain check because today's lunch is actually on Gianni." Luke regards me with amusement in his eyes.

"Well, that's very nice of him." I feel relieved that I don't have to dig into my credit card and at the same time I feel bolder of spirit because I want to find out more about my companion. "You know, in my experience, when someone gets a freebie people expect something in return."

Luke laughs at my comment just as our coffees arrive. "Good grief!" he exclaims. "How old are you, forty; fifty?"

"You're implying I'm too cynical for someone young." I now regret having made the comment in the first place and I have to defend myself.

Luke says, "I guess, but I don't really know you well enough to judge." He stirs one sugar into his coffee and I add one into my cappuccino while feeling a little put out with him, treating me as if I were a child. He's right in one thing, though, he doesn't really know me and yet for some reason I can't let his comment go without a comeback.

"If you must know, I'm twenty-three, and you should never prejudge people. One thing I learned is that we never really know the kind of life someone's had at any age, so younger people can be quite mature just as older people can be immature. It all comes down to their life experience, I guess."

Luke reaches across the table and pats my hand. "I'm sorry. Of course you're right, and I agree with what you say about not prejudging people. I should've reacted in a different way, but the last thing I want is to make you feel uncomfortable by asking you what kind of life you've had so far."

He really hit the nail on the head and now I do feel uncomfortable. My fault, but I'm not about to divulge my entire life story to someone I met yesterday just because he thinks I'm cynical. "Thank you," I tell him. "I appreciate your candour." Luke nods, but says nothing. I remark, "Well, let's start again, shall we? And you can tell me why people are making bookings in advance to see you. You're not some kind of celeb, are you?" I smile at him.

Luke smiles back. "Okay, I'm willing to reveal a small part of my life and tell you why I'm a 'regular'."

"I'm all ears." Just then, the pizza arrives and we dig in and I'm relieved we moved past our previous discussion.

Luke takes a few bites of his pizza and then refreshes his mouth with mineral water. "How do you like the salami?"

"Great," I respond. "It's smokier than the Italian style, but at least not as spicy."

He agrees and tops up my glass with water.

"So," I say before picking up another slice of pizza, "tell me why you're a regular."

"I'm a musician and I do a gig here every other Saturday."

My heart jolts with excitement—a fellow muso! I say nothing, however, and let him continue talking.

"I live in London, as I mentioned to you at the hospital, but I spend a few months out of the year here in Berlin. My main gig is at a place called Ku-dorf."

I'm impressed. "Wow, that's great! Ku-dorf is the largest nightclub in Berlin, so you must be pretty good."

He smiles. "Why? Did you expect me to be bad?"

"No. I meant if you perform at Ku-dorf then you pretty much got it made."

"It's not what you think, Sam. Having a couple of gigs pays me enough to live on, but I wouldn't say I've got it made. I don't seek to make it big, in any case. Fact is, I'm a bit of a lone wolf and I like my life the way it is—uncomplicated."

Suddenly, I'm bursting to tell him just how much we have in common, minus the money, that is, and at least he can afford to live on his income. I feel his gaze on me as if he's trying to work me out, but I'm not yet ready to reveal too much about myself. "I can understand where you're coming from," I say instead. "I'm also a lone wolf and I live in London, as you've learned from my health card, and for the past eight years I've been coming to Berlin during the week surrounding the 4th of July." Luke throws me a curious glance and waits for me to continue, but I don't disclose why I visit Berlin yearly, instead I say, "I'm a muso, too, as it happens. I busk in the streets more than anything else, but I do manage to get a number of gigs from time to time. In fact, now and then I play at The Treble and Bass at Covent Garden."

I detect a look of real interest in his eyes. "Well, we have more in common than I thought. While waiting for the ambulance yesterday, I had a feeling you were a fellow muso."

"How so?"

"When I helped you sip water from the bottle your hands touched mine for a moment and I felt the calluses on your fingertips. Mostly guitarists have those."

"You're very observant," I reply and we then go on talking all afternoon and late into the evening about our music and passion for living a life without ties and our earlier exchange about cynicism totally forgotten.

While we converse, I keep having a sense of déjà vu because it feels as if we've known each other for years and we agree on so many things. Something seems so right about our encounter and I don't necessarily mean in a romantic sense, even though I find Luke attractive and I'm drawn to him, but I mean an encounter tantamount to finally having a feeling of close friendship and belonging. Somewhere during our conversation I learn Luke is twelve years my senior so he could turn out to be the older and wiser friend I never had.

Chapter 4 - Robert

The demobilization (demob) of the US armed forces began in May, 1945, and continued through 1946. Berlin was still a broken city and it would be years before it claimed back pieces of its former glory.

What used to be the city center was a complete wasteland with parks, especially the Tiergarten, having been denuded of trees so Berliners could use them for firewood. Buildings in commercial and business centers were destroyed and any structure still standing in what was considered to be a strategic location was totally degutted.

I presumed the Nazis themselves would have destroyed much of their capital rather than hand it over to the enemy, but not much had survived aside from average type buildings, now mostly uninhabitable. There were some exceptions, however, like the Brandenburg Gate and the Olympic Stadium, the latter built for the 1936 Berlin Olympics. I read somewhere that the Brandenburg Gate was commissioned by the Prussian Emperor, Frederick William II in the late 1700s, so the gate had a good run of luck over time. Its original name meant 'Peace Gate' and this might end up being a positive omen for the future. As for the Stadium, the Nazis were determined to make the 1936 Olympics a memorable showcase for Aryan physical superiority, and the place still stood, but the physical superiority had come down a notch or two. How is that for irony?

In the end, the only structure that proved to be useful was the Berlin transport network with its underground subway, the U-Bahn; the above-ground S-Bahn plus a network of tramlines, many of which had been destroyed. Some areas of the U-Bahn had also sustained damage. Despite this, the transport system kept the population moving and the train network was the only lifeblood of the city, which the Allies made sure kept running along. At the time of our arrival, automobiles were few and far between and gasoline was still in short supply, but once the Allies took over the city they slowly began to make the place more livable.

Meanwhile, people were starving and looked through the city wreckage in the hope of finding something they could use or sell in exchange for food. Children begged in the streets for cigarette butts from occupying soldiers and if they were lucky they could swap the butts for edible items, but if they couldn't get any food they would turn the butts over to their fathers to smoke.

There weren't many jobs to be had either, and families economized by living together with other families in the wreckage of buildings that still stood, and these were the lucky Berliners. Others, especially young women and girls without family or friends, were forced to turn tricks—prostitution in exchange for a chance at survival.

During this time, the setting up of military government organizations was a priority and the Allies requisitioned well-positioned real estate in what was left of the city. As it was, the former Luftwaffe district headquarters in Berlin-Zehlendorf, which still had some buildings left standing, became our US Headquarters in the city.

Once the war ended for those of us in Europe, we wanted to know when we could go back home. Unfortunately, it wasn't going to be immediately or easy. The demobilization was predicted to be a huge exercise plus the war in Asia was still raging with the Japanese who were not looking to give up any time soon, so many of the European divisions were sent off to fight yet another war.

I was fortunate. My division was not selected for the war in Asia. In fact, it looked like we would be held up in Berlin for quite some time while the Allies went about organizing demob, not just for Germany, but for the whole of Europe.

In the end, things worked out very well for me. I was commissioned to work at US Headquarters in Berlin, assisting in all things administration for the big demob project.

This was just as well. I liked the work, I was safely housed and fed, and above all, I met my destiny—her name is Clara.

Chapter 5 - Samantha

<u>6th July, 1985, Berlin, Germany</u>

After our long chat yesterday, Luke and I walked the streets of Berlin by night and then he dropped me off by taxi at my hotel. He invited me to his gig for Saturday evening and I accepted, pecked his cheek goodnight, and exited the cab. I was exhausted and went straight to sleep. Funny how chatting for so long tired me out incredibly, but when one is alone most of the time they're not used to talking for long hours as Luke and I did at Gianni's.

This morning I slept in till late and I discover Herr Groth left a tray outside my door with coffee and assorted pastries. Bless the man! After a shower, I sit by my window and eat hungrily while I watch the people of Berlin passing by.

I'm looking forward to tonight's gig, but I try not to get too excited about seeing Luke again. Being a lone wolf means one doesn't become attached to another person. Sure, two people can be friends or even lovers, but there needs to be a sense of independence and freedom between them—this is what flying solo or being a lone wolf means to me.

I really like Luke, at least what I've learned about him so far, and I have a feeling I can become attached to him in some way, but I don't want this. Alone is safe, alone means free. And I already made my mistakes early in life and hopefully I've learned from them and now have the wisdom of my earlier years to fall back on.

Ironically, it seems to me Luke feels the same way or at least that's what he says. I still don't know him well enough to judge nor do I believe I'll see him again after tonight. Luke is here for a few months, but I'm due back in London. My week long pilgrimage to Berlin has come to an end. My father did not show up, just as in past years, and with each additional year that goes by the less I expect him to appear. I don't really know why I even keep coming back here. I don't see the point anymore. To date, I haven't been able to find very much information about him and I can no longer afford to pay private investigators in Europe and America to try and trace my father's movements.

All I know is that after the war my father worked in the military based in Germany for about three or so years until he was shipped home to America. Interestingly, it turns out he became a musician somewhere along the way and supposedly lived in the States for a while. This was way before I was born and my birth certificate states I was born in London, which leads me to presume that after the war my father came to live in the UK where he later met my mother.

As for being a musician, this could be during the time he lived in the States. I can't remember what he did there nor did he tell me if he was ever a professional musician. Perhaps it was just a hobby with him, playing the odd gig here and there, but what I do remember is that he was a travelling salesman for homeware items, so he travelled a lot within the UK.

Then, when I was eight years of age, my parents separated and consequently agreed to a divorce. I was never given a reason for the split-up, but I could tell even before my father left home that things were not right with him and my mother. Whenever my father was home there used to be violent arguments with a lot of screaming and breaking of crockery. It was during these times that he talked about Berlin and meeting me there one day, but he said he first needed to go back to the States to wrap up some business. He also promised he would try to send for me, but if somehow things did not work out as planned we should meet on July 4th by the Berlin Wall instead. He would write and send for me.

At the time, I thought he meant a few months at most as he had to save money for our new life together. Despite this, I was upset at having to wait, but if it meant I'd be reunited with him for good it was worth the waiting. So my father left and then there was silence. No letter, no telegram, no call.

Luke glances up from his set-up of instruments, speakers, and musical paraphernalia to wave at me. He's standing on a smallish makeshift stage located towards the back of the café near the bar and I cross the floor from the entrance to reach him. The place is packed with patrons while waiters swish past, laden with trays full of food or coming back from clearing a table. It's only seven-thirty and Luke goes on in one hour.

I reach him and take his extended hand as he helps me up onstage. "Well, you certainly have enough here for a whole band," I comment, taking in his electric and bass guitars, a keyboard, drums, saxophone, and more.

"I sometimes perform as part of a group, like a casual band," he explains. "It all depends on the crowd Gianni's get. For instance, this gig will incorporate more rock music because of the 4th of July festivities, but say for Valentine's Day the mood would be smoother, slower, more romantic, that sort of thing; so for some gigs I perform on my own and for others I need a band."

"That makes sense; you're eclectic with your gigs, matching the mood with the times of year."

Luke nods. "Something like that. I have three guys on tonight with me, they're the ones I usually work with at Ku-dorf."

"And when you're in the UK?"

"I work gigs at London nightclubs, well-known pubs, and special functions such as weddings, that sort of thing. I work with a regular small group when needed and I play solo when appropriate; it all depends on what the gig is."

I'm impressed, but before I can ask him more questions he grabs my hand and leads me offstage and towards the kitchen at the back of the café. "Listen, I have forty-five minutes before I'm on, just enough time to grab something to eat. Care to join me, brown eyes?"

"That'll be great, thank you; but what's with the brown eyes?"

"I haven't come across too many girls of Irish descent with red hair and dark brown eyes; usually their eyes are green or hazel. Of course, with a surname like Kelly and your colouring I presume there's Irish blood in your family."

I raise an eyebrow and remark with a touch of sarcasm. "You presume? And you're an authority on this, how?"

He smiles and ruffles my hair. "You're so easy to tease."

What a smartarse! He must have a bit of the Irish himself with that kind of banter, but I don't comment on anything because we enter the kitchen and Gianni's waiting for us, holding two plates with Italian panini and a side salad for each. *"Ciao, bella!"* Gianni greets me and puts down the plates on a small table at the back of the kitchen. "Coffee and mineral water for two?"

"Thanks, Gianni," Luke says and then turns to me. "Eat up, my girl."

I don't wait to be told twice. The food looks delicious and I'm starving, but I'm not Luke's girl.

Gianni's is jam-packed by the time we finish eating and the only place Luke finds for me to sit is in a corner of a small passageway leading to the toilets. This doesn't exactly provide a good view of the stage, but I can see from one side of it. The group plays covers from different rock bands and in between they slip in an unknown piece here and there, which I'm sure is one of Luke's compositions. He did mention to me that he writes his own songs and oftentimes plays them in between covers.

I get caught up in the spirit of things and enjoy songs from selected icons such as Rolling Stones, Led Zeppelin, David Bowie, Elton John, Queen and the list goes on, but more than this I'm captivated by Luke's voice. He's the lead singer and possesses a rich voice with a lower range that has the capacity to reach all the way up to a tenor. His voice range is incredible and it's not in any way contrived. Luke's just a pure natural.

By midnight the band is still playing and the crowd keeps calling out for more. Despite the small breaks they had in between sets the boys in the band look tired, but they're not about to finish any time soon.

I'm tired, too, and I have an early flight to London in the morning so while I'm mesmerised by the incredible gig I still have to get some sleep so I can get up at six, pay my hotel bill, and get to the airport on time.

Luke doesn't know I'm leaving tomorrow. I couldn't find a way to tell him. It's not like I'm a close friend and the last thing I don't want is for him to think I'm looking to stay in order to get to know him better. If I'm honest with myself, however, I admit I would like to get to know him and develop a closer friendship, but he'd think I'm being presumptuous, so in a way it's a good thing I can't afford to stay on; I need to get back to work.

I glance at my watch and I'm shocked—it'll be one in the morning if I wait for another fifteen minutes. I'm fairly sure the boys will put an end to the gig soon so this is my one chance to leave before Luke notices I'm gone. Without wasting another moment, I walk through the kitchen in order to avoid being seen by Luke and I leave by the back door of the building. When I get to the main road, I'm able to flag down a taxi immediately for the short ride back to my hotel.

Herr Groth is working late and sees me come in, so I take the opportunity to settle my bill as this will buy me a little more time to get ready in the morning. "*Danke schön, Fräulein Kelly,*" he says, handing back my credit card and receipt slip. "Have a good trip and we hope to see you next time."

I wonder if there is going to be a next time, but I simply smile at Herr Groth and wish him a good night. Once in my room, I put out clean clothing for the morning but decide to shower immediately because I'm sweaty and the smell of smoke is clinging to my hair. It seems most of the café patrons were smoking the night away and being a non-smoker I hate the smell that clings to me after having spent time in a smoky environment. This is one of the health hazards of music gigs.

———◉———

I hear a telephone ringing somewhere in the hotel and tell myself to be sure and complain to Herr Groth for allowing the phones to ring so loudly. I grab the spare pillow on my bed and put it over my head. This muffles the ringing, but it doesn't stop it. I toss and turn, starting to get annoyed, but then my eyes flick open and I'm fully awake. It is then I realise it's my phone ringing. I glance at the digital clock on the bedside table, it reads 01:48. My heartbeat speeds up because I know who the caller is and although anxious to speak with him I'm also thrilled. Good grief, what is the matter with me?

I pick up the receiver, but before I say anything Luke's voice comes through loud and clear, and sounding concerned. "What happened to you? You left without a word. For a moment, I thought you felt sick and went back to the hospital, but one of the kitchen hands who stepped outside for a smoke said he saw you flag down a taxi and heard you give the driver the address of your hotel."

I switch on the lamp on my bedside table and sigh. "I'm sorry," I say as I run my fingers through my hair. "I waited until almost one, but I was buggered so I decided to come back to the hotel and sleep."

"Why didn't you let me know?"

I sigh again. "I wanted to, but you were about to start a new set and I didn't want to bother you," I reply, feeling guilty. "I loved the gig, but I was really tired, honest." Luke doesn't respond and so I keep talking, "It's my fault, I guess, but I didn't know what to do."

He finally speaks. "What do you mean?"

"My week in Berlin's up and I have an early flight back to London in the morning, so I have to get up at six."

Luke sounds thoughtful, "I see." I wait for him to go on and after a few moments he says, "Why didn't you tell me earlier in the evening? Why run away?"

"I wasn't running," I explain. "But look at it from my point of view: we've only just met and spent most of our time together. We have heaps in common, at least I believe we do, but I've only known you for two days, so what would you think of me if I told you I had to leave the next day? Would you think I'd be telling you this so you can ask me to stay longer or would you be relieved that I was going?" I pause and then continue speaking before he has a chance to say anything. "I never expected to meet someone like you. I mean someone who has so much in common with me, and I feel that we could become really good friends, but I must go back to work so it's best to move on. I wanted to tell you, please believe this, but I couldn't find the words without sounding presumptuous." There is a long pause and I think the call is lost. "Luke, are you still there?"

"Yes, I'm sorry. I was just thinking. Look, it's late and you need your sleep and yet there's so much I wish to say to you. I don't suppose you're willing to stay on an extra day?"

I'm so tempted to say yes, but I wouldn't feel comfortable doing this on such a short acquaintance. I barely know the man, plus one more day won't solve anything. "I'm so sorry, Luke. If I had more time I would consider staying, but I think it's best that I go. I really have to get back to work." I then try to sound cheerful when I suggest, "But you work in London, too, so perhaps we can continue this when you're back there."

"You're right, of course," he agrees, albeit reluctantly. "How can I reach you?"

I give him my phone number and he tells me he plans to return to London in September and will look me up. "Take good care of yourself, Sam. I wish you a good summer season with your gigs, and I look forward to September."

I thank him once again for all he's done for me and we ring off.

Chapter 6 - Robert

<u>1945/46, Berlin, Germany</u>

There wasn't much by way of entertainment in post-war Berlin, so some of the personnel from US Headquarters applied for permission to start a club for the Allies where people could go for a beer and dance to live music. A few buddies who worked in my division were musicians from New York, all of whom made a tidy sum in the many nightclubs of that city prior to the war.

The powers that be granted us permission for a club, albeit with a number of strict rules. Our superiors were not exactly enamored with the idea of a nightclub as this would take us away from our regular work in order to run the club, but with personnel morale in mind entertainment was seen as a dire necessity. We already had a book club, a chess club, and weekly baseball games, but you just couldn't beat the excitement of music and dancing washed down with a beer and in the company of a pretty girl.

Our superiors warmed to the idea in the end and made available a large basement, which had access to a street exit in the rear of the building we occupied. Therefore, armed with the rules and conditions in mind, we set about painting the room, putting down a dance floor surrounded by an odd collection of tables and chairs recovered from the wreckage of other buildings in the area and which we could mend. We also built a stage for the musicians, a bar for the service of drinks, and the set of double doors at the entrance from street level were fixed and painted. It took us about two months to put things together, which we did in our free time, but the end result was worth it and we named the place the 'Victory Club' in commemoration of our victory in Europe.

Our club was not exactly Harnack House, a vast and luxurious estate that had been found intact in 1945, in the American-occupied zone. Harnack House became and remained a venue for social gatherings and events. It was like a country club with luxury hotel accommodation and the kind of place where invitations were issued for important press conferences and receptions. Notables such as Harry S. Truman and Dwight D. Eisenhower visited Harnack House immediately after its confiscation by our forces. Of course, this was a place for people of high rank and VIPs, and there was no comparison between Harnack House and our humble Victory Club, but we were thrilled to have a club for ourselves.

How we managed to get the project up and running, I will never know but morale was up, the guys couldn't wait for opening night, the band put together a repertoire and somehow managed to find musical instruments, especially from a number of friendly locals who knew where the Nazis stored them for occasions when they marched or held receptions for Hitler. Aside from this, although so many buildings were destroyed, many items managed to survive, one of which turned out to be a grand piano from the now-destroyed opera house, the Berlin Staatsoper.

When rehearsals began, the guys in the band decided they needed a second trumpet player and one of my buddies from the admin office put me forward as a candidate.

I learned to play the trumpet in high school and picked it up fairly quickly. Ollie used to say I was a natural and he encouraged me to join the school band. Therefore, when my name was mentioned, the guys in the band asked me to audition. I was both terrified but excited, and I could barely function when I auditioned; however, I somehow managed to go ahead. My mouth was dry as a desert and after having had no practice whatsoever I was sure I'd lost my lip. Irrespective of this, I still auditioned in front of the guys. I played a solo piece plus one accompanied by the band, and in the end I got an enthusiastic round of applause. I was in!

We set our opening night for two weeks after we put the finishing touches to the Club and sent out invitations to all personnel at headquarters, which included the Women's Army Corp (WAC). The WACs had joined us in Berlin from their post in France, where they worked on high-level communications, admin and conferences; a number of them were transferred to Berlin for the Potsdam Conference held by the three Allied powers at the time: US, Britain and Russia, and in the end a number of WACs became a permanent fixture.

We were relieved there were females we could invite to the club; otherwise, dancing would have been a sad affair. Our superiors made it clear the club was only open to Allied personnel of both sexes and the occasional spouse of visiting officers. Members of the public, especially ladies of the night, were not permitted.

Fortunately, by December 1945, the War Brides Act was passed and service personnel could marry their German sweethearts; this evened up the number of females. As a result, the club thrived and crowds grew to maximum capacity, and the Victory Club became the go-to venue for the Allies and now for their German wives.

Meanwhile, I realized once I returned to the States I had a career if I chose music. The guys in the band took me under their wing and encouraged me to look them up in New York after the war as they might be able to help me secure an on-going gig. This made me very happy and I couldn't wait until our division was sent home, but life had other plans for me, at least in the short-term, and then Clara stepped in.

It was a freezing January night and my turn to do close-up at the club, which usually took place by midnight. We took turns tidying up and securing the place before going back to our digs. On this particular night, or I should say morning because it was close to two, I was doing close-up with Joey, one of my buddies. We had a special function for our division leader's birthday hence the late closing time and now we hurried through our routine and parted at the corner of the street. Our digs were within walking distance with mine to the left and Joey's in the opposite direction. We said our goodnights and I held my coat and scarf around me tightly in order to ward off the cold weather. I was sure it was going to snow and I couldn't wait until I got back to the warmth of my barracks.

I walked fast, wrapped in thoughts of becoming a New York musician, when I heard a scuffle from across the street and turned my head toward the noise. Two men in uniform were accosting a young woman. They were speaking in French and it was obvious they were very drunk. The girl was sandwiched between them, struggling to free herself while the men laughed at her unsuccessful attempts to escape. One of them put his arms around her waist and roughly pulled her toward him, and he started to kiss her. The girl cried out in German: *"Bitte lass mich in ruhe!"*(which meant something like 'please let me go'). The men laughed and while one of them held her the other started to raise her skirt and she screamed in fear.

Without thinking, I ran across the street with one of my hands in my pocket, shouting in English while waving my arm. "Stop right now! You're in the American sector and I'm armed. You're under arrest!" I drew out a small baton from my coat pocket, which I liked to carry for self-defense when I had to do the close-ups on my own, and in the dark it looked as if I was holding a gun. Of course, it was fortunate these brutes were the worse for drink and they believed me. One of them shouted something I couldn't catch with my poor French, but whatever it was it had the right effect because they instantly released the girl and ran off as fast as their legs could carry them.

The girl slid to the ground and sat on the freezing pavement, holding her knees and rocking back and forth while she cried.

"Bist du okay?" I asked in my limited German. She nodded but stayed seated on the ground, weeping. I drew out my handkerchief and offered it to her while I helped her to her feet. At first, it looked like she was going to struggle, but then she said in halting English, *"You help me, American?"*

I reassured her. *"Yes. My name is Robert. And you?"* She was a slip of a thing, no older than sixteen or seventeen years of age, very slim (for lack of food, I thought), huge eyes and short white blonde hair. I stood almost two heads above her and my heart broke for her. She gazed at me and I thought she didn't understand what I'd said, but she was trying to calm herself. She dried her tears, blew her nose, and managed a tremulous smile. *"I...am Clara,"* she spoke in a soft voice.

And it was then, when I took in the picture she made—a defenseless waif fragile as a china doll—that I fell in love.

Chapter 7 - Samantha

Jul/Aug, 1985, London, England

The moment I open the front door at my digs in Sloane Square, Miss Brand appears in the parlour, hobbling on her cane and with a big smile on her face. "My dear, Sam! I'm so glad you're back."

I put down my travel bag and give her a gentle hug even though I'm not usually one for hugs. In fact, the only hugs I remember came from my father on the occasions when he was at home from his travelling job. His was the only affection I ever knew during my childhood hence the reason why I felt so close to him, especially when he taught me how to play guitar in his spare time, although this didn't happen often because of his job. Despite his many absences, however, I still learned enough from him to enable me to teach myself, and on the occasions when he was home I used to play for him and he'd hug me and tell me he was glad I inherited the Kelly genes after all. Apparently, we came from a musical family, but not all Kellys chose to play.

My mother, on the other hand, was always distant with me. I seemed to be a hindrance rather than a daughter and I never knew why. So when I came to live with Miss Brand five years ago, I began to learn what it was like to have a mother and in a short period of time, Miss Brand practically adopted me even though I never took this seriously. Why would she want to adopt me?

"So how was it, my dear?" Miss Brand always wants to know the details whenever I have been away.

I take her arm gently and guide her over to the kitchen where I know what is to follow: tea and gossip. I tell her about the trip, the places, and the people, but I leave out the fainting incident or she'll worry and keep me talking for hours and I need to take a nap because I'm exhausted after my trip.

Totally captivated by the Independence Day festivities, Miss Brand claps her hands like a young girl on an adventure and when I finish my commentary she goes on to bring me up to date with the latest gossip at Apple Court, where she lives in a three bedroom apartment located in an early art deco complex of twelve.

Miss Brand is in her late eighties, and I have a suspicion she relives her youth through me. This explains why she wants to know every little detail of what I get up to. She's a well off lady who used to live with her older spinster sister, Anne, until she passed away at the ripe old age of ninety-two. The apartment belonged to the sisters and as neither married, Anne willed her half of the apartment to her younger sister, and Miss Brand has been taking in boarders since.

People always ask me how I can afford to live in Sloane Square, a posh part of London, and I tell them I'm only a boarder, but the reality is that I walked into a kind of job for which I never applied.

When Anne passed away, Miss Brand could not face the prospect of going into aged care and she knew she needed help if she were to stay living independently in her beloved apartment. After all, it was her home and the sisters had lived here for over sixty years after they inherited the apartment from a wealthy aunt who was the only family the sisters had after they lost their parents to the Spanish flu.

The sisters came from a gentle but impoverished background due to a large investment which failed, leaving the Brand family having to rent after they had to sell their own home to repay debts. So when the sisters moved into their inherited apartment, they were cash poor and as a result they used their talents to earn a living.

Miss Brand is a wonderful pianist and she tutored students from home, while Anne used her own talent in fashion design, a lifetime love of hers, and she became an exclusive fashion designer for wealthy ladies in the affluent parts of London.

During their time together the two sisters saved a nice nest egg for their retirement. After what had happened to their father, losing everything the family owned, the sisters learned that security was far better than gambling on the stock market where many lives had been ruined, and they figured they were better off putting their money in the bank. When Miss Brand told me about this, I took her advice and started depositing my small savings into a bank account, hoping they'll hold me for the proverbial rainy day.

I live simply and the rent I pay is a token amount to cover my share of the power and phone bills plus the few times when I organise a domestic/personal helper to assist Miss Brand if I have to travel away from London. At first, Miss Brand and I decided to put the whole arrangement to the test and in the end it worked out well for both of us: she got to stay home instead of having to move into aged care and I got to live in a lovely place near the centre of London and its many attractions, where I usually busk. Not only this, but additionally I feel I picked up a kindly mother along the way.

———————◉———————

A week after my arrival from Berlin, I receive a call from the owner of The Treble and Bass. "So how was your trip, Sam?" Tom Gerrard asks. He knows I go to Berlin every year and he's known me for about four years now.

I say the usual without mentioning my accident. "It was great, thanks, but I missed London."

"So no news of your father, I take it." Tom is the only person aside from Miss Brand who knows about my annual pilgrimage to Berlin in the hope that I'll finally find my father waiting for me by the Wall.

"Well, you know how it is," I reply and change the subject. "I haven't heard from you since my last gig at the pub about six weeks ago, so who's going on holidays this time?"

Tom has a regular number of musos who take turns performing at The Treble and Bass and I usually fill in when one of them is off sick or on holidays.

"Oh no, it's much better than that," Tom says with a mysterious laugh in his voice.

"Don't tell me someone's lost their mind and they're getting married!" This is a standing joke among most of the musos I know. We're all free spirits and marriage doesn't fit into our lives.

Tom laughs again. "You live for your art, but look at me: I run a successful pub and I'm married with three kids and another one on the way."

"Oh, congratulations! I hope all is well with Helen. When is she due?"

"Plenty of time to go yet and Helen still wants to host, but I put my foot down and she finally agreed to work part-time."

Tom's wife is the host at The Treble and Bass and despite being a mum she loves what she does and works fulltime. She pretty much runs the restaurant part of the pub and organises all kinds of events such as special dinner parties, theme functions, and even small weddings. "Well, I hope to see Helen soon to congratulate her in person."

"And you will," says Tom. "The reason for my call is to ask whether you'd be interested in a regular gig." My heart starts to beat with excitement, but I say nothing and wait for him to continue. "Jeff landed a gig with an up and coming band in the States and it looks promising for him, so I'm wondering if you'd like to take over his two nights at the pub."

I feel like yelling out in delirious happiness, but when I go to speak I find I'm speechless.

"Sam? Are you still there?"

Thankfully, I recover my voice. "Yes! Of course! Wow!"

Tom chuckles. "That's better. I thought you were going to turn me down."

"Are you kidding me?"

"I know how talented you are and how hard you work. Our patrons like you and you've never let me down, so why would I be kidding you? I want you to know that I've had my eye on you for some time, but I simply didn't have any vacancies to offer you, except for filling in when someone couldn't make it.

"My guys have been with me long term, you see, but I always kept you at the back of my mind in case something opened up, and now I can offer you a steady gig."

I feel tears rolling down my face. What Tom said gives me the validation I've been seeking since I started performing. I never thought of myself as truly talented. I know I can play and sing and I do it well, but coming from Tom, a man with years of experience working with professional performers, it means so much more. Suddenly, I think of Luke and his incredible voice and musical talent and for once I don't feel awed, even by him. I know he's far superior to me, but according to Tom it seems I can hold my own. "Tom, I don't know how to thank you," I say, "but you can count on me."

"Well, my dear, drop by early tomorrow afternoon and we'll go over the details."

"Will do. I'll be there with bells on!" I ring off, but I still stand in the hallway with the telephone receiver in my hand and a wide smile on my face.

———◆———

Jeff's last gig at The Treble and Bass is on Saturday, 27th of July. It'll be a farewell performance featuring Jeff and his small band of two. I will also feature on this particular evening so Jeff can introduce me to the audience. I'm terrified but excited at the same time. Jeff's band will not accompany him to the States; it's only Jeff who's making the move to America.

"Chris and Marcus are not part of any group," Jeff explains at our handover session after my meeting with Tom regarding details and conditions. "We simply play as a trio for the sake of accompaniment for me, and the arrangement suits us quite well."

"I always thought you guys were a group, I didn't realise the boys were accompaniment." I swallow a shot of Baileys Irish Cream to steady my nerves and ask myself how I go from being a solo performer, mainly playing covers as a fill-in, to managing a band. And small as it is, it's still a band.

Jeff gives my hand a gentle squeeze. "Hey, don't worry. It'll work out well. You probably know Chris and Marcus have other gigs in London, so they don't need this gig. What you don't know is that they requested to play with you."

I throw Jeff a look of surprise. "They did?"

Jeff laughs. "Of course they did. They saw you perform heaps of times over the years, and it was their suggestion that Tom consider them to become part of your new gig. They also like the idea of having a trio arrangement with a female lead."

I'm not sure whether to believe this, but Jeff seems to be dead serious. I feel a blush rise to my face and I'm thankful we're in the dim atmosphere of the pub. "Well, thank you. I'm flattered." But secretly, I'm not sure if the guys really wish to do the gig with me because they like the idea of having a female lead or they simply wish to keep their jobs after all.

Jeff runs a hand over his bright orange hair and regards me with his baby blues. I used to have a thing for him for a while, but I never acted on it and neither did he. Just as well because he's now moving on to bigger and better things.

"Sam, you must believe in yourself. You have a great husky kind of voice that can also hit the high notes and it doesn't matter what you sing because you can reach both the highs and the lows. There aren't many who can do this, you know? Most of the time we choose songs to suit our voice range, but so far you've been able to handle quite a variable repertoire."

I think of Luke again and his incredible voice range. Could it be that I'm a little bit like him? And why do I doubt myself so much, anyway? After all, I don't think Jeff is being insincere, so I guess it's because no one ever gave me much feedback, especially when busking, but in hindsight I admit I must have done rather well or else I wouldn't be here now.

Once all arrangements are confirmed by both Tom and Jeff, I prepare to break the news to Miss Brand over dinner. On the evenings when I'm home, I normally cook for both of us. I also do the grocery shopping and keep the house clean. Miss Brand insists on doing something for herself and so she cooks and tidies up around the place when I'm out. I agree as long as she takes it easy. I also help her with bathing and this is the only thing I never allow her to do without someone being present, in case she has a slip and fall. Miss Brand tells me I mollycoddle her, but I know deep down inside she's relieved that not only do we get on, but that my time is flexible and therefore I can look after her.

"By the way," I say while we eat our dinner of roast chicken with baked potatoes, pumpkin, and a fresh green side salad, "now that I have a fixed gig I no longer have to busk in the streets, so my time will be more regular and I can plan activities easily."

Miss Brand regards me with affection. "My dear, I'm so happy for you. You work so hard and you deserve to do something you love, but I must confess I didn't like the idea of you having to busk in the streets with our type of weather, especially in winter; plus who knows what other dangers lurk around the city."

I smile. "Miss Brand, you know I'm a careful girl. Besides, the locations where I busk are always full of people, particularly during the day. As for inclement weather, there are many porches and porticos where I can take shelter."

"Well," Miss Brand sighs with relief, "but at least you now have your fixed gig, as you call it, and I'm very proud of you."

I'm moved and take a sip of water so she can't see my eyes, which are getting a little teary. No one's ever told me they were proud of me.

Miss Brand luckily doesn't notice my emotional response and she goes on to say, "And my dear, don't you think it's about time you call me Dora?"

"Oh, I never thought to do so. I was brought up to show respect for my elders. This was ingrained in me at school." Nothing of the sort is true, of course. My father was away, working hard, my mother ignored me, and I went to a rough school where we were little devils, even when the punishment was harsh. But I did learn some things, so when I met Miss Brand and walked into the job of companion, of course I showed respect, and over time the name stuck. Calling her Dora now would feel strange.

"Well," Miss Brand says, looking a little impressed by my manners, "Miss Brand it is if you wish, but don't forget I'll also answer to Dora," she adds with a smile.

For the rest of our meal we talk about my timetable so we can make new arrangements for my companion duties. There will be times when I have to go to the venue to rehearse and this will take place during daytime hours, and Tom did tell me that I could still fill in if something didn't clash with my set gig. I agreed to this arrangement as it would not only help my savings grow, but it would also give me more variety in the music I play.

The Treble and Bass didn't just have gigs at night. Helen, Tom's wife, hosted high teas on Friday and Sunday afternoons where live music was played in a quiet ambience with either piano or guitar. The gig was usually performed by a middle-aged lady named Joan and if she was off sick or couldn't make it for any reason, Helen used music tapes instead.

However, when I came along to fill in at The Treble and Bass, Helen discovered that I could play classical piano as well as modern music, plus I sang ballads and other songs on the guitar. Helen liked my style, as did Tom, and I became the 'relief' musician, which eventually led to my latest gig.

Chapter 8 - Robert

1945/46, Berlin, Germany

Between my broken German and Clara's limited English, I somehow managed to put together a picture of her life.

After she recovered from the shock of the attack by the French soldiers, I offered to escort her home, but she said she had an errand to run first. I wouldn't think of letting her walk on her own so I accompanied her and while we walked in the cold night air we talked, and I even made her laugh a few times when trying to express myself in her language.

I learned Clara's surname, which is Meyer; she no longer has any family—they all perished in the war—so she was fortunate to get work from a local baker who used to be a good friend of Clara's father. Mr. Schmidt and his wife, who also lost family to the war—their two sons—ended up taking in Clara when she lost her parents and two siblings in a bombing raid.

The Schmidts gave Clara a home in their house/bakery, one of the few structures that still survived, in exchange for helping out with housekeeping duties plus giving Mr. Schmidt a hand with the bakery. This all transpired shortly before Hitler committed suicide on April 30, 1945, and Germany fell apart. Clara was fifteen years of age at the time and turned sixteen in July of the same year.

I asked her why she was out on the streets at such a late hour and she said she was running an errand for Mr. Schmidt as his supplier had run out of yeast and the new shipment was not expected until around two in the morning. As a result, Clara was asked to go and pick up the goods, but when she was a couple of blocks away from the bakery she was accosted right there and then by the French men.

Clara explained that bakers usually work at night in order that their goods are fresh and ready to go by early morning, and Mr. Schmidt needed the yeast immediately if he were to finish baking the bread on time. He sold his goods through a window that looked out onto the street from his small bakery and by five in the morning there was usually a long queue of people wrapped around the corner of the block.

Berlin was starving, but those with good connections managed to obtain the raw materials with which to make their products. This was all they could do until the Allies established a government of sorts. Rations were inadequate as much of the infrastructure in Germany had been destroyed and even when the Allies arrived, it was a mammoth project to get food to people across Germany. The Allies were unable to cater for such a multitude of displaced people and with so few of them back at work in their farms food production was still very slow. Consequently, those with money or valuables to trade turned to the black market in order to supplement their inadequate rations, but this, too, was difficult. The destruction of Germany was massive and it would take time to restore the food chain.

About an hour before he opened the bakery window each day, Mr. Schmidt sent Clara to the black market, which was located at the wasteland that was once the Tiergarten. He sent some of his bread through Clara to share among the destitute. He told Clara he did this in memory of the two sons he lost in the war. Clara said Mr. Schmidt had a good heart and he liked to think that perhaps at some stage during the war someone out there may have helped his own sons, and so he wanted to reciprocate.

It was almost three when we reached a small cottage about half an hour away from my barracks and I hoped no one from US Headquarters would see us. They patrolled the city and suburbs and if they found me wandering around at that time with a German girl I'd be in a heap of trouble.

Clara knocked softly on the door of the cottage and I stood a short distance away in the darkness, stamping my feet against the cold. Fortunately, Clara returned within a few minutes holding a cloth bag which I presumed held the yeast. I took it from her and hand in hand we started to walk across the city. It was almost a full hour's walk from where we first started, close to where I found Clara near the bakery, which was a couple of blocks away, but I still had at least half an hour to return to my barracks, and this would put me there rather close to dawn.

On arrival at the bakery, we didn't have time to talk nor did we dare in case Mr. Schmidt became suspicious and decided to see what was going on. For good measure, we parted a few doors down from the bakery, but not before I asked Clara if she would see me again.

In answer, she stood on her tippy toes and planted a sweet kiss on my cheek. I waited until she went into the bakery and I took note of the street address. Clara would soon be receiving a letter from me.

Chapter 9 - Samantha

Jeff's farewell performance goes off with a bang and his usual following of fans have him playing encore after encore. Meanwhile, I'm backstage trying not to vomit from nerves. I should never drink alcohol on an empty stomach and short of a Valium tablet appearing magically in my hand it's impossible to be calm.

In between sets the band takes a ten minute break and I get to see Jeff and the boys three times during the evening. They give me much encouragement and this works until they go back onstage for the next set during which time I rush to the 'musicians' bathroom and heave.

I finally lose track of time between all my visits to the bathroom and suddenly Chris pops his head in the small foyer located next to it, where I'm half sitting, half reclining on a very old sofa chair which is covered in stains and has probably been utilised by many anxious musicians while awaiting their turn to go onstage. I don't even see Chris until he taps my shoulder; I just want to disappear and find myself at home in bed and Miss Brand fussing over me with a cup of hot cocoa.

"Sam, you've got five minutes. Get ready!" Before I can answer, Chris is gone and I manage to stand and grab my guitar. It is then I remember I didn't warm my fingers; my first song is Hotel California by the Eagles and I'm the one doing the guitar instrumental. Oh, my God, I can't even remember the first note! Then, by some benevolent force of nature, I feel myself being propelled forward and before I know it I'm onstage being introduced by Jeff.

I have no idea what he says to the audience, but it's a good sign when they applaud. I then hear the three beats from the drums, which is our cue to start playing, and I launch into the intro of the song. My fingers seem to know what to do without me having to think about it plus my voice actually works when I sing the first verse of the song, but the biggest sign that all is going well is the fact that no one has yet thrown wet, rolled up toilet paper rolls at the stage (or at my face) and the audience is actually listening.

I still feel as if I'm in a strange dream, but then the sound of applause and whistles explode into my brain and I realise the audience is really clapping while the boys are taking bows. This means we must have finished the song.

Jeff puts his arms around me and kisses me on the lips. There are more whistles from the audience and then I wake up from the dream and realise this is no dream—it's actually happening. I hide my face against Jeff's shoulder and start to cry.

The crowd calls for an encore—an encore from me this time—but Jeff announces another break before the next set. He knows I need time to breathe, gather my emotions and calm right down before we go back on.

When we return from our break, I have two more songs to sing before Jeff performs his last song for the evening, which will be one of his own compositions. And as soon as we're onstage, I launch straight into Fleetwood Mac's 'Rhiannon' and I close off with Phil Collins' 'One More Night' where I play the keyboard with Jeff doing lead guitar and backup vocals for me. The crowd loves our performance and they keep asking for more. The high atmosphere in the room energises me to the point where I can go on singing even though I feel spent after my pre-performance nerves.

Jeff launches into his own composition—Travellers—a song about friends who take different paths in life. I accompany him with rhythm guitar and backup vocals while Chris and Marcus belt out the music with the bass guitar and drums while Jeff plays lead guitar and sings; and when he sings I listen to the lyrics of the song even though I know them by heart, but somehow tonight, in this incredible atmosphere, the lyrics seem to take on a special meaning for me and I'm suddenly reminded of my short interlude with Luke. We kind of became friends or were on our way to doing so, but at the same time we were travelling on different paths and so we parted.

He has my phone number, however, but I never heard back. It's been three weeks since my return from Berlin and so much has happened to me; yet now I wonder where Luke's road is taking him. He's probably playing at Gianni's and Ku-dorf, but as I always say 'life can change at the snap of two fingers' and he could be anywhere right now. I shake my head to disperse these thoughts, which make me feel melancholy. Thankfully, the song we're performing comes to an end and the loud applause and whistles from the audience shake me out of my rather morose reverie.

Jeff says his goodbyes to everyone and thanks each of us in the band. The crowd calls for more, but Jeff looks beat so we take one last bow and finish up. The patrons start to disperse just as I straighten up from my bow and it is then that I find myself looking into the eyes of Luke Hart.

After having a farewell drink with the band and the staff of The Treble and Bass, everyone goes their own way. I grab my guitar case while Jeff and Luke have a few words. It turns out they played together at Ku-dorf some years back. I join them when the two men finish their drinks and shake hands. "Wish you all the best in the States, Jeff," Luke says. "And don't be surprised if I turn up there one day."

I say nothing, but the thought of Luke one day going off to the States somehow disturbs me, and I almost jump when Jeff ruffles my hair and brings me back to the present. "Keep an eye on this one when you're London," Jeff tells Luke with a wink. I feel myself blush, but the men don't seem to notice and Jeff gives me one last hug and kiss. "You did really well tonight," he says when he releases me from his arms. "Take care, and perhaps I'll see you one day in the States, too." We smile at each other.

Jeff says a final farewell to Luke and goes backstage to sort out his music equipment. "You two can go," he calls out from behind the stage, "I told Tom I'll lock up."

"Will do, and safe journey!" I call out to Jeff and then turn to Luke, saying casually, "There's an all-night café around the corner if you feel like a coffee. I'm in need of one after tonight's excitement."

Luke takes my guitar case from me. "Lead on MacDuff," he says with a smile.

We walk into the night and I'm glad I have my leather jacket with me; although summer, it's kind of nippy at this hour. Luke doesn't seem to feel the cold in his jeans, white T-shirt and long-sleeved black shirt. "So what gives?" I say conversationally as if I'm making a remark on the weather. "Weren't you supposed to be playing in Berlin tonight or something?"

"I should've been, but I heard about your debut and I just had to come over and see you perform."

"How..." I'm surprised and lost for words, but I make an effort to recover instead of sounding like a teenager who just met her rock idol. "I meant to say, how did you know?"

"Someone who saw you at Gianni's remembered seeing you at The Treble and Bass on the night Jeff made his announcement about leaving for the States and mentioned you as his replacement. Last week, I ran into this guy at Ku-dorf and he told me."

I'm still surprised. "Really? How can someone remember after seeing me a couple of times? It's not like I'm famous," I remark.

We turn a street corner and I point to a small café called Sunflower. "So where are the flowers?" Luke asks.

"It has a Van Gogh theme inside," I explain and we head towards the half-empty café. We sit at a window table and Luke admires the walls in the place, which have been painted with a collage of Van Gogh works. The café itself consists of a French country style room with small round timber tables and Bentwood chairs.

"This is really cosy," Luke remarks. "How come I never heard of this place?"

I shrug. "It's away from the main drag and a nice place to unwind after a late night out on the town. A lot of musos come here; I'm surprised you don't know about this little haunt."

Luke glances at the menu card on our table. "Well, I don't remember ever coming here. So do they have a waiter or do we order at the counter?"

"Counter," I say and order a cappuccino from him. Luke insists we have something to eat. I'm not hungry, but I agree to his suggestion of sharing a slice of carrot cake and I go to take some money from my jeans pocket, but he waves it away and heads for the counter returning within moments and carrying a tray with our coffees, a thick slice of carrot cake and two forks. "Thank you," I say when he sets down our order. I try a bit of the cake and nod my head. "It's very good," I declare, "and so is the coffee."

Luke tries the cake and agrees. Meanwhile, I wait for him to tell me more as to why he made the trip to London. He reads my eyes. "I wanted to see you, okay? And this was the perfect opportunity. Unfortunately, we didn't have much time to hang out in Berlin."

"Hang out, doing what?" Where is he going with this? Is he teasing me?

"I meant jamming," he says. "We talked so much about music and I thought we should have a jam session together."

"Oh, but why didn't you say so back then? Not that we had enough time," I remark.

"Well, you just disappeared that night and when I rang you in the early hours you told me you were leaving that very morning. If I'd known beforehand how little time you had left in Berlin I would've arranged something prior to your departure."

"Yes, but why would you want to do that? You'd only just met me."

Luke sighs. "Why are you so suspicious? There's no agenda here, you know?"

"So first I'm cynical and now I'm suspicious." I smile briefly so as not to come across too strong with my opinions, but I feel the need to explain. "Look, it's not you; it's just that I've always been rather guarded with people."

He sips his coffee and regards me thoughtfully for a moment. "That's right. I forgot about what you said—not judging people if we don't know what kind of life they've led."

I nod. "At least you were listening."

"Okay, so I'll come to the point." He gazes into my eyes and I pray I don't blush and make a fool of myself, and thankfully I don't. "It's obvious we have a lot in common and I knew even then that we could become good friends. I know we say we're lone wolves, but sometimes we need to have a friend we can trust and these days there aren't many around. I guess I just had a feeling you and I could be friends—the type you can trust, that is. And look, if I'm wrong and you don't agree, that's fine, too."

His sincerity warms my heart and I have a sudden impulse to hug him, but I don't. I remain in my seat and play with my empty cup. "You're right, of course," I concede. "I also felt a connection between us, but I guess it takes me longer to trust. Having said this, I'm glad you came to see me."

Instead of meeting his eyes I keep playing with my coffee cup. My face feels a bit flushed and I'm sure I'm blushing. I feel his finger under my chin all of a sudden and he tips my face slightly so he can see me eye to eye. "And that's a good start," he says and leans across the small table to kiss the tip of my nose.

Now my face is burning! I seem to be cursed with this blushing impediment, but I try to remain cool. "How about some water?" I suggest and go off to the bar to buy a couple of bottles. When I return I'm back in control, but Luke's smile tells me I didn't fool him. I give him one of the water bottles and take a long drink from mine.

"There's another reason I came to see you," Luke discloses. "I've known Jeff for some years, as I mentioned earlier, and I also worked for Tom. I didn't tell you this, but I used to have a regular gig at The Treble and Bass before I started to divide my time between London and Berlin."

"This explains why everyone was chatting with you."

"Yes. I know a lot of people here. When I arrived, however, Tom pulled me aside. You were backstage so you didn't see us talking. He asked if I'd be willing to do a gig every second Saturday."

I say nothing and wait for him to continue.

"I used to play every Saturday at Tom's place with my band, which dissolved once I went to Berlin. After I left, Tom replaced me with Max Welling to fill every other Saturday plus he brought in Jeff. Both Max and Jeff could only commit to every second Saturday so this worked out well for a while, but now with Jeff going to the States, and Max has been offered a full gig in Edinburgh, his home town, Tom's replacing both of them with you. He knew you were ready to do a fixed gig for quite some time."

I'm confused. "So what are you saying? That Tom wants you to take over Max or Jeff's time slot every other Saturday?" The look on my face must've warned Luke to be careful with his next words.

"No, no, no," he shakes his head. "Tom wants the stability of having an artist running a fixed gig every week," Luke clarifies. "He just came up with an idea when he saw me tonight and asked me to run it by you, but if you're not comfortable with it nothing changes. Tom made it clear that Thursdays and Saturdays are all yours."

I'm not sure of Tom or Luke now—so much for friends you can trust—but Luke did say 'only if I'm comfortable with Tom's idea' so I stay silent and let him continue.

"Tom says you and the boys will perform every Thursday and Saturday, as was agreed between you, but he feels it would make a nice change if every other Saturday I perform along with you guys. This would open us up to playing all sorts of songs, including duos, harmonisation, doing backup vocals for each other, that sort of thing. Chris and Marcus are good at backup, too, but with all due respect to them they're not wide-range singers as we are. So this'll call for a bit of experimentation between the two of us. Tom wants you to have a think about it and if you don't feel it'll work out, then I won't take the gig."

I'm now glad I allowed Luke to explain. The idea is actually brilliant and I know immediately that it'll work really well with the two of us. Just the range of songs we can add to our repertoire is potentially limitless.

Luke regards me pensively but says nothing. He obviously wants me to take my time to think the proposition through. I don't need to, however; I know it will work and I merely reach across the table and squeeze his hand while I give him a nod and a smile of approval.

Chapter 10 - Robert

<u>1946, Berlin, Germany</u>

It's been six months since I've written in my journal. I have been so busy I barely had any time to myself.

We celebrated Christmas a couple of weeks back and we've now entered into a very busy 1946 with this mammoth demob project. No one seems to know when we'll be done in Berlin, but I'm not in a hurry to go back stateside just yet.

Since Clara agreed to see me after our first meeting, we had to juggle our time so we could meet privately. This presented a number of problems: when to meet, where to meet, and how much time we can spare.

When to meet was the easiest; I had a couple of hours between the end of my shift at US Headquarters and playing with the guys at the Victory Club. The club turned out to be such a success that we expanded the days we were open from five to seven nights per week; therefore, to cover the extra shifts we drew up a schedule so each of us could get at least two nights off per week. Playing music was fantastic, but it was also exhausting, especially when we worked fulltime during weekdays and half days on weekends. So with time off between work and the club, I was free to see Clara for a limited time.

Meanwhile, Clara worked overnight, helping Mr. Schmidt at the bakery by taking bread to distribute at the Tiergarten black market and then returning to the bakery to assist with the long line of people waiting to get their ration of bread. Once done, Clara slept from dawn until about noon and then helped Mrs. Schmidt with the housekeeping and preparing the main meal of the day, which consisted of an early dinner. After this, Clara's time was her own until she joined Mr. Schmidt back at the bakery in the late night.

This enabled Clara and I to meet for about two hours, after her early dinner in the late afternoon, which coincided with the couple of hours I had free between work and the club. Weekends did not change for Clara and though I only worked half days during this time as a result of the amount of work we had to get through, plus the club being at its busiest, we still managed to have our time together.

Where to meet presented a more difficult challenge. It was obvious I couldn't go to the Schmidts' place—they didn't even know I existed—and I had no justification to bring Clara to the Club since she was not yet of age. I couldn't even pass her off as a sweetheart under the War Brides Act because the minimum qualifying age is eighteen years, and even if I had been able to get her into the club we wouldn't have had any private time together. When I thought about the club and some of the GIs already bringing their German girlfriends, inspiration struck.

The club didn't open until 8:00pm so I smuggled Clara into the musicians storeroom, where we kept our equipment locked up, and this is where we spent time alone. I had a key to the storeroom and so did the other guys in the band, but they had no reason to arrive early, plus I made sure Clara and I were in by around five-thirty in the afternoon and out by seven-thirty, and even if one of my buddies saw me, I'm sure they would be discreet. We always had each other's back. So in the precious two hours we shared together, I started to teach Clara to speak English while she corrected my German. We lay on a bunch of storage blankets in one corner of the small room and simply talked about life and what kind of future we wanted for ourselves. We laughed, joked around, cuddled and kissed. This was all the time we had and after a few months of getting to know Clara better I still loved her to distraction, just as I did from the very first time I met her.

Chapter 11- Samantha

Luke is due to fly back to Berlin at six in the morning; it's now close to four and we're still sitting at Sunflower drinking coffee. Once I agreed to our arrangement we launched into a deep discussion on what we could do with the gig and time flew by all too quickly.

I glance at my watch. "Luke, you're going to miss your flight!"

He doesn't seem concerned. "I can always catch the next one," he replies. "Now, how about I start in September? I'm sure you'll want to settle in with the band plus have time to get used to your own style. And you'll probably want to compile a list of the songs you wish to play more regularly and others that you keep for special occasions. I'll do the same while in Berlin and we can revise the lists when we get together."

"Good idea," I say. "We also have to work on new stuff, come up with some experimentation, and I suppose you'll want to play some of your own compositions."

He gives me a surprised look. "You don't have a problem if now and then I play one of my own songs?"

"Not at all. In fact, I happen to have some of my own, too," I throw him a cheeky smile.

He smiles back. "Ok, I get it. I take it this means I have to audition for you and vice versa," he says, and quickly adds, "I mean, we both wish to approve of what we're going to play, right?"

"Of course," I reply and peek at the time again; this time Luke gets it.

"I'm sorry. What was I thinking? You probably haven't slept for hours with the excitement of Jeff's farewell gig."

I nod. "Thank you for understanding. It's just that with all the anxiety about playing those solo songs plus wondering what the audience would make of me, I'm really beat."

Luke stands up and grabs my hand. "Come on, I'll see you home." He picks up my guitar case with his other hand and we walk out into the night.

We're lucky to find a cab immediately and I give the driver my address. Luke raises his eyebrows when he hears I live in Sloane Square, but he says nothing about it and instead remarks, "I'm keeping the gig at Ku-dorf and I'll give up Gianni's gig. I know a good guy in Berlin who'll replace me at Gianni's, anyway. So how about I come back here by end of the first week of August and stay for three weeks? This'll give us ample time to prepare for September, which is when I'll start with you guys."

"Whatever works for you is fine by me. I'll be working with the boys and if you join us for rehearsals we can get used to each other's style that much sooner."

"It's agreed then," Luke says. "By the way, Tom has a spare room at the pub and he's offered it to me at a low price, so I'll be living there whenever I'm in London."

"I didn't know Tom had rooms," I remark with surprise.

"It's only the one room upstairs at the back of the building. It used to be spare storage in the old days, but the stairs leading to it are deep and narrow and not practical for moving bulky musical equipment up and down. In the end, Tom converted it into a small studio flat for the odd guest, and I used to rent it from him when I played here before I moved to Berlin. London rents are expensive and by renting from Tom I don't have to book hotels every other Saturday."

"Makes sense to me." I get the feeling Luke's waiting for me to reveal how I can afford Sloane Square and while I don't mind him knowing about my living arrangements this is not the time to tell him; besides, the taxi's now a few blocks away from my place and I really need to get some sleep.

The alarm clock goes off at seven-thirty and I groan, my eyes only half open, and all I want to do is pull the bedcover over my head and keep snoozing. This is the usual time I get up to make Miss Brand's breakfast, although she usually makes it herself, but I also help her with bathing even though she's flexible with my timetable, especially if I've been performing the previous evening.

As I jump out of bed to get ready I wonder if this is going to work out. I didn't exactly go into detail when I told Miss Brand about my new gig. At the time, I had no idea about days and schedules, but now that I know how things stand I'm going to have to discuss arrangements with her and I wonder whether I might have to find another place in which to live. Paying a domestic/personal helper to cover for me on the odd occasion when I'm absent is one thing, but doing it on a regular basis is something I can't afford to do despite the improvement in my upcoming earnings.

I throw on a clean T-shirt and a pair of jeans and run down to the kitchen to prepare breakfast. While I poach eggs and make toast, I decide not to mention anything to Miss Brand just yet. It's only early days and I'm not even sure how things will pan out in terms of my working hours, and good thing I waited before speaking to Miss Brand because the days fly by so quickly that I barely have time to rehearse with Chris and Marcus.

The boys have their own outside commitments and can't always rehearse at a time that suits all three of us. Tomorrow, however, we have our first gig since Jeff's departure and I feel like we achieved nothing. It's early afternoon and we've been going through the original repertoire, which Jeff put together, and I manage to down at least three coffees to keep myself alert.

"Take it easy," Chris pats me on the shoulder when we stop for a break.

Marcus joins us and puts down a plate with a sandwich right in front of me. "At least eat something while we talk."

Looking at the sandwich suddenly awakens my hunger and I take a bite. "Thank you," I say.

"Who wants some water?" Chris asks.

We all do by the look in our eyes. We're tired and dehydrated with all the energy we spent while rehearsing and now it's time to re-energise.

"Look," says Marcus, "we can fall back on the current repertoire and simply add a couple of new songs we haven't done yet. Jeff left us with a wide choice of songs and artists, you know?"

Chris nods. "Marcus is right, Sam. Besides, the existing crowd will understand we need time to diversify our repertoire and in the meantime they can enjoy the songs we usually play. Plus don't forget," he adds, "for all we know we'll get a different crowd from the one that came to see Jeff."

My eyes widen in fear. "Oh, my God, I didn't think of that! What if no one comes?"

The other two laugh. "Are you kidding?" Marcus says. "This place always rocks, no matter who's on; that's Tom's promise to his patrons. He always says: if you want good music come to The Treble and Bass."

"Well, that's good to know," I say sarcastically, "but what will he say if we bomb out?"

Chris replies, "Have you forgotten how wild the crowd went when you did those solos? I certainly didn't see anyone running for the door. Frankly, I think you're underestimating yourself."

"I agree," Marcus says.

I sigh. "Okay, you guys. Thank you for putting up with me. I really appreciate your encouragement and I love you both." I give each of them a hug and they look at me as if I've truly lost it. "What?" I say.

"Well," remarks Chris, "I guess we weren't prepared for our female lead to give us a cuddle."

"Just a 'thank you' hug," I correct him, "not a cuddle. So let's get back to work." And work we do.

Thursday's our first gig without Jeff and this will give us the opportunity to see how the crowd reacts. The boys tell me Jeff did more ballads and soft rock on Thursdays for those who want a little romance or more sedate dancing rather than hard rock, but Saturdays get wilder and pretty much anything goes.

By late afternoon, we have a pretty good repertoire that incorporates rock, blues, and ballads. For the time being we stick to music covers the crowd enjoys. As for our own compositions and other experimentation, we'll wait until Luke arrives so we can work as a team.

Chapter 12 - Robert

<u>1947/48, Berlin, Germany</u>

After almost three years in Berlin my demob orders finally came through. I'm going home!

My darling Clara will follow a few months later, in early 1949, traveling with yet another shipment of German wives. Since December, 1945, from the time the War Brides Act was passed, a huge number of GIs married their German sweethearts and by the time Clara was getting ready to leave for the States some thirteen thousand marriages had taken place between American soldiers and their German girlfriends.

Thinking back on all the times Clara and I met for those two precious hours in the late afternoon made me realize how far we've come and how close we've grown, and the fact that we managed to keep our secret. This was mainly because Clara was too scared as to what the Schmidts would say if she told them about me. She regarded them as her parents and respected them as such, but I also believe she was waiting to see how things would turn out between us.

As it happened, it was on Clara's eighteenth birthday that we finally consummated our relationship. We stood barefoot on the blankets in our usual meeting place and Clara looked away, a flush on her cheeks, while I lit a single candle that cast a weak golden glow around us.

I started to undress her gently and whispered words of reassurance and love in her ears. She was a virgin and still spooked by the incident with the Frenchmen who had tried to attack her on the fateful night we met. Prior to this, she had never known the touch of a man and when we finally started seeing each other I gave her the time she needed to trust me.

Once naked, Clara began shaking like a leaf. I kissed her lips softly and proceeded to divest myself of my clothes, except for my boxer shorts. I was fully aroused, but I didn't want to frighten her and spoil the moment. We lay back on the blankets and I planted soft kisses all over her while I gently explored her body with my fingers, and after a while she raised her hips to admit their entry. She was so wet that she barely felt any unease when I finally took off my boxers and entered her fully. She made a low mewling sound and then pulled me deeply into her with her legs wrapped around my waist. I will never forget this sweet passion for as long as I live.

On Christmas Day, 1947, Clara finally took me to meet her people. We had already married and after submitting all documentation to US Headquarters, Clara was cleared to receive her permanent US visa. Full approval for the visa came through just before Christmas and the timing was perfect for us to get the Schmidts' blessing.

By this time, Clara's English was fairly fluent albeit with a soft German accent, but even this was slowly disappearing. My German was fluent, too, but I spoke it with an American accent that gave me away. This was not a concern for me as I wouldn't need to speak like a local, something Clara would have to do when she arrived in the States. Despite the fact that almost four years had passed since the war ended, Germans were not exactly welcome in Europe and America. Therefore, with my Irish surname and a near-American accent Clara would pass muster.

So we went to the Schmidts' humble home for tea and the best apple strudel I've ever tasted. The fact that I was able to express my compliments to the cook in German, in this case Mrs. Schmidt, seemed to bring us a little closer as a family, but this was not so apparent when we first arrived, bringing Christmas gifts by way of a couple of Virginia hams, Christmas pudding, a few blocks of chocolate, a basket of fresh fruit and French champagne.

The Schmidts were a simple and humble people and although I could see the amazement in their eyes at the amount of food we brought, I knew they were overwhelmed at our display of such sumptuous fare that seemed to faze them. Fortunately, once Clara told them the whole story of our meeting, courtship, and marriage, the Schmidts realized just how much in love we were, and I'd like to think they recognized my common sense in taking it slow while getting to know Clara.

The Schmidts understood the reason we kept our relationship a secret, it gave us time to recognize we were fated to be together. They were the old-fashioned type of parents and happy that Clara and I didn't rush to make a decision to join our lives together. So in the end I was accepted as their son-in-law with a big hug from Mr. Schmidt and an even bigger one from his wife. Their blessing was given and we all sat down to eat.

Chapter 13 - Samantha

<u>Aug/Sep, 1985, London, England</u>

Luke arrives in London after the first week of August and the boys and I bring him up to date since he last saw us. It's early morning and we're sitting at a small table at the back of the pub drinking coffee and munching on toast.

"What time did you get in?" I ask.

"Late last night so I'd be rested for this morning. I did my gig at Ku-dorf yesterday evening, but I was gone by eleven and caught the midnight flight to London." He then addresses all of us. "Last night was your first Saturday together, right? And what about Thursday night, did it go according to plan?"

We all go to answer at once, but Chris gets in first. "We decided to do the softer stuff on Thursdays, like soft rock and ballads; and Saturday was wild, baby!" he grins. "We just let loose."

Marcus rolls his eyes. "You're like a kid," he reprimands Chris, who is the youngest in our group at only twenty years of age.

Luke glances my way, but I say nothing. I wait until Marcus, the eldest of the two boys, at thirty, gives his feedback. "In my opinion," Marcus says, "I thought we did the right thing. Jeff left us with a great repertoire that pretty much covers all the stuff we did with him. There's a lot to pick from, but in the end we wanted to try out the audience and see what went down well with them, so we thought Thursdays might be better with the mellow, soft rock and ballad stuff; after all, people tend to go home earlier if they have to work the following day. And on Saturdays we can go all out and anything goes."

I nod in approval when I feel Luke's eyes on me. "Sounds good," Luke remarks.

"So you're here for three weeks now?" Chris asks. "What time are we rehearsing?"

Luke glances my way again, reminding me I'm the group leader. "It's either an early one, before the pub opens, or we have to find another venue." I then turn to Chris and Marcus, "Can you guys manage mornings from eight and rehearse for a couple of hours two days a week?"

The boys look at each other and I turn to Luke and give him a knowing smile. He and I both know Chris and Marcus like to sleep in. Luke winks at me and turns to them. "Guys, we're only talking three, four weeks at most to make everything gel. After that we only rehearse whenever we introduce new material."

The relief on the boys' faces is almost comical. "Oh, that's cool, man," Chris says and Marcus nods his agreement.

We leave it at that and agree to rehearse the following day, which is Monday. The boys depart and Luke and I are left alone. I glance at the wall clock behind the bar and the time has just gone nine-thirty. Tom will arrive in an hour or so to open up and Luke and I can keep working in the small foyer behind the stage or in the studio unit he's renting from Tom. All this time I've been wondering what it looks like, but I won't ask to see it unless Luke brings it up. I don't want him thinking I'm being too familiar.

"Feel like another coffee?" Luke asks. "You seemed deep in thought just now."

"I'll make the coffee," I offer, "and then you can tell me what you've been up to." I go off before he can see me blushing. What is the matter with me?

Upon my return, I find Luke gathering the repertoire lists we've been working with. "If you don't mind," he says, "why don't we continue from the studio? It has a table and even a kitchenette, and we'll be more comfortable there than sitting in the foyer."

Good grief, he must've read my thoughts! I hand him his coffee. "You said the stairs are deep and narrow so help me out in case I trip and pour coffee all over your head."

He laughs and takes his cup. "Come on then. Up we go."

The place is small but comfortable; it even has a large window overlooking parts of Covent Garden. The studio area consists of a double bed in one corner with a night stand and wardrobe on one side of the room, and a half circular table by the window with the view. A large Edwardian screen divides the studio in two where the other side houses a small partitioned room converted to a bathroom with its own vanity and shower cubicle and next to it is a narrow timber kitchenette with a built-in minibar fridge, small counter, drawer dishwasher and some storage shelves. The place is neat and tidy and the furniture and décor mainly come from the Edwardian period.

"It's comfy and rather soothing," I comment and take my cup to the table by the window. "Where do you suppose Tom got all the Edwardian stuff from?"

Luke joins me at the table. "I think he purchased the place with all the furnishings intact."

"Well," I remark, "at least it's not Victorian. I never liked the heavy timber furniture of that period plus all the clutter and ornaments filling a whole room so that there's very little space left."

"I agree," Luke replies. "Mind you, I'm quite flexible and will sleep in an empty room with a mattress on the floor if I have to."

"Yes," I nod, looking at nothing in particular. "I can relate to that."

Luke reaches out and puts his hand over mine, but I'm not ready to share my story with anyone.

"I can relate, too," he replies. "Want another coffee? I also have mineral water in the fridge."

"Any chocolate biscuits to go with that?" I grin and his smile makes me want to be closer to him physically, but I chastise myself silently and while Luke makes the coffee I say, "So how did Gianni take it when you left the gig?"

"He was disappointed," Luke replies from the kitchenette, "but he's happy with Mick, the guy I introduced to him, so everything's cool."

"Well, that's good."

"And you, if you don't mind me asking, what's the deal with Sloane Square?"

I laugh. I knew this was coming. No one seems to be able to resist asking how I can afford to live in a posh area. "Oh, all right!" I give in. "I'll tell you over coffee."

Luke's face appears around the corner from the Edwardian screen and he throws me another one of his smiles. I try not to react, but my body has different ideas. Meanwhile, he disappears back into the kitchenette and within a couple of minutes he brings out the coffee things with a plate of chocolate biscuits and two mineral water bottles. Once he settles at the table, he says, "Okay, out with it, Sam Kelly."

I sigh in resignation, have a sip of coffee and begin talking. I tell him the story about boarding at Miss Brand's and walking into a job that I wasn't expecting. Luke doesn't interrupt, but I know he has questions. I may not be ready to tell him my entire story, but somehow I feel I can talk to him and trust him.

When I finish the part of the story I wish to reveal, I notice him observing me in a thoughtful manner. "What?" I ask.

"So you said you've been with Miss Brand for five years; that would make you eighteen at the time, but where were you prior to that?"

This is one of the difficult parts for me to share with anyone. "Busking around London," I reply and sip more coffee, but Luke's all-seeing eyes have no intention of backing off. I finish my drink and throw him a guarded glance. "Let's just say I was a child of the streets for a while."

His eyes don't react in any way, which is a relief to me. I've always hated the sympathetic looks and soft words I used to get whenever I had to explain myself. Luke, on the other hand, remains silent as if waiting for me to continue, and I find I can't help myself—I just feel I have to tell him more.

"My parents split up when I was eight and my dad, who was born in the States, went back there. I stayed with my mother waiting for Dad to come back and fetch me. He said he would take me to live with him, but he disappeared." I pause and take a swig of water. "Cut a long story short, my mother worked a nightclub gig, she was a singer and wanted nothing to do with me. I imagine a kiddie made her feel older so she turned me over to welfare and I don't need to explain how that went. But after eight years in many foster homes and running away at the first opportunity, I ended up on the streets and by age sixteen I was making my own living." I look away from Luke; I don't want to see pity in his eyes and when I sneak a peek in his direction he's getting up from his chair and coming round to my side of the table. He then gathers my face gently with his two hands and softly kisses my slightly parted lips.

I must have blushed to the roots of my hair after his gesture and I shoot up from my chair and make my excuses to go to the bathroom. "I'll be right back."

Upon my return, I see Luke clearing the table and spreading the repertoire lists on it. He also adds more lists from his own Berlin gigs plus a whole bunch of music scores for compositions that I don't recognise.

I sit opposite him and feel comfortable in his company despite our earlier interchange so I take another swig of water and put on my business face. "This is a hell of a lot of material," I comment while flipping through some of the lists and glancing at the music scores. "May I?"

"Be my guest," Luke says.

I pick up a few of the songs and know immediately these are some of his own compositions; their range is wide in style and some seem experimental. I take a while to play the notes inside my head and he remains silent. When I'm done, I put down the scores. "These look great," I finally say. "It must've taken a long time to produce so much stuff."

"It's a passion of mine. It doesn't matter whether others like my songs or not. I simply compose them because they're an expression of who I am, and I take the opportunity to play one or two when I do a gig. It's nice to see what kind of reaction I get from the audience."

"Well, from what I can see I feel people can't help but like them. I know I do," I remark. "I see aspects of rhythm and blues, soft rock and jazz ballads in these, but you also have a range of rock and roll from soft to hard rock, so there's something for every taste here."

Luke smiles. "You know your music styles, I see."

I misunderstand him. "Please forgive me, I don't mean to be patronising."

He grins. "I didn't mean that. I'm simply pointing out that you know the different styles of music. You'd be surprised at the number of musos that don't and to some of them it's all noise."

We smile at each other and I suddenly wonder what it would feel like to be passionately kissed by him. I quickly immerse myself in the work and give thanks he can't see inside my head, which I shake to clear my thoughts. Luke's waiting so we can get on with choosing the covers for Saturday's gig and here I am, mooning around like a teenager.

Chapter 14 - Robert

As soon as I docked in New York, I said my farewells to the muso buddies who traveled home with me and we promised to keep in touch. George Hutton, who played in the Victory Club, reminded me to look him up. He had some contacts in the business and was confident that with my skill on the trumpet I would be able to find work in one of the jazz clubs on 52nd Street, a renowned jazz mecca in New York.

I thought about this while taking the train to White Plains, New York, where my parents live. They were expecting me, having received my telegram which I sent prior to my departure from Germany. Although I missed Clara so much that it hurt, I was at the same time excited and looking forward to seeing my family again. It just seemed so surreal that since 1943, when we shipped out to Italy, I would see them again in the next few minutes. Then, my heart sank—Ollie would not be going to see his family; he would not celebrate a reunion with them or with me, and here I was: young, healthy and married to boot.

I often wonder whether there's any justice in life—we didn't start the war and yet many of us did not come home. My heart went out to Ollie's parents, knowing that each day would be an empty day for them, especially as I had come back from the war alive and well. I'm not sure whether my parents told them I was arriving today and I wonder if I should visit them at some stage. I wish to pay my respects, but at the same time, seeing me alive, it would bring back the pain at the loss of their only son.

I couldn't think of this now, but I would like to see Ollie's parents if possible. My thoughts then turn back to Clara—my family knows nothing about her. Since I married her, I wanted to write to them with the news but something stopped me from doing this. Perhaps it's because of Clara's nationality, but she's not a Nazi, I argue with myself, she's merely a citizen of Germany who got caught up in Hitler's war. She's a sweet, innocent girl who would never harm anyone and her parents are kind people who helped those in need as much as possible, plus Clara is so gentle that anyone with eyes would fall in love with her immediately, just as I did.

When the train arrived at my destination I immediately recognized my parents. For five years I hadn't seen them, but they looked almost the same as they did back in 1943, only their hair was grayer and my dad's hairline had started to recede.

They stood there, hand in hand, looking out for me; they hadn't yet seen me, but a huge smile suddenly appeared on their faces when they spotted me exiting the train and walking onto the platform. I was in civilian clothes by now and I imagine in their eyes I had filled out a bit. I had gone away a boy of eighteen and now, at twenty-three, I was a young man in a suit and ready to take on the world.

I put down my luggage and trumpet case and we embraced. My mother had tears running down her face and she kept touching me, to make sure I was real. My father patted my back and welcomed me home. I didn't have any siblings, so for five years my parents had been a duo and today we became a trio again. I was delirious with happiness and thanked God I got home safe and sound to be with my family.

We lived a ten minute ride by car from the station and while Dad drove, Mom filled me in on all the news. I knew it would take a lot more time than ten minutes to bring me up to date, but she sounded so happy chatting that I let her go on. We had plenty of time to catch up properly. Besides, I wanted to find the right moment to tell them about Clara.

<u>Disaster strikes!!! As I write in this journal I'm on an evening train back to NYC. I can't believe this is happening!</u>

After arriving home, my mom, dad and I lounged around for most of the day swapping our news and just feeling happy being together. We spoke of Ollie, of course, and they advised it'd be best not to see his parents until they had time to get used to the idea that I was back. Mom pointed out that I would be a huge reminder of Ollie because we'd been best friends and always inseparable. I was practically Ollie's brother and this would only bring back the pain of his loss, so I agreed to wait a couple of weeks before I went to see Ollie's parents.

By late afternoon, we pretty much covered most of our news and Mom made dinner. We talked right through the main course, dessert and coffee while I entertained them with stories of the Victory Club. I didn't talk about the terrible conditions in Berlin or all the awful things I witnessed during the past five years; I wanted to keep things on a positive note. My parents enjoyed hearing about my musical talents plus the important work I did in the demobilization of our troops, and they were very proud of me.

Mom refilled our coffee cups and asked if anyone wanted seconds with the apple pie she made for dessert. I opted out since I was full after a sumptuous dinner of roast beef, baked potatoes and roast vegetables plus all the trimmings, but I accepted a second cup of coffee. In my mind, I decided this would be the perfect time to tell them of my marriage. After all, our reunion had gone really well and we were so happy to be together again that I didn't see any reason to delay my news.

I figured if I waited for days they'd think it strange that I held back, especially about something this important, so I finished my coffee and announced with a big smile, "I have big news I'd like to share with you." They looked surprised and seeing my smile they waited expectantly. I felt rather nervous, but I had the floor and it reminded me of the first time I played a trumpet solo at the Victory Club. The audience waited with a smile for me to begin while my mouth went suddenly dry. There was no going back and so I started to play and in the end I was applauded, congratulated by my peers, and the audience called out for an encore. This is now what I saw in my imagination, except that I didn't play the trumpet this time, I simply announced I met a wonderful girl and after three years of going steady we got married.

My parents looked at one another and then turned to me. The expression on their faces remained neutral, but I hadn't yet finished the rest of my story. They said nothing and waited for me to continue. I felt my mouth go dry and took a sip of water before going on, but all of a sudden I couldn't come up with the words I wanted to say and I realized my error in bringing this up so soon, but now it was too late. I couldn't take it back and I couldn't keep going forward either; unlike the solo trumpet episode, I suddenly knew this would turn out to be a nightmare rather than a triumph.

My father broke the silence in the room and asked with a serious tone in his voice, "She's not a WAC, is she? You would've written to us about it if you'd met a girl from back home." I was still unable to speak and he went on, "You're talking about a dirty German! It's not enough they killed millions of innocent people, but now they're marrying Americans because we destroyed their country and America's still the land of milk and honey. But if you think I'm going to tolerate a Kraut in my family, you can think again! And if you don't like it, then I no longer have a son."

All I remember after his horrible words is my mother breaking into tears, but I wasn't sure if it was because I married a German or because my father's ultimatum made it clear that he'd rather lose a son than tolerate a German daughter-in-law.

Somehow, I picked up my belongings and walked out from my childhood home. I found myself walking toward one of the main roads in our area where I caught a cab to the train station, and now I'm about fifteen minutes out of New York city. It's very late at night and I have yet to find a hotel.

Chapter 15 - Samantha

Our first Saturday gig with Luke is fantastic. I'm amazed at how many regulars remember him after his time away from London. While performing, I throw a quick glance Tom's way and I see a huge smile on his face which doesn't seem to want to leave him. It's obvious he considers our band a hit and this gives me a sense of relief and elation.

During the breaks people surround Luke, hoping to chat with him and I have to admit he deserves all the praise he gets from the crowd. His talent knows no bounds as far as I'm concerned and I have to wonder why he never made it to the big time. I still know very little about him and I make up my mind to put this to rights; after all, he knows a lot more about my story, but he doesn't give much away about his unless it's to talk about music.

In the gig, we take turns singing songs while the other harmonises or does backup vocals, which at times also includes Chris and Marcus becoming involved. We also try an experimental soft rock duo that works out really well with Luke and me singing. Finally, Luke closes the last set with one of his own compositions, a soul/R&B ballad. And after the final song for the night, the crowd calls for an encore, but we put an end to the evening. It's past midnight and we've been playing for four hours, so we're exhausted.

"You look beat," Luke says into my ear while the crowd finally starts to disperse.

I pick up a small towel from my guitar case and dry the perspiration from my face and hair. "Good grief!" I complain. "With all the smoke in here I stink like someone who hasn't had a bath for a month."

"You and me both," Luke replies.

"Hey, you guys!" Chris calls out, and Marcus remarks, "That was one hell of a gig."

Chris passes around bottles of water. "Drink up! We need to rehydrate."

We all drink thirstily from our bottles and meanwhile Tom approaches and slaps Luke and me on the back. "You guys click so well together. That was an amazing gig."

"And let's not forget our backup talent," Luke remarks.

"But of course. I meant all of you, and the crowd loved you." We thank him and Tom adds, "By the way, I'm closing up now so you're welcome to leave your stuff here. You look exhausted and need rest rather than having to pack up your equipment."

"That's right," Chris says cheekily, "where the hell are our roadies?"

We have a laugh and Chris and Marcus agree to leave their stuff overnight and pick it up the following day. "Before we open, mind," Tom warns them.

"I'll make sure your stuff is safe," Luke tells the boys and turns to Tom. "You okay if I use the storage downstairs?"

Tom nods. "Good idea. I'll give you the key for the street door on that side of the building so the boys can pick up their stuff without having to trudge through the public area. Just make your arrangements." He takes out a key from his key ring and hands it to Luke. "Your responsibility," he says.

"Don't worry. It'll be okay." Luke takes the key from Tom and turns to the rest of us. "If you guys don't need your equipment over the weekend I'll keep it locked up until Monday morning, when we rehearse." The boys agree and leave for home while Luke turns to me, "What about you? Do you want to leave your stuff here?"

"I'm actually performing tomorrow afternoon," I tell him.

He throws me a look of surprise. "What, here?"

"Yes. I'm filling in for Joan. She performs during high tea twice a week on Friday and Sunday afternoons, but she's off with a cold and asked if I would fill in for her tomorrow. It's only for two hours."

A pensive look appears on Luke's face. "Suggestion," he says. "How would you like to do this together?"

"Why would you want to do that?" I'm bursting to know what he's up to, but I feign disinterest.

HEROES

"I never played at a high tea," he replies. "It would give us a chance to try some of the slower numbers."

"There's not much by way of lyrics, though," I inform him. "High tea's more for background music, both contemporary and classical."

"Oh, well, no worries." He starts to gather his music scores in preparation to retire. "Goodnight, Tom!" he calls out, only to discover Tom's gone home and we're alone. "Okay, so how about I escort you home? It's almost one in the morning so the tube's not an option."

"It's okay," I reply. "I've walked home later than this before."

"Not if I'm around," he says. "At least let me get you a taxi."

I don't want an escort and I don't want to get a taxi, I say silently to myself while Luke stands there, waiting for me to respond. I admit much to my shame that all I want is to stay with him.

He regards me thoughtfully, during my moment of silence, while I stand near him saying nothing, but I realise he's waiting for my answer. I don't know what to say. Although I lived in foster homes and on the streets for years, my experience with males is rather limited—at least the type of experience that one would consider to be tender and loving, and most of my experiences were anything but that. "Look, forget it," I suddenly say, "I'll call for a cab." I turn towards the bar for the telephone, but Luke reaches out and grabs my wrist, bringing me closer to him.

"It's really late," he says, "and I have an idea, but I don't want to seem presumptuous. It's silly for you to go back home now. I simply should've offered you my studio." My heart jolts for a moment and I can't think of what to say, but Luke continues, "What I mean is, you're better off here so you don't have to rush around tomorrow. You had a big night with the gig and you should sleep in to recharge your batteries, so if you're okay with it just take the studio. Have a hot shower, sleep in all you like, and tomorrow you'll feel more refreshed."

"I can't take your room. You're tired, too, and I'm sure you also want to shower," I tell him.

He seems to realise he's still holding onto my wrist and lets go. "There's a fold-up bed that Tom keeps in the back storeroom. He sometimes stays here when his team work late doing stocktake, so I don't mind sleeping in the storeroom while you have the studio."

69

I make up my mind. "In that case, I'll accept your kind offer, thank you. It'll make things a bit easier rather than rushing around." I then hesitate, not knowing how to put what I wish to say without making it sound like a come on, which is not at all my intention.

"Something wrong?" Luke asks while I stand there, looking indecisive.

"Well... It's just that this'll sound unusual and I don't want to give you the wrong impression."

"Try me," he replies.

"It's to do with my past and some of the places where I slept. I have to admit that I feel safer with a person I trust in the room, so would it be an imposition for you to bring in the fold-up and sleep in the studio?"

"I totally understand and can even relate; it can happen to guys, too, you know?" he replies. "It's not a problem for me, so go on up and get ready. There are fresh towels on the top shelf of the wardrobe and I have plenty of T-shirts that'll serve as a nightshirt for you. Everything else you need is in the bathroom, including some new toothbrushes. I have a habit of leaving them behind whenever I travel so I usually take a whole bunch with me. I'll be up in about twenty minutes."

I nod but say nothing and take off for the stairs with my cheeks burning. I never thought I'd ask a man I knew for such a short time to share my room, but the fact that Luke can relate to what I said reassures me, and I know I can trust and feel safe with him.

The shower revives me and I feel refreshed once I get the smell of smoke out of my hair. I do a quick blow-dry, brush my teeth and slip into a white T-shirt. Then, my curiosity takes the better of me and I go back for a peek at the contents of Luke's wardrobe. I know so little about him and I remember reading somewhere that people's belongings often reveal a lot about them.

Luke's T-shirts are either black or white, why is that, I wonder? He has two pairs of blue jeans, aside from the ones he's currently wearing, and in my estimation he seems to be partial to an American kind of look, hence the reason I thought he had a rebel air about him when we first went out in Berlin.

Moving on, there's a well-worn black leather jacket, a couple of pullovers, a pair of black half-calf leather boots and two pairs of white sneakers. Okay, so maybe he likes that young, cool type of look or he simply feels comfortable in this kind of clothing. I then chastise myself. What am I doing wasting time with this? The man's going to be back at any moment and I don't want to be caught snooping through his things. I shut the wardrobe door just as I hear footsteps outside the studio and I run for the bed where I sit with the bedcover over my knees although Luke's T-shirt reaches below them and therefore I look quite conservative.

Luke walks in with the fold-up and deposits it at the other end of the room, away from my bed. "Find everything okay?"

"Yes, thank you. I feel human again."

"Well, it's my turn now, so feel free to go to sleep if you want. I'll keep it quiet. And good thing I don't make a habit of singing in the shower!" He laughs at his own joke and this brings a smile to my face.

When he disappears into the bathroom I lie back on the bed, trying to relax. The only light in the room is the bedside table lamp, which casts a soft glow and I begin to feel sleepy with the rhythm of the shower running in the bathroom.

———————⊛———————

It's raining and far too cold for the thin, ragged blanket to protect me from the weather despite my luck at finding a sheltered doorway at the back of an off-licence. The shop is shut and the lights are switched off so I set up in a sheltered corner space of the doorway with an old sleeping bag serving as a kind of mattress and the thin blanket for cover. I fall asleep immediately, holding on to my guitar case.

As the freezing cold invades my body, I slip in and out of consciousness while shivering uncontrollably. I'm so exhausted that I manage to stay asleep, but not for long. I hear a kind of shuffling noise nearby and I wake up to find someone trying to pull the guitar case away from me. I'm still dazed with sleep and at the same time fear screams out silently from inside me.

A middle-aged man in a scraggly raincoat is trying to steal my guitar, but he seems to change his mind and instead he punches me in the stomach and I'm winded with the pain of it. Before I can move, I feel his weight pinning down my body and his hand is fiddling with the fly of my jeans while his swollen penis sticks out of his pants. His intentions are more than clear and my only thought is to fight for my life, no matter what!

A sharp knife appears at my throat and I spring into action, trying to escape from under my attacker. He brings his face closer to mine and it is then I smell the alcohol on his rancid breath. He's still under the influence and none too steady, but his weakness suddenly becomes my strength.

I push him away from me with whatever force I can muster and then grab hold of his disgusting member and pull it with all my might. He lets out a scream, especially when I twist the repulsive thing, but he manages to stand up and kick me in the ribs. The pain is so acute that I double over as I wait for the man to drive his knife into me. This is the end and I wait for death...

My eyes open wide and I find myself sitting up in bed, sobbing loudly and with my arms flailing as if I'm still fighting with my assailant.

Luke suddenly appears, switching on the bedside lamp with one hand and drawing me to him with the other. "It's okay, Sam! It's okay!" he reassures me. "It was a bad dream. You're safe now, there's nothing to fear."

Crying against his bare chest, I say, "Did I talk in my sleep?"

He gathers me closer and produces a bunch of tissues from the bedside table drawer. I take them gratefully and hold them to my face to dry my tears. "You were yelling," he replies, "and it seemed as if you were struggling with someone and then you woke up crying."

I regard him with new tears in my eyes. "I'm so sorry I woke you, I didn't think I'd have nightmares if you were here."

Luke sighs and caresses my hair. "There's nothing to be sorry about, it wasn't your fault; it's probably old memories that resurfaced, especially when you told me about feeling unsafe when sleeping alone. So please know I'm here for you if you need to talk or just to be with someone, okay?"

I nod and search his eyes and see the care and genuine concern in them, and I'm grateful his gaze doesn't show pity for me. It crosses my mind that this man may have had his own fair share of bad times, especially as he mentioned he could relate to my situation and that it could happen to guys, too.

He remains silent, gently holding me close and as my body rests against his, the remnants of my bad dream dissolve into the ether and a warm feeling of affection for Luke takes over me. I can't explain why, but I suddenly feel so close to him and his touch arouses in me the kind of desire I haven't felt in years.

Luke's still watching me, saying nothing, but his soft touch says it all. I gently move closer within his embrace and dare to touch his lips with mine in a kiss that is tentative but with a promise of passion. He responds and our kiss deepens to the point where our mouths explore each other while my hands travel over his body as we somehow ease off our clothes.

Luke caresses me with his hands and lips, touching, kissing, tasting, as I lay back on the bed with him by my side. We take our time feeling each other, trying to find a style to suit our bodies, and with Luke giving me the chance to show him what I want.

I feel so safe with him and know I can trust him, and I can't resist the acute pleasure of his body next to mine, so I wrap my legs around his hips and bring him into my body. He enters me easily and we slither in the wetness inside me. I hold him in place as his thrusts grow from their smooth movement into a crescendo that releases our passion and brings us both to climax.

The sound of a door slamming downstairs wakes me and at first I feel disoriented. I rub my eyes, look around the room, and then I see Luke, fast asleep next to me. My face suddenly grows hot as visions of our lovemaking flood my mind. I search for my discarded T-shirt and find it just as Luke awakes. I slip it over me and sit up in bed while he remains lying back with arms behind his head.

"Good morning," he greets me with a sleepy smile.

I get out of bed immediately, feeling shy after what took place between us and I rush for the bathroom while calling out, "I have to leave, it's getting late and I need to get my music scores, plus I want to check on Miss Brand. But I'll make us coffee before I go." I dress in my clothes from last evening and still wear Luke's T-shirt, which is clean and fresh, and once I go through my morning ablutions I come out to find him standing in his shorts. "My turn next," he says. "And yes, coffee's great, thanks."

I make coffee and toast and by the time Luke comes out of the bathroom fully dressed I'm finishing making the bed. He suddenly takes me into his arms and kisses me to the point where I start to consider skipping breakfast and making love again, but he releases me with a warm smile and we sit at the table as he says, "I'm famished, and you?"

I blush and hate myself for not being able to control my desire. I know he can see my feelings written across my face and I'm not sure how to respond after what happened between us. I may have lived in the streets, but I never had an experienced and mature lover like Luke.

"I think Tom's downstairs opening up. Didn't you hear the back door slamming?" I say as if the kiss didn't affect me.

Luke glances at his watch. "Damn! It's almost eleven. I have to clear up the stage and put everything away or Tom will have a fit."

I sigh with relief that I don't yet have to face what we did last night. I don't know how Luke feels about what happened, but I don't want to dissect our union or feel embarrassed that I was so easy with him. "I need to get home to Miss Brand," I remind him. "Good thing I told her last week that with the gig being new and all, I might be required to work later than usual and I'd probably stay in the area. Anyway, Miss Brand knows she's to wait for me before she has her bath. I help her in that department in case she has a fall."

I'm blabbing too much and feel foolish, but Luke puts me at ease by speaking as if we're simply having a conversation about every day things. "You're very good to her and I'm sure she'll understand. Now, let's go down together and I'll let you out via the back door. Does that work for you?"

"Yes," I reply. "I'll be back around three to set up for high tea; it starts at four so I have plenty of time."

We finish breakfast quickly and prepare to leave, but not before Luke kisses me again. When we draw apart we laugh as if we're kids getting away with having done something naughty and I say, "We don't have time to talk about this now, but even though last night was wonderful I want you to know that you're under no obligation to me."

"The thought never entered my mind. I don't play games with people's feelings, but I do agree we should talk. Will you stay here tonight?"

I nod with a shy smile.

Chapter 16 - Robert

<u>1948/49, New York City, USA</u>

I arrived back in the city feeling shell-shocked and checked into a cheap hotel on the fringe of Clinton or Hell's Kitchen, as it is known. The district has mainly been home to Irish-American immigrants although other nationalities populate the area. The place is full of tenements, boarding houses full of prostitutes and businesses run by gangs. Crime is rife on the streets and witnessing a murder in the middle of the day can be commonplace. The closest I've ever been to Hell's Kitchen was prior to the war when I caught a show at a Broadway theatre with some friends.

I was fortunate to come from English-Irish ancestry that went back to my great grandfather, who made a small fortune in stocks and other investments. He was an adventurer from the stories I heard about him, but he was an adventurer with a nose for business and thanks to him the Kellys never wanted for anything nor did any of them have to live in Hell's Kitchen among the gangs, the criminals, the poor, and the homeless.

I was brought up at my parents' home in White Plains where the streets are safe and the neighbors friendly; therefore, the shock of Hell's Kitchen when I arrived after the unpleasant incident with my parents was almost too much to bear and as I sat in my small and sparsely furnished hotel room, if one could call it that, I realized there were three things that would get me through this phase in my life: 1. Hell's Kitchen is affordable for someone like me, just out of the military and with a small amount of savings. 2. New York City is the jazz mecca for all serious musicians and the majority of jazz clubs are practically on top of Hell's Kitchen, especially the area that runs from 52nd Street, between Fifth and Seventh Avenues.

I was sure I'd be able to find somewhere to live near work a little farther from the outer perimeter of the area. I was also convinced that I would secure a gig in one of the many jazz clubs springing up all over 52nd Street.

And saving the best for last: 3. My darling Clara will be joining me in four months' time.

The thought of my love brought a smile to my face and my heart longed for her so much that nothing else mattered. I would live in a tent if it meant we could be together forever.

Daydreaming about the future, I can also see a way to mend things with my parents. Once settled into a musical career and doing well, plus if Clara and I are blessed with a child, I'm fairly sure my parents will relent. I know in my heart that they wouldn't be able to reject a grandchild and I believe that if they give Clara a chance they will learn to love her.

The war ended less than four years ago and times are already changing. We're in one of the best countries in the world and opportunities are there for the taking if one is prepared to work hard. I'm young, fit and healthy, and so is Clara, and this will be our time to build a new life based on love, music, and hopefully a young family.

I can't wait until all this happens, especially Clara's arrival, but in the meantime I have some contacts to connect with in the music business. I remember George Hutton reminding me to keep in touch. So once I find a gig I can look for a suitable home on the edge of Hell's Kitchen—not exactly an elegant location, but at least an area fit for musicians, singers, artists, and more.

Chapter 17 - Samantha

<u>Aug/Sep, 1985, London, England</u>

While I assist Miss Brand to bathe, I tell her about last night's gig and what a success it was. Although I don't want to bring up the subject of Luke into it, I can't help my enthusiasm when I describe his voice range to her and, being a musician herself, Miss Brand can appreciate what I'm talking about.

"It sounds wonderful, my dear. How I wish I could have heard him sing," she remarks. "Oh, if only I were your age," she sighs with melancholy.

I reach out for shampoo and while I massage it into her hair I reply, "But Miss Brand, at least you've had an extremely interesting life, plus your skill on the piano is extraordinary. In fact, I'm surprised you never thought of becoming a concert pianist."

"Thank you, dear. In my day young girls were only encouraged to give recitals at rich people's homes in the hope of meeting a prospective husband rather than performing for the public. Isn't it ironic how over time women have had to fight and keep on fighting for their rights?"

"I agree with you; a woman's lot has always been tough." I grab the handheld shower and start to rinse her hair gently. Miss Brand relaxes into the scalp massage which I follow up with hair conditioner and a final rinse.

"Sam," she says when I help her out of the bath and into her bathrobe. "I hear you sing many times when you practice in your room and you have a lovely voice, so I take it when you sang with this young man the two of you harmonised beautifully."

I blush, damn! If only she knew what happened after the music she'd be thoroughly shocked. Thank goodness she can't see my face while I blow-dry her hair. "It's fortunate our voices fit well together," I say and change the subject. "Miss Brand, I forgot to tell you that I'm filling in for another musician this afternoon. She's off sick with a bad cold and she normally does the high tea gig, and after that I have to keep working on the repertoire with Luke for next week's gig so I'm afraid this will take us far into the night and I'll stay overnight at the boarding house near the pub, which I sometimes use when working late. But I'll be back tomorrow evening, so will you be okay until then? If you need anything from the market I can go now."

Miss Brand walks into her bedroom and sits in her reading chair. "Thank you, my dear, but I'll be fine. I think you're burning the candle at both ends, though. Is that wise?"

I suddenly feel concerned by her question. What if she's trying to tell me that our arrangement is not working out for her? "This is only until the band finishes rehearsing and Luke and I agree on the songs we're going to perform. After this, he goes back to Berlin and from beginning of next month he'll be commuting to London every other weekend for our gig."

A smile appears on Miss Brand's face. "Oh, Sam, who is going to look after you, my dear? I was young once, albeit from a different time, but I can see in your face how you feel about this young man."

I blush again. Crap! "I'm... I mean... Well, I do like him and we're on our way to becoming good friends. Beyond that... well... I'm not one to fall hard for someone. I'm a lone wolf."

Miss Brand laughs softly. "A lone wolf? Sam, all I'm trying to tell you is that if this is the guy for you, then you should go for it." She sees the surprise in my eyes and goes on to explain. "Despite the restrictions for ladies during my youth, I once fell madly in love with a pianist I met at a recital I attended and we had a whirlwind romance, but not one that led to marriage. Our parents found us out and broke us up. According to them, we were too young to marry and there was always the question of money. Our respective families were relatively well off at the time, but the Great War was looming, fortunes were easily lost, and this seemed to be the biggest impediment to our union.

"In the end, my Edward went to war and was killed in action." A few tears gather in her eyes and she quickly wipes at them with a tissue. "After this I didn't want to live anymore, but I went through the motions for the sake of my family, especially my sister to whom I was very close." She takes a moment to gather her thoughts and then looks at me with love in her eyes. "You've become like a daughter to me, my dear. You know I keep telling you this and I don't want anything bad to happen to you. I know very little of your background, but I feel it wasn't an easy path and so I tell you this: be a lone wolf if you must, but if this Luke is the one for you, grab him any way you can and hold on to him. Life's not a dress rehearsal, as some say, and I for one agree with them. So I quote to you from Horace's 'Odes', which were published way back in 23 BCE: *'Carpe diem quam minimum credula postero'*, which translates to pluck (or seize) the day, trusting as little as possible in the next one."

I'm overcome with emotion and allow my tears to flow freely as I cross the room and give Miss Brand a warm hug. "I never had a person I considered to be a loving mother so I'm honoured that you see me as a daughter. I value your caring about me as I value your wonderful advice and guidance." I kiss her warm cheek and add, "And from now on I promise to call you Dora."

We smile at each other and she says, "At long last I get you to call me by my first name and I have this young man, Luke, to thank for it even though he's not aware of our discussion. So Sam, when you next see him make arrangements for afternoon tea; I want to meet this Luke of yours."

———————⊙———————

I pack a small overnight bag that I'll leave at Luke's with a few of my things and when I arrive at the pub I let myself in through the back door, taking a peek in the storage room where I see Luke's been hard at work putting away all our equipment. To my surprise, I spot a baby grand piano behind the main stage and this is when I bump into Tom.

"Whoa, there!" Tom takes hold of my shoulders to steady me.

"What's this?" I point to the baby grand.

"You did agree to fill in for Joan, right?"

"Yes, but Joan usually uses one of the keyboards or the old stand-up you have in storage," I refer to an old stand-up piano that Tom was thinking of donating to the Salvation Army until Joan insisted the real McCoy always sounds better for elegant occasions.

"Oh, that!" Tom laughs. "I thought you knew she finally convinced me to buy a baby grand and show off our style. I must say, though, the lady's got class, and high tea somehow tastes better with music coming from a baby grand."

I shake my head at this notion, but I have to smile as well. Joan is a real perfectionist. "So you're telling me I'm playing the baby grand?"

"I am."

"Then why isn't it onstage?"

Tom sighs. "You musicians are so picky. Have you any idea how much that piano weighs? We couldn't even lift it with me, Luke, and one of our other guys."

"So what happens now?" I ask, trying not to blush at the mention of Luke.

"Well, Luke came up with a great idea. I have a number of large screens, like the one in his studio, so we're partitioning the stage away from the dance floor and we can wheel the piano over to the front of the screens and that's where you sit, surrounded by a set-up of tables and chairs bordering the dance floor so you'll be at the forefront of the action."

"But no one told me I'll be out front!" I protest. "I'm wearing jeans because I thought I'd be mostly out of sight onstage, away from the patrons. I thought this was just background music. And why didn't anyone telephone me so I could've brought an appropriate outfit to change into?"

Tom pats my shoulder. "Simmer down, Sam. Go and see Luke. He tells me he's got everything in hand." Before I can say anything, Tom wishes me well and he's off back to the bar.

I rush up the back stairs to the studio and Luke swings the door open, pulling me inside and slamming the door behind us. He gathers me in his arms and kisses me deeply, and I forget everything else and enjoy the moment.

When he releases me I'm about to speak, but he beats me to it. "Joan forgot to tell you about the piano, right?" I nod, still recovering from his kiss. "She rang this morning and sent a friend along with a number of dresses and shoes that you may want to wear. She's slightly taller than you, I believe, but she said you're both quite slender and you also have the same shoe size. She apologises for the inconvenience, but she's totally out of it with this cold and she forgot to tell you about the new arrangements."

I put down my overnight bag, which I've been holding onto all this time, but Luke makes no remark about it. He simply points to the wardrobe where there are three coat hangers holding three different style of dresses, each with a pair of matching shoes.

I glance at my watch; it's almost three-thirty. "I have just enough time to get dressed and decide what I'm going to play."

"Need any help?"

"No. I won't be long. I decided to stick to classical stuff once Tom showed me the baby grand. Good thing I brought quite a bit of music scores with me. I'm thinking Beethoven, some Chopin nocturnes and Mozart. They're my favourite boys in the 'classical band'." I smile at Luke and then turn and go off to the bathroom to put on some make-up; good thing I thought of it. One has to look classy with classical music.

Luke appears at the bathroom door. "I'll be downstairs watching, and about tonight..."

I turn and look at him. "What about it?"

"We're still on?"

"Yes. Unless you changed your mind."

"Of course not, but you'll be tired after the gig so I thought I'd take you out to dinner and we can have an early night."

I smile. "Thank you. I think we'll both need it after all the equipment you've been lugging about downstairs, plus we have rehearsals with the boys tomorrow morning."

"That's right. I'll see you downstairs." He kisses my cheek and leaves me to prepare.

Joan's dresses are not my style, but there is one that catches my eye. It's a silk 1920s number in a deep forest green designed as a sleeveless shift with a low waistband and a hand-stitched braided hem with tiny pearls. For shoes, I go with the ballet-like slippers covered in small black sequins that are Joan's choice for this particular dress. I leave my hair loose, apply some make-up, and I'm ready.

When I arrive downstairs, I have butterflies in my stomach. It's been an age since I played the piano and I pray I can carry it off without mishap. I take a seat at the baby grand and throw a quick glance at the audience. Luckily, Luke's not sitting out front so I feel more relaxed. I know he's probably watching me from behind the scenes, but as long as I don't see him I can focus on the task ahead.

I play for two hours with a ten minute break for every half hour. A waiter drops by during my first break and hands me an espresso as he whispers, "From Luke." He then tops up my glass with fresh mineral water and goes on his way. I take a sip of the coffee with a smile on my face. I still don't know much about the man, but he's certainly gallant and thinks of everything.

The ten minutes fly by and over the next hour and a half I dazzle the audience with my favourite piano sonatas from Mozart and Beethoven, and in between I slip in one or two Chopin nocturnes.

While I play, I'm transported into a world where all is good: there's no homelessness, all children have loving parents and don't have to grow up with abuse, family and friends gather round and they don't abandon you, and all the beauty in the world is there for us to enjoy, protect and pass on to the next generation.

I come out of my reverie to a sound that feels like thunder and when I glance towards the audience I see them on their feet, applauding, smiling at me, and calling for an encore. I feel humble and tears gather in my eyes. Music is so very powerful that even if you're out in the streets busking it can still transport you into other worlds.

I feel someone's hand taking mine and I find myself eye to eye with Luke. He says something I can't hear because the audience is clapping like mad, so he gets closer and speaks into my ear: "You're so beautiful." He takes a quick glance at the audience and turns back to me. "Are you up for an encore?" I nod in response, and in full view of the audience he kisses my lips softly before he lets go of my hand and leaves me to it. I finish with a Chopin nocturne and then take my bows at more applause, whistles, and smiles.

Tom appears next to me with a bunch of roses, which he deposits in my arms, and he escorts me backstage while the crowd sit back to finish their afternoon tea. Luke's waiting for us with a smile on his face and he relieves me of the bouquet and the music scores I have tucked under my arm. "Isn't she wonderful?" he says to Tom.

"Why didn't you say you played classical music?" Tom addresses me. "You're incredible! Where did you learn to play like that?" Before I can reply, Tom goes on, "Never mind. I want you to consider playing a special high tea—just classical music once a week with really posh furnishings and an elegant crowd; black tie only."

My head is spinning and I grab hold of Luke's hand, but I turn to Tom. "I don't know. I have to think about it. I don't want to take Joan's gig away from her. Besides, it would clash with my band gig."

Tom says, "You let me worry about that. Just think about it and I promise you nothing will change the band gig or Joan's high teas. I'm only asking for two hours or so once or twice a week; we can make it something like a cocktail-do for the crowd that wants to have drinks prior to going to the theatre."

While Tom is excitedly planning my future, I glance at Luke and he comes to the rescue. "Sam needs to rest, Tom. Don't forget we've got rehearsal tomorrow morning with the boys."

Tom looks thoughtfully at the two of us. "Of course, and Sam, you take your time and we'll talk when you're ready. And if you guys don't mind me asking, I take it you're together?"

"Why do you ask?" Luke says rather firmly.

"Simply so I know who's living in the studio for insurance purposes, nothing more."

"Fair enough," Luke replies.

Tom says, "You guys go and rest. I'll see you tomorrow."

Luke and I go into the studio and the moment he closes the door he puts down the flowers and music scores, and leads me to bed where we lay fully-clothed in each other's arms and fall asleep.

———————◆———————

It is dusk when I awake and coming up to eight in the evening. Luke's fast asleep on his back, but his eyes open when he feels me move and he turns to face me. "I think we needed that, don't you?"

"Most definitely."

"So what now? Shall we go out to dinner or would you rather we postpone it for some other time and order in this evening?

I agree. "Staying in sounds nice, plus I've yet to take off these clothes. I wrinkled Joan's dress."

"Can I help you with the clothes?" he says with eyes full of meaning.

I sit up in bed. "Tell you what. You order in while I go and change. How about something from Casa Della Mamma? They're nearby and they deliver."

"Okay," Luke sits up and goes for the telephone. "I know them well; I used to eat there regularly when I worked for Tom. Anything in particular that you want?"

"Something light. They do a great stracciatella soup."

"Done!" replies Luke while I go to the bathroom and change into a sleeveless cotton nightshirt and wash the makeup off my face. When I return, Luke's in his shorts.

"You don't mind, do you?" he says. "It's kind of stuffy tonight, besides I don't wear pyjamas. I hope it's okay if I stay in my shorts."

"Fine by me." I hang Joan's dress on a coat hanger to air it and hopefully get rid of some of the wrinkles. "How long will the food be?"

"They said about forty-five minutes or so. Sunday nights are big for ordering in. I can always get dressed and go to pick it up myself."

"Don't be silly. We're relaxing, and I'm not all that hungry. I simply wanted to know how much time we have."

"For what?"

"What do you think?" The look I give him is unmistakable, and this time I don't blush at all.

Chapter 18 - Robert

Found a place to live and it came before the gig rather than the other way around as was my original plan, but after looking for suitable digs for two or three weeks and not finding something within my budget, I finally made a decision and settled on a two-bedroom apartment just off 59th Street, only a few blocks away from Hell's Kitchen.

The area is busy, noisy, full of bars, hotels, restaurants, and of course the jazz clubs that fill 52nd Street and spill into the streets in between. I signed a lease for twelve months and spent much of my savings on paying rent in advance but this got me a small discount from the landlord and with the extra savings I was able to purchase some used furniture, household goods, and a couple of suits and shirts for me to wear. Aside from my army uniforms all I possessed was what fit into my suitcase when I left my parents' home and much to my amazement, I discovered the clothes were a tight fit. I'd have thought I would've lost weight after the war, but the army fed us well in Germany and once in the States food was aplenty.

I've been keeping busy, sorting out our apartment in preparation for Clara's arrival and in between I usually look up or call on contacts to find a gig. In my spare time, I practice older and more recent jazz pieces so I can offer variety during auditions; this takes care of my daytime routine. During the evenings, I go out for a meal at one of the cheap eating places around my area and then I visit a few clubs to check out the competition.

I did the round of calls to the guys with whom I traveled back home on demob, but it seemed most of them scattered to the seven winds; even George Hutton was unreachable. In the end, I discovered he moved west to California to establish a career in film, so once I ran out of contacts I started to look at newspapers and entertainment magazines even though mine is a word-of-mouth kind of business. I also took to frequenting as many jazz clubs as I could afford. It's expected for patrons to buy alcohol, so I can't very well sit on a small shot of bourbon or a beer all evening. It helps when I stand at the bar, somewhere in a dim corner, so no one can see how little I drink and the barman is too busy to care.

As the weeks wear on, I finally receive a letter from Clara. She's excited about the apartment, as I had written to her once I secured it, and in the letter she also asks after my parents, but I decided to wait until she arrives so I can explain the situation in person.

I'm not even sure that I want to tell her the truth about what happened, but she'll think it strange if I don't introduce her to them. I don't want to think about this right now and I'm sure we can work things out once Clara arrives, which she confirms will be on December 20. This is still two months away, but I will attempt to contact my parents. Perhaps, with Christmas on the way, they'll relent and allow me to introduce them to my wife.

Meanwhile, I step up my visits to the jazz clubs and eventually I make a couple of new contacts with potential promise. None of the places I visit are well known, but to make it in this business one has to have contacts, exude confidence and be influential. I discovered this is not me—I've always been kind of shy, but I became a good trumpet player because I had the encouragement and support of my buddies at the Victory Club. I don't want to be back at war, of course, but how I miss those wonderful days. Not only that, but things are changing faster than most people thought, and this includes the good old-fashioned values we lived by prior to the war. These days, however, it seems to be dog-eat-dog and everyone's in a hurry to get to the top or introduce ideas and concepts that will make them big money.

Kindness and consideration are fast becoming a thing of the past, especially in the big cities, and people without determination discover theirs will be a very long and slow path to a successful life, if at all.

In terms of the music business, the first change after the war came with the gradual disappearance of the big bands and artists like Arti Shaw, the late Glenn Miller, Benny Goodman, and others that simply faded into history only to be replaced with crooners, pop singers, and bebop.

The first time I heard of bebop I knew it wasn't my kind of music. Bebop was a fast tempo type of jazz with complex chords and fast rhythm changes, and this made it the kind of music to listen to rather than dance to due to its fast tempo. Fortunately, around the same time, another style emerged, which was made up of smaller jazz groups, and this became known as cool jazz, which tended toward calm and smoothness.

I began to study this style by going to clubs where this kind of music was played and where eventually R&B was born. Rhythm and blues originated from African-American music and it's a mix of jazz, blues, gospel, and other styles, but in my estimation the music's fun and sexy, and above all people love to dance to it.

It was during this time of learning to play new styles of jazz that I got talking to some musos, many of whom were great guys with long experience and especially those who had served in the war and were helpful to fellow soldiers. In the end, after a number of auditions with a few groups, I was accepted at a small club called Big Charlie's, just off 52nd Avenue.

Big Charlie was both the owner of the club and the leader of our small group and for someone called Big Charlie, the man was a skinny African-American fellow that stood at 5'4 ft, but his temper was more like 10 ft. Despite this, people respected him, especially as Charlie dealt in a world of high competition and he had no time for nonsense. He worked us hard, but he looked out for us and we respected him because not only did he treat us like family, but he was one of those very rare people that don't seem to exist so much these days—that being people with integrity.

The pay wasn't much, but it was enough for rent and living costs, and I was finally a fully working musician in NYC. Who would've thought?

Chapter 19 - Samantha

It turns out our food delivery is early and just as things are getting interesting the doorbell rings loudly, startling us. Luke jumps into his jeans and T-shirt and goes to the back door downstairs where all goods and deliveries arrive. While he's gone, I set the table and when he returns we sit to eat. I open the window fully to air the room as the night is warm and humid.

"Perhaps soup is not the best dish for a summer evening, but at least it's light," I remark.

Luke agrees. "I'm not that hungry in any case."

"We also need to talk," I remind him. "We said we would."

"I know."

"I meant what I said about you not feeling under any obligation to me after what happened between us." Luke says nothing and I continue, "And I meant it about the lone wolf thing, too. I've always been pretty much alone and I saw what relationships can do to people; my parents being one big example. Besides, aside from our common love of music, I know nothing about you."

Luke puts down his spoon and takes a sip of the red wine we've been drinking with dinner. "Being a lone wolf because of bad relationships isn't the point; even good relationships can hurt a person. In my case, I was adopted from birth. I know nothing about my biological parents, but I was fortunate to be adopted by a wonderful and loving couple," he pauses momentarily and has another sip of wine. "But get this: at age ten, I find myself totally alone, and it had nothing to do with their relationship. My adoptive parents were instantly killed in a car accident and I lost the only familial love I've ever known."

"Oh, my God!" I say, horrified.

Luke nods. "That's right. One minute I'm part of a loving family, the next I'm doing the usual rounds in foster care and constantly changing schools. I didn't last too long living that way, but I was lucky to have a good friend with whom I kept in touch, and his family let me crash in a caravan they had at the back of their property. I was already into the music scene at the time and when I turned sixteen I took care of myself by busking and getting gigs, just as you did."

I reach out and touch his forearm in mutual sympathy. "We've both had a bad run it seems, but we managed to turn things around, at least to a certain extent. I didn't tell you my father marched into Berlin with the Allies in 1945, did I?" Luke shakes his head and I go on. "He loved Berlin; he always talked about it when I was old enough to understand. Dad was a musician, too, you see? But for some reason, while he was still married to my mother, he held a travelling salesman job in London. I could never understand this because I knew music was his life. Anyway, I think I mentioned to you that he planned to bring me up and he promised he'd call for me to join him. What I didn't add was that he also said if something kept us apart he'd meet me by the Wall on the 4th of July, American Independence Day. Unfortunately, I never heard back from him since, so I guess all relationships can affect a lone wolf after all."

Luke takes my hand in his. "Is that what you were doing in Berlin this past July?"

"Yes. My mother didn't know where my dad was and according to her certain money he promised never materialised, at least that's what she said at the time. In any case, I don't know where she is today and I don't want to know, but for the past eight years I've been going to Berlin and waiting by the Wall for Dad." I pause to gather my emotions for a moment. "You know, I even made inquiries via private investigators to see if I could track him down. Last I heard, he was playing in a jazz band in New York on 52nd Street, but this was way before I was born. It seems he played there for two years with a band, but by 1950/51 the trail went cold. The thing is when he split up with my mother, he told me he was going back to the States and would send for me, but there seems to be no trace that he ever returned to America around the time I was eight.

"Anyway, now that I'm making more money, I'm thinking of re-opening inquiries. The one thing I do know is that his name doesn't appear on the death register here in the UK or the US. And even the German death register has no record of him. I'd like to think there's some other explanation and that we'll see each other again, but then why doesn't he meet me by the Wall?" Luke squeezes my hand to lend me comfort and I realise there is no answer to my question and there may never be.

After dinner, we lie in bed watching a movie on TV, which doesn't seem to be making any sense to either of us. I'm not sure what Luke's thinking, but the vibes I pick up coming from him are exactly the same as those I'm feeling so I take the TV remote from his hand and press the off button.

He turns to me, "What are you doing? I was watching that."

I smile knowingly. "Yeah, like I don't know what's on your mind."

He can't help but smile back. "And what is on my mind?"

"Exactly what's on mine," I reply and place the TV remote on the bedside table. His eyes follow my every move, but he stays silent as I take off my nightshirt and he removes his shorts. I straddle him and discover there's no need for any other movement, except having him enter me. It's obvious we're both ready to climax—and we do.

We stay as we are for a few moments, silent, merely gazing into each other's eyes, and I find myself wondering if this is how two minds can be as one. Is this the real thing or is it only unadulterated lust? I get the eerie feeling that Luke can read my mind, especially when he brings my body right up against his and we kiss deeply and passionately, and for a moment I truly believe our minds can be as one after all. When we finally come up for air we lie back in bed and fall asleep in each other's arms and by around four in the morning we suddenly wake up. I pull on my nightshirt and Luke his shorts. "So what now?" he asks in the darkness.

"I can't sleep," I tell him. "There's so much on my mind. How about you?"

"I'm not sleepy, either. How about we finish the wine?"

"I think water is our best bet. Healthier, you know."

"You're right, plus it's still so warm out there."

"Then water it is," I say and go to fetch two bottles of mineral water from the fridge. We sit up against the plump pillows on the bed and drink while we talk. "I have something to confess," I say.

He smiles my way. "So this is like kiss and tell?"

"Except that I haven't slept with a celebrity," I reply and he laughs at my humour.

"I thought I was the celebrity," he plays along.

"Stop it. I'm trying to be serious."

"Okay, go ahead. I've been reprimanded."

"When I lived on the streets it was terrible. I never knew if I'd be safe and wake up unharmed the next morning or if someone was going to put a knife to my throat and rape me. I was still a virgin at the time." Luke stays silent, but I know he's listening carefully. "I was fortunate in a way. Sure, I was attacked a number of times, but I always managed to escape, and after a few months of this I had enough with the fear and anxiety of trying to stay safe so I decided to sleep during the day and wander the streets by night; at least I felt safer that way." I pause and drink some water.

Luke shakes his head. "It amazes me in this day and age how we don't have enough safe shelters for the homeless. As for foster care, I heard too many horrible stories of neglect and abuse, but nothing is ever done to fix the problem."

"I know," I reply. "You were fortunate to stay in your friend's caravan, but in the end I was lucky, too. I met a small group of street kids my age; they were mainly musos and they took me in. As a group we were safer and we looked out for one another, and it was here that I met Declan. He joined us shortly after I was taken in. At seventeen, Declan was only a year older than me and he was by far the most incredible pianist. He was a genius like Mozart and Beethoven." I pause again for some water and to gather my emotions.

"So what happened?" Luke says after a period of silence from me.

"He taught me how to play piano, even though I already knew how, but under his tutelage I flourished and so we busked together around London—he with his battery-operated keyboard and me with an old spare I borrowed from one of the other kids in the group, and whenever we played in the streets people just stopped and listened. They loved us and we became regulars around London's West End. We even had offers made to us; more especially the offers were for Declan, but he refused them all. He told me he needed to be free and that he couldn't play to order. Although he could play all the classical pianists in the world he composed his own stuff, and that was his dream." I sigh as I remember Declan's handsome face with his shoulder length brown hair and soulful dark eyes. "Long story short, he was my first and only love and after he left I've never been with anyone else until I met you."

"You said 'after he left'. What happened?"

Tears well in my eyes and unfortunately the light of dawn reveals them to Luke. He puts an arm around my shoulders and hands me a bunch of tissues.

I cry for a while, but in the safety of Luke's arms I know I can finish the story. "Declan, like all geniuses, had a very complex mind and an even more complex personality. These special people are capable of incredible things, you know? But at the same time they're so fragile they can break very easily, and this is what happened to Declan. The offers to play at concert level were many, even the London Philharmonic Orchestra was after him. Declan was certainly recognised as a Mozart or a Beethoven or both, but this wasn't what he wanted. So he stopped with the busking and kept composing while I went back to my guitar and busked around London, which eventually led me to the odd gig at The Treble and Bass."

"And?" Luke prompts me. "You haven't finished."

"No, I haven't," I remark with sadness in my voice. "We stayed together for a while in a cheap boarding house, thanks to the money we made busking, and then he was gone. One day, after my busking rounds, I came back to the boarding place and the police were waiting for me. It seemed everyone knew Declan around the West End by now, so the cops knew exactly where to find me. And then they told me—Declan took his own life. He jumped into the Thames and never came back up.

"I burst into tears and cried like I've never cried before and the cops stayed with me all afternoon, comforting me and making me cups of tea. They were really nice, and in the end I was asked to identify the body. Declan had no family, not even one friend, except for me, so the cops couldn't find anyone else to formally confirm his identity."

I move away from Luke and sit up in bed. "I'm going to make coffee. Would you like some?" He nods and I put on the coffee and get some brioche out of the fridge. I figure we may as well have a very early breakfast and if time permits go for a walk before Chris and Marcus arrive for rehearsal. "Breakfast at the table or in bed?" I ask from the kitchen.

"It's comfy here," Luke replies. "Need any help?"

"No. I'll bring it in."

While eating the warm brioche and sipping our coffee from mugs, Luke changes the subject. He knows I'll open up to him if I need to do so. He's now my lover, and he's also my friend, and after exchanging our stories we may be something closer still.

"While you were performing at high tea yesterday Tom had a word with me."

"Oh, that Tom! He doesn't miss a single opportunity, does he?" I remark, sounding somewhat annoyed.

"You can't blame the guy, Sam. He runs an expensive establishment that needs to remain a success. God only knows how much he pays in overheads; besides, I have a feeling you will approve."

I have a hunch this will involve us in some way and I'm still not pacified, but I admit whatever Luke has to say could be to our advantage and we both need the money after all. "Okay, so what gives?"

"Even before you finished playing yesterday, we both knew this was going to be a huge success for the pub so Tom put out some ideas he'd like us to consider."

I bite on a bit of brioche. "And these ideas are?"

"Well, he told you yesterday, didn't he? He wants to create this pre-theatre type of cocktail-do while you play classical music on the piano."

"I know this already and I think it's going to clash with our gig," I remark.

"Just settle," Luke admonishes me with a smile. "I haven't finished yet, you fiery Irish lass." I make a face at him but let him continue. "The gig stays the same, Thursdays and Saturdays from 8:00pm, and for the classical gig Tom suggests two performances starting at six and only running for one and a half hours each Friday and Saturday. What do you think so far?"

I finish my coffee and pass the empty mug to him so he can place it on the bedside table. "I guess Saturday's the problem. I'll need some resting time before our other gig and the cocktail do will only give me a thirty minute break, assuming there are no encores."

Luke explains, "Tom says we, the guys, can cover the first half hour of the band gig, which means that you join us onstage at eight-thirty instead of eight. This gives you a full hour to rest from the classical gig and Tom still pays you for the extra half-hour's rest."

I raise my eyebrows. "He thinks of everything, doesn't he? But who's going to cover for me while you're at Ku-dorf?" Luke smiles enigmatically. "What?" I say, suspicion in my voice.

"Well, I was saving this for last. Tom wants us to do the band gig together every week. He said the feedback from this past Saturday's gig was incredible and people are raving about us already."

I feel a jolt of excitement within me for I know this means Luke will move back to London and we can be together. Then I frown because I'm doing this for myself—the lone wolf is softening her own rules: don't get attached; don't give up your freedom; and above all, don't fall in love.

"Sam?" Luke brings me back from my thoughts. "Something wrong?"

"You're willing to leave your Berlin gig for me? What about the lone wolf thing?"

For once he sighs with frustration. "Sam, listen to me," he says in a serious tone. "I am a lone wolf; I go my own way; and I do what I want. For me, it's never been about fame and fortune because they would only end up owning me, but choosing my own gigs makes it possible for me to be free. Besides, I'd also like to come back home to London." He caresses my face and continues, "I still have some business in Berlin, but I only need to be there for a few days once a month, if that. This is all that's holding me in Germany. The gigs I had there were a bonus for me; they just came up and they enabled me to make some extra money."

"So this has nothing to do with me?" I don't know whether to feel happy or relieved.

"I won't lie to you; from the moment I met you I knew we had a special connection, but even something this special could turn out to be short-lived. All my life I've gone with the flow if it felt right. What we have feels right, but this is early days. I want to be with you and see how things turn out, but I don't want you to do the same if you feel this isn't for you."

He's right, and I say, "I'm a lone wolf, too, and if I find the love of my life then I'd want to be with him, but in order to find the real thing I realise I have to take a risk and open myself up to love." I then change the subject abruptly. "I'll go see Tom and tell him I accept and do the classical gig, but I'll do it in memory of Declan because without him I wouldn't be the pianist that I am. As for the band gig, I really love it and I knew when we joined forces on Saturday just how fantastic this can be for all of us.

"The boys want you in the band, too, and we want to stay together as a group so we can come up with a name for it, and who knows, eventually we may even cut an album of our own compositions. And if you have to go to Berlin for a few days for whatever business you have there, we'll cover for you just as you'll cover for me when I do the classical gig and need to rest. I'd like to think we're a family here and I'm blessed that I went from nothing to this: more gigs, meeting you, having our own band with the boys, and seeing where life takes us."

Luke reaches across the pillows and kisses me deeply. When he releases me I get out of bed with a blush on my face and walk towards the kitchen with the empty coffee mugs, but then I stop and turn towards him and try to get back at him for making me blush. "By the way," I announce with a cheeky smile on my face. "Dora wants to meet you."

Luke frowns. "Dora? Who's Dora?"

"She's Miss Brand to you, and she's intent on checking you out, babe!"

Chapter 20 - Robert

1949/51, New York City, USA

I'm on top of the world right now and I have much to give thanks for. Clara's on her way to NYC plus I love my music gig.

Playing at Big Charlie's six nights a week is tough work but rewarding. There is never a dull moment and since I joined the band I've made good friends and they brought me up to date with the latest music styles.

Thankfully, when I was frequenting clubs for a gig, I got to learn some of the music by ear as I couldn't afford to keep buying music scores, but just listening to the music night after night the notes got stuck in my head and this served me well when I auditioned for my current gig.

Our repertoire is huge as our patrons like variety, and half the time we play without sheet music—jazz is the kind of music where you sometimes 'jam' together and see what comes out. And this, I love.

We come up with so many pieces of music that remain unwritten, except that they stay in our heads. At one point, we thought we might write it all down and see whether we could sell the music scores, but there's no time for this, at least not now. We're kept super busy while patrons seem to enjoy our experimentation alongside popular tunes by better known musicians.

The most important thing, however, is that my loving Clara finally arrives next week. Time's flown for me since I picked up the gig at Big Charlie's and all of a sudden it's December and the 20th is looming closer and closer. Clara's ship arrives early morning and I'll be there to meet her and even spend our first day together before I have to go to the club. I can't wait until I take Clara in my arms. She's my life and always will be.

I guess the only that shadows my happiness is that my folks refuse to talk to me. I telephoned a number of times to no avail. My father answered all calls and the only thing he asked was: *"Did you get rid of that German woman?"* And when I said I wish to have a chat with him and Mom, he simply hung up on me. I couldn't get him to listen and somehow it's always he who answers the phone when I call. I don't even know how my mother is doing or what she thinks about the situation; therefore, I ended up sending her a letter, hoping she would at least read it and try to understand my side of the story. To date, I've sent about five or six letters, but they all came back 'Return to sender' and the envelopes had not even been opened.

My heart broke at this situation and I didn't know what else I could do. My father fought in the Great War and I can understand his hate of Germans, but we're talking about a civilian who took no part in the war and she's only a young and loving girl, so where is my father's compassion and understanding? He must know that thousands of GIs married their German sweethearts by the end of WWII and I haven't heard any negative comments about this among the American population. Sure, everyone hates the Nazis and wishes we'd caught Hitler alive to punish him for the evil he brought into this world, but how does this translate to an innocent young girl who worked hard and helped others?

After a couple of months, attempting to open communication lines with my folks, I had to face this was not going anywhere and I was on my own in terms of blood family. Moving forward, it will just be Clara and me, and though my heart has truly broken I've learned to accept that parental love is never conditional, but I still like to think there are some parents out there that will at least tolerate their new German daughters-in-law.

Chapter 21- Samantha

Aug/Sep, 1985, London, England

At rehearsal with Chris and Marcus the next morning, Luke and I sit around a table having coffee with the boys and discussing the new changes for the band. Luke says very little and lets me do most of the talking; he still considers me the main member of the band, but I feel rather overwhelmed considering how much more experienced he is in the music business.

Chris stirs his coffee and at the same time runs his fingers through his curly brown mane which almost reaches his shoulders. He looks like an innocent child with his large green eyes that right now look sleep-deprived. "Late night again?" I remark.

He shrugs. "At least I have a love life."

"What's that supposed to mean?"

Before Chris replies, Marcus jumps in. "It means I have to listen to him and his newest girlfriend bonking all night, and the friggin' walls are paper thin!"

I try not to laugh, but Luke intercedes. "Settle down you two. If you can't handle something this simple how are you going to handle a permanent gig?"

"Well, if this gig pays enough I can afford to move out," Marcus says to no one in particular and folds his arms across his chest.

I roll my eyes and catch the amusement on Luke's face; then I turn to the boys. "Look, you guys, this is serious. We're talking about a future that could benefit all of us, plus we'd be a real band, one that not only does covers but also our own compositions. So if you want to be a part of this you're going to have to develop more self-discipline."

The boys look contrite and Marcus says, "Sorry, Sam. I, for one, am ready to take this on. Imagine if we end up having our own label!"

I lean across the table and pat his shoulder. "Exactly. Just think of all the girlfriends you'll both have to play with." The boys are at attention now, especially young Chris.

"I'm in, too," he declares.

"Okay, so you know the deal. We play our usual nights, but Tom also said he'll hire us to outside parties under The Treble and Bass company name and we split the earnings with him equally. I guess Tom's looking to become our agent." I turn to Luke to see if he has a comment on this.

"That's right," Luke says to the boys. "I've known Tom for years and he's an excellent agent and manager. You may not know this, but before he got married Tom used to manage a number of bands and he did really well getting gigs, even arranging live concerts, tours and studio recordings, but the hours were crazy, and then he met Helen and decided a family was more important in his life, so he sold the agency and purchased this place with the proceeds."

The boys look impressed, and I say, "Moving on, if you're both in, be prepared to work hard." The boys nod their assent. "And lastly, I'd like to suggest a name for the band and get your feedback, and of course feel free to suggest any names you may have in mind."

Luke turns to me. "I've been thinking about names for the band, but to date I rejected them all. What's your suggestion?"

"Well, I also rejected all the names I came up with and I was running out of ideas, but then I started to think about a name to describe what our band does rather than who we are. So I figured what we do is get ideas from music and its different styles from a broad and diverse range of sources, and so I came up with 'The Eclectics'. Any thoughts on that?"

Luke winks his approval at me and I know immediately that he loves it. Chris and Marcus don't seem too bothered to try and find another name, they simply smile at the same time and Marcus says, "Makes sense to me—that's exactly what we do."

We smile at each other and we all shake hands. We are a band at last!

———◈———

After rehearsal, the boys go their own way and Tom arrives with Helen. "No need to update us," Tom says, "we just ran into Chris and Marcus. They're thrilled about the band, and its name is just right for you guys." Tom then takes Luke aside for a word and I go to Helen and give her a big hug.

Helen and I stand at the same height of 5'4ft and Tom and Luke are both 6'2ft. Why am I thinking about this, anyway? For a millisecond, I put myself in Helen's shoes—married to the man I love and having his children. The love I see in Tom and Helen's eyes when they look at each other, even from across the room, is the kind of love I fantasise about, although I never believed it could exist. I shake my silly romantic thoughts away and step back from Helen. "You're positively glowing; and congratulations on number four, but you're not even showing yet."

Helen's smile is so incredibly beautiful that I think I'm going to shed a tear. I tell myself to get a grip and focus on my companion; she's absolutely gorgeous with her natural white blonde hair that almost reaches down to her waist and eyes of green like emeralds. Helen is fortunate to be a woman who is truly loved.

"Sam," Helen's voice breaks into my thoughts, "you're looking so well these days, and I'm absolutely thrilled about the cocktail gig you agreed to do. Tom hasn't stopped raving about your talent with classical music and I look forward to organising the gig. I think it needs a woman's touch, don't you? Plus I'll be your helper with wardrobe and such things. Is that okay?"

I smile at her excitement. "Of course it's okay. But Helen, you have to think of the baby and not overtire yourself."

"Don't you worry, my dear," she replies. "If anything needs doing Tom will help out, as will Luke," she throws a quick glance Luke's way and turns back to me. "I know he cares for you very much and I'm thrilled for you both." I blush, but Helen doesn't seem to notice. She looks in the men's direction again while they're still engaged in conversation a few feet away from us. "Look at them, so handsome, yet so different—one, a blond god with the sexiest blue eyes, and my Tom, a dark-haired, dark-eyed tall bear of a man."

I laugh. "Helen, don't let them hear you or it'll go to their heads."

"Tom knows better than to strut around like a peacock; he knows he's not 'movie star' material, although he is to me. As for Luke, we've known him for years and we never saw a single sign of vanity coming from him. He's impervious to all sexual offers, even in the face of hordes of women throwing themselves at him."

I feel a stab of jealousy in my heart and Helen sees right through me. She gives me a hug and speaks close to my ear. "Sam, don't worry about what I said. I chatter too much, but I thought you might like to know that Luke's always been very choosy, extremely so. He's no sucker for a pretty face without a brain. He's the kind of complex man who needs someone with substance, a woman that can stimulate him intellectually." Helen releases me but stays close. "Tom mentioned you're together and that Luke's very private about the whole thing; that's why Tom covered up his gaffe the other day by telling Luke about having the right names of the occupants for the studio insurance."

"It's okay, Helen," I say, not wanting to hear more about the hordes of women going after Luke, and I remind myself that I'm a lone wolf—I fly solo—but who am I kidding?

"I'm sorry if this makes you feel uncomfortable, but I need to say this to you. Since you came into the picture, the change in Luke has been remarkable. He's lighter of mood and smiles all the time as opposed to being serious and very private, like he was before he met you. Look, I'll say this and then I'll shut up for good about it; I don't know whether you're aware of his life and the loss and hardship he endured. He had a hard road to travel during his early years and he's not one to mess around with others' feelings or use people.

"Sam, I've seen the way he looks at you, plus he's very protective of you, my dear, so all I can say is he won't break your heart. I know I'm a romantic, but I'm also a good judge of character."

I say nothing. What is there to say? If Luke's serious about me, then I'm sure he'll let me know when he's ready. I feel fear all of a sudden, though, and I can't deal with the fact that Luke and I could end up together for good. I think back to what happened with Declan and me. I thought we'd end up together, I believed in the love I found with him, and then he took his life.

Helen's voice suddenly breaks into my thoughts. "I'll leave you now, Sam, but let's meet to discuss your wardrobe for the cocktail gig. And please be reassured that what I said to you is for your ears only; I won't even discuss it with Tom."

I'm relieved to hear Helen say this and I paste a smile on my face. "Thank you, Helen, and I'll call you to discuss the wardrobe."

It's past eleven and Tom just manages to open the doors in time for the first patrons. Helen disappears into the kitchen to catch up with the staff, and Luke grabs my hand and draws me to the rear of the pub where we store our equipment.

"What are your plans for today?"

"Actually, today and the rest of the week will be a busy one with the band and the classical gig, plus I need to rehearse my classical pieces. I'm still a little rusty with some of them so I won't have too much time for anything else because I also have to do a shop for Dora and I'm going to cook and freeze some meals for her to cover for the nights I'm at the pub."

"How is this going to work out for you long term?"

"I discussed it with her and she refuses to let me go. She says she can manage, but I'm not sure how this is going to pan out, especially if we start doing gigs outside of Tom's pub on top of everything else."

Luke picks up the tinge of sadness in my voice and draws me to him, caressing my hair. My legs turn to jelly and all I want is for him to take me to bed, but now is not the time. He tips my chin so our eyes meet and kisses my lips softly. "Just remember I'm here to help, too," he says. "There's no reason to hurry just now; first we need to see how things turn out over here and later we can worry if there are more gigs offered to us."

His words comfort me and I feel more reassured. As exciting as my life has been recently, too much, too soon scares me and the thought of the future is at once filled with happiness but at the same time marred with anxiety. "You're right," I say, knowing that if things get too crazy I can always count on him. "So what's on your agenda?"

"I'm going to revise the song lists for both Thursdays and Saturdays; we have so much material that we can go for months, never having to play the same song twice. I also have to call Berlin and break the news to Marc, the manager at Ku-dorf, and tell him I'm giving up the gig. I know a couple of guys who'd be great as a replacement so this could tide things up quicker for me and I can move the rest of my things back here."

"You mean furniture and stuff?" I never asked Luke exactly where he lived while in Berlin.

"Yes and no. I rent a studio near Ku-dorf, but it's fully furnished. It's more the personal stuff I need to deal with like the rest of my clothes, books, music CDs, and some more of my equipment. I have two guitars over there and all the paraphernalia that goes with them."

"Sounds like you're going to be busy."

"That I am, but I'll get it done as soon as possible, especially if one of the two guys I recommend to replace me is engaged by Marc."

"Well, I'd better be getting along," I say. "We're all busy bees."

"We sure are, but things will settle in time." He then draws me to him again, his lips close to mine. "So do you want to stay here with me until I go to Berlin?"

I blush and wish my feelings were not written all over my face for the whole world to see, but at least Luke doesn't seem to mind. We share a passionate kiss and when we break off he says, "Tell Miss Brand I'm stealing you from her—at least for the nights—but make a time for us to visit her. I have a feeling I'm going to like that lady."

I smirk. "You'd better have your wits about you, mister. Dora Brand is a force to be reckoned with, and I believe she has a weakness for younger men."

He laughs. "Good grief! I have a feeling you two are going to be big trouble." And with that, he slaps my rump softly and sends me off as he calls out, "Six o'clock this evening for that early dinner we missed out on last night."

Chapter 22 - Robert

<u>1949/51, New York City, USA</u>

My darling Clara arrived today and it was like a dream. So many months apart, so much longing for each other, so much anxiety in case something went wrong and she would be delayed, and so much worry on my side when I would have to explain to her about my parents. But when I saw my love coming ashore along the ship's ramp with all the other brides, all of my concerns vanished—at least for a while—and suddenly Clara was in my arms at the back of a taxi taking us home the long way, as I requested, so she could see parts of New York City.

On the way, she took in the incredible skyscrapers, which she had never seen before, except on postcards I used to send to her while we corresponded. She was amazed at the height and presence of the Empire State Building and she fell in love with the Art Deco features of the Chrysler Building; she also loved the bridges that led to the different boroughs of New York from Manhattan, and the mad busyness of the city. Her eyes shone with wonder and she could barely speak from the excitement. I felt a little concerned because when excited Clara would sometimes revert to German, and I didn't want to start our lives in New York with a negative experience if someone made a racist remark.

Clara is as beautiful as any New York girl and I noticed many male eyes, including the cab driver's, turning her way. She seemed to think this was funny, but I could tell she enjoyed the attention. I was so proud of her and how far she had come with her English. She still had a slight accent, which was a mixture of US English and German, but somehow it came out sounding like soft Irish-American, and for this I was grateful because nobody would think to question her, especially with a surname like Kelly.

The moment we arrived at our home, she seemed a little unsure by the crowded area with its multitude of clubs, theaters, eating places, boarding houses, and the tenements not too far away from us. She made no comment, but she looked a little anxious. I reassured her that it was safe here and our home was close to my work, so she could come over and watch me perform any time she wished. I also reminded her of the theaters and shows we could take in from time to time in addition to the fact that we were close to everything—shops, restaurants, cafés, bars, the city, and the waterfront.

This seemed to reassure her and I then gave her a tour of our apartment. She liked it well enough but didn't say much. I could understand how overwhelming everything must seem to her, especially after having come from a city that had been flattened by all the bombing during the war and then having to leave her parents behind. They might only be adoptive parents, but they were the only link she had left with Germany.

I took her suitcase to our bedroom and she stood across the bed from me. Her large and luminous brown eyes held such love in them that I couldn't wait any longer. I approached her and started to undress her, my eyes never leaving hers. She remained passive, but at the same time I sensed the passion in her. She finished undressing herself while I took off my clothes and we stood facing each other, naked.

I took her in my arms and kissed every part of her, starting with her mouth and finishing at her feet, by which time we were lying in bed with her moaning as my lips travelled from her erect nipples down to the wetness between her legs. Clara jolted in surprise when my tongue invaded the depths of that mysterious inner place, but she raised her hips slightly so I could enter her more easily. She climaxed immediately, groaning with the passion of the act, and then I withdrew and entered her with a smooth thrust that led us both to the most intense peak of pleasure.

I had several sexual encounters during the war and I never felt anything, except release when I climaxed; but with Clara, what we did was so intimate and sublime that I could never imagine myself doing this with any other woman.

Chapter 23 - Samantha

Aug/Sep, 1985, London, England

The early dinner turns into an early night. I decide to go back to Sloane Square to spend the night there and Luke will come over the following day for afternoon tea. We are both tired after the hard day's work filled with rehearsals, meeting with the boys regarding the band, Luke catching up on some things to do with his Berlin gig, plus sorting out more lists of songs he wanted to revise. And me, stocking up on groceries for Dora, checking out my wardrobe to see if I have something to wear for the cocktail gig, but above all is the discussion with Helen about Luke, which I need to contend with in solitude.

After breakfast, I help Dora with her bath and then go back to my room to check out a couple of outfits that may be suitable for the classical gig. I still have to get back to Helen for suggestions on what to wear because I don't have enough variety of stylish clothes to choose from. I'm not a dress or skirt person, but I do have some nice blouses to go with silky black pants and there is also a cream satin pantsuit that will complement a gauzy chocolate brown blouse.

While I'm sorting through my clothing, I cannot help but keep thinking about Helen's comment regarding the hordes of women throwing themselves at Luke, and him not being impressed by a pretty face but instead by intellectual stimulation.

It doesn't help that I lay awake half the night thinking about this already. At first, I thought if Luke wanted to be with me, and I with him, then there was no problem. Unfortunately, things are always different in the light of day and all my doubts came back to haunt me.

Why is Luke with me? I'm much younger than he is, not necessarily in age, although he is thirty-five years to my twenty-three, but I think it has more to do with life experience. Sure, I had enough life experience, too, with a rough journey while growing up, and in this Luke and I have the same thing in common—both alone due to life's circumstances, living in and out of foster care and then being homeless. I believe this is a big draw for both of us because of our similar backgrounds and our work, but where he's ahead of me is in life experience with more maturity, having had many lovers and relationships, for I know he's no monk, and when it comes to sophistication he wins over me hands down.

I throw the cream satin suit I've been holding all along back into the wardrobe while I go on torturing myself with more thoughts of Luke. What does he see in me? Do I stimulate him intellectually? Perhaps I do in music because this is what we both do, but other than this what else do I know? I only know about classical music and I play the piano, but this is hardly the equivalent of having a formal education. I'm well read, but mostly in fiction and not the classics, philosophy, history, and so on. Meanwhile, Luke's seen a lot more of the world than I have and I know he's a prolific reader and has vast knowledge on a wide number of subjects.

What about sex? The question suddenly pops into my head. This is the subject I've been trying to avoid the most. I only ever made love with Declan, a young boy genius, but not yet a man with sophisticated sexual experience. Then I blush at the thought of Luke, a man in every sense, and I hate myself for having this blushing problem, especially when he's around. It's like all my emotions show on my face for anyone to see and I wish I could cultivate a poker face instead.

I shake my head in frustration and sit on the edge of the bed to compose my chaotic emotions, but then the questions start again: is my lovemaking experience enough to satisfy a man like Luke? I kind of initiated sex with him the first time due to that horrid nightmare I had, but does this make me look sophisticated or simply someone playing a cheap trick to get him into bed? I'm not exactly a beginner, but mine are not the skills of a seductress, either, and in the end I have to wonder whether my lovemaking plus other skills are truly enough to satisfy a man like him. And as if this is not bad enough and we end up getting together for good, am I going to be enough for him in the future? I stand up and walk back to the wardrobe, grab the black silky pants and throw them across the room with all my strength.

Well, that was childish, and I go on to admonish myself because I'm behaving nothing like a lone wolf and I feel as if I'm a failure. I'm about to throw myself on the bed to cry into my pillow when there's a knock at the door. I jump up with a feeling of tension, but then I hear Dora's voice calling out to me and I calm down.

"Sam, dear, are you in there?"

"Yes, yes. One moment." I rush to the wardrobe mirror to check my face and ensure I'm not blushing; then, I open the door as if I haven't a single care in the world. "Dora, come on in," I invite her. "Excuse the mess, but I'm trying to work out my wardrobe for the cocktail gig."

Dora looks around the room. "Well, there isn't much here, dear, but I'm sure we can do something with those nice silky pants and that cream satin suit." She doesn't ask why the offending garments are lying in a corner of the robe almost crumpled to death. "I only came in to ask if you'd like some lunch. I'm making a light repast seeing as your young man is coming over for afternoon tea."

My young man! As if I need reminding. "Oh, right, of course. I'll join you for a bite and then I'll go down the road to Astor's and get some of their tea cakes. Is that okay with you?"

Dora agrees. "And I'll make my famous cucumber sandwiches," she adds excitedly.

I tried Dora's sandwiches on previous occasions and she really is good at making them taste scrumptious. I figure this must be from all those tea parties Dora used to give when she was younger.

"One thing, Dora," I remark. "Whatever you do, don't call Luke 'my young man'. Let's just treat him as a friend."

Dora looks surprised. "But Sam, you're sleeping with the man." I'm about to protest, but she continues. "No, no, my dear, if you're having sex with Luke then he's your young man. I'm no prude, mind, and I know this generation doesn't worry too much about it, but I'd hate to think you two are involved just for the casual sex."

And of course I blush again. "No, Dora. We are very close friends and I believe we're heading towards something more serious. I'm not one for casual sex, either, I assure you."

This seems to pacify her. "I believe you, Sam. You're too sweet to give yourself to just anyone and this is why I can't wait to meet Luke. He must be really special for someone like you to go for him, and if I'm right I believe you have feelings for him that you're not yet ready to reveal."

I breathe a sigh of relief and kiss her cheek. "I knew you'd understand, and thank you for your support. Now, let's go and have some lunch."

––––––––––

Luke is not due until four so after lunch Dora takes me to Anne's inner sanctum. This is the third bedroom in the flat and it has remained just as Anne left it. I never went inside the room, but when Dora opens the door and bids me to enter it's like I've walked into an Aladdin's cave of fashion. My eyes run over benches and sewing tables all over the room, which is also full of shelves containing the most exquisite materials. Dora points out each of them to me: there are silks, satins, velvets, brocades, laces, beaded and sequined fabrics, crepes, chiffons, cotton, damask, taffeta, and much more. I'm absolutely astounded at the beautiful rainbow of colours and textures reaching out to me. "Lovely, aren't they?" Dora remarks. "And these are not the only things Anne left behind. Have a look inside the big wardrobe behind you."

I turn around and see a huge robe that takes up one entire wall of the bedroom and I open its doors to find the most incredible pieces of clothing; there are garments from different times, some dating back to the 1920s. There are pants, long and short skirts, cocktail dresses of all kinds; and then I see the bags, shoes, and other accessories, most of which match certain dress designs, and I gasp at the beauty before me and realise that I really don't hate dresses after all; I only avoid the cheap, ugly ones that are within my budget, but to see this display one would have to be blind not to admire the artistry before me. Anne might not have been into music, but she was an artist all the same.

"Dora," I remark with awe, "there are no words to express this incredible collection Anne put together."

Dora does not respond and I detect a few tears rolling down her face. She must miss her sister so very much. I put an arm around her shoulders. "Thank you for sharing this with me. I feel privileged that you allowed me to see Anne's art."

Dora says, "I miss Anne like anything; but my dear, I know for a fact that Anne would love it if you selected your wardrobe for your cocktail gig from her collection."

Now, I almost burst into tears, but I manage to stem them before they fall. "I'd be honoured to accept, and not only will Anne's spirit be with me on opening night, but you will be sitting at the best table in the venue, watching me play the piano."

"Oh! But this is wonderful, Sam!"

"I was planning to invite you this afternoon, when Luke arrives, but after seeing this and being given the opportunity to wear some of Anne's designs, I just couldn't wait to tell you."

We hug and Dora exclaims, "Oh, my dear! It's almost two and I haven't made the sandwiches, plus I have to dress to meet your young man. And yes, I feel he's yours, but I promise not to mention this in front of him." She gives me a conspiratorial smile and we go back to the kitchen.

"I'm off to Astor's," I announce. "I won't be long and then I'll help you with the tea things."

<hr>

Luke arrives right on the dot of four and I let him in the hallway. He gives me a brotherly kiss and hands me a bunch of pink roses as he whispers in my ear. "These are for Miss Brand." He then takes off his leather jacket. It is a rather cool day outside and while he hangs it up in the hallway's coat rack I quickly take in his appearance.

He's wearing a black long-sleeved silk shirt, what looks like newly ironed black jeans, and black leather boots. His hair reaches down to his shirt collar and the long fringe falling over his eyes still tends to hide his expression even though it looks like he's had a trim at the barbershop. I try not to smile, but he's certainly made an effort to impress. When he's ready, I hand him back the flowers and lead him into the sitting room, which looks out onto a small well-kept garden. All apartments in the complex that are located on the ground floor share the same floor design as Dora's.

"Have a seat," I point to one of the chintz sofa chairs nearest the window. "I'm just giving Dora a hand. We won't be long." As I go to pass him on my way to the door, he catches hold of my hand and pulls me gently towards him.

"Hey! You're supposed to behave," I whisper. He takes a quick look to make sure no one is approaching and kisses me. I don't make much of an effort to escape him, but I know Dora will be waiting for me. "Later," I whisper and take off for the kitchen, but within a few moments I'm back in the room, carrying a tray with all the tea things while Dora follows behind holding a plate of cucumber sandwiches and another with the cakes from Astor's.

Luke stands up immediately and takes the plates from Dora while I arrange all the tea things on the sitting room table.

Dora is wearing one of her loose afternoon dresses, designed by Anne, and her white hair is gathered in a soft chignon and held in place with mother-of-pearl combs that I helped to secure. She looks really elegant and the softness of her appearance belies her age.

As for myself, I decided to make an effort, just like Luke, and instead of my usual casual apparel I'm wearing a pair of black silk pants with a white finely knitted, long-sleeved top which accentuates my figure.

Dora and I sit on a two-seater lounge adjacent to Luke's sofa chair and I immediately make the introductions. Luke reaches for the bunch of pink roses he brought with him and hands them to Dora. "Miss Brand, it's finally a pleasure to meet you and I hope you like the flowers. I should've asked Sam if you had a favourite kind."

I throw a quick glance at him as he's looking rather shy and I almost laugh, but the moment doesn't last too long when Dora addresses him. "My dear young man," she says with a smile, "please relax. I'm going to call you Luke and I insist you call me Dora, and we're going to be good friends. This, I knew the moment I saw you and it has nothing to do with Sam." She then turns to me for a moment. "Sam, please serve the tea." Then she turns back to Luke and says, "To be honest, I'd have to say that if I were young again I'd have a fancy to run away with you."

This makes Luke smile with a bit of a blush on his face as it's probably the last thing he was expecting to hear and I stop midway from serving the tea in fear that I might drop the teapot. "Oh, Sam," Dora admonishes me, "don't look so surprised; let's have some tea."

Luke winks at me when Dora's not looking my way and while I continue serving he says, "I would consider that to be a pleasure, Dora." She gives him a big smile and I relax, secretly knowing she approves of Luke already.

For the rest of the visit we chit chat while having our tea and then I tell Luke about having invited Dora to the cocktail gig and he assures her that on the day of the debut he will personally collect her and ensure she gets home safely. Dora's thrilled and a big smile appears on her face.

"And by the way," I address Luke, "I never told you that Dora could've been a concert pianist."

Dora briefly explains how she came to take in pupils after the sisters lost their parents and their home. How ironic, I think as she tells her tale. She was fortunate, however, that her aunt came to the sisters' rescue; otherwise, Dora and Anne would have had a rough time of it.

"Will you play something?" Luke asks Dora while they're engaged in a conversation about classical music.

"Well, it has been many years since I've played. My hands these days are not what they used to be, but I will play something if you later sing some of your songs for me. Sam tells me you write wonderful compositions of your own."

I catch the shyness in Luke's eyes and I can't believe it, but it disappears almost instantly; he obviously knows how to hide his emotions better than me. "It will be my pleasure, but I didn't bring my guitar."

I jump in. "That's okay! I have mine here and you can borrow it."

"Very well," replies Luke, "but I'd like to hear Dora play first."

So for the next half hour Dora totally and absolutely entrances us with playing my favourites: Beethoven, Mozart, and Chopin. She may not have played for ages, but she's incredible, and so much better than I am. When she finishes, we applaud and I remark, "Well, Dora, you put me to shame. There's no way I can play at that level."

She gives me a kindly smile. "My dear, you will play at that level if you give me a couple of hours of your time every day prior to the debut. I'll be more than happy to tutor you."

I thank her and commit to this goal, and Luke heartily agrees. Then, it's his turn to play. I bring him my guitar and he plays a couple of ballads, ones that even I haven't yet heard. The music is composed in order to emphasise Luke's vocal range and I know if he had ever gone professional he would've been snapped up.

When he finishes, Dora praises him highly and assures him she's not just saying this for the purpose of being polite. "You can be sure that I'm a hard critic, Luke. Your voice and range are fantastic and you can more than hold your own with many of the current famous musicians."

Luke seems touched by her comment. "Thank you for your honesty, Dora. I appreciate it."

"My dear," Dora says. "I like your spunk and I wholeheartedly approve of you."

I blush at the way Dora gives her approval, which sounds like Luke's come to ask for my hand in marriage, so I quickly collect the tea things and take them to the kitchen before Dora or Luke can see my red face.

Chapter 24 - Robert

1949/51, New York City, USA

With Christmas five days away I can no longer put off telling Clara about the break with my family, but I just don't know how to do it. Since her arrival, we've done nothing but make up for our absence from each other and we pretty much spend the days in bed, making love and sleeping. When I get home from Big Charlie's it's usually way past midnight, but Clara always waits up for me even though I tell her she doesn't have to.

Instead, she greets me with something light to eat in case I didn't have time to grab a meal at the club and later we relax and talk about the future and what it may bring. We then go to sleep and in the very early hours of the morning I turn to her and touch her between her legs. She moans and stretches like a cat and I enter the warmth of her being, thrusting gently into her. We play this game and try to drag it out for as long as we can until one of us can no longer resist; we then climax together in a storm of passion that leaves us spent but satisfied. Once we're up, we shower and dress and Clara makes breakfast.

This morning was my last opportunity to talk to her about my parents as I've run out of time. Today is Christmas Eve and I realize I can no longer delay the discussion, so while we have our coffee and toast I bring up the subject. I tell her that she's probably been wondering about my parents.

She says she's been waiting for me to tell her about them, but that she felt all along that something wasn't right between my family and me.

I feel ill at ease telling her what transpired between me and my parents, but there is no way I can avoid this unpleasant situation and so I tell her the whole story from the time I arrived home and the many attempts I've made to try and communicate with my folks.

Clara's eyes show nothing but compassion for my situation and she comforts me, telling me she understands and that people will never be able to change after what the war has done to them. Many people were broken and this is something that will stay with them for the rest of their lives.

Her acceptance of the situation amazes me in one so young, but then I realize the suffering and sacrifice Clara went through during the war and I feel she's the strongest and wisest out of the two of us. While Clara can understand and forgive, however, I am filled with rage and resentment—rage at what the war did to millions and resentment at ignorant people like my parents, who cannot seem to understand. It also occurs to me that I must learn to let go and move on with my own life. I have to accept that in one way or another we have all been damaged and now we have to live with the circumstances in our respective lives.

I am thankful for Clara's insight of the situation and feel blessed that I met and married her. I guess the war, while wreaking havoc, also brought people closer together and each of us has the opportunity to see the glass half full or half empty. Clara is an optimist and, therefore, someone I can learn from. As long as she's in my life I know I will always see the positive side of things.

Chapter 25 - Samantha

We leave Dora's at six, but first Luke and I help tidy up and wash the dishes. While I finish in the kitchen, I can hear Luke and Dora chatting in the sitting room and Luke's asking her about her piano days and whether she played at recitals. I can't quite catch the entire conversation, but I know Dora took to Luke so much that they're already talking like close friends.

Before we leave, I confirm with Dora that I'll see her late morning for the piano tutorial. Dora is ecstatic at the prospect of not only tutoring me, but she goes as far as to admit she feels life is energising her again, despite the usual arthritis, and that she's now a part of our band.

Luke and I assure her that we couldn't do without her, not after we found a musical kindred spirit. Dora laughs and hugs us both. I can't believe the change in her, even though she always tries to maintain a chirpy countenance, but Luke seems to have charmed her for good and this makes me happy.

We say our goodbyes and decide to get a taxi back to the pub. "That went well," Luke remarks as the taxi drives away from Dora's place. "She's an amazing lady."

"So now you know why I'd be loath to leave her. She's like the mother I never had and as far as I'm concerned she's my family."

Luke gives my hand a squeeze. "And what am I?"

I squeeze his hand in response and say closer to his ear, "I'm not sure about that yet, but I think for now you're my lover."

He glances at me questioningly and says, "Not that lone wolf thing again."

I let go of his hand. "I'm not sure what I am, Luke. I agreed when you said we'll see where this goes, so this is what I'm doing despite a number of issues I'm having trouble with."

I see the concern in his eyes. "Why didn't you say anything before? You know you can trust me, no matter what's troubling you." I look down at my fingers, which I twist and untwist because I can't seem to sit still. Luke notices them and places one of his hands over both of mine. "Can we talk later?"

This is the thing I've been trying to avoid, but at the same time I realise I need to be honest with him. I'm too afraid to let him become the centre of my life and I know where I'm heading already, and this scares me. "Okay," I say.

We arrive at the pub and go up to the studio from the building's back entrance. "I'm going to take a shower," Luke says. "What do you want to do about dinner?"

"No dinner for me. I'm still full from Dora's tea party."

"Same here," he replies, "but there's some stuff in the fridge in case we get hungry later."

"And let's not forget the kitchen downstairs doesn't close until ten at night," I add.

Luke turns to gaze at me before entering the bathroom. "Are you okay?"

"Of course," I reply. "While you shower I'm going to ring Helen and tell her about Dora's sister's wonderful designs. I'm sure she's going to want to see them."

"That's right. Dora told me the whole story about her and Anne, using their talents to make a living when their parents passed on."

"She told you all this while I was washing the dishes?" I'm not surprised because Dora took to Luke immediately and I have a feeling she'll eventually tell him she regards him as a son. But wouldn't that make him my brother? I cringe at the whole ridiculous thing and am thankful it's not family blood that Luke and I share.

"I'll only be a few minutes," Luke says and disappears into the bathroom. Meanwhile, I call Helen and invite her to Dora's place tomorrow, after my tutorial, to view Anne's designs. Helen is thrilled and I give her Dora's address and ring off. Then I grab a clean nightshirt from the stuff I keep at Luke's and I go to shower as soon as he comes out of the bathroom.

When I'm done I find Luke reclining in bed, leaning against a whole bunch of pillows. He pats my side of the bed, motioning for me to join him. "Do you feel like watching a video?"

I sit next to him and pull the bedcover over me. It's a cold evening and there's a chill in the air. "Up to you; it's too early to go to sleep."

"We can always talk," he remarks. "You seemed anxious in the taxi and I thought you might want a friendly ear."

I'm not prepared for this. I don't even know where to start. It's one thing to imagine what I want to say to Luke and another when I'm confronted with him in real life. "Maybe this isn't such a good idea."

"Sam, you don't have to say anything if you don't want to." He takes my hand and caresses it. "I'm always here if you want to talk." He kisses the back of my hand before he releases it.

I'm still in two minds about what to do, but I think I should confide in him in spite of what he may think of me. I expel a sigh of resignation and turn to him. "Okay, I'll tell you, but you must promise not to judge me."

"I don't judge, Sam, especially if what you want to say is from the heart," he reassures me.

I look down at my fingers, which are twisting again, and then I speak. "Well, it all started with a remark Helen made about you and this got me thinking about us." I take a peek at his eyes and I see the curiosity in them. He's probably wondering what Helen has to do with any of this, but he doesn't interrupt and waits for me to continue. "Helen said she knew we're together and she was really happy for us, but then she said I was fortunate because over the time she and Tom have known you they saw hordes of women throwing themselves at you." I feel myself blush and another quick glance at him tells me he's rather surprised at what I'm saying. I go on, "Helen said you're not after a pretty face and that you look for intellectual stimulation, and this got me thinking about why you're with me." I pause for a moment and then say, "Do we have any bottled water?"

Luke jumps out of bed immediately and returns within seconds holding bottled water for each of us. I open mine and take a long drink. Luke says nothing and simply waits until I'm ready to continue. "To cut a long story short, what Helen said played around in my mind and I started to question myself. Why me? Why do you want me? I'm so much younger than you in many ways, and I don't mean age difference but more like lack of sophistication and intellectual life experience. As for sexual experience, I've only learned from that one boy. He was very loving with me, but he wasn't yet a man." I drink more water as my cheeks grow hot. "So then I wonder what I bring into this relationship. If there's a future for us, am I going to be enough for you or are you going to take off with a highly sophisticated and experienced woman? I ..." And then I can't go on anymore. I don't even want to look at him because I know I'm blushing bright red.

Luke remains quiet while all this is going on and I feel like crawling under the bedcover to hide there for the entire night. I must sound like a confused, inexperienced teenager to him and perhaps I should just go back to Dora's.

Luke still hasn't uttered a word and I take the risk of glancing his way only to see the beginnings of a smile on his face. I find my voice. "What? Is this funny? I pour my heart out to you, and you think it's funny?"

Luke shakes his head while trying to stem his smile and he gathers me in his arms, where I cannot escape. I bury my face against his chest, still berating myself for being a fool and sounding like a clueless virgin.

"Apologies for smiling," Luke says as he brings my head under his chin and strokes my hair in a calming manner. "I'm not making fun of you at all. The smile is what I call an endearing smile. You're adorable, so why can't you believe it?" I feel myself relax and lean into his embrace. "What you said took guts," he continues, "and all the points you brought up are legitimate, but this doesn't mean they apply to either one of us."

"How so?"

"For starters, you only have Helen's opinion about this so-called horde of women and the fact that I prefer someone who's intellectual and sophisticated. She's right in one respect, however, and that is I don't go for a pretty face and an empty brain, plus one thing she doesn't know is that I don't sleep around with just anybody.

"Yes, I'm choosy, but what appeals to me is someone with the right energy, someone who makes me laugh, and someone with a bit of an Irish temper." He stops here and kisses my forehead before he goes on. "Whether you believe it or not I don't have time for flings or one-night stands and all the complications they bring. Those things don't turn me on at all. Sure, I've had a number of relationships, even a couple of which I thought were going somewhere, but they didn't work out. So this is where we are at present: we met, the energy was there, I felt it immediately the moment I saw you, and I knew I had to pursue this and find out whether you're the one. I'm hoping you will be and that we both feel the same in the long term, but only time will tell.

"As for you, thinking you're not enough, please promise me you will never think something so negative about yourself. There are plenty of people out there willing to put you down, so don't make the mistake of doing it to yourself. You're a strong young woman with a tough upbringing; you're a survivor; and despite this you made it happen for yourself. You went from abandonment to finding someone like Dora, who loves you to bits and then you started to make a living from your music. So you have the strength and the talent plus you're a caring person. You're not a spoilt brat nor are you ignorant.

"Helen mentioned intellectual stimulation; well, you stimulate me with your incredible knowledge of music, your singing talent, your humour, your warmth, and the fact that you look after a senior lady who considers you to be her daughter. You make sensible decisions and irrespective of what happened about the disappearance of your father you still carry on searching for him and haven't given up, but above all your genuine desire to help others, if you are in a position to do so, is far higher than being some intellectual person. In any case, I consider you as intellectual: you're well read, you're curious about things, you converse intelligently, and you learn from many different sources, including life. Should I go on?"

I shake my head. He made his point.

Luke adds, "So know this, I've come to love who you are and I want to be with you. I didn't want to tell you this so soon, in case I spooked you, because you have this thing about being a lone wolf. But now that you brought this up, I can open up fully and tell you how I feel, and don't confuse sex with love. Love is much bigger than sex so I don't know where you get the impression that you're not enough to satisfy me. I assure you I'm very satisfied, thank you very much; besides, if you're ever in doubt about something sexual you've only to ask and I'll be more than glad to 'tutor' you—just as Dora said about your piano playing." He grins at his own humour while I feel tears run down my face, wetting his chest.

"What's this?" he remarks and hands me a few tissues.

"What you said, it made me cry. It's beautiful and though I am a lone wolf, it seems I found another lone wolf to love, so I guess you're stuck with me."

He dries my face with another tissue and looks into my eyes for a few moments before his mouth descends on mine and we lay back on the bed removing our nightclothes.

Chapter 26 - Robert

<u>1950/52, New York City, USA</u>

Christmas came and went and before we knew it a whole year passed us by and we were now on the eve of 1951. Over the past twelve months, Clara and I kept living to our usual routine of going to bed late and waking up early mornings, when we made love, or we slept in and then had the day to ourselves.

We often went for walks around the neighborhood, all the way to Central Park and sometimes beyond. We enjoyed going to the top of the Empire State Building to count all the skyscrapers from the viewing platform and see who counted the buildings faster. We frequented Midtown Manhattan with all its shops and major stores and pretended we were rich and could buy whatever we wanted. We visited art galleries and museums all over Manhattan and I even took Clara to the opera on her birthday, and on my free night from the club we'd sometimes go to check out other jazz clubs and have a dance. Clara also started coming with me to Big Charlie's some nights to listen to the music and wait for me to finish work so we'd go home together.

Meanwhile, I still grieved for the loss of my parents and although I sent them a Christmas card I never heard back from them. Clara and I were trying to start a family and I would have loved to tell my folks that a grandchild was on the way, but much as we tried Clara did not fall pregnant. This was a disappointment for both of us, but we were still young and healthy and there was no reason why we could not conceive.

On the financial front, our rent went up but my pay from Big Charlie's didn't. The club was due for some refurbishment and Charlie argued he could get another year or two before he invested in a new look, but over time my buddies in the band and I could see this might never come to pass. I already knew that a couple of the guys had received offers from other venues and they were considering making a move. This got me thinking about my musical career, which was going nowhere and most importantly things were already tight for Clara and me, and we couldn't stretch the dollar any more.

Aside from all this, another problem was looming on the horizon. The crime in our area was increasing and Clara began to fear living there. The Irish gangs were tougher than the Italian mafia and there were often turf wars where many got killed. On top of this, even though it wasn't yet as bad, a couple of Puerto Rican gangs began to infiltrate Hell's Kitchen and everyone knew things would have to get much tougher before the district was cleaned up. Unfortunately, even the police were corrupt and mostly turned a blind eye, and if they were not corrupt they still turned a blind eye out of fear for their own safety and that of their families. This put more pressure on Clara and me to move out of the area, but without more money we could go nowhere and secretly, at the back of my mind, I was glad Clara had not yet conceived. I couldn't think of anything worse than bringing up a child in such an environment.

Clara noticed my worries just by looking at my face. These days, I didn't smile so much nor can I remember when I last had a good belly laugh. I was under pressure and responsible for a wife, possibly a child in the near future, and to find safe housing so I could protect my family.

I didn't say anything to Clara or to my buddies at the club, but I decided to start looking around for other gigs. If I could find something that paid decent money I would be able to move us out of this place and we could have a better life.

I noticed of late that Clara reminisced more about Germany and the rest of Europe, particularly the UK, where she holidayed with her family prior to the war. Subsequently, she started to drop hints about gigs in Europe, especially in major cities like London. Besides, I knew for a fact that America was not her style with its imposing buildings and skyscrapers, and where people were brash and in a hurry all the time. Clara couldn't get used to the loud and fast American culture and while I knew she would bear living in the States for my sake, I didn't have the heart to expect her to live in a place she could not take to.

In the end, I decided to keep on searching for a gig in New York, but if I couldn't find something that paid decent money I would have to consider Europe, and London was the place to be.

Jazz in London was not as popular as in the States, but it was growing and went from strength to strength. Rhythm and blues, jazz, and calypso were popular. One of my band buddies had a brother playing a gig in London and he said Soho was being populated by jazz clubs and there would always be a place for American musicians—at least for the foreseeable future. My buddy, Jimmy, said, *"If I were you, I'd go there. You don't have children yet and this frees you up to grab new opportunities."* I thanked him for his frankness. He had two kids and the move would prove too disruptive for his family, but Clara and I were still free and we didn't have a family to think of.

Chapter 27 - Samantha

The alarm clock goes off at seven and I open my eyes to discover I'm still in Luke's arms and he's looking at me. "Good morning," he says after switching off the alarm.

I stretch but make no effort to get up. I feel warm and safe lying against him and I wish we had all day to stay in bed and make love. I suddenly blush when I remember our night of passion and I smile. Luke plants a chaste kiss on my lips, however, and then slaps my backside playfully.

"Time to get up," he announces. "We have a really busy day ahead."

"Awww!" is my response.

"Have pity on me," Luke feigns exhaustion. "You're insatiable, woman, and I'm too old to keep up with you."

I laugh. "I didn't see you struggling, and three times in one night was no mean feat."

"That's it!" Luke laughs with me. "You've been counting. Get away with you or you'll make us late."

I kiss him and go off to shower. "Coffee for me, please," I call out from the bathroom.

When I'm done, I dress and towel dry my hair. Luke's waiting at the table with coffee and croissants and I join him. "I'm starving," I help myself to a couple of croissants while he pours me a cup of coffee. I can see he already drank one cup himself and he's onto his second.

"So you have your first lesson with Dora after rehearsal with the boys this morning, and then Helen's joining you to view the wardrobe?"

Time for business, I remind myself, and I push away images of our lovemaking, which still keep popping into my mind. "That's right," I reply. "What about you?"

"I'm meeting with Tom after rehearsal regarding the date for The Eclectics debut. Luckily, I placed the guy I sent to Marc for the Ku-dorf gig and as a result I don't need to go back to Berlin so soon, which gives us more time to get ready for the debut, plus Tom wants to have a bit of extra time to work on your cocktail gig so he can do it in real style and promote it properly; he's going to meet with you about that."

"Hold on a minute. We're a band now, so shouldn't Tom meet with all of us about The Eclectics?"

"We're only talking dates because my travel plans have changed and Tom needs to know when I'm going to be around for good so he can launch The Eclectics," Luke clarifies. "I finished compiling the song list for the band and we can discuss it with the boys at rehearsal. You saw my list and you know how much material I have so I need to consult with you guys and decide what we want to play this coming Thursday and Saturday."

"Okay, that's fine. But what's this about Berlin?" I grab another croissant and Luke refills our coffee cups.

"The business I mentioned to you regarding Berlin is that I'm a kind of agent for a few of the clubs over there and I find the entertainment for them. I usually audition bands, singers, backup vocalists, etc, and when I have a placement request I send the customer a list to choose from."

"Oh! So in a way you're a bit like Tom, except you don't run a pub."

Luke nods. "Exactly. It's a casual thing that developed over time because of my own gigs in Berlin and through them I met many people in the business, both artists and club owners."

"And this is why you have to go to Berlin a few days a month or so?"

"That's right, although I mostly do business over the phone with the artists I already know. It's only when I have new artists to audition that I go in person."

"Wow! That sounds really fun. How come I never thought of it?"

He smiles. "Because you're too young and impulsive."

"Hey!" I protest.

"Just joking," he says. "I know you're capable of doing anything you put your mind to, but I can't resist stirring you and your Irish temper."

I stick out my tongue at him and start to clear the table.

After rehearsal with Chris and Marcus, Luke goes through the songs we select to play for this coming Thursday and Saturday. He already knows my preferences, which I gave to him earlier, so I can leave for Dora's place and my piano tutorial. The boys watch me pack a whole bunch of music scores into my shoulder bag.

"Don't know how your fingers don't drop off, Sam," Chris remarks. "Almost two hours of guitar playing and now classical piano. You're a smart cookie." He blows me a kiss for luck and I return the gesture.

"Thank you," I say. "Let's just hope my fingers don't cramp up during tomorrow night's gig." I place my guitar in its case and leave it with Luke. "Must dash now. Have fun all!" I wave at them and I'm off.

I make it to the tube station just in time and once I'm sitting on the train I close my eyes to rest. As much as it was magical to make love with Luke all night, I was beat. I played it cool in his presence at breakfast this morning, but I could do with a few hours of sleep to recharge my batteries. Images of the night flow through my mind, however, and my eyes suddenly fly open when someone announces the Embankment stop, where I need to change for Sloane Square. I pick up my bag and rush towards the sliding doors, almost missing my step and tripping on the platform. Fortunately, someone grabs a hold of my arm to steady me and I thank the old gentleman who came to my rescue. I then rush across the platform when I see my tube connection arriving. Dora's place is about a ten minute walk from the station so the clear and cool weather refreshes me as does the strong coffee Dora offers me upon arrival.

"My dear Sam, have you slept in?" she regards my puffy eyes.

"Quite the opposite," I reply, momentarily forgetting who I'm talking to.

Dora laughs. "You forget I, too, was young once, and though I didn't engage in sexual athletics all night I can imagine you must be extremely tired. Besides, who can resist that young man of yours?"

My only response is a big blush and I bury my face in my coffee. Dora ignores my looks and makes for the parlour where her grand piano stands. I follow while sipping on my caffeine shot.

The next two hours are excruciating. Dora has me warm up with some scales, as if my fingers haven't worked enough already during rehearsal, and then we move onto the pieces I will play at the gig debut.

"It's not that you don't know the actual piece," Dora explains when I complain at having to do scales and play short pieces with the metronome ticking away. "It's all in the rhythm, my dear. You play beautifully, but an experienced ear will pick up if you're not playing according to the tempo of the piece."

I sigh. "I do understand what you're saying but aside from you, I don't think anyone will pick up on it. The gig's about cocktails prior to going to the theatre so I'd say most patrons will be too tipsy to pick up on my tempo."

"Really, Sam!" Dora admonishes me. "It doesn't matter who doesn't pick up on what you play and how you play it; what matters is that you're playing the piece as it should be played to the best of your ability."

I look down in shame. "I'm sorry, Dora, of course you're right and I know with your help I'll become a better piano player.

Dora pats my shoulder. "All right, dear, no need to beat yourself over the head, but may I make a small suggestion?" I nod and she says, "Do try not to have too much sex the night before you're due to perform. Modern music, you can fudge through, but don't insult our favourite maestros. Somehow, I don't think Beethoven, Mozart and Chopin would approve."

I'm not sure whether to laugh or look contrite with shame. In the end, I simply give Dora a hug.

Helen arrives at around one and I let her in and offer her tea in the sitting room. She accepts and I rush into the kitchen to put on the kettle while I finish a sandwich Dora had prepared for me after the tutorial.

When tea's ready, Dora and I join Helen in the sitting room and we chit chat about fashion design and Anne's work. Helen is a fan of vintage fashion and she can't wait to see what Dora has in store to show her.

After tea, I clear up while Dora takes Helen on the grand tour and I hear squeals of delight coming from Helen, followed by words like wonderful, magnificent, exquisite, and so on. I join them once I'm done in the kitchen and find them chatting like old friends already. Although Dora is into music she still shares Anne's passion for fashion design. I hide a little smile, thrilled for Dora that she has found yet another kindred spirit.

"Oh, Sam!" Helen turns to me when I enter the room. "This is incredible, beyond words really. Anne was so talented; and Dora, what wonderful taste you have."

Dora wipes away a tear at hearing such praise for Anne and I feel for Dora. There is nothing more horrible than being separated from the one you love, the one who is meant to be with you forever until death. This doesn't necessarily have to be a lover; it can be a sister, brother, parents, other family, good friends, and so on. I see Luke's face in my mind all of a sudden and I wonder whether he'll turn out to be my destiny and I his.

"Sam!" Helen calls out and startles me out of my thoughts. I turn to her. "Sam, you look as if you're in another world, but in the meantime Dora and I have come up with a plan."

Dora suggests we go back to the sitting room for more tea and I follow them.

"Sam," Helen says again while Dora refills our cups although the tea is lukewarm by now. "Dora and I are going to start a kind of partnership. I'm going to rent items from Anne's wardrobe for Joan's high tea gig and for your own cocktail gig, and this could expand to other venues where vintage fashion is needed. I have so many contacts I can introduce to Dora. I'm even happy to help out at this end, you know."

Helen is far too excited and I'm sure she's forgotten she has enough on her hands with her kids, the expected baby, and the hosting responsibilities. Then again, Helen thrives on what she does and she's full of energy, so who am I to bring this up, not that I would.

"That sounds wonderful, you two," I tell Helen and Dora. "All I ask is that I get to choose what I wear."

Helen laughs. "Oh, Sam, you're so stubborn sometimes. I promise you that once Dora and I are through with you, you will look divine for your cocktail gig."

I wouldn't go that far, I think to myself, but what the heck—if Dora and Helen are happy with their arrangement and it's good for Dora to be able to make use of Anne's designs, plus meeting all sorts of interesting people, why should I worry about what dress they suggest I wear? I don't want to spoil their enthusiasm.

———◆———

When I get back to the pub it's past four in the afternoon. Helen left around three, but I stayed chatting with Dora about the new venture with Anne's designs. She was so excited working with Helen that I felt she needed a cup of chamomile tea and a nap. So when she finally dropped off, I left.

When I enter via the back door, Tom and Luke are chatting in the storeroom about Tom's plan for launching both The Eclectics and the cocktail gig. I don't wish to disturb them, but they hear me come in and Tom calls out, "Sam, is that you? What have you done to my wife? She called a while ago and was so excited that I didn't get heads or tails of what she was talking about."

I join the men. "What a day!" Then I give them a rough rundown on how things went and more importantly about the new partnership Dora and Helen are going to form.

"Isn't that too much for Helen with the baby on the way?" Luke says.

Tom laughs. "You don't know Helen. The woman's unstoppable. Even I don't have a say, but I do have concerns about this Dora; she's elderly, isn't she, Sam?"

Now it's my turn to laugh. "Yeah well, she may be elderly, but she's so determined that once she makes up her mind to do something nothing can stop her. I think meeting Helen brought them together as 'spirit sisters' born a generation apart, but nothing's going to stop them plus they're going to make me wear a dress!" I protest with a smile.

We all share a laugh and then Tom says, "Well, I'm glad you walked in when you did. I'm thinking of launching The Eclectics in two weeks' time, two Saturdays from the one coming up this weekend. Then, two more weeks on from The Eclectics debut, I'm launching you with 'Classical Cocktails'. I'll need more time to promote this gig with photos, posters, some press if we can get it, and VIP invitations to the opening night. So what do you think of the name, Sam?"

"It has a nice ring to it, especially now that I'll be wearing all sorts of vintage fashion designs, courtesy of Dora and Helen." I grin, but I'm rather nervous about this particular gig on top of which everything is happening too quickly and I keep hoping I will be able to cope. "Tom," Luke says, "do you mind if I borrow Sam for a while? We still have to go through a number of song lists."

Huh? I wonder what Luke's up to because I've already been through the song lists with him. Tom's none the wiser, however, so he nods. "Yeah, you guys go. Sam, I just wanted to give you the dates so you can start preparing."

"Don't worry. I've already started." I give him a quick smile and turn to Luke. "I'll see you when you're done here. I'm just going to freshen up."

As I climb the stairs leading to the studio I hear Luke saying something to Tom and then he runs up the stairs to catch up with me. I open the studio door, with Luke following right behind me, and close it while I throw my bag with all the music scores on the table and I sit on the bed.

Luke grabs a couple of water bottles out of the fridge and offers me one. I take it and have a long drink while he sits next to me quietly. "Thank you," I say when I finish drinking. "It's been a long day."

"Do you want to tell me about it?"

I sigh. "Not really."

Luke accepts this without trying to find out what's going on with me. He knows I'll tell him if I want to. I feel better because he's not one of those people who need to know everything about a person or they pester them to death. Just thinking back on the whole day is too much for me right now. Too many things happening, all good of course, but I need to rest and then

I'll be able to take it all in bit by bit rather than rush into an emotional maelstrom about gigs, dresses, playing complicated piano pieces, starting a new band, the excitement of my ever growing love for Luke and a whole lot more. I'm aware Luke steals a glance at me now and then as we sit there in silence, and suddenly I smirk.

"What?" Luke says when he sees the expression on my face.

"You'll love this one on top of everything else that happened today."

"And what's that?"

"Dora told me I should slow down on the 'sexual athletics' but on the other hand she said, and I quote: "'Who can resist that young man of yours?'" I smile as I notice a little colour appear on Luke's face. "Hey, don't tell me you're shocked?" I tease him.

"Shocked, no; worried, yes! The woman may be elderly, but she's a bit scary. Remind me to watch my back, and never leave me in a room alone with her." This seems to break my earlier rather morose mood and we both break out into laughter.

Chapter 28 - Robert

1952, New York City, USA

Sometimes life keeps dealing us one kick after another until we fall to our knees and wonder what will happen next. If we're lucky and when we least expect it, something good will suddenly happen which can change our lives, and in this instance I'm happy to say that we were very lucky. Thanks to Jimmy from the band at Big Charlie's and his brother, who lives in London, Clara and I are soon to set sail for England. We are bound for Soho, an area filled with nightlife and jazz clubs to equal NYC.

Jimmy's brother, Mike, is a trumpet player at the iconic 100 Club, a venue often frequented by American GIs which introduced the jitterbug dance to London and which was subsequently banned from many other venues because some of the dancers complained of bruises sustained by flying heels as their GI partners threw them around in jitterbug frenzies, and this sometimes hurt other dancers within their proximity.

Prior to the 100 Club offer, however, I looked around for another gig outside of Big Charlie's and though I received strong interest from a couple of clubs, the money just wasn't going to be enough. Meanwhile, Clara's heart was set on Europe and since my mission for reconciliation with my parents never eventuated I figured I had nothing to lose. As a result, I asked Jimmy to help me get in touch with his brother in Soho and one day, quite out of the blue, I received a letter from Mike, who advised he had spoken to his boss at the 100 Club and on Jimmy's say so, who used to work at the same club prior to the war, Mike's boss decided to offer me a job. One of his trumpet players was leaving for the States and the boss took me on faith because he knew he could rely on Jimmy and Mike's word.

While Clara and I waited for our immigration approval from the UK, I kept corresponding with Mike, who was very helpful in providing information about the cost of things and where to live cheaply, hopefully safer than in Hell's Kitchen. Mike mentioned Covent Garden was a decent enough area close to the West End theatres and Soho. It was a place mainly for working folk, not the rich, but Mike assured me it was safe enough to live in and for less than what we paid for our two bedroom apartment in New York, Mike said we could rent a decent terrace house.

Clara was happy when I told her about our situation and how we would be able to live better in London. She asked if I was sure that this was what I wanted. I could tell she felt somewhat guilty for what had transpired; however, I was quick to point out that I didn't see a future for us in New York and there was no point in staying here with the cost of living going up. Moreover, we had family in Germany and Clara and I would be able to visit them any time. Since I lost my own family, I was grateful the Schmidts welcomed me to theirs.

After a couple of months, we were surprised to receive our immigration visa approval and we were told the visa was expedited because I already had a job waiting for me in London, and this put us ahead of other candidates who had yet to find employment. This was excellent for us as we could now get on with organizing things toward our departure.

That evening, I took Clara out for dinner and dancing. This was to be our farewell to New York City, which gave me the start I needed in order to get the experience that came in helpful for us to be able to live in the UK.

Chapter 29 - Samantha

<u>Aug/Sep, 1985, London, England</u>

The Eclectics debut is upon us and The Treble and Bass is jam-packed to full capacity with new and regular patrons. I peek from behind the black curtains, which divide backstage from the front, and I've never seen the pub so busy. My legs feel rubbery all of a sudden, my stomach seems to be pasted to my back and I'm sure I'm going to throw up at any moment.

I thought it scary when Jeff first introduced me to the audience at his last performance, when I was a real beginner, but now I'm more confident and gig-savvy and yet, when I see the crowd cheering and calling for us to come out onstage, my courage fails me. Chris, Marcus and Luke are getting ready to go on and chatting at the same time about the first cover we'll perform to launch the show. Meanwhile, I sit down cross-legged on the floor with my head in my hands in the hope that I can pull myself together.

"Five minutes, everybody!" Tom suddenly appears backstage to wish us luck. He has a huge smile on his face, especially as we got some press in the local papers a few days prior to the launch. The response was so huge that Tom had to get printed tickets to sell ahead of time so we wouldn't have any problems with the number of people attending, which met capacity requirements under safety laws. "You guys are going to be great," Tom exclaims and looks my way when he sees me sitting on the floor. "Hey, when I say 'guys' I mean you, too," he jests.

It is then Luke spots me and comes to my side with a bottle of water. I shake my head, thinking it's going to make me feel worse while Luke glances at me and turns to the boys. "Marcus, Chris, get ready just in case you have to go out there on your own. If you do, play any instrumental piece you can think of and I'll join you guys as soon as possible."

Tom addresses Luke with concern, "Do we need a doctor for Sam?"

Luke scoops me in his arms. "No, she'll be okay. Tom, go out there and say a few words before you introduce us; that should buy us a few extra minutes." Tom nods and disappears behind the curtains. I can hear the roar of voices, whistles and applause, and Tom takes the microphone and starts talking. The boys are almost ready to go on and Luke takes me to the back storeroom and deposits me on Tom's fold-up bed. He disappears and returns within a moment, carrying a glass with what looks like a shot of Baileys Irish Cream; he knows it's my favourite. He sits on the edge of the fold-up and holds me in a sitting position with one arm.

"Listen to me, Sam. You're having a strong case of stage nerves. Trust me, I know this because I've been there, done that."

I'm about to say something, but I cling to him with both my arms around his neck; he shifts back a little so he can see my face. "What I'm about to do is something I don't approve of, and you shouldn't feel pressured into doing it." He then says to himself, "Good God, what am I thinking?" And he seems about to change his mind, but I sit up and shake him by clutching at his shirt.

"This is no time for regrets!" I yell at him while I'm still trying to flick off the anxiety attack, but I can feel my strength beginning to come back. "What the fuck do you want me to do?" I never speak to Luke this way, but it's time one of us makes a decision. "Tell me!" I shout close to his face.

The look of doubt in his eyes disappears and he shows me the glass in his hand. "I crushed a small dosage of Valium in here, so if you drink this you'll feel calmer. The other option is that we cover for you, and on hindsight this might be the best solution."

I look at him in disbelief. "Are you kidding me? This is the launch, damn it!" I snatch the glass from his fingers. "What's this dosage you're talking about?"

"Five milligrams."

I almost laugh my head off. "Oh, for God's sake!" I remark, snatch the glass from him, and swallow the liquid in one gulp before I throw the glass away from me and send it crashing into a corner of the storeroom. "After the life I led I've been on a number of medications, including Valium, with dosages much higher than this one!"

Luke regards me with surprise in his eyes. "How was I to know? Are you still taking drugs?"

I let go of his shirt. "This is not the time to discuss it, but no. I rarely need to take something to calm me down. Now, let's get the hell out there and do this gig. We'll deal with my drug history later."

I don't know whether it's the Valium, Luke's concern for me or the fact that my strength is coming back, but whatever it is I grab his wrist and pull him along with me on the way to the stage.

The gig goes off with a bang and by midnight we wind up. The Valium with the Baileys did the trick and I performed my best without anxiety or fear creeping in. The crowd calls for encores and Chris, Marcus and I gaze in Luke's direction to see what he wants to do. He's been singing most of the night and playing guitar while we accompanied his tempo and supported him with backup vocals and harmonisation. I sang a number of songs myself, plus Luke and I performed a couple of duos.

The audience is still calling out for more, however, and finally Luke nods to the rest of us and shows us two fingers, meaning we'll do two more songs and finish up. We're done by a half hour past midnight and with final bows we go backstage with the sounds of cheering, whistling, and clapping from the crowd behind us.

Tom meets us out back. "If you guys keep going this way I'm going to have to find a bigger venue." We laugh at his remark, but the look on our faces tells him we're exhausted. "Off you go, all of you," Tom says. "Tomorrow morning I'll get a couple of my guys to move everything into the storage room. You guys deserve to sleep in."

None of us reply, but Tom knows we agree with him and are grateful. Chris says in my ear, "If this keeps up we'll be able to convince him to get us a couple of roadies."

I give him a hug and kiss him on the cheek. "Trust you to think of that one, my lad, but they call them 'roadies' because they travel on the road with the bands." Chris makes a face at me and he and I are the first to disappear. He goes out the back door and I go up the stairs to Luke's place. I shout a good night to Marcus and Tom and then enter the studio and collapse on the bed.

Luke follows a moment later and finds me stretched out with arms above my head. He looks spent himself and I shift over so he can lie next to me, which he does. "What a night!"

"It went beyond our expectations despite my false start," I remark. "I do apologise for that, by the way. I unleashed my temper on you and I had no right to do so. You were simply supporting me, for which I am very grateful."

"How are you feeling now?"

I turn to him and kiss his lips softly while I grab his hand and pull him gently to follow me. "Where are we going?" he asks.

"We're sweaty and smell of smoke," I reply and pull his hand a little harder as I stand up. "We need to shower and get some rest. C'mon, let's go."

"Go where?"

"To shower, where else?" I answer.

"Okay. You go first."

I keep pulling him along with me. "We'll save more time if we go in together. Just a quick shower and then some shuteye.

He follows me into the bathroom and we peel off our sweaty clothes and enter the small shower cubicle where we wash each other, including our hair. The steamy water cleanses away my tiredness and I feel completely relaxed, but at the same time I can't resist the touch of Luke's wet and naked body against mine, and I don't need to turn around and look between his legs to know where he's at.

Luke puts his arms around me from behind and his hands rove over my body. I'm immediately consumed by a wave of arousal that awakens every cell in me and I lean back against him. His mouth takes possession of mine and then he kisses my neck, ears, and shoulders while his hands travel lower and he reaches the place between my legs where he holds me in place and enters me, teasing, thrusting one moment and easing off the next. I feel a climax building up but manage to delay the moment of pure ecstasy as he keeps thrusting gently into me, smoothly and deeply until I reach a release so strong that I feel a cascade of orgasmic pleasure that brings tears to my eyes.

———◆———

I suddenly wake up and find Luke gazing at me. I stretch and realise we're both naked under the sheets and this brings back a picture of what we did in the shower, and of course I blush. Luke smiles and plants a kiss on the tip of my nose. "Still tired?" he remarks with a meaningful grin.

"Oh, stop it! And don't forget you started the funny business," I throw at him.

"Yes, but you were the one that dragged me into the shower in the first place," he returns with smugness.

I sit up and quickly hold the bed sheet against me. Luke regards me with humour in his eyes. "I think you can stop the maidenly act. I know exactly what you look and feel like."

"Fine!" I say, not mad at him but at myself, for feeling so self-conscious. "How about you make some coffee?"

"Is that an order?" He's still teasing me.

"Yes."

"Very well," he replies and gets out of bed, stark naked.

"Put on your shorts!"

He gives me a mock army salute. "Yes, Captain Kelly." He pulls out a fresh pair of shorts from the wardrobe and while he's at it he grabs one of my nightshirts and throws it at me with a smile. "There you go, now you can feel less vulnerable." He goes into the kitchen and I hear him putting on the coffee and taking stuff out of the fridge. A few minutes later, he brings a tray with our hot drinks and warm brioche and he sets it on the bedside table, handing me my coffee and brioche on a plate. I'm starving after our nightly antics and so must he be because both of us eat and drink in silence until we finish.

"More coffee?" Luke tops up my cup when I nod and he also refills his own.

"Thank you for making breakfast," I say.

"You're welcome, you fiery Irish lass who throws glasses across the room," he replies. "You're not half Russian by any chance?"

I roll my eyes. "Okay, so I was overcome by anxiety, but when you brought the drink and were going to give it to me, all of a sudden you hesitated so I made the decision to drink it myself. There was no way I was going to miss out on the debut and let you guys down as well as Tom and his pub. I really don't know what came over me."

Luke caresses my hair and plants a soft kiss on my lips. "You know I'm kidding when I call you fiery or bad-tempered, right?" I nod, and he continues, "I'm not proud of what I did, Sam. It's not the sort of thing I would do. If you had come up with the idea yourself, that would've been a different story, but I felt terrible suggesting it. It was like I was pushing you to take drugs."

"Luke, you forget it was I who snatched the glass from your hand and drank the stuff, so in the end it was my decision, and I made it."

"It's just that I had a drug problem during the early years of my life and the impact on me was pretty bad. I won't go into details now, but in the end I came off the hard stuff and at least I never smoked again, and I only drink lightly. I take care of my health, especially my throat. If something happens to my voice that'd be the end for me."

"Explains all the water we drink," I respond. "I still take Valium from time to time. I used to get really bad panic attacks in foster care plus growing up on the streets, and I'm still hypervigilant at times, but these days I'm finally beginning to feel safer. I don't smoke either, and never have, and I only drink very little. So it seems we have yet another thing in common. But Luke, don't feel bad. I'm glad you came to my rescue or I would never have been able to go up on that stage. The odd gigs in the past were not as important as what is happening now, and it was this that freaked me out. It was our debut, one with a future attached to it if things go well for us."

"Sam, things will go well, and remember that now we're together, we're safe. We have a good future to look forward to so just think about that. And I should ask if you're okay for the Classical Cocktails debut."

I nod. "After what I went through last night I think I can handle anything," I reassure him. "By the way, where did you get the Valium from? I don't carry any."

"Tom takes them for anxiety and he keeps some at work just in case."

"He knows? Oh my God, how embarrassing!"

"Relax, Miss Kelly," he reassures me. "I took it without asking; he won't miss it."

"Well, that's a relief."

"Yes, and I won't be doing it again." He then changes the subject, "By the way, I decided to go to Berlin tomorrow. I need to meet with Marc and make sure he's okay with the guy I sent him, plus I want to audition a couple of new people who've been referred to me. I also have to pack up my stuff and have it shipped back here."

I wish I could go with him, but I don't bring it up. He'll be busy plus I have to keep going with my piano tutorials and meet with Dora and Helen regarding my wardrobe for the cocktail gig. "How long will you be gone?"

"I'll be back by Thursday. Don't forget we're sold out again."

He's right. The Thursday Eclectics gig sold out as soon as the Saturday gig was full. We're already becoming popular and I know Tom is in discussions with outside venues that want to hire us in the near future. This will take a bit of time, however, until we have time to settle down as a band.

Chapter 30 - Robert

<u>1952, London, England</u>

We arrived in London during midsummer and I was pretty much put to work immediately. I was very lucky, though, to have Mike as a friend. He made our arrival a lot less stressful by arranging a rental terrace for us and showing us around the district prior to my debut at the 100 Club. My pay from the club is adequate, making easier to meet living costs and put aside some savings.

The other plus, unlike New York, is that London has an old world charm that echoes the rest of Europe. After the war, when I was stationed in Berlin, I sometimes traveled while engaged in the demobilization project and I was fortunate to visit cities like Paris, Rome, Amsterdam, Brussels, and others—all cities built hundreds, if not thousands, of years ago; all of them before America saw its first pilgrims. In Europe, people are entrenched in their culture, customs and values, and they don't take to change easily, but this gives their home countries a patina of permanence along with a rich heritage of being.

Customs are passed from father to son, mother to daughter, and family to family down the centuries and even millennia. As people grew and developed along with civilization, they clung to their ways, but at the same time they were able to incorporate the old with the new.

The closest I got to this in the States was when visiting the smaller country towns, where strong tradition is still honored. American cities, however, grew so fast, as did the people which populated them, and with the speed of growth something was missed and cities such as New York were an example of the brashness with which modernity became the norm and older values lost.

Our terrace in Covent Garden is charming and it even has a tiny patch of earth at the rear of the house suitable for growing vegetables or a small garden. The house has its living quarters downstairs and two bedrooms upstairs. It is fully furnished with some cheap pieces but also a number of rustic ones that add to the ambience of the place. The main windows are located in the sitting room with a northerly aspect while the one in the main bedroom upstairs also faces north, which gives the place a sunny aspect all day long. We're close to transportation and amenities such as the market, bakery, butcher, etc. In all, Clara and I are happy with our home even though some pockets of the district look impoverished, but walking around and having a look at the people that live in the area we feel the place is safe and nothing like Hell's Kitchen. Mike confirmed this was the case when I told him. Covent Garden wasn't a bad area; it was just where working people lived in a district that was safe enough.

When I started work at the club I found my boss, Steve, to be a likeable man, and when I played a few pieces for him he was indeed pleased that Jimmy and Mike's endorsement of my musical skills was spot on. Steve welcomed me to the 100 Club family and gave me my work schedule, which runs from Wednesdays to Sundays. The official club hours are seven to midnight, but more often than not we don't finish until two or three in the morning, hence the reason we're given two full days off to rest.

While Clara started to make a home for us, she also met some of the neighbors and happily reported she passed as someone from Irish descent. She was excited that at last her German accent had disappeared for good and I was relieved for her because at the back of my mind I still worried about what life would be like if anyone discovered she was German. Some people, I realize, will never forget what the Germans did in the war, but they easily forgot that not all Germans were Nazis.

In a short period of time, while I slept late after working nights at the club, Clara took to making bakery goods in order to sell at the local market. After her life in Germany, helping out Mr. Schmidt at his bakery, she certainly had the skills with which to venture into her own little enterprise and when she shared her idea with me I saw no harm in her doing this. Keeping busy could only enrich her life rather than sitting at home and waiting for me to come back from work. Besides, we still had two days during the week when I had my time off and we made the most of them by exploring London and all its beauty.

Chapter 31- Samantha

<u>Sep, 1985, London, England</u>

We spend the rest of Sunday stocking up on groceries, tidying up the studio, and then we go for a leisurely walk around the district where we have lunch at a local café. In the later part of the afternoon, we go through more song lists to expand our repertoire plus Luke wants to experiment with harmonisation and find more duet type of songs that we can perform together. In the evening, I make spaghetti Bolognese and we watch a video before having an early night.

At dawn on Monday, Luke packs an overnight bag and puts on the coffee, meanwhile grabbing his leather jacket out of the wardrobe. I wake up and stretch. "Is it time already?"

"My flight leaves at eight-thirty so I'm catching the airport tube at seven." Luke goes to check on the coffee and I glance at the bedside clock. It's just gone half past five so we have a little time together. "Want some brioche?" Luke calls from the kitchen.

"I'll get it," I call back, "you finish your packing." I get out of bed and bump into him as he's coming out of the kitchen. He gives me a quick kiss and goes into the bathroom to get some toiletries. "I'll call you this evening, but it'll be late. I'm meeting Marc at nine so I should be back at my hotel by eleven. Is that okay with you?"

"Sure," I respond while buttering the brioche and serving the coffee. "I've got my tutorial with Dora late morning and Helen's coming over later to choose my wardrobe for the classical gig."

Luke comes out of the bathroom and packs his shaving kit, a new toothbrush and other essentials into his overnight bag. I follow him with the coffee and brioche, which I set on the table. "Am I staying in the studio while you're away?"

He joins me and we have our breakfast while we talk. "It's up to you. You're free to do as you like."

"Yes, but seeing as Tom lets you rent this place for very little money he may have issues with me staying here all the time."

"Tom won't have a problem with that. It's early days yet, but the band seems set to be a regular drawcard so I don't think he'll quibble over who stays at my place." He finishes his breakfast and glances at his watch. "I'd better get going." He checks his overnight bag to make sure he has everything he needs and then puts on his jacket over a long-sleeved T-shirt. When he's done, he gives me a hug and we kiss. "Be good while I'm away," he says with a smile, "and if you can't be good just wait for me to return." We laugh and I walk with him to the studio door. He's about to step out but then turns back to me. "So do I ring you here or at Dora's?"

"Here," I reply.

"By the way, I left you the phone number of where I'm staying, just in case you need to reach me. It's on the kitchen bench, but we'll definitely chat tonight." He turns to go and then stops again and turns back to me with a serious look in his eyes and says, "I love you." And before I can react he's gone.

———— ◉ ————

I go to Dora's early and help her with her bath while I tell her about The Eclectics debut on Saturday and how we're fully booked for this coming Thursday. She's very excited for me and wants to hear every tiny detail about what went on. I give her a rundown while I finish blow-drying her hair, but I leave out the shaky start I had at the gig. No one, except Luke, knows about my past and the drugs that kept me going.

"So how are things with Luke?" Dora asks while I help her dress.

"They're good," I reply, trying to sound casual. I'm still in shock at Luke's parting words and I don't know how to interpret them. What does 'I love you' mean these days? Even friends say it to each other and it's no big deal, but the look in Luke's eyes when he said it to me makes me think he is truly serious. On the other hand, however, we've only known each other a short time and while our sexual relationship is incredible, I know that no matter how good it is now there will come a time when things will slow down and even wane. Isn't this what happens in most relationships? Or is it that when true love is involved the sexual side of things keeps going, and it may even get better with time? Unfortunately, I don't have the wisdom to judge any of this, except for the short time I was with Declan, but I can't rely on my limited experience with him. He lived a troubled life and though he told me he loved me it still didn't stop him from committing suicide.

"Off with the fairies, Sam?" Dora's voice brings me out of my reverie.

"I'm sorry. It's just that I have so much on my mind with all the stuff that's happening," I reply. "Luke and I are doing well. This morning, he left for Berlin to tie up some loose ends. He's really busy in London now so he decided to move back here for good."

Dora claps her hands excitedly, like a little girl in a candy store. "Oh, I have a feeling things are getting serious!"

I laugh; Dora's such a romantic. "It's not like that," I say. "Luke still has business in Berlin, but we're all so busy with the band now that this is purely a financial decision for him."

"Is that what he calls it, dear?"

"Dora, please behave and let's do the tutorial before lunch." I'm really not ready to explore my relationship with Luke right now.

"Very well, Sam," Dora says. "I made some sandwiches for us; and I take it Helen is coming over today?"

"Yes. I think she said she'll be here by two so we'd best get on with it." We go directly to the parlour and for the next two hours I immerse myself in the wonderful world of my 'classical boys' in the band.

At lunchtime, Dora and I sit in her kitchen and we munch on the sandwiches she made while I make coffee for myself and a cup of tea for Dora. "There's one thing regarding Luke that I need to discuss with you," I say after we finish chatting about my performance during the tutorial.

"And what's that, dear?"

I sigh, not sure whether this is the right moment to bring it up, but while I regard Dora as the mother I never had I want to be direct with her and get her feedback on the issue. "Well, now that Luke's basing himself in London, he's living in a studio at the pub and he suggested I live there with him." I watch for Dora's reaction to this piece of news, but her face is unreadable.

"Well, Sam, this is really up to you to decide."

"I just want your feedback on this. I mean, I would still come here to help you with things and of course I'd visit, too. It's just that spending so much time with the band business plus the new classical gig, I'm over there a lot more than I am over here so it makes sense for me to be there with Luke."

Dora reaches out and pats my hand. "Oh Sam, you don't have to ask for my feedback. It's your life and you can do whatever you want with it."

"Well, I don't want to lose the connection with you and although this means loss of income for you, unless you decide to get another person to board here, I want you to know that I'm not asking for payment in order to give you a hand with the household and personal care stuff."

Dora doesn't say anything for a moment and I can tell she's controlling her emotions. I refill her tea cup and top up my coffee to give her time until she's ready to respond. She sips her tea for a moment and then addresses me. "I don't mean to get emotional," she says. "It's just that despite your own problems, here you are offering to help out an old lady and not even asking for anything in return. My dear, you're so rare! There aren't many in this world that would do something like this."

I breathe a sigh of relief. "So does that mean you're okay with the arrangement?"

"If I had my way I'd have both you and Luke living under my roof fulltime—and for no rent! After all, I feel I have a family around me when you're here. I'm not sure, however, that this is an arrangement you and Luke would accept. I already told you I consider you a daughter and although I've only met Luke once, in my heart I know he's the one for you and that makes him family."

I'm stunned by Dora's disclosure and I don't know what to say, but I'm saved by the doorbell ringing. I jump up from my chair and glance at my watch. "Good grief! It's two already and that'll be Helen. I'll go and let her in; and Dora, let's finish this conversation after tomorrow's tutorial." Dora nods with a smile.

After I greet Helen, I tell her and Dora to go ahead and pick my wardrobe as they see fit and I will model for them when they make a final choice. They agree and I take my leave. I have a meeting with Tom at three to discuss the Classical Cocktails gig.

"You look a bit dishevelled, Sam," Tom remarks when I rush into his small office at three on the dot.

"I wanted to get here on time so I ran from the tube station. You know I had to escape from Helen and Dora, right? Had I stayed there, I wouldn't have made this meeting."

Tom laughs. "Coffee?"

"Yes, please."

Tom picks up the phone and orders coffee and pastries from the kitchen. "Okay," he says, "let's talk about the launch. Nothing like this has been done to date and I managed to get a TV spot to promote Classical Cocktails. How do you feel about being interviewed?"

"I don't know. I've never been in front of the cameras before."

"Well, it's not as scary as being in front of a huge crowd like you were on Saturday night," Tom remarks. "This'll be a one or two minute spot and an excellent opportunity for us to mention The Eclectics as well."

"So you'll be in the spot, too?"

He nods and I feel a wave of relief wash over me. I never thought I'd be on television. "I'll introduce the Classical Cocktails concept and then the interviewer will ask you a few questions. We might even slip in some footage of you playing the piano, but we'll see what the guy wants."

The coffee and pastries arrive with a jug of iced water and as soon as the food attendant leaves I go for the water and drink a whole glass while Tom pours the coffee and offers me a pastry. I keep wishing Luke were here, but Classical Cocktails is my gig entirely and it's time I learn to negotiate my business on my own.

Tom says, "I've also organised a press conference via invitation only."

"What does that mean?" I ask and take a bite from a cinnamon roll.

"I think we should have a closed 'VIP-by-invitation-only debut' for the press and other important business contacts of The Treble and Bass."

"You mean I debut for them privately and a few days later we have the real debut?"

Tom refills our coffee. "That is exactly what I mean, so I need to know when you'll be ready with the pieces you're planning to play and we can use the VIP function as a dry run. Oh, and I have a photographer coming in to get some shots of you so I can order posters and leaflets. I'll get onto Helen to work with you on the outfits. Just pick two or three and let's see how they turn out in the photos."

At this moment, my head starts to swim a little and I wish I had a Valium. I'm beginning to understand how a lot of famous artists start on their journey with drugs. The pressure to perform is huge and here I am, worrying about a couple of pub gigs. I couldn't possibly imagine being famous and performing in front of tens of thousands of people.

"What's wrong?" Tom's voice breaks into my thoughts.

"How do you mean?"

Tom's gazing at me. "You've gone a bit pale. Are you okay?"

"Sure, sure," I lie. "We've been so busy lately that I haven't had much by way of sleep."

Tom pats my hand. "Well, be sure you get enough rest because we have a lot to do between now and the debut."

I finish my coffee and stand to go. "Anything else? If not, I'm off to have a siesta."

Tom says, "Don't let this unsettle you, Sam. You have our support and we're all here for you. Go have your sleep and leave matters to me."

"Thank you, I appreciate it," I say and leave the office.

I sleep the afternoon away, what is left of it, and by eight I put on a video and sit on the bed, leaning into a whole bunch of pillows while I have my dinner: a roast chicken salad I ordered from the kitchen downstairs. I really had no energy to cook after the day's excitement and it's a relief that I don't have to order in from a restaurant and wait around for the food delivery.

It's almost ten when the video finishes and I get ready for bed, starting with a refreshing shower. My hair's clean, but I wash it anyway and while I do I picture in my mind what went on only two nights ago in this very shower cubicle. I shake my head to disperse the erotic imagery my mind conjures up and I quickly finish showering and drying my hair. I put on a fresh nightshirt and socks, but I feel cold for some reason so I go back to bed and get under the covers. The evening is rather cool, but not enough to switch on the heating.

I close my eyes and try to relax after my busy day; my body feels warm and I can feel myself drifting into a peaceful sleep when the shrill ring of the phone startles me. I glance at the bedside clock, it's almost midnight and I sit up and pick up the receiver, but before I can say anything Luke's voice comes through loud and clear.

"Sam, were you sleeping?"

"Yes, but I'm glad you rang."

"I just got in from my last meeting of the day. I didn't realise how late it is."

"Oh, the time difference. It's past one in the morning over there, right?"

"Yes. I should've known you'd be asleep by now."

"Well, I'm one hour behind you, but I had a good nap this afternoon so I'm okay to chat unless you wish to get some sleep."

"I'll chat with you first, my love." There he goes again. The 'love' word. I'll just have to ignore it. This isn't the time to bring it up, so in order to distract him I briefly mention what Dora said regarding living arrangements plus I tell him about my meeting with Tom.

"Wow!" Luke exclaims. "I'm gone for one day and everything changes."

"Yes, you're missing out on all the fun here. The whole debut thing is bigger than I thought and rather daunting," I confess, "but my only consolation is that you'll be here when it all happens. You will be here, right?"

"Just try and keep me away," he replies. "But you sound like there's something else going on. What's bothering you?"

He knows me so well, but I don't want to go into details now about living arrangements or why he calls me 'my love' or even all the stuff Tom wants me to do. I simply want to hear his voice and so I say, "Let's leave all the talk about me until you come back. Right now, I want to hear about your day and what you've been up to."

Luke tells me about his meetings with various club managers, including Marc, who was impressed by the guy Luke introduced. The auditions for a couple of new singer/guitar players went well and Luke has them earmarked for a couple of clubs off the Ku-damm, and lastly there are the personal effects Luke is shipping over.

"The next two days are jam-packed," he tells me, "so I'll be out and about until late. If I don't ring you don't worry, but if for some reason you need to get in touch with me the number I gave you is where you can leave a message at any time. I'll be back late Wednesday night or first thing Thursday."

"Will do," I reply, "and you should get some sleep." I hesitate for a few seconds and then I say, "I miss you. Stay safe and I'll see you soon."

Luke wishes me a good night and we ring off.

Chapter 32 - Robert

<u>1952, London, England</u>

While I'm enjoying my new gig at the 100 Club, Clara is baking up a storm and becoming a regular stall vendor at the Covent Garden market.

A neighbor in our street runs an outdoor fruit and vegetable stall at the market and when she heard Clara was looking for a small space in which to sell her bakery goods the neighbor, Mary, approached her and after a chat, plus the fact that they seemed to get on really well, Mary offered to share part of her stall for a small fee so Clara could sell her goods. The arrangement was made and Clara took up the option of selling her goods three times a week.

In a short time, our kitchen turned into a bakery and Clara has been so involved in her venture that she positively glows with happiness. I am so glad for her because I can imagine how dreary it has been for her when I come home and sleep during the day as a result of my late hours at the club. So now Clara bakes during the night and when I come home from my gig we manage to have some time together until Clara leaves for the market early morning, and then I sleep until it's time for me to get ready for work.

It's a hard life for us, but we're making the most of it by spending my days off together, stealing a few hours here and there when Clara stays up late to bake, and it's during this window of time that we also make love. Above all else, Clara wants a baby, but as hard as we try she can't seem to conceive. She saw a doctor when we were living in New York and he couldn't find anything wrong with her, but Clara won't give up and we keep trying in the hope that one day we may be blessed with a child. In the meantime, we manage to achieve the kind of rare happiness and contentment that often evades so many people. Clara and I are companions, friends, lovers, and soul mates.

Sometimes, it frightens me to think of just how lucky we are irrespective of the fact that up until now Clara can't conceive, but I always think things could be worse, especially if we want something too much. For my part, I don't worry as to whether we'll have children or not; I leave this to fate. I'm not a religious person, but I believe that if we ask too much of life we may get something much worse in return. This thought haunts me and I feel shivers run up and down my spine whenever the thought pops up. Clara is not as philosophical as I am and she seems to take things in her stride, but she's not one to give up on dreams. At present, she has her work to keep her busy and she's making friends via her bakery.

Speaking of friends, Mike and I have become close buddies and we get on really well. He looks upon me as an older brother seeing that Jimmy, his real older brother, is settled in New York for good. Mike is five years younger than I, but at twenty-three he seems a lot savvier to my twenty-seven years. Perhaps it's because the war in Europe ravaged England and the rest of the Allied nations for so many years that while the US delayed going to war, England and other European nations practically starved despite the aid America sent to Europe; a large part of which was sunk in the Atlantic thanks to the German U-boats. And yet, England fought on and managed to keep the Germans at bay while other nations fell under the tyranny of the Nazis.

The irony is that while we were in the US, dancing to the jitterbug, we remained totally unaware of the danger creeping toward our shores. Pearl Harbor was the wake-up call for America, one which none of us will ever forget and one that finally made men out of boys.

Chapter 33 - Samantha

Sep, 1985, London, England

The days seem to fly by and Tuesday and Wednesday are a blur. On Tuesday at Dora's, Helen pops in before I start my tutorial and she and Dora take me through ten outfits they agreed upon for both the by-invitation-only debut and the public debut. I spend at least two hours modelling the outfits for the women and these are not the only things I model; there are shoes, accessories such as jewellery, hats and other head wear, bands, clips, and more.

It is lunchtime by the time we finish and Dora invites Helen to stay for sandwiches and coffee. We sit around the kitchen table and while I eat quietly the other two are bubbling with ideas.

"We'll have to take in a few of the outfits," Dora remarks and turns to me. "Sam, you're very slim and bordering on the skinny side."

"Don't worry, Dora. I haven't dropped any weight." Even as I say this I'm lying. With all the goings-on, the nervous energy spent on the gigs, plus my very active sexual life with Luke, I've lost some weight, but not enough to make me look gaunt. Besides, I'm sure when things settle down my natural weight will stabilise.

Dora turns to Helen. "I still think the outfits need taking in."

"Don't worry, Dora. Even if we don't take them in no one will notice as Sam will be sitting down at the piano for the majority of the time."

I look from one to the other. "Helen's right," I remark in the hope that Dora will let it go. Dora remains quiet on the subject for the moment, but being the perfectionist that she is I'm sure she will bring this up again.

Helen leaves after lunch and I have my tutorial with Dora. Time flies and before I know it it's mid-afternoon when I finish. "You've improved quickly, my dear, much faster than I expected," Dora tells me. "You know the music well and it's simply a matter of correcting your tempo so I think by end of this week you can practice on your own."

"Thank you. I wouldn't have been able to do this without you." I hug her and feel just how fragile she is and this worries me. "Are you coping okay with all the extra activity?" I ask with concern.

Dora looks surprised. "Why Sam, what do you mean?"

"Well, it's just that so much is happening plus I haven't been spending as much time with you as I used to, and then there's the partnership you're going into with Helen. You don't think this is too much?"

Dora gives me a kindly smile. "My dear, if anything I feel alive again. Not that I didn't feel alive before—I mean since you came to live here—but being involved in something this exciting really helps. You know I'm not one to sit at home living on my faded memories of youth. I simply wish I could be young again and be free to do the things young people do these days. I must confess I still think about my Edward; we had so little time together." She pauses for a moment to gather her thoughts and then says, "I see you and Luke being so much in love and you're able to be together freely, without the conventions of the past." I know immediately what she means and I feel the colour rise to my face. Dora smiles, "Don't be shy, Sam. The fact that you can be intimate with him is part of being in love as well. I did have some intimacy with Edward, but it was too short-lived and we were separated by our families and then the war, and though I don't like to ruminate about what 'could have been' I do wish I had the freedom people have today to express their love, both in sentiment and physically."

I don't know what to say; convention truly frowned upon pre-marital sex in Dora's time even though intimacy is a part of being in love, as Dora put it, but every now and then I think modern times are so much more complicated. These days one never knows what a person means when they say they love you or if they're even going to be there for you if things get difficult, like someone becoming ill. So many people get dumped and end up alone and this makes the mind boggle.

I remark, "At least you did have some intimacy with Edward and this is something you can cherish for the rest of your life. It won't take away the 'what may have been if life had dealt you both a different card', but I know that no matter what age we live in there will always be problems that seem insurmountable and we'll always reflect on the 'what may have been' side of things."

Dora sighs. "Very true and this is why being involved in something exciting, like my project with Helen, gives me something to strive for even if it's not what I would choose had I the power to conjure up the past."

"I agree, Dora," I reply, "and for as long as humans have been and will be on this planet, no matter whether it's past, present, or future, we will all have moments when the 'might have been' rears its ugly head to taunt us."

"My dear, you've got that right." Just then, the clock in the hallway strikes four. "Oh, look at the time! I've made you late," Dora exclaims.

"Not at all, but just before I go, about what you said yesterday regarding living arrangements, whether or not I end up with Luke is irrelevant. I wish to stay with him, at least to see where our relationship takes us, but I don't wish to leave you unless you ask me to. Like I said, I will help you with the household and personal needs, and this I will do because you have become my family. I may not sleep here, but if you're unwell or something troubles you, you've only to call. Of course, if you choose to find a new boarder I'll understand."

"I agree with you, Sam, in that you need your time to be with Luke and see where your relationship takes you. As for me, I'm grateful you're happy to help me out and that I can call you if I need to. I don't really wish to take in a boarder, especially now with the partnership bringing in some extra money, plus I can still cope financially in any case. So I accept our arrangement for the time being."

I look questioningly at her. "For the time being?"

"Until you know in your heart whether Luke is the one," she clarifies.

"Thank you, and please don't be concerned about anything; you can't get rid of me that easily." I give her a big hug. "I'll see you tomorrow."

I go back to the studio, heat up some soup for dinner and after a hot shower I get to bed early and fall asleep almost immediately. The following morning, I join Chris and Marcus for another rehearsal even though I don't feel we need it.

"You guys," I address the boys during our session, "I think we're doing okay and don't need to go over these songs again. Let's wait for Luke; I know he's adding a whole bunch of stuff to our list of covers, plus we need to practise a couple of his compositions. What do you say?"

"I agree," says Marcus. "I think we're doing okay and we already know the songs we did last Saturday."

"I second that," Chris chimes in.

"Well, unless Luke adds any new stuff between now and this coming Saturday, I say let's wait until he gets back."

The boys agree and we finish our session with a coffee before I go off to my piano tutorial. Today, I'm modelling the wardrobe again chosen for me by Dora and Helen. Dora contacted Helen and was insistent on taking in the outfits that looked a little large on me, so in the end Helen agreed to come to Dora's and help with the alterations. I should have warned Helen that Dora would turn out to be a perfectionist and when I arrive at Dora's I sigh in resignation, seeing that I promised I'd wear whatever outfits she and Helen choose for me in whatever size, but I draw the line at having my hair swept up with bands or clips of any kind and this leaves Dora and Helen with no choice but to agree. However, they are happy I put myself in their hands in regards to the dresses and shoes.

It takes ages with the modelling of the outfits, so much so that Dora insists I stay for dinner. Helen takes her leave to go home and look after her family and I glance at my watch; it's just after seven. I haven't yet heard back from Luke as to when he'll arrive so I assume he's coming back very late tonight or early tomorrow morning.

I get back to the studio by nine and Luke's not back nor did he leave a message for me with anyone downstairs at the pub. I wonder whether I should call the number he left with me, but I decide not to. After all, chances are he's still doing business, and if he's not back by tomorrow I'll call then.

After a long shower I go to bed; it's still rather early, but I'm quite tired due to all the activity of the last three days and tomorrow will be yet another busy day and night. I drift off while thinking about all the things that need doing and next thing I know I hear a noise at the door as if someone's trying to get in. I feel disoriented because I thought I had just dropped off to sleep, but when I glance at the bedside clock I'm shocked to see that it's close to three in the morning and suddenly I feel frightened that someone's broken into the pub.

I sit up in bed and switch on the bedside lamp just in time to see the studio door open and Luke walking in. I sigh with relief, but before I can say anything I see him drop his overnight bag on the floor while he's trying to take off his leather jacket, and for some reason it seems he's struggling with it.

He looks kind of strange and I blink my eyes to make sure I'm not dreaming, which I'm not, and without a word to me Luke finally takes off the jacket and even in the weak light of the lamp I can see his white T-shirt is saturated in blood, covering his right shoulder and upper arm area. Luke is grimacing in pain and I jump out of bed and go to him. I switch on the main light and I see the pale look on his face.

"My God! What happened?" I take hold of his good arm and gently walk him to the bed and he sits.

"I was grazed by a bullet, but I'll tell you about it later. I'm okay. Just get an old towel or something so I don't stain the bed. I need to lie down." He sounds exhausted.

I rush to the bathroom and come back with a couple of towels and sharp scissors. "Stay as you are for a moment while I cut off the T-shirt," I tell him and proceed to cut the back of the shirt and slip it off him. I try not to wince when I see the bandage covering part of his shoulder and upper arm, totally soaked in blood, and I carefully help Luke to lie down. I cut the bandage and when I take it off I see a bleeding wound on his upper shoulder which looks like a deep gash, but it's hard to tell what it is exactly as there are stitches holding the wound closed.

"Don't worry about the blood," Luke says. "The doctor told me to lie down and rest for a couple of days, but I had to come back home and I obviously unsettled the wound."

"Did the doctor give you painkillers?"

"Yes, and I'm due to take some, but I held off because I need some scotch to calm me down."

He still looks pale and I can tell he's in terrible pain, but mixing alcohol with painkillers is too risky. I cover the rest of him with a blanket and brush his hair back with my fingers. "Let me ring Tom and we'll take you to the A&E," I say.

"No!" Luke replies in a sharp tone. "You must promise me you'll keep this to yourself."

I'm confused, but I don't argue with him. I am, however, afraid for him. "Very well," I tell him, taking over the situation. "But I'm calling the shots. I'll make you a hot toddy with a little bit of scotch so it's diluted and you eat something before you take the painkillers. Agree?"

Luke nods with a weak smile. "Trust me to fall for Nurse Ratched."

I feel reassured when he says this; if he has time for humour he can't be that badly off. I always say that if men had to put up with painful periods or the agony of childbirth the human race would have become extinct a long time ago. Despite my thoughts on the subject, however, I rush to the kitchen and make his toddy with a dash of scotch, honey and lemon; then, I cut a large piece of brioche, heat it up and add butter and honey on it and bring it to him on a tray that I rest on the bedside table. Luke is able to sit up by himself, which is another reassuring sign that he's starting to feel a little better. I put a whole bunch of pillows behind him so he can rest back when he's ready. "Where are the painkillers?"

"In my bag, inside the shaving kit."

I find the tablets and read the label, which is written in English. "It says two tablets every four hours," I bring them to him. "When was the last time you took them?"

"By the time I got to the airport in Berlin." Luke puts out his hand for me to give him the prescribed amount of tablets and then I grab a bottle of water for him.

I watch him drink the toddy, eat the brioche, and take the tablets with half a bottle of water. When he's done, I take the tray back to the kitchen and rummage in the bathroom's first aid kit for disinfectant and bandages. "Did the doctor give you antibiotics?" I ask when I come back and start cleaning his wound and rebandaging his arm.

"He gave me some to take just in case, said to keep the wound clean and be careful how I use my arm so I don't reopen the gash. It's just a flesh wound and I know I look like a stuck pig with all this blood, but I had to make the trip back. It couldn't be helped."

"Well, I can take you to the A&E after you've had a rest," I say. "And I'll call Tom when it's a decent hour."

By now the colour started to return to Luke's face and he's looking much improved. "No, Sam. I told you I don't want anyone to know about this."

"But how are you going to perform tonight at the gig?"

"I'll get Marcus to play lead guitar and I'll stick to singing."

"That's going to look a bit suspicious, don't you think?"

"I'll tell the boys I strained my shoulder. Overall, I'm fine and there's nothing stopping me from being able to perform."

"As you say," I reply, "but you have to be truthful with me. I promise I won't tell anyone what happened if you promise to tell me everything."

"Deal," Luke says and reaches out with his good arm, bringing me closer to him so he can kiss me. "This is better than any painkiller," he whispers against my mouth.

I pull back and laugh. "Yeah, right! Don't overdo it, mister. You men suck even when you're laying it on thick."

Luke can't help himself and grins. "And you're scary, Miss Kelly. Trust me to get mixed up with a crazy Irish gal."

Chapter 34 - Robert

1952/53, London, England

Christmas 1952 is approaching and Clara wants to go to Berlin to visit her parents. I'm all for it and hope I can get some extra days off. At work, I discuss this with Steve. The club is open every evening, except for Christmas, but seeing as I've been putting in extra hours and sometimes even covering for guys in the group if they are too ill to work or something else comes up, I asked not to be paid but instead to clock up the extra hours for a time when I might need them. Steve allowed me to do this and when I asked to redeem these hours he was okay with it. He told me he was happy with the way I worked and, seeing as I had family in Europe that I hadn't seen in years, he gave his approval for a whole week.

I never told anyone, not even Mike, that my wife is of German origin. The guys think I'm off to Ireland with Clara and I let them believe it.

The following day, I went to work slightly earlier and booked train tickets to Berlin and when I arrived home from work I surprised Clara with the news. She was over the moon and couldn't wait to telephone her parents and tell them the happy news.

We were set to depart in the early morning the day before Xmas Eve and the train journey would take about nine hours, depending on schedules running to time and the weather. While London was having a milder winter it seemed Berlin was full of snow. Had we been well off financially, I would have purchased plane tickets with British European Airways, which flew from London direct to Berlin in less than half the time it would take for the train to make the trip. In any case, I'm still grateful to be able to travel because I clocked up those extra hours at the club and as a result Clara and I will get to spend five days with her family.

Meanwhile, although our financial position is not exactly the best, Clara and I are doing well. Her bakery stall is growing and she now plans to go four days a week to sell at the market. She's getting regular customers and Mary, the woman who owns the stall, asked Clara if she'd like to get a bigger stall between them and go halves on the rental fee. Clara agreed and the women decided to start the new venture in the New Year. It seems 1953 is going to be a good year for us all and if we're lucky we might even be able to save up for a deposit on a home.

The one thing marring our happiness is that although we keep trying for a baby it just isn't happening. I know Clara feels like a failure because she hasn't been able to conceive, and she confessed this to me, but I explained that the problem could lie with me. What if it's my seed that's infertile and why didn't I do something about this before? Therefore, I secretly went to see a doctor and had a fertility test. The doctor told me it would take a while to get the results, especially with Xmas coming up, but this was okay with me. I'd rather get the news after our trip to Berlin. No matter what happens or what the result might be, I don't want to spoil our trip to the Schmidts'. I have a feeling that if we both relax and have some fun, who knows what may happen? Up until now we had to get over the stress of New York and how we existed on so little money, the violence of the area and then having to immigrate to another country in the hope that we could start again and make ends meet.

Now, I have a job that pays reasonable money, we have a decent home, Clara has her bakery venture, and she's enjoying it, plus she's also closer to her parents. All these blessings may be what our bodies need in order to conceive.

Chapter 35 - Samantha

Sep/Dec, 1985, London, England

I wake up at dawn and get out of bed slowly so as not to disturb Luke. As far as I can tell he slept and no blood broke through his bandage. Today, I decide to miss out on my tutorial and tell Dora we have a big meeting about tonight's gig; I can make up for the tutorial by having a longer session some other time, and once the shops open I'll go to the pharmacy and stock up on bandages and other supplies while Luke will probably meet with Tom to give him the story of his fictitious strained shoulder. I wash my face, brush my teeth and then head for the kitchen to make coffee.

"Ouch!" Luke suddenly shouts and lets out a few swear words.

I rush back to the bed and find him sitting up. "Are you okay?"

"Yes. It's just that my shoulder's really sore, but once the muscles warm up it should be okay."

"Let me check the wound. I have to clean it and change the bandage."

"Not now," says Luke. "I smell coffee and I need some."

"Very well," I reply and give him a cheeky smile. "You know, I rather like having you under my thumb, so I might get you to go out there and get yourself shot more often." I kiss him and return to the kitchen to finish breakfast.

"You're trouble, Sam Kelly, but wait until my shoulder heals and then I'll show you."

I laugh from the kitchen. "Yeah, yeah, like I'm really afraid of you."

"Hurry up with that coffee, woman!" he calls back.

I make some toast to go with the coffee and join him back in bed. "Okay, I'm ready to listen to your secret and how you got into this state."

While we have our breakfast, Luke makes good on his promise. "I belong to a secret group made up mostly of musicians called Musos for Freedom or MFF. How much do you know about the Berlin Wall?"

"I know what everyone else knows," I answer. "The Wall was built to prevent people from escaping East Berlin and making their way to the West or to any of the democratic countries in the world. People have been oppressed for far too long by the Soviets and East Germans and they live a drudgery of a life, so I don't blame them for wanting to escape to freedom."

"Exactly," Luke says. "You may or may not be aware, however, that there are a number of organised groups which assist people to escape from East Berlin plus there's a number of European nations that give sanctuary to escapees.

"Even West Germany provides sanctuary from East Berlin. This is a highly dangerous thing we do and many are wounded or killed; this includes people assisting in the escapes. Our group's affiliated with a number of other groups based here in West Berlin and we have some British and American people aiding in the escapes."

My blood runs cold as Luke tells me his secret and the thought that one day he may never come back terrifies me, but I stay quiet and wait for him to finish his story.

Luke says, "Our group's been around since the Wall went up in 1961; it was founded by a bunch of musicians from all over Europe. I joined them after a close friend of mine was killed, trying to escape back in 1975. He was only twenty-five at the time and newly married with a baby on the way."

I squeeze Luke's hand in sympathy. "That's horrible. I'm so sorry for your friend and his family. I can't possibly imagine how after a war that killed millions of people, the Communist regime keeps killing. Hasn't there been enough death already?"

Luke replies, "I don't know, Sam. There's no perfect system of government in this world, but the right to be free should be a human right that applies to all of humankind."

"You know, I often wonder what the people on the other side of the Wall think of us, especially on the 4th of July. It must fill them with longing to be free when they see the fireworks from our side and this so sad," I pause for a moment, reflecting on those who cannot be free and I pray that one day they will be able to embrace freedom. I turn back to Luke. "Your business trips to Berlin, are they all related to assisting in escapes?"

"No. I really do have a business where I represent musos, but I sometimes combine the trip for both purposes: my business and taking place in assisting an escape."

"So who shot you?"

"The East Germans patrol the area and it was simply a matter of bad luck."

"Was this just on the other side of the Wall?"

"No. This was a Baltic Sea escape attempt. We often get help from the Danish and Swedish fishermen. All we do is meet the escapees at the border, close to the sea. Usually, the area's less fortified compared to the Wall, perhaps because the East German guards would rather stay closer to their towers and take shelter from the weather, especially when it rains or snows. Whatever the case, they just happened to be there and saw us making contact with the escapees, and that's when all hell broke loose.

"They killed all ten escapees with their machine guns, including one of our guys. It was horrible. The guards just kept shooting the same bodies as if killing someone once was not enough. The bullets kept coming and these poor people were mowed down as if they were nothing. I was very fortunate that only one bullet grazed me, but I also have a feeling the guards knew we were from the West and they held back, except it was too late for our guy; perhaps his was a stray bullet like mine, only he was killed.

"There were two other helpers with us and they came to no harm, thank goodness, plus the fishermen from Denmark opened fire, which scared off the East Germans and instead of shooting back they retreated, and this gave us long enough to pick up the body of our fallen friend plus reach our vehicle and drive away."

I don't know what to say. I need time to digest this. "I'm very sorry about your colleague getting killed plus all those poor escapees. I can't imagine how horrible it must've been for you and your friends to watch this savage bloodshed."

Luke doesn't say anything, he simply nods and closes his eyes as if he's reliving the whole thing all over again.

"Luke, you need to rest now, but first let me change your bandage," I say, gently taking off the old one and feeling relieved to see the blood stopped seeping out and the stitches held. I dab the wound with more disinfectant and then apply a fresh bandage. "You're doing better, but I think you should rest today if you want to perform tonight. I'll go to the pharmacy to stock up, but I'll stay with you all day until the gig. I'll look after you."

Luke remains still as if he's resting. Sleep is the best healer for him right now so I pull the bedcover over him and watch him for a few moments as he sleeps. I then move close to him and whisper in his ear, "I love you."

By ten in the morning I'm ready to go out so I silently leave the studio and head for the pharmacy and afterwards to stock up on some groceries. I ring Dora from a public phone booth outside the grocer's and tell her the white lie about having a meeting regarding the gig and that I'll work extra on the piano tomorrow. We set up an early afternoon session so I can sleep in after tonight's gig and we ring off.

At the grocers, I buy the usual staples plus I get some readymade meals so Luke and I can stay in without having to call out for food. While waiting to pay at the check-out, I catch sight of a newspaper headline about Berlin. I grab a copy of the paper and scan the news article. The headline reads: *"Massacre in the Baltic - East German guards given licence to kill."* I read on and the story that unfolds is exactly what Luke told me about last night.

"Miss, can I help you?" A male voice addresses me and I look up, startled.

"Oh, I'm sorry," I say to the cashier and hand him the items I purchased, including the newspaper. Once done, I make my way back to the studio and while walking I read the rest of the article and my blood runs cold. I'm so very afraid for Luke; what if next time his luck runs out?

Back at the studio, Luke's up and about and drinking coffee at the table. He looks fine, but I can tell he's still in pain. "Hey there," I say. "I went shopping for a few things including bandages, which I'm going to change for you when you're ready. Did you sleep okay? Are you in pain?" I drop my purchases on the kitchen bench and come back to him.

"I just took my painkillers," he replies, "and I've been waiting for you so you can help me shower. I have to cover the shoulder with some sort of plastic so the wound doesn't get wet."

"Let me top up your coffee first; I need one, too, after this bit of news." I put the newspaper in front of him and he starts to read. "Do you want some toast?"

He nods, engrossed in the article, and I go to the kitchen and put away the groceries and make fresh coffee. I bring out coffee with toast and top up Luke's cup plus fill my own. Just before I sit down I quickly check his bandage, which still seems to be dry and holding well, but I'll have a better look once I help him shower. A sudden wave of love overtakes me and I lean down and gently kiss Luke's injured shoulder, then I kiss the other shoulder, and then I kiss his lips.

Luke pulls me towards him so that I straddle him while he's sitting on the chair. He's only wearing shorts and I can see that despite his shoulder pain there is nothing wrong with his other equipment. He holds me in place and our kiss grows deeper as our coffee grows colder. I pull away softly and break the kiss. "Good morning to you, by the way," I remark, "but nothing's going to happen until we have you rebandaged and you call Tom about tonight and let Marcus know that he's playing lead guitar."

"Since when did you become so bossy?" Luke complains.

"Since you went and got yourself shot!" I stand up and sit on another chair. "Coffee's getting cold and time's ticking away. It's just past eleven and Tom's probably down in his office by now."

"I hope you don't expect me to go down there in my shorts."

"Just talk to him on the phone and then call Marcus. After that, you'll be resting all day."

"You really are Nurse Ratched," Luke says, "but under the circumstances I'll do as you say. Just remember, however, that I will deal with you once I feel better."

"Shut up and eat," I reply, but I blow him a kiss and once again I'm filled with that overwhelming feeling of love. I remember I told him I loved him when he was asleep and now I wonder if he heard me. "So what do you think of the news article?" I say in order to distract myself from my other thoughts. "I was wondering if someone from your group rang it in."

"Yes, the head of MFF is based in Berlin. We reported what happened when we returned and he rang through all the details to as many newspapers as possible. He has good contacts in the press."

"Do you think the Wall will ever come down?"

"We can only hope. Free nations and activists are fighting for this atrocity to come to an end, and maybe one day it will." Luke finishes eating and stands up. "I'm going to give Tom and Marcus a call."

The gig is a huge success and Luke performs without any issues. Marcus is fantastic on lead guitar while Chris covers drums and I back him with bass and rhythm. By midnight, I can see Luke is ready to retire. I notice the pain in his eyes, but no one else is the wiser; only I know he's been shot.

We take our bows and the usual shouts of 'encore' come from all around us. Luke brings the microphone close to his mouth and waits until the crowd quietens down. When they do, he addresses the audience. "Thank you all very much for joining us tonight. We appreciate your support and would love to do just one last song..." And here the crowd goes crazy again, yelling out 'encore, encore'. Luke smiles at the audience and waits until they stop shouting and whistling.

"Some of you may have read the papers today or watched the news about the massacre by the Baltic Sea in East Germany." The crowd goes wild again and applauds; I can even spot a few people in the audience drying their tears, hugging one another or holding hands with the person next to them in a human chain made by the audience.

Luke takes in the energy from the crowd and he becomes emotional when he says: "Tonight there is only one encore; one special song that will live on in our hearts, a song in honour of the victims from this act of barbarity and the selflessness of the escape assistants who put their lives on the line to free the oppressed and helpless. Please feel free to sing along with us and never forget that together we can change the world."

The audience erupts in applause, whistling, shouting, and calling out: Love! Love! Love! Luke takes a moment to watch people hugging, laughing, crying, whistling, and then he turns to us and gives us the three beat cue to start playing and we launch into David Bowie's 'Heroes'.

Chapter 36 - Robert

<u>1952/53, Berlin, Germany</u>

After the war ended, the Schmidts continued working at the bakery and they still kept up their distribution of free bread for the needy. Over the next five years, however, life started to become much more costly and the Schmidts decided to move to a less expensive area of Berlin that suited them financially and geographically, plus Mrs. Schmidt had extended family living there, including a married sister with three children. The sister and her family lived in Treptow, a district situated southeast of Berlin's city center. Treptow, which is in East Berlin, consists of residential neighborhoods with cheaper housing and green spaces along the Spree River and the Schmidts were happy to be close to family, especially now that Clara was married and living in London.

The Schmidts met us at the train station on the evening of our arrival and although the weather was very cold the snow held back as if it were waiting for us to get to shelter. After hugs and many tears of joy from the Schmidts and Clara we all bundled into a cab to take us to the Schmidts' cottage which, like their previous home, had a bakery attached to it from where Mr. Schmidt did his work.

Though my German is fairly fluent by now, I still have an accent but can still communicate quite well. During the drive to the cottage we mainly spoke of our journey and the weather. I think Germans are more careful than what Westerners say in public. Theirs is a more regimented culture than the one we Yanks have, but then these people live in a country that's still divided into four sectors, like Berlin itself, and I've been keeping up with news from Germany since I left in 1948. Somehow, I can't get rid of the feeling that things will get worse moving forward.

We celebrated Christmas in style with traditional foods like roasted goose, braised red cabbage and dumplings, and we finished with mulled wine and a platter of festive cookies. Germans celebrate their Christmas on Christmas Eve and this is a day when families spend time together decorating the tree, preparing food, wrapping gifts and so on. As we sat down for dinner, it started to snow and the happiness on everyone's faces was something we will always remember—the perfect Christmas.

The following day, Mrs. Schmidt's sister and her family joined us at the cottage along with a few of their cousins and while everyone was exchanging gifts, I was accosted by the men in Mrs. Schmidt's family to talk about my time in New York as a musician. Clara smiled at me while I was surrounded by the men and the love in her eyes was radiant. I blew her a kiss across the room and kept chatting as the women gathered together to serve more food, including some great apple strudel.

Our time in Berlin flew by much sooner than we wanted and tomorrow we leave to go back to London. By now, I'm like a son to the Schmidts and I know I'm going to miss them terribly. Clara and I invited them to visit us in London at any time and although they accepted I somehow know they won't come. It's not a money matter; besides, I would pay for their travel costs, but I have the impression that while the Schmidts put on a happy face there is something worrying them and I sometimes catch a look of fear in their eyes.

Chapter 37 - Samantha

Within a week Luke is back to playing guitar, his wound is on its way to being healed and his stitches removed by a doctor in London. I accompany him to his appointment and afterwards we go for a coffee at a nearby café.

"I'm glad this thing is healing," he remarks. "It would've happened faster, but I couldn't risk going to the doctor when I first arrived back in London."

"How come?"

"I can't very well show up at a doctor's rooms with a bullet wound, can I? Doctors are obliged to report this kind of thing to the police; this is why I waited for the wound to start healing."

"So how come this didn't happen in Berlin?"

"We have a few doctors that work with our group. I was lucky one of them is based in Berlin, so he patched me up when we returned from the Baltic Sea mission."

My blood runs cold every time I read or hear about the Baltic Sea and my fears for Luke grow every day; I really don't know if I can live with it. I feel terrified every time I think about what happened, so much so that I almost jump out of my chair when Luke's hand covers mine.

"What's wrong?" He regards me with concern. "You've gone pale."

I pull my hand away and have a sip of coffee, warming both my hands by cradling the cup. "I'm sorry, I just got spooked."

"By what?"

I sigh and know within myself that I must tell him how I feel. Our relationship's been growing more serious and I've yet to come to terms with the time when he said he loved me, plus my own declaration of love when he was asleep. Since then, Luke hasn't verbalised anything about loving me so I pushed the whole thing to the back of my mind, but just sitting across from him now I still can't find the words to tell him. I know I have to say something, but what? Luke waits for me to reply and the look of concern in his eyes is still present. "I don't know what it is, but it's important that we talk about it."

"Whatever it is, Sam, I'd rather you tell me instead of keeping it to yourself and agonising over it."

"I know, I know."

The waiter approaches our table and clears the empty cups. "Would you like anything else?"

"I'll have another cappuccino, please, and more water," I say immediately while Luke nods at the waiter.

"Make that two." The waiter goes on his way and Luke turns back to me. "Okay, so what is it?"

"You're probably going to think I'm an idiot, but sometimes I have trouble expressing my feelings," I explain. "Anyway, before you went off to Berlin you told me you loved me, but I didn't know whether this was a real 'I love you' or merely one that people use loosely, such as when you say 'I love you' to a friend."

Luke regards me with the beginnings of a smile. "So you did hear it," he says. "I thought you didn't catch what I said so I let it go for the time being. I thought I was rushing you somehow."

I feel the colour rise to my face and wish the waiter would hurry up with the coffees and give us a moment of distraction so I can think of what to say, but I can see the guy is still at the counter, waiting for the barista to make the coffees. "Well, I did hear it, but I wasn't quite sure how to take it. I figured if you wanted to talk about love you'd do so again."

"Then, why did you tell me you loved me the night after I got shot?"

Now my cheeks are really burning hot. "I thought you were asleep."

Luke reaches across the table and takes my hand in his again. "Sam, why don't you just tell me straight out what it is you want to say?"

The coffees finally arrive and I could kiss the waiter for interrupting, but in an instant he sets the coffees and water glasses on the table and then goes back to his other duties. "I'm trying to tell you! Just give me a moment." The sound of hesitance in my voice is not lost on him. He smiles again and I envy his look of calm. It's the life experience thing, I remind myself. He's older and wiser than I am. "Okay," I say, "I didn't know if you meant it so I kept thinking about it and then discovered I felt the same way, but I was afraid to bring it up in case it was a friendly 'I love you' rather than the real one."

Luke laughs softly and I catch the loving look in his eyes. "See? This is why I love you, my fiery Irish lass," he says. "You're all contradictions: a little girl looking for reassurance, one who helps others in need, but one with the strength to carry on after the kind of life she led before we met. You dealt with homelessness and Declan's suicide, something that would break most people, but somehow you picked yourself up and kept going.

"Then, we met and it was like we've known each other for years and you relaxed and trusted me with a lot of what happened in your life, including dealing with the disappearance of your father. You're a passionate young woman who doesn't hold back; one minute you're a frightened little girl and the next a woman of mettle, and all I want to do is make love to you, live with you, laugh with you, and even cry with you, and of course 'jam' with you. So yes, I do love you for real, both as a friend and a soul mate."

I'm speechless for a moment and feel tears well in my eyes. Luke sips his coffee to give me time to gather my emotions. Finally, I say, "I love you, too, and I feel just as you do, but Luke, after what happened to you in Berlin and the dangerous stuff you're into, this is something that scares me. I know I couldn't bear losing you. It was bad enough when Declan left this world. And ever since my father disappeared, I've been alone and abandoned by all, but I managed to survive all that and now that I'm older and slightly wiser I know my love for Declan was a childish kind of love—he was someone to cling to—but with you I feel it's the real thing and so I can't lose you. On the other hand, we did say we're lone wolves and I have no right to expect you to stop what you're doing. We're both free people travelling through life in a way that suits each of us, but what happens now that we're together? I tried not to fall for you simply because I knew that one day something like this might come up, and now I don't know how to move forward from this point."

Luke gives my hand a squeeze. "We'll figure something out, I promise. The main thing is that we communicate openly, no matter what. We don't need to rush to come up with an answer right now. Do you agree?"

I sigh with relief. "I do."

The rest of the week is filled with the TV interview Tom arranged for us to introduce Classical Cocktails. The interview's short, but Tom makes sure he gets the message out there and I answer a few questions posed to me by the interviewer. I don't say very much as I'm not used to being on TV, but I speak calmly and clearly and this gets me through.

A couple of days later a photographer takes a few shots of me, posing with the baby grand and wearing different outfits selected by Dora and Helen for each shot. Tom is having these made into advertising posters that will be pasted all over the West End and at other strategic points in London. He also contacts friends of his who work in the press and they promise a write up in the entertainment pages.

All is moving very quickly and I am now less than two weeks away from the 'by-invitation-only VIP event'. I catch up with Dora and do extra time on the final tutorials and then I take to practising on the baby grand at the pub during early mornings, before the pub opens to the public.

This leaves me with little time for anything else, except dropping in on Dora to help her out, having rehearsals with the band and discussing new songs we want to introduce to our ever-growing repertoire. During one of these discussions Luke says, "I've introduced a number of my own compositions, but I see I'm the only one. Do any of you have your own songs that you'd like the band to play?"

I'm the first to reply. "I have some songs I've been working on, but with the Classical Cocktails gig coming up I don't have time at present."

"Well, maybe when things settle down," Luke says.

"We'll see. Right now my plate's too full."

"Fair enough," Luke responds and then turns to the boys. "Marcus, Chris, what about you guys?"

"Count me out, man," Chris says, "I'm just a muso so don't ask me to compose. It's bad enough for me to write a postcard, let alone a song." We laugh and then Marcus adds, "I'm the same as Chris, only I can compose a postcard, but when it comes to music I simply like to play in the band and I'm happy playing covers."

Luke replies, "Very well, but I've heard you two sometimes playing instrumental pieces and riffs that sound great, and if you want you can contribute that sort of thing and we can all work together to turn it into a song."

"That's a great idea, Luke," I remark. "I never thought of that, but you're right. Sometimes just a few notes or riffs can lead to a great song."

Chris says, "This is why Luke's such a cool muso."

Marcus agrees. "I've heard a lot of your own stuff, man, and if you don't mind my saying I think you should be cutting your own records."

"Thank you, guys. I appreciate your feedback, but I'm not aspiring to cut my own records; it's not my thing," he says, modestly.

I notice the subtle shyness in Luke's voice and wonder why he never tried to bring out his own album. He did tell me, when I first met him, that he never looked for fame because in the end fame ends up owning a person. At the time, I wasn't sure if he was putting it on, but after having experienced the quality of his work and talent, not to mention his incredible voice range, I have to wonder whether all this is going to waste because the world will never get to enjoy it.

Luke told me I had talent in both voice and the way I play the guitar and piano, and he even saw a couple of my own compositions, which I came up with just for fun, but I never felt I was good enough to reach the dizzy heights of fame, and for me this wasn't related to modesty but rather the fear of not being able to cope. The thought brings Declan to mind and his incredible compositions, his overall genius would've been enough to make him go to the top, but inside something in Declan was broken and even if he'd reached the heights of fame I still believe he would've taken his life in any case.

"Hey, are you okay?"

I come out of my reverie when Luke's hand covers mine. Chris and Marcus have gone and I'm sitting with Luke at one of the back tables in the pub. It's not yet eleven, and the place is quiet, but Tom will soon arrive. "Yes, I'm fine. I kind of let my mind wander for a moment. I didn't even notice the boys leave."

Luke kisses my hand and gently pulls me to my feet. "Why don't we go upstairs? I feel like making your mind wander again, but for a much longer time." The meaningful look in his eyes sets my heart thumping faster and my legs feel weak.

Chapter 38 - Robert

<u>1953, London, England</u>

My fertility test results came back normal and the doctor told me the problem was not with me. He suggested Clara get checked out and gave me a referral for her to consult with a gynaecologist. He also said oftentimes first conceptions could take a long while, even years, and Clara and I should not worry.

When I returned from seeing the doctor, I discussed the situation with Clara. She was surprised that I'd kept the whole thing a secret in the first place, but she understood that when it came to delicate discussions such as fertility men found it a touchy subject; it's something to do with their manhood, she said.

Right now Clara is in an excitable state of mind, having seen her parents after so long and now looking forward to her new stall venture with Mary. She has grown from the shy young girl I met all those years ago to a confident and enterprising young woman, and there is no stopping her. She's a strong person with a great capability to love all of life. Every time I look into her eyes I see a brilliant light of being. Despite the hardships of her past, and whatever is in store in her future, Clara shies away from nothing. She said she would visit the specialist in due course, but right now she has a business to deal with.

This doesn't bother me; we're young and healthy, and I know in due course we may conceive. I feel that now is not the right time to start a family in any case. I've only just started to save money toward buying a home for us plus Clara seems to be enjoying her growing business.

Meanwhile, I love my gig at the club and Mike has practically become the brother I never had. When we both have time off work, Clara and I usually have him over for dinner, but to date I never told Mike about Clara's background, especially as she sounds like a regular Londoner these days.

Mike is still single at twenty-five and in no hurry to find a wife, but he is a handsome guy and I notice how the females at the club eye him all the time, hoping he'll ask them out. I once remarked jokingly that Mike was getting on, but he laughed it off, simply saying he hadn't met the right girl. But I saw the way he looks at the women in the club and it's obvious he finds many of them attractive. I thought perhaps Mike was shy and needed a bit of encouragement. I brought this up once when we went out for a drink after one of our gigs and Mike confided in me.

Although he's white with amber-colored eyes and dark wavy hair, Mike is half English, half Jamaican. His mother was fair with green eyes and alabaster skin; his father, however, was a black man. Theirs had been a very difficult marriage due to the racism of the times back in the 1920s (and even in the fifties things are still tough), but their love endured and they sacrificed many things to remain together until they passed from this world.

This also explains why Mike's brother, Jimmy, went to live in New York. He resembles his younger brother in looks, but despite this he copped quite a bit of bullying and bashings, especially as a child in the UK, so he moved to the States at a young age and New York City was the place to be, especially for a muso. People seemed a lot more tolerant in the larger American cities.

When I shared Mike's story with Clara the first thing she said was *"We'll try to find him a nice girl"*. There is nothing more exciting for a woman than matchmaking, I tell her, and she replies, *"That's because women have to look out for each other in a man's world."*

Chapter 39 - Samantha

<u>Oct/Dec, 1985, London, England</u>

Early one morning, Luke's stuff arrives from Berlin. He rushes downstairs and he and the delivery guy make a couple of trips up and down the stairway until everything is deposited in one corner of the studio. Luke signs off on the delivery slip and gives the courier a tip. When he closes the door, I come out of the bathroom still wearing my nightshirt. "Coffee?" I call out.

"And brioche, thanks," Luke replies as he starts to go through the boxes and a couple of small trunks. When breakfast is ready I bring everything to the table. "Come and get it while it's hot."

Luke washes his hands and joins me. "It all seems to be here. I'm going to go through each box after we eat. It's a good thing I sent these off prior to the Baltic Sea operation; otherwise, I'd have to return to Berlin. There was no way I would've been able to pack all this with only one arm."

Just the name of the city gives me the shivers where once it gave me a feeling of excitement, but I don't say anything to Luke. He said we would work something out about his trips there and I hope we do. Instead, I say, "While you're going through your stuff I'm off to Dora's. She wants me to try on the outfit for tomorrow night's private debut one final time and Helen will be there, too, so don't expect me back any time soon."

"How are the tickets going for the public debut?"

Luke finishes his coffee and tops up his cup, but I shake my head when he tries to top up mine. "I'm cutting back on caffeine until after both debuts are over and done with; I'm jittery enough already as it is. And the public debut is fully sold out," I tell him. "Tom really did a good job with the press and that TV spot." My stomach lurches with fear and I try to ignore it. "By the way, did you rent a tux? It's black tie, you know."

"I'll be behind the scenes for your first debut so I don't need a tux, but I'll rent one for the official debut. After all, I'll be bringing a guest with me," he winks my way, "and I'm already worried about her."

"How so?" I wonder what he's up to.

"Didn't I tell you not to leave me alone with Dora? I think she must have been a man-eater in the old days."

I laugh. "You think you're so cool with the ladies and you're afraid of a little old one?"

"The old ladies are probably the scariest; they have life experience for one thing. And as for being cool with the ladies, as you put it, where did that come from?"

I give him a knowing look. "I'm not blind. While you're up on stage singing your head off, I get to watch all the young babes with stars in their eyes when they look at you."

Luke breaks into laughter. "You forget Chris and Marcus are good looking guys and compared to them I'm the old man in the group. I'll be turning thirty-six next year; time flies!"

"You're right, of course," I tease him, "you're an old man and nobody wants you."

He stands away from the table and pulls me up with him. "You're a bad liar, Miss Kelly. I happen to know you want me for yourself." He then kisses me to the point where I can't resist even though I have to get ready to go to Dora's. He knows what I'm thinking and I know what he's thinking, but now is not the time. Luke kisses the tip of my nose instead and sends me off to the bathroom so I can get ready for Dora's while he goes back to checking his delivery items.

I step out from behind one of the huge Edwardian screens when Tom mentions my name after a short introduction about Classical Cocktails and the concept that the audience has been invited to experience on this special 'by-invitation-only' debut night.

When I join him to the sound of applause, I feel my legs turn to rubber and pray I don't make a fool of myself by tripping over and baring my knickers to the audience. Thankfully, my outfit is a pantsuit, albeit from the 1920s; it feels quite comfortable, covers my legs, and I know I look good in it.

The outfit consists of a beaded slate-grey sleeveless shift that reaches to just below the knee and a pair of loose satin black pants. The shoes are flat, ballet-like slippers with tiny black beads to match the pants. The only thing I'm not sure of is the narrow hand-worked headband made of tiny black pearls, which ties like a delicate coronet around my head. My hair hangs loose, barely touching the top of my shoulders with its natural waviness, and I wear very little make-up with only eyeliner enhancing my eyes and a dash of muted red lipstick. The final touch is a pair of black onyx oval earrings dangling from my ears and the overall look is simple but elegant. I never did like gaudy or showy outfits.

"Ladies and gentlemen," Tom addresses the audience once the applause ceases. "If you wish to take photos, especially for those of you in the press, I ask that you wait until the end of the performance so as not to distract our pianist. We will hold a photo and interview session once the performance comes to an end. Thank you and enjoy!"

Tom leads me to the baby grand piano where he kisses the top of my hand and announces to the audience, "Please welcome Miss Sam Kelly." There is another round of applause while Tom leaves and I'm left alone onstage. My throat goes dry and I take a few sips of water from a glass left for me on the piano.

There is a space of a few seconds where the entire room is silent and the audience is waiting for me to begin. My only thought is of Luke and how much I love him, and it is with this feeling in my heart that I launch into my favourite Chopin nocturne, Nocturne in C# minor, a beautiful romantic piece that celebrates love. I then follow through with a few other Chopin nocturnes and Mozart sonatas, and finally I end the recital with a silent tribute to Declan, thanking him in my mind and heart for his love, for saving me at a time when things were dire in my life, and for perfecting my piano technique. I say goodbye to him from my soul by playing his favourite piano piece—all three movements of Beethoven's 'Moonlight Sonata'.

By the time I'm done, one and a half hours have elapsed and I'm exhilarated despite feeling tired. The audience bursts into loud applause and I take a few bows. Then, without waiting for Tom, some of the guests, especially those from the press, take photo after photo of me and I begin to feel overwhelmed at the energy around me.

I suddenly feel a hand taking mine and bringing it to his lips and I turn to see Luke in a tux—so he wore one after all—leading me backstage as Tom's voice radiates from the microphone, advising the guests that there will be a fifteen minute break before the photo and interview session takes place. In the meantime, Tom invites the guests to order their favourite drinks, compliments of 'Classical Cocktails'.

Luke takes me back to the studio and sits me on the bed while he fetches some fresh water for me, and I drink it thirstily. "You were brilliant! And this is why I stayed backstage. The emotions you conjured up in me with the music made me fight the tears threatening to fall down my face, but don't you tell anyone I said that."

I set my glass on the bedside table. "So you decided to wear a tux, I see. I'm honoured," I tease him. "As for the tears, no need to worry, your secret's safe with me, you cry baby." I smile and ruffle his hair.

Luke replies with a smile, "I'll make you pay for that later, my love, but right now I call the shots." He glances at his watch and pulls me up with him. "We have to go back downstairs and get the press out as soon as we can; we don't have much time to set up for our gig. Remember, you're not required to come on until eight-thirty, okay? We'll cover for you so you can rest awhile."

The press takes photos as soon as I rejoin them and a few of them throw me some questions. Tom stands beside me and also takes part in the interview. Meanwhile, the rest of the audience begins to depart and a few minutes before eight everyone is gone and Luke and the boys set up the stage for our gig.

I go back upstairs and change into my regular gear of jeans and T-shirt, but I leave the make-up on seeing as it's minimal. I make myself a quick sandwich, as I didn't eat anything since lunch, and then I put up my feet for a short while knowing that if I lie down now I'll fall asleep and miss the entire gig.

I can hear them starting to play downstairs and before I know it the time comes for me to join the boys. I appear onstage just as Luke finishes singing a hard rock song, and the audience applauds and whistles. Then, the lights are dimmed and a spotlight shines on me as I go directly to the standup microphone, located front stage, while Luke moves to the keyboard and Chris and Marcus man the guitars. The whole atmosphere in the pub changes from the high energy of rock down to the magic tranquility of a lake as we launch into Fleetwood Mac's 'Songbird' with me singing lead vocals. As I sing the beautiful lyrics of this song I feel Luke's vibes all around me again and in my mind I also see fragments of Declan, fading peacefully into another world.

I'm also aware of many in the audience, swaying from side to side, some with tears in their eyes, others hugging and kissing, and in my heart I feel the love I bear for both Declan and Luke. Declan, who left the world too early in life, and Luke, whose love supports me to the end of time.

The moment the song is over and some people are still drying their tears, the lights come back up and we launch into some soft rock to lighten the mood. The gig finishes at around one in the morning with people still calling out for encores, but we've gone over one hour from our usual finish time and we've had enough. The audience applauds and cheers during our final bows and then they start to disperse while we tidy up onstage and leave the main equipment to be put away the following day.

Tom congratulates us for a top night and hints that an additional gig with The Eclectics wouldn't go astray, but he lets it drop when he sees the tiredness on our faces. "We'll have to talk about this at some stage, guys and gals, but for now off you go and rest. Goodnight all!"

We bid everybody goodnight and Luke and I retire to the studio where we quickly shower and go to bed, falling asleep almost immediately.

I wake up just before dawn and the room is freezing. We forgot to switch on the heating before we went to bed, but we were so hyped up after the gig that we felt warm at the time. I quickly hop out of bed, switch on the heat and come back under the covers. The bedside lamp goes on and I find myself looking into Luke's eyes.

"I forgot, too," he remarks. "Surely, it wasn't this cold when we went to bed."

"Well, it's friggin' cold now. Do you have an extra blanket anywhere in your personal possessions? If not, we'll have to invest in one."

Luke holds out his arms to me. "Come here, my love. I'll keep you warm. And yes, I have a few blankets I brought back from Berlin. It gets positively freezing over there."

I move into his arms and our body contact starts to generate heat. Luke switches off the lamp and we relax silently for a while. I try to go back to sleep, but I'm wide awake now. Just the proximity of Luke's body is enough to energise me and it seems he feels the same because he's also awake. "So what now?" I remark. "It's too early for breakfast."

Luke draws me closer to him. "I agree, but it's never too early for keeping warm." And with this said, he pulls off my nightshirt and his mouth takes mine in a deep kiss that leads to the tenderest lovemaking I've ever experienced. In truth, this is the kind of lovemaking I have never experienced to date. What Luke is doing to my body makes my blood run hot, not only to my face, but to my entire being. He tastes my body in every way until he reaches that private area between my legs and with his tongue he teases my inner being, invading the most vulnerable part of all.

I am totally unprepared for this and so very shy that I want to put a stop to what he's doing, but at the same time my body is so aroused that the whole thing becomes a tug-a-war between my body and my brain, and within seconds my body wins and I climax several times to the point where I can't think anymore; I simply enjoy the pleasure until it slowly subsides.

Luke lies back beside me and brings me into his arms once more, where I hide my face against his shoulder. "What is it? Did I hurt you?" He tries to look at my face, but I won't let him so he switches on the lamp.

"Nooooo!" I bury my face deeper in between his neck and shoulder. "Switch off the light!"

He laughs softly, endearingly. "Don't be silly," he says. "I presume this is your first experience, but it's nothing to feel shy or awkward about, not if you're with the person you truly love."

His words are like balm to my tumultuous emotions and I finally move back a little so he can see my face. "I am with the person I truly love; it's just that I wasn't prepared for this." I kiss his lips and when I move against him I notice he's hard. Luke doesn't seem to be fussed about it, but I straddle him, take him inside me and within a few seconds he achieves release.

We sleep in until around ten and then have breakfast in bed. The weather turned stormy overnight, but we thankfully have all of Sunday free. I worry about Dora because I haven't seen her since Friday and I give her a quick call while tidying up in the kitchen. Dora sends her congratulations and also assures me that Helen has been around to tell her all about the press debut of Classical Cocktails. She also reassures me that she was okay bathing as Helen was present at the time and helped her. I feel guilty, but at the same time I realise I'm burning the candle at both ends. We ring off and I make a note to come up with a regular arrangement for Dora.

"Any coffee left?" Luke calls out after I finish my phone conversation.

"I'll make another pot. I need one, too."

"Whatever happened to cutting back on caffeine?" he asks.

"You."

There is laughter coming from the bedroom. "Me? How do I make you drink more caffeine?"

"Keeping up with you has turned out to be a big surprise," I reply with innuendo in my voice.

Luke says with amusement, "You really are funny, Sam Kelly. Thousands of girls would kill for what you got this morning."

Now it's my turn to laugh. "Ah, not only overconfident with his lovemaking skills, but you do notice the babes eyeing you after all!"

Luke is still laughing when I come back to bed with our coffee and brioche. "I love it when you get all uppity," he remarks. "It's an invitation for me to tease you."

"You wish," I reply, "but now I need to talk to you about something serious."

Luke glances my way with concern. "Are you okay?"

"Yes," I reassure him. "It's just that I've been meaning to tell you this, but with everything that's been going on I pushed it aside for another time." Luke sips his coffee and waits for me to go on. "It's a decision I made about the search for my father."

"How so?"

"Well, at first I thought having more money would facilitate things, but in the end the only information I have about him, which I obtained from various investigators in the past, is simply going round in circles and in all these past years I got nowhere with it."

"So what do you know about him?"

"I think I mentioned some of this, if you remember, and I just don't think there's much more to find out. Basically, I know the trail in the States went cold around the early fifties, when my father immigrated to the UK. At one point, it was thought he returned back to the US after the split-up with my mother, but no real proof was found of this. It also seems he worked as a musician in a jazz band before coming to live over here.

"I don't know what kind of work he did prior to my birth, but when I was old enough to understand I knew he was a travelling salesman. He didn't have any gigs nor did he try to look for any. All I know is he taught me music, mainly guitar."

"So did any investigator in the UK check out whether your dad ever worked as a muso over here?"

"They did, as a matter of fact, but in those days gigs were often paid in cash, so there are no tax records to confirm this, but my father's tax records for his salesman job were intact, which means he worked as a salesman from 1962."

Luke is intrigued. "So to what date do the tax records run?"

"They match to the time of the split-up, around 1970, when he tells me he's going to the US. I was eight at the time and he said if somehow things didn't work out he'd write and let me know. Of course, this never happened because he seemed to have disappeared and not even my mother had a clue as to his whereabouts."

"I think you told me about checking the death registers, right?"

"Yes. The death registers were checked in the US, UK and even Germany." I sigh, despondently. "I'm at the point now where I realise I have to let this go. If my father were alive, I know he'd be looking for me in London and Berlin, but it seems he's disappeared from the planet and my life is different now, plus I have to live in the present. At least I kept looking for him in Berlin for some years, but I still came up with nothing. Anyway, I just wanted you to know of my decision. I figure if destiny wants us to reunite it'll happen and if not then I'll accept that something bad happened to my dad and he's gone forever."

Luke pats my hand. "You're strong, Sam. You may not think so at times, but I can feel it, and I know that whatever happens, you will face it. Just remember, I'm with you for good."

"I know you are and I love you for it," I say and peck him on the cheek. "Shall we have another coffee? We have that 'other' subject to talk about."

Luke nods knowingly. "Yes to another coffee and some more brioche, and yes again to discuss Berlin."

"I won't be long." I get out of bed and head for the kitchen. It amazes me how in tune our minds are, and Luke almost always knows exactly what I'm thinking. I'm still worried about his Berlin activities, but I can't expect him to give up something that obviously means so much to him. At the same time, I don't want to lose him. Our relationship is solid and I feel he completes me and I complete him. We are no longer lone wolves—I know that now—and if something awful happens to him it will destroy me.

I return with our coffees and brioche and Luke sets everything on the bedside table. "It's almost noon, you know?" I point out. "Why don't we order a late lunch today from the pub?"

"Good idea, but first let's get this out of the way." Luke takes a bite of his brioche and washes it down with coffee. I do the same and wait for him to speak.

"I've been thinking about our previous discussion," Luke begins. "I must confess the shooting at the Baltic Sea opened my eyes to the danger involved in what I do. I never thought of it before, but things have changed and we're not exactly lone wolves anymore."

Once again, Luke reads my thoughts and we're on the same track about the lone wolves.

"I love you, Sam, and I want to spend the rest of my life with you. I hope this is where our destinies take us so the last thing I want is to get myself killed." I shiver with fear when he says this, but I wait, saying nothing, and he says, "The work with MFF is very important to me and before I met you I took some crazy risks, but now I realise something has to change. So after some thought on the matter I decided that while I still want to be a part of MFF, I can still play a role at a lesser risk level."

"So how do you achieve that?"

"There are three parts to an escape operation: one is preparation by the organisation helping escapees; two is the actual escape; and three is leading the escapees to sanctuary. In the ten years that I've been with MFF, I pretty much took the riskiest missions, which are the ones assisting in the actual escape, such as the Baltic Sea mission."

"So there are three levels of danger," I remark.

"Yes."

"But what happens now? Are you going to involve yourself with other activities that are less dangerous?" Suddenly I can see relief on the horizon.

"Well, yes and no," Luke replies, flattening my hopes. He notices the expression on my face. "Hey, it's not as bad as you think," he says. "The main danger is if one is caught aiding an escapee, but there are ways and there are ways, you understand? I know what I'm doing and I now know to stay away from the actual escape operations like the last one I did."

"So give me some examples."

"We help escapees by providing them with forged papers so they can get out by themselves and we supply them with Western clothes like jeans, sneakers, T-shirts, stuff that doesn't exist in East Germany, so escapees can pose as tourists. There are also groups that have helped to tunnel under the Wall from West to East Berlin. In fact, one of the most famous tunnels was dug by a group of students from West Berlin, which led to the basement of a building in East Berlin. They were able to get a large number of people out that way.

"There are many other examples of escapes that I can give you, but I think you get the idea," Luke takes a moment to finish his coffee. "There's a big industry of people who give of their time to help those in captivity, so it doesn't just end there. When we get an escapee we still have to house them for a while until we deck them out with clothing, papers, maps, train tickets, some starting out money, and so on. We even hold English speaking classes to throw the East Germans off the scent if the Stasi, the secret police, follow these people into the West in order to apprehend them; this has been known to happen before. Anyway, I could go on telling you about all the ways in which we help people and how each of the organisations that often work in conjunction with each other assist in the rescue process."

"So you're happy to step out of the dangerous level?"

"Yes. And it's not just because I'm with you. The bullet wound episode taught me a big lesson and I realised that I can still help people by doing so many other things, one of which is the gigs I find for the musos I represent through my so-called agency."

I jump up and hug him, almost spilling my cold coffee leftovers all over him. "You sneaky man, you sure kept that quiet!"

He laughs. "Well, I never lied. I simply told you half the story and now you have the whole picture."

Chapter 40 - Robert

1955/59, London, England

These days I don't get much time to write in my journal, but I thought I should try to keep it going. This is still the journal Ollie gave me all those years ago and even back then I was never much of a writer.

Clara and I continue living happily in London and we're both so busy that our time together is not as long as we'd like it to be. While my gig is going well, plus I got a small increase in pay, the income from Clara's venture started to flourish and by 1955 she started running her own stall with a view to moving indoors into a shop at Covent Garden. To date we don't have enough savings to purchase a home in any case, but growing Clara's business makes more sense at present and she's sure it could get to the point where we would eventually have enough to put down a deposit on a house.

Over the years we still kept trying to conceive, plus Clara was checked by the specialist in London and given a clean bill of health. No one knew exactly why she couldn't get pregnant, but that didn't stop us from trying. Despite our busy lives we still make time for intimacy both in companionship and sexually. Clara and I are friends, lovers, and husband and wife. Our union couldn't have been better and even if we never have a child I know we will be together for the rest of our lives.

Another thing to report is that the Schmidts never did come to visit us, just as I thought when I last saw them. At the time, I picked up a vibe, especially from Mr. Schmidt, but I couldn't put my finger on it, except that there was an element of worry and fear around him, and it wasn't until Mrs. Schmidt sent one of her regular letters to Clara, where she mentioned shortages of consumer goods, the expensive standard of living, restrictions in travel, and other issues that it all finally clicked in my head.

HEROES

The fear I saw in Mr. Schmidt's eyes during our visit to Berlin confirmed in my mind what was happening and I felt my blood run cold. I didn't dare share this with Clara as I didn't want to worry her, but I knew Mr. Schmidt regretted his purchase of a cheaper home in East Berlin, and making a move now from East to West would be a lot more expensive and too late due to the political situation building up.

I managed to obtain German newspaper clippings from, Joey, my buddy at work, whose cousin, Carl, lives in West Berlin and keeps Joey informed. Carl is in touch regularly and looking to come and live in London; perhaps even join us at the 100 Club as a double bass player. Joey reads the newspaper clippings to keep up to date with what's happening, especially as he knows of musician friends that live in East Berlin where things are changing very fast and for the worse.

One of the news clippings mentioned the movement of people still taking place between West and East Berlin, but it is not as significant or as common as the movement from East to West. During the immediate post-war period, there were some individuals that moved from West to East for various reasons such as family ties, job opportunities, cheaper housing—as with the Schmidts—or for political reasons, particularly during the early years of division, when the situation in the East was still stable.

While I was stationed in Berlin, I started to notice this movement of people to the East, but I didn't think they realized that the Communist regime had other things in mind for the future of East Germany.

Chapter 41 - Samantha

Nov/Dec, 1985, London, England

The official debut of Classical Cocktails goes so well that if I didn't know any better I would think I've been playing for the London Philharmonic Orchestra. The area, which is jam-packed to capacity, gives the illusion that we are inside an opera house.

Tom went all out and engaged stage prop consultants to turn the pub into what looks like a theatre minus the rows of seats; instead, guests are seated at round tables, each accommodating four to six people and surrounding a special stage the prop consultants put in place to showcase me playing the baby grand. Walls are covered in silk from top to bottom with a reproduction chandelier at the centre of the room plus small light sconces around the perimeter of the walls.

Helen and Dora chose an outfit for me similar in design to the one I wore the previous week. The shift and pants in this outfit, however, are the same colour and made from softly patterned, off-white damask with cream court shoes to match. I wear no jewellery, except for a pair of pendant pearl earrings and this time I allow the women to brush back my wavy hair off my face with a mother-of-pearl clip fastened at the nape of my neck. My make-up is light and I refuse eye shadow so Helen applies eye pencil to enhance my eyes and she accentuates my lips with muted red lipstick.

Once I'm ready, the ladies leave to sit at their table where they will later be joined by Tom and Luke. Luke had gone to pick up Dora earlier in the afternoon so she and Helen could help me dress and when finished, the ladies donned their own evening wear in Luke's studio.

When six o'clock strikes, Tom appears onstage and welcomes the audience to Classical Cocktails. After introducing the concept, he calls out my name and Luke escorts me onstage and kisses my hand before he leaves me at the baby grand. The sound of applause is rather loud considering I haven't yet played one single note and while I anxiously prepare to play I notice a whole bunch of waiters wearing jackets and bowties, heading for the guest tables with trays full of different cocktails and hors d'oeuvres.

Once the waiters withdraw and the room goes quiet, the lights are dimmed and I immediately launch into my repertoire. This time, I deviate slightly from last week's list by still keeping my favourites but also adding scores from Schubert, Liszt and Rachmaninoff. I'm so intent on getting through this without making a mistake that I don't even remember to take a break; thankfully, no one interrupts me. I simply play straight through the program for one and a half hours and when I finish I feel, rather than hear, the thunderous applause coming from the audience.

It is at this point that Luke comes to escort me offstage once I bow to the audience. Meanwhile, Tom goes straight to the microphone and thanks the audience for attending the event. Shouts of 'encore' can be heard here and there, but Tom explains the concert was played without a break and I needed to rest.

The audience applauds one last time and begins to disperse. Tom and the boys immediately start to set up for The Eclectics gig while Luke leads me to the studio and pours me a glass of wine while I sit on the bed.

I sip my drink in silence for a while and feel the wine's warmth spread through my body. Luke picks up the phone and talks to someone for a few moments before he joins me.

"What's going on?" I ask, still sipping wine and feeling as though I'm coming down from a high.

"Helen suggests she take Dora home seeing as we're on in half an hour." He gently rubs my neck and shoulders.

"That's a good idea," I reply. "I forgot we're back on tonight." I lean into his massaging hands and feel so relaxed that I could fall asleep right now.

Luke sits next to me and draws me close with one arm around me. He plants a soft kiss on my cheek and I lean my head against his shoulder. "I'm going to tell Tom to bring forward the Classical Cocktails event. It's madness to have you jump from one gig and into another with very little time in between. How about we make it at five-thirty until seven and you finish right on time with only one encore if requested? At least you'll have a full one and a half hours to rest before you join us at eight-thirty."

My eyes close while my head rests against his shoulder and Luke takes away my almost empty wine glass. He gently lays me on the bed without bothering to take off my shoes and covers me with a warm blanket. "You sleep as long as you need, my love," he says softly in my ear. "We'll cover for you tonight, but if you wish to join us come down after you've had a good rest and something to eat."

I nod and the last thing I feel is the tender touch of his lips on mine.

———◆———

I open my eyes suddenly and the studio is in total darkness and, when I switch on the bedside lamp and sit up, I jump when I notice the time on the clock, which is just past nine. I put on a pot of coffee and a couple of bread slices in the toaster while I undress and change into black jeans and a long-sleeved black shirt with a white singlet underneath. I pull my hair loose and run a brush through it while I step into a pair of black leather boots.

I'm so hungry that I devour the toast with plenty of peanut butter and honey plus I splash extra milk into my super strong coffee. It takes me less than five minutes to eat up and then I brush my teeth and apply some of the lipstick Helen used on me this evening. I quite like the muted red shade and it adds colour to my face.

The sound downstairs attacks my ears after the lovely sleep I had, but the coffee helps to wake me fully and now I wait backstage until the boys decide to take a break. In the meantime, I peek through the dividing screen and see Marcus on the drums, Chris on keyboard, and Luke on the hybrid guitar while singing Led Zeppelin's 'Stairway to Heaven'. I feel really guilty for not coming down sooner as this song has a complex guitar instrumental and I should have been playing rhythm to help out. Just at that moment, Luke happens to turn as if he feels a presence behind him and he signals me with one finger of his hand, meaning the break is coming up after this song.

The boys meet me backstage at break time with special hugs from Marcus and Chris, who both attended the Classical Cocktails debut this evening. "You were awesome, Sam!" Chris says, stealing a quick kiss from me. Marcus pushes Chris aside as if he was a piece of furniture and plants a kiss on my lips, too. The boys know I live with Luke, but that doesn't stop them from kissing me, and even though they jokingly tell me they're younger and cooler than the 'old man' they make sure this is stated loudly enough for Luke to hear.

Luke simply turns to us and laughs. "I may be an oldie to you, guys, but experience calls the shots, if you know what I mean." This shuts up the boys and we head to the small foyer area behind the stage to get some cool water. Chris and Marcus are both smokers so they go out the back door to have a smoke in the lane behind the pub.

I turn to Luke the moment we're alone. "I'm so sorry about leaving you for so long; I just needed some shuteye. But what made you sing that song? You could've gone for something simpler."

"The audience called for it." Luke caresses my hair, my face, and my shoulders before he brings me to him and kisses me even though he comes away with half my lipstick on his mouth. He grins and reaches for his handkerchief and wipes his and my lips clean. "You've got time to touch up if you want," he says.

I shake my head and wrap my arms around his neck, returning the kiss while standing on my tippy toes.

We finish the gig at around two in the morning as the crowd won't let us go. They call for encore after encore and we can't deny them. The energy's so intense that none of us feels tired anymore, but when Luke and I retire to the studio we rip off our clothes and brush our teeth. We don't bother with anything else, except switching on the heating and crawling under the blankets after which we zonk out in seconds.

The telephone rings for a long while, waking us up, and eventually Luke takes the call. "Hello?" his voice sounds croaky.

I open my eyes and peek at the clock. It's close to noon. "What now?" I whisper.

Luke elbows me gently and I glance at him as he puts his index finger across his lips. "Yes... okay," he says into the phone, "lunch at one then. See you later." He rings off.

"Who is that and what's the deal with lunch?" I ask and reach for a robe that's resting at the end of the bed. I shrug into it before I go to the kitchen and get bottled water for both of us. Luke says nothing until I return and we take a long drink of the cool water. He pulls on an old T-shirt but stays under the covers. "What happened to the heating?"

"Who knows? I remember switching it on though," I reply. "By the way, am I wearing your dressing gown?"

"I believe you are," Luke says.

"Explains why it's so big on me. Do you want it back?"

He smiles and shakes his head. "Just get into bed."

I check on the heating and it is off so I switch it back on and then join him.

"That was Tom," Luke says.

"And?"

"And he wants to have lunch with us."

We meet with Tom at exactly one and he leads us to a back table in a quiet corner of the pub. A waiter approaches us and Tom orders the Sunday special, which is roast chicken with all the trimmings. For drinks, I choose a small light lager and the guys order the same, but they make it a large one. The waiter leaves with our order and Tom says, "Apologies for calling you on your day off, but I wanted to speak with you two."

"So what's up?" I ask.

"First of all, Sam, I have to tell you that your performance last night was incredible and I'm not sure why you're playing in a pub when you could join an orchestra—not that I wish to lose you."

"Thanks, Tom. I'm glad it went well. I must say I was anxious about the whole thing, but in the end it all worked out," I reply. "As for joining an orchestra, that's not my style. I love playing the piano, but only if I can choose to play what I want and when I want to play it. I've always lived my life as a free agent and I would find playing with a proper orchestra restrictive."

Our drinks arrive and we pause until the waiter leaves. "So what is it you want to talk to us about?" Luke addresses Tom after he takes a drink.

"Well, this is to do with The Eclectics gig," Tom replies. "I've been approached by a number of club owners who want to engage you guys to play at much bigger venues, but this would mean expanding your repertoire with your own compositions. These guys don't mind covers; after all, they're popular and people enjoy the variety of songs you perform." Tom pauses for a drink of his lager and continues. "The interesting part of all this, however, is that a couple of agents that caught your act expressed an interest in representing you if the band only plays its own compositions, plus they're talking about touring the main cities in the UK once you guys cut your first album."

This is bombshell news and I pick up my glass and drain half the drink. Luke remains silent, sipping on his lager and Tom gazes at us from one to the other, trying to read our thoughts.

The food arrives and this gives us a break while Tom cuts the chicken into different sized pieces and we help ourselves to our favourite cuts plus a variety of roast vegetables. Luke passes around a small basket filled with warm bread buns and I take two and butter them. We eat without referring to Tom's news and instead stick to chit chat until lunch is finished and we're offered dessert and coffee, both of which I accept after not having eaten anything decent since the toast from last night.

"That was wonderful," I remark, feeling satiated.

I catch a smile in Luke's eyes and blush; I know exactly what he's thinking and it has nothing to do with food.

"More coffee, anyone?" I signal the waiter, directing him to the coffee pot and he nods from a distance while another waiter approaches, clears our table and sets down clean coffee cups.

Once the refilled coffee pot arrives, the talk turns back to business and Luke says, "This is big news to absorb, Tom."

"I knew this would happen when you guys turned into The Eclectics. You just gel so naturally that the crowd loves you. I'm still getting huge amounts of feedback from people that attended. I've also had mid-size venue owners that want to engage you for special occasions, plus I want to ask if you would consider expanding your gig nights to incorporate Fridays."

Luke and I glance at each other and I remain silent while he turns to Tom and says, "Sam and I wish to discuss it between us plus we have to consider what Chris and Marcus have to say."

"I understand," Tom replies. "So I'll leave it with you guys and we can talk in a few days?"

"That'll be fine," Luke says and turns to me for my feedback.

"Yes," I remark. "We need time to digest this, no pun intended," I refer to the ample meal we've just eaten.

We laugh and Tom gets ready to leave. "Thank you, guys. Chat soon."

Luke and I go back up to the studio, our plan to go for a walk thwarted by the miserable weather, but at least the studio is warm and we can relax.

"I'm getting out of these jeans and into my pyjamas," I announce. "It's nice to know I don't have to go to piano tutorials or to model an outfit for the gig or even rehearse with the boys before our next gig."

"What you're saying is that basically it's nice to do nothing, at least for today," Luke remarks.

I smile and jump on the bed in my winter pyjamas. "That's exactly what I mean."

Luke undresses and gets into his pyjamas, too, and we get under the covers, watching the rain fall outside the studio window.

I sit back on the pillows and stretch my arms. "Aaaahhh, this is great!"

Luke regards me with amusement. "And this is life—when simple pleasures make you happy. If you can achieve this state of mind you'll want for nothing."

"Except for you," I reply and glance at him with a meaningful look he could not possibly misunderstand.

"Good God, woman! You're going to be the death of me yet," he exclaims in a dramatic voice, but I detect the desire underneath his tone.

"Well, you'd better enjoy it while you can, mister, because in a few years who knows where you're going to find the energy," I tease.

Luke starts to tickle me and we end up in a tangle of arms and legs, but then we slow down and our bodies meld into another kind of tangle that has kept humankind going for millennia.

Chapter 42 - Robert

<u>1959/61, London, England</u>

Clara noticed that things were not quite right with her parents and she showed me her mother's latest letter. I understood immediately where this was going. Mrs. Schmidt wrote that all was well with the family and that she and her husband were keeping busy with the bakery. She also wrote about mundane things such as the weather, her flourishing herb garden, how one of Clara's cousins was helping out at the bakery, and other day to day things. Gone were the complaints at the standard of living, shortage of consumer goods, travel restrictions, etc.

I sensed Clara was seriously worried and I reassured her about her parents plus promised I would do all I could to gather information about the situation in East Berlin. For this, I turned to Joey, who is still receiving newspaper clippings and letters from his cousin, Carl, and other friends in West Germany. The picture they paint is not at all promising.

One article mentioned that the allure of economic prosperity, political freedom and opportunities available in West Berlin made it a far more attractive destination for individuals seeking a better life. The stark contrast in living standards and freedoms between the two sides of the divided city led to a significant net migration from East to West Berlin. This explained the fear in Mr. Schmidt's eyes and his wife's short letter to Clara. The government was watching and looking for a way to stop a mass exodus.

I was aware from my time in Berlin that after the defeat of Nazi Germany in 1945, the country was divided into four occupation zones controlled by the Allied powers: the US, UK, France and the Soviet Union. But even back then political differences between the Soviets and the Western Allies started to emerge, leading to the division of Germany into East (under Soviet control) and West (under Western Allied control) and this division soon laid the groundwork for future tensions, which is what is now taking place.

For starters, the Soviet-controlled East German government faced economic challenges, especially in the aftermath of WWII. The country was heavily damaged during the war and the Soviets extracted reparations from East Germany, exacerbating its economic difficulties. The West, on the other hand, received aid from the Allies, which helped to rebuild Western Germany's economy and contributed to stark economic disparities between the two regions.

In my opinion, this was a powder keg waiting to explode. The Soviet-backed government in East Germany implemented repressive policies to maintain control over the population. This included censorship, surveillance, and suppression of dissent. The lack of political freedom and human rights abuses led to dissatisfaction among East Germans and this was the reason why many sought to escape the repressive regime and improve their economic prospects by moving to West Germany. As a result, the loss of skilled labor became a significant concern for the East German government.

Berlin, which is located deep within East Germany, became a focal point of tension between the Soviet-run government and the Allies. In 1948, just before I received my demobilization orders, the Soviets blockaded West Berlin in an attempt to force the Allies to abandon their presence in the city. This led to the 'Berlin Airlift' during which the Allies supplied West Berlin by air. The crisis heightened tensions between East and West and this solidified the division of Germany.

The newspaper clippings had nothing good to say about the situation and the more I read, the more alarmed I became, especially for Clara's parents. I had no idea what would happen next, but my fears now reflected what I saw in Mr. Schmidt's eyes.

Right now, I can only comfort Clara and hope to reassure her. Beyond this, however, there is nothing I can do, except wait and see how the situation in Germany develops.

In the meantime, Clara and I keep very busy, she with the growing business and I with my gig. Joey still keeps me updated with news of what is uncoiling in Germany and Mike, who also has musician friends living in East Germany, joins in with Joey to explore the idea of extending help to get these musos out of East Berlin. Meanwhile, Carl is successful in obtaining his visa to the UK.

Chapter 43 - Samantha

<u>1985/86, London, England</u>

Luke and I are of one mind and it sometimes scares me how often we think along the same lines. Even though I met him in July, merely six months ago, I feel as though I've been with him for years. We have so much in common and get on so well, not just as lovers but as best friends. Of course, I have no other comparison, except for my time with Declan. He was very good to me, but it was difficult to live with a genius and he was often moody and uncommunicative. Still, I loved him in my own way, but at the time I didn't see the signs. I didn't even know what he thought and I certainly never suspected he would take his own life.

I grew up in a hurry after Declan passed on and I vowed I would never again get into another relationship, and this is where the lone wolf thing came from. I became afraid to open up to others, especially if it was about something intimate, but I took a risk with Luke. I don't know what it was that made me come out of my cocoon; perhaps it was Luke's energy that helped me along. He made me feel safe, wanted, cherished, special, and I never had that in my life.

"Hey, Miss Kelly!" Luke's sudden voice makes me jump from my seat at the breakfast table. He kisses me softly. "I'm sorry I startled you. Are you okay?"

"Yes. I guess I was away with the fairies." The rain from last night hasn't stopped and I feel a chill in the air even though the heating is on.

Luke goes to the kitchen and comes back with coffee and toast. "Hungry?"

"Yes."

He pours out the coffee while I butter a piece of toast. "So what's on your agenda today?" Luke says. "I've yet to find extra storage downstairs for my Berlin stuff."

"And I'm off to see Dora," I reply. "I think it's time to sort out the living arrangements for her, especially if we're going to incorporate an additional gig night for The Eclectics."

Luke remarks, "I know we only spoke to Tom yesterday, and we'll get back to him in due course, but I want to share my thoughts with you about the proposition and get your feedback."

"Shall I tell you what my feedback is before you tell me what you would do?" In my mind I already know what I want to do and unless I'm totally reading him the wrong way I'm sure this'll be what Luke has in mind, too.

Luke nods with a smile and a knowing look in his eyes as he waits for me to continue.

"I want to do what I think will make me feel free," I pause in case Luke wants to say something, but he simply waits in silence for me to keep going. "I'm okay with the extra Friday gig for The Eclectics. I think three gigs are more than enough, plus I also have my two piano gigs and this alone will keep me busy.

"The one-offs, like Tom said he'd hire us out for special occasions, is okay with me, too, as long as we all agree to some guidelines. For instance, no more than one gig a month or at most a maximum of two. After all, I don't want our own gig here to clash with the others. Besides, most people in need of a band for special occasions generally hire them for the most important night of the week, that being a Saturday, so I think this'll present a problem, but we could make an exception if we wish to work around it.

"As for playing at really big venues with mostly our own compositions or taking on an agent and becoming a real band cutting records and touring the country, I'm afraid that's not for me."

I finish my coffee and wait until Luke is ready to respond. His smile alone already tells me that I hit the nail right on the head.

"So you don't want fame and fortune?" Luke says.

"No. While money's important because we all have to live and pay bills, I don't believe that fame and fortune can buy freedom, at least not for me. I've seen famous bands split up over money or other issues, while some go crazy with alcohol and drugs to the point where they jeopardise their health, plus they never know who their real friends are because everyone wants a piece of them. I've seen the suicides, the failed relationships, the unhappiness, and the fact that these people can't even walk down the street before they're recognised by fans and mobbed.

"Anyway, that's not for me; not that I expect to be famous because I don't think my compositions are good enough, but I think yours are excellent and you have what it takes to be famous.

"Last of all, I realise poverty and homelessness can also make one go on drugs, live with violence and crime, and much worse. Mostly, however, I see these two things: 'fame and poverty' as one extreme at either end, but there's a lot of space in between from where I can choose rather than be forced to go one way or the other."

Luke sits there, regarding me thoughtfully.

"Well?" I say after a while.

"Well what?" Luke replies. "You ought to know by now that we're of one mind."

"Are you sure, Luke? An opportunity like this comes once in a lifetime, if one is lucky."

"I'm sure," he replies. "But like you, I'm happy with what I do. I make a living out of music, I call the shots as to where I go and what gigs I play, and in essence I'm free."

"You're not doing this because of me, right?" I know he's not, but I just want to make sure.

"You know me better than that, Sam," he says. "I know how important the lone wolf concept is to you, but now we're two lone wolves and don't forget: wolves hunt in packs."

I smile. "That's a good one."

I spend most of the day with Dora and arrive late morning to assist her with bathing. I later make a trip to the market to stock up on groceries and for lunch I make potato and pumpkin soup and we eat it with chunks of freshly baked bread and lashings of butter. It's a great lunch for a cold winter's day.

"You spoil me, my dear," Dora says.

"Not enough, I'm afraid," I reply. "I must confess that lately I've been worrying about leaving you on your own so much."

Dora pats my hand. "My dear, Helen and I have become great friends and I see her at least twice a week, if not more."

"How's the business going?" I'm curious to see what these two are up to and this momentarily distracts me from what I want to say to Dora.

"Helen found a great shop for rent, not too far from Covent Garden, and she and Tom agreed to take it on as a costume hire place; not just hire of Anne's designs, but also for party wear and artist costumes for those that can't afford to buy their own."

"That's an excellent idea!" I exclaim. "But how is this going to fit in with Helen's baby?"

"She's not expecting until March."

"Well, that's only four months away," I remark. "Christmas is just around the corner."

Dora smiles. "Don't you worry, Sam. Helen's an incredible person and she's lucky to have Tom; he's a very supportive husband. In any case, I'll be putting in some hours at the store when it opens."

"You're going to work?" I say, totally surprised.

Dora laughs. "Oh Sam, you'll discover this when you get old and grey like me but inside you still feel as though you're young and you have your entire life ahead of you, and yet you know that no matter what you do you can't turn back the clock."

I suddenly feel depressed even though at present I'm too young to be able to put myself in Dora's shoes. Still, when I assist her around the house or I see her in pain, this brings me to the awful conclusion that we're all going to get old and die one day—that is, unless we get hit by a bus and die young. No one knows when their time will come.

Dora takes a look at my face and says, "My dear, don't look so morose. You have years and years to worry about that, but hopefully it's very far in the horizon."

I nod agreement while deep down inside I wonder who the hell invented life and had to make it so complicated to boot. Dora waits for my response and I push the gloomy thoughts away. "When's the store opening, and what hours will you work?"

"We're opening right after the New Year. Hours are flexible, but I can manage two days a week. Helen will do the same until the baby comes and then we'll see. I suggested taking on a young person that can look after the store when we're not there."

"That sounds sensible, but make sure you get a strong young man rather than a female. The costumes can get quite heavy, plus you need someone who can move shelves around and lift large items and heavy boxes, that sort of thing."

"Good suggestion," Dora agrees. "And I'll make sure he's gay."

"Gay? Why?" Dora never ceases to surprise me.

"Without stereotyping gay men, I find that usually these boys are very much into fashion and they understand the principles of elegance and refinement."

I stare at Dora as if I'm looking at someone from another planet. "Where do you get all this from?"

"Oh, Sam, plug in," Dora replies. "Now, how about we have a cup of tea? And, dear, do close your mouth."

I love Dora so much and how I wish she could be young and enjoy our generation, but when I hear something like 'plug in' I know there's no age barrier between Dora and today's way of life; deep down inside she's one of us.

While we drink tea, I finally bring up the subject of Dora's living arrangements. "With the extra gigs I'm finding it difficult to keep up with assisting you and much as I want to help I'm usually wiped out after a gig, especially on the days I have Classical Cocktails followed by The Eclectics. On these occasions, I tend to sleep quite late the following day, mainly because our gigs never finish on time; we mostly keep playing into the early hours when we're supposed to finish by midnight."

"My dear, I don't want you to worry about this," Dora says firmly. "You have to stop feeling guilty and understand that circumstances have changed both in your work and personal life."

"Yes, but I still want to help you despite Helen and your upcoming work at the store. You're the only family I have, Dora, and I don't walk out on family."

"Luke's your family, too, Sam."

"Luke can take care of himself, plus we have an agreement between us that we let each other be when it comes to doing something that's important to us." I want to tell Dora about Luke's Berlin activities, just to give her an example, but I keep quiet as this is Luke's secret.

"I've also been thinking about our arrangement of late. I'm not blind and I see how you're stretching yourself in all directions because you think these are obligations you must fulfill." I'm about to interrupt, but Dora continues, "Now, Sam, you listen to me for a moment. I have a suggestion that may suit us both."

When I get back to the studio, I can barely walk in. Luke unpacked all the boxes from Berlin and there is stuff absolutely everywhere, most of it covering the furniture and the floor.

"My God! I thought you said you didn't have much stuff," I exclaim.

Luke's sitting cross-legged on the floor and going through three boxes full of LPs, single vinyls and music cassettes. "Hello to you, too," he replies, "and don't drip on anything."

I pick my way across the floor carefully and head for the bathroom where I dry my hair and peel off my clothes, which were drenched along with the rest of my body when I came out of the tube station and walked to the pub.

"How's Dora?" Luke calls out.

"She told me to 'plug in,'" I answer with sarcasm, but this is obviously lost on Luke because when I come out wrapped in a bath towel he barely looks up. He's like a kid who just discovered an Aladdin's cave full of treasures.

I head for the wardrobe and pull out black woollen leggings and singlet plus a white pullover and warm socks. "Why's the heating off?" I ask but get no reply. Luke's totally absorbed in his activity so I switch on the heating and think about dinner. It's past seven and I'm hungry. "Do you want to order something from the pub? I cooked lunch for Dora so I don't feel like cooking again."

"Huh?" This from Luke.

I go up to him and slap the back of his head. "Hey, I'm talking to you!" I exclaim in frustration.

Luke throws me a look of mock annoyance. "Don't hit me, you fiery Irish witch!" And before I can turn and walk away he stands up and grabs me around the waist, bringing my body against his.

"Let go!" I struggle within his strong embrace and feel helpless because I can't free myself unless I resort to violence.

"I'm never going to let you go," he whispers against my ear and then he's kissing me like he hasn't seen me in years.

My struggles die down immediately and with my arms around his neck I pull him towards the direction of the bed. At first, Luke pretends he's unmovable, but after I return his kiss, deeply and ever so passionately, he lifts me in his arms and carries me to bed, making sure he doesn't step on any of the stuff littering the studio floor.

The bed is covered in clothing, blankets, shoes, and other personal items, but Luke manages to make some space and he deposits me on the bedcover. I barely have a chance to draw breath as he assaults me with another kiss, and before I know it we're both naked.

A while later, we dress and Luke starts to put aside some of his belongings so we can actually walk around the studio without tripping. "I keep saying this, but you're insatiable, you know," Luke remarks.

I laugh. "Look who's talking. It wasn't me who started this."

"You hit me over the head!"

"And that turned you on, did it?" I tease him.

"Anything you do turns me on," he plays along.

"Then, I'll have to be sure to hit you next time I want sex."

Luke laughs. "You won't have to. I want to make love to you every time I see you."

Like an idiot, I blush, and Luke regards me with meaning in his gaze. "Stop it!" I say. "All I want to know is if you feel like ordering dinner from downstairs and now it's almost eight and I'm starving."

"Okay, my love, I won't tease you, and I'm starving, too. Just order whatever you want while I finish up clearing some space in here. I can't put all this stuff in Tom's storage area. He needs the space; besides, anyone can have access to it down there."

Just before I dial the phone to order our food, I say, "I may have the answer to that, but I'll tell you over dinner." I dial the pub kitchen while Luke continues to tidy up and after I order dinner I clear the table and the rest of the bed. I put a down quilt on top of the bedcover; the quilt is one which Luke brought over from Berlin and while I finish tidying up, our food arrives and I bring it to the table. I ordered pasta carbonara and a large Italian salad. Luke stops what he's doing and joins me. "Wine or mineral water?" I ask.

"How about a bit of both?"

"Very well," I reply and bring a bottle of cabernet sauvignon plus sparkling mineral water and some Italian bread to mop up the salad dressing.

"This looks good," Luke says as he uncorks the wine bottle and serves our drinks.

We eat in silence for a while, not only were we hungry to start with, but after our session in bed we need to replenish our energy.

"Okay," says Luke after he finishes his pasta and starts to pick at the salad. "What answer do you have to my storage problem?"

I'm munching on a piece of bread and wait until I swallow. "I had a very interesting visit with Dora." I tell him all about the news with the costume store Helen and Dora are going to run. "This means all of Anne's designs are going to be transferred to the store."

"That Dora's a plucky lady," Luke comments. "And what's this thing she said to you? 'Plug in?'"

I laugh. "Yes! So you were listening to me when I came in. Anyway, I never expected Dora to be so 'with it.'"

"Should I ask what it is you were talking about?"

"Not meaning to stereotype gay men because they're into fashion, elegance or some such, and Dora's going to employ a gay guy to help out at the store once she and Helen open up in the New Year. I asked her how she knew about gay men being keen on fashion, elegance and I think she mentioned refinement, and then she told me to 'plug in.'"

We both have a good laugh and Luke says, "I told you she's a plucky lady. I really like Dora."

"Well, that's good," I reply, "because after discussing how busy I've become and how I feel bad about not seeing her as often, she understood and told me not to stretch myself so much. The thing is that I still want to keep in contact with her and help her out, so then she suggested we might like to move in at Apple Court, but she also said she'd understand if we don't want to move."

Luke says, "How do you feel about that?"

"I guess there are pros and cons to everything. This is why she said to talk it over with you and whatever we choose to do is fine by her."

"You know, lately I've been thinking about moving out of here. The studio's okay for a single person, but a bit more room would be great. More importantly, however, is the fact that I don't want to leave you here by yourself when I go to Berlin."

"Why do you say that?" I try not to think of him going off to Berlin, but I know at some stage he will.

"You'd be all alone here at night, Sam," Luke replies. "And while the place has an alarm system it wouldn't be too difficult to break in, and what if you're harmed? There's so much crime out there."

I get up for a moment and go to the kitchen to put on a pot of coffee. "But that could happen at Apple Court as well," I remark.

"Yes, but the place is a residential complex with a whole bunch of flats, and although Dora's an elderly lady at least there would be two of you. And we don't hear much of burglars breaking into residential buildings while the occupants are sleeping there. Sure, it happens, but not as much as break-ins into places of business where something of value is kept, like cigarettes, alcohol, and even money. Any burglar worth his salt would probably break into Tom's safe without a problem."

I never thought of that. "Well, thanks for planting this in my head. I'm sure if you're not here I'm going to stay awake all night now."

"You could stay at Dora's when I'm away," Luke responds.

"Not if she takes on another boarder. I can't use her place as a hotel."

"Okay," Luke says, "so what's the deal?"

I come back with the coffee pot and fill our cups. Luke picks up his and sips on it.

"The deal is Anne's room, where her design wardrobe is kept. In reality, it's the actual master bedroom, but once the garments are transferred out to Helen and Dora's store, the room, which also has an ensuite, is ample for a couple. Not only this, but the storage space Anne had built for her designs is perfect for all your Berlin things and then some." I can see I have Luke's undivided attention and I continue, "Dora suggested we might like to take that room for ourselves and use my old bedroom, which is also fairly roomy, and turn it into a sitting room with a sofa, TV, and so on.

"Dora's room is out the back, off the main bathroom, and she has the sitting room and the parlour where she plays the piano, so she has plenty of space for herself. She even suggested we may want to use the parlour if we want to practise, of course not so loudly that the neighbours will complain. Finally, we share the kitchen and, like a family, we eat together when we want to."

"Well, she thought of everything," Luke replies, pensively. "So she's willing to share her home in exchange for what?"

I sip some coffee and say, "I go on helping her with household things, personal care, and grocery shopping, which you could help with as well, except for the personal stuff. She would love to live with a family, and I am her family. She also mentioned you becoming family, too. She really took to you, Luke, plus she's really looking forward to working with Helen and, therefore, becoming more involved in something she can share with others."

"What about rent? After all, we're talking Sloane Square," Luke points out.

"She doesn't want rent," I reply. "I just told you: she wants a family around her and wants to live out her days in her own home."

Luke regards me with a thoughtful look in his eyes. "And what if she becomes extremely ill, Sam? You must think of this because you can't go to any gig unless she's okay."

"I thought of that, too, and as long as she can be at home I would engage a nurse to look after her irrespective of whether I go to a gig or not. Even if I'm home I'm not a qualified nurse, and if Dora needs to go to hospital it's understood it will be the last resort. Dora's set on dying at home if possible and I know many people can do that as long as they have the right medical support. So my answer to you is, yes, I'm prepared for that eventuality."

Luke runs his fingers through his hair and sighs. "I don't know what to say; I have to think it through. But, Sam, I'm not going to live off an elderly lady. If we move in with her, I insist on paying rent." I laugh softly and Luke says, "What's so funny?"

"Dora said you'd want to pay rent. She calls you a man of honour. Isn't that nice? She said to tell you she doesn't want rent money and that she'll make sure you pay in a different way." Suddenly, Luke's expression changes to one of deep concern and I burst out laughing. He waits until I control myself and then I tell him, "No, she doesn't want to have sex with you, but she would if she were closer to your age." Surprisingly, Luke actually blushes for the first time since I met him.

When he composes himself, he says, "So what does she want?"

"I already told you: a family, good friends, and that we'll be around when her time comes. Her sister died at home with Dora holding her hand; she wants the same, and if I have it in my power to do it, I'll make sure that's what happens, whether we live with her or not.

"We can put some money aside in a bank account in case we need to hire a nurse or whatever. I won't let Dora spend her own money when she's not asking us for rent, and we can pay the power bills and groceries. So think about it."

"It seems to me you've already made up your mind," Luke remarks.

"I have and I would move in with her, but not without you. I don't expect you to move in, either, if this is not what you want. I'm still happy for us to live in the studio or get our own rental elsewhere."

Luke beckons me with his index finger and I go to him. "Sit on my lap," he says, already enclosing me in his arms. He gazes into my eyes and kisses me and when he stops I am awed by the love I see in his eyes and I feel a tear roll down my face. Luke wipes it away with his finger and says, "I love you."

"And I love you," I reply with emotion in my voice.

Chapter 44 - Robert

<u>1961, London, England</u>

Miraculous news! Clara's officially pregnant and the baby is expected in February, 1962.

When the doctor confirmed the pregnancy both Clara and I could barely speak. We were so surprised that we didn't know what to say. How can someone conceive after twelve years of trying? What brought on this wonderful miracle?

Clara was crying tears of joy while I asked the doctor whether there was an explanation for what happened. The doctor said he had seen a number of cases similar to ours, where couples failed to conceive for many years and then, quite spontaneously, they conceived and no one knew the reason why it took so long. The doctor also suggested Clara may have conceived but lost the fetus during a heavy period, without being aware her body had rejected it. Her medical history showed her menses could be quite heavy at times or perhaps it wasn't the menses after all, but a miscarriage. In any case, whatever the reason, Clara and I were past caring.

The doctor said the first trimester was the most important and as Clara was fit and healthy there was a good chance the baby would come to term. He further advised Clara on diet, not to lift heavy things, and above all not to stress too much—anxiety was always a danger to health.

For the next few days, Clara and I walked on cloud nine. We just couldn't believe we would soon be a family of three. We also discussed the running of the bakery. I suggested she close it, but she didn't want this. Assuming everything went well, she had every intention of maintaining the business even if she had to bring in an assistant.

Although I argued with her to give it all up and that I would quit music and get a job with better pay and benefits, Clara would have none of it. Instead, she talked to Mary, the lady with whom she used to share the outdoor market stall, and an arrangement was agreed between the two of them—Mary would move her fruit and vegetable stall inside the bakery and at the same time she would run the bakery for a percentage of the takings while Clara had time off with the baby. I wasn't too sure about this, but for a little fragile thing, Clara had an iron will and when she made up her mind about something that was it.

Eventually, after a few rows, I accepted the arrangement between Clara and Mary; as long as Clara felt well we would keep the store going. I did extract a promise from Clara, however, that should she feel too tired or sick I would close the store myself.

Clara agreed, albeit reluctantly, but she understood this was something that could affect the baby. And this was not the end of what Clara had in mind to do; much to my surprise, she announced that now was the time for her to visit her parents. She hadn't seen them in years and couldn't very well go and see them once the baby arrived as she would be busy with the child and going back to work part-time.

This idea was even worse than the one about keeping the business open. I knew that what was happening in Germany was a powder keg waiting to go off and the last thing I needed was to have Clara trapped in East Berlin, especially as travel restrictions were in place. Clara argued that with a British passport she was safe, and she was right. As a UK citizen, she could travel to either side of Berlin without a problem, but what worried me most was if things somehow got worse. The political situation was unstable at present and I didn't like Clara going there in the first place. She wanted to stay with the Schmidts for at least a month; after all, she hadn't seen them for so long and she wanted to be with them.

I would not have hesitated so much if I could accompany her, but there was no way I'd be able to get a month off work. I told Clara I may as well leave work altogether and get a new job when we returned from Berlin.

Clara would not accept my suggestion and for a few days we didn't talk to each other. This is the first time I can remember having a disagreement between us and not talking for days, but it wasn't a simple issue and it weighed heavily on me because while I could understand why she wanted to see her parents at such a crucial time in her life, at the same time I had fears about her traveling to Berlin alone and even though the UK passport would provide her with protection there was always the unexpected. I would feel better if I simply quit my job to go with her, but she wouldn't have it. She said we needed to keep saving so when the baby was born we'd be financially viable and still have the bakery to fall back on.

In the end, after a whole week of silence, I gave in. Much as it was against my better judgment, I realized I had to let her go. Clara was ecstatic when I told her and she was all over me, hugging and kissing me, but I did ask her to promise me one thing, and this was that when she arrived in Germany she would book herself into a hotel in West Berlin and she'd only visit her parents during the day. Additionally, if the parents could see her in West Berlin it would be much better.

I also mentioned West Berlin had better standards in medicine and hospitals so should something happen to Clara she would at least be in good hands. It was bad enough that I agreed to let her go, but if I knew she kept to the West side, safe in a hotel and close to high quality medical care then she could go. Clara promised she would do this and would also telephone me from the hotel every day to reassure me all was well.

I felt a small measure of reassurance knowing that being in West Berlin most of the time would be safe for Clara and I booked her passage to Berlin by airplane rather than have her sitting on a train for over nine hours. Clara complained that it was too expensive, but she saw the sense in traveling for a shorter time so she would arrive refreshed and rested for the baby.

I prayed I made the right decision in letting Clara go to Germany on her own, but I told myself I would try to get a few days off from work and fly to Berlin to surprise her. I didn't tell her this in case it couldn't be done, but I would do all I could to ensure things went well.

Chapter 45 - Samantha

<u>1985/86, London, England</u>

Luke and I meet up for coffee with Chris and Marcus at Sunflower café a couple of days after our lunch with Tom, and Luke informs them of the proposal put forward.

The boys glance at each other and then turn to us. "So what're you going to do?" Chris speaks first.

Luke replies, "This isn't just about Sam and I, it's about the future of our band and what we want to do with it."

"We'll do whatever you decide," Chris says.

Marcus rolls his eyes at Chris. "Wake up, man! What Luke's asking is for our feedback. Do we want to go for it and end up being rich and famous or do we stick with what we're doing and, while it won't make us rich, at least we're free to do what we want?"

"I just want to meet chicks, man, but I could use a bit more money," Chris replies.

I try not to laugh. "You're so cute, Chris, that girls will always go after you, but when it comes to the money side of things fame and fortune are not guaranteed. We have to work really hard to make it happen and at the same time realise that it may never come to pass."

Chris seems undecided. "I don't think it's for me, you guys, despite the chicks," he responds and then turns to Luke. "Hey Luke, does this mean I'm out of the gig?"

"I never said that," Luke responds.

Marcus glances at Chris and then says, "Don't mind him, man; aside from the chicks, I don't think he knows what he wants."

Chris blushes and I take pity on him so I put my hand over his and say, "Don't worry, Chris, whatever happens we won't let you go."

"Thanks, Sam." He squeezes my hand. "You're alright, and I don't mind telling you the truth. I actually enjoy what I do, but I'm not sure this is what I want to do for the rest of my life. I guess I don't have the ambition to go all the way."

This is the first time I hear Chris confessing to something so important. I turn to Marcus. "And you, what do you think?"

"I know we joked about this when things started to go well for us, but I never thought we'd be given the opportunity to go for it. On the other hand, like Chris, I just want to do what I want, and right now it's just playing gigs of my choice."

Luke remarks, "So what you're saying is that both of you are happy if things stay the same."

Chris and Marcus nod, and Chris adds, "But with a little more pay."

Luke glances my way and then turns back to the boys. "Thank you for the feedback, guys. Sam and I already discussed this between us, but we didn't want to influence you with the decision we made, which is pretty much the same as yours. Aside from the proposal put to us by Tom, there's also the question of doing the odd one-off gig for special occasions, but we've yet to hear on that."

"So we're okay then? That is, we stay the same?" Marcus says.

"Yes, we're okay," Luke responds.

<hr />

With Christmas ten days away I haven't had time to plan anything even though in past years at Sloane Square I always had Christmas lunch with Dora. I never celebrated the festivities, especially during my troubled childhood, but for the sake of Dora I'm happy to help her prepare a traditional Christmas lunch and as neither of us has other family, Dora suggested some time back that we invite any neighbours from Apple Court who also find themselves alone. So we gave birth to our own little tradition and each year we invite anyone from the complex whose circumstances matches ours.

When I saw Dora last week she brought up the Christmas lunch and I accepted immediately without consulting Luke. Did being a couple with him count as having family? Dora didn't mention Luke and so I telephoned to ask her.

"My dear," Dora exclaimed, "of course Luke must come. You may be a couple, but neither one of you have extended family, isn't that right?"

"True," I replied. "So who's coming this year from Apple Court?"

"Well, there's Mrs Bennett, whose hubby passed away three years ago, and she has no children or other family, but you know this already; then, there's a new neighbour, Mr Adler, who recently moved in; he's a musician by the way."

"And anyone else?"

"Yes, Mr Danvers, whom you also know."

Mr Danvers is a retired soldier and widower in his late seventies; his only son died during the war.

On the Sunday before Christmas it starts to snow and Luke and I stay in bed most of the day. With various Christmas functions at The Treble and Bass, where we were hired to play for private functions plus performing in our own gigs, we were due for a break and Tom gave us two days off on full pay.

"It was decent of Tom to give us the time off and with that nice little bonus to boot," I remark while drinking coffee that Luke made midmorning along with toast. "Considering the amount of free hours we put into our gigs it's the least he can do."

Luke replies, "Don't forget we're supposed to finish by midnight, but we often go into the early hours of the morning only because the audience wants us to keep playing, so it's not up to Tom to give us extra pay."

"True. I hadn't thought of that."

Luke savours his coffee with satisfaction. "Aaahhh! There's nothing like being in bed with a beautiful girl, drinking hot coffee as we watch the snow falling outside."

I throw him a questioning look. "What's got into you all of a sudden? And if you're thinking of sex you'll have to wait, I'm trying to have breakfast here."

Luke regards me with amusement in his eyes. "Trust you to go straight there, my sexy Irish lass, but I hate to disappoint you. I was merely thinking of how cosy it is in here with you, the coffee, and the falling snow outside. No other agenda, I promise you."

"Well, snap out of it because I need to get back to Dora regarding the Christmas lunch I told you about and she needs to know whether you're attending."

"Of course, I am," he replies. "Where else am I going to go? I don't have extended family; you're my family."

"Nice try, but even this isn't going to get you laid right now," I remark saucily. I feel so loved by him that I can't help but make a joke of it lest tears well up in my eyes. I'm still getting used to being loved by Luke and it's often difficult for me to tell him just how much I love him while deep down I'm secretly afraid that I don't deserve to be loved and that this whole thing has only been a beautiful dream and I'll wake up from it at any moment to find myself back on the streets.

I sip my coffee to buy time and recover from my emotions before I say, "I'll call Dora later today. She's a stickler for a traditional Christmas and she's also going to need help with decorating the tree."

"Well, you can count me in for that. I take it I'll be doing all the hard work?"

I playfully stick my elbow in his ribs. "Get real! Anyone can decorate a tree, but stuffing a turkey's a totally different story, especially when you have to rip out the guts."

Luke makes a face. "Then I'll leave the turkey to you, my love; you know best." He gently kisses my lips and says, "Just remember how much I love you."

I don't know what to say so I sip the rest of my coffee nice and slow and Luke suddenly changes the subject. "By the way, I had a chat with Tom while you were playing your piano gig yesterday."

This had the desired effect of distracting me. "I thought we were going to see him together," I remark.

"We were, but he had another proposition that just came in and which I think will work out really well for the band, plus this won't clash with our current gigs at all."

"Let me top up the coffee first," I say and rush to the kitchen for the coffee pot. I top up our cups and warm up some brioche while I'm at it and then go back to Luke. "Okay, so keep going."

"Tom wants to know what we thought of our last chat and I saw no harm in telling him, especially after we already discussed it between us and with the boys."

"So how did he take it?"

"He said he thought we'd choose to stay as we are and he's fine with it. In fact, he brought up whether we'd consider the extra gig night on Fridays, which he had in mind for a while now, plus the gig won't clash with anything and the feedback coming in is really positive."

"That sounds reasonable."

"I thought so, too, but of course I told him Classical Cocktails needs to start a half hour earlier so you can get more rest, plus we still have to discuss the extra gig with the boys."

"So is this the proposition Tom came up with?"

"No. He was actually approached to see whether we'd be interested in playing at the Hammersmith Odeon two Sundays per month. The promoter introduced the concept some time ago and it's really working out well: a band that not only plays the popular covers from the last two decades to the present, but also one that can introduce some of their own compositions. The big plus is that this is a stand-up gig with a capacity of five thousand people.

"These kids just go there for the dancing and even singing along with the band, but they also like to discover new songs from up and coming artists. The promoter has a band doing this right now, but they're going on to try and make the big time so this clears the way for a band like The Eclectics."

Now I'm blown away. "Wow, this is incredible! Imagine us at a venue where the likes of The Rolling Stones, The Beatles, David Bowie, Queen and other icons performed in past years." I'm so excited that I almost spill the coffee all over Luke while I kneel on the bed, jumping up and down as though it were a trampoline. Luke smiles at my childish display, but he stops me before I actually spill the coffee.

"Do you think the boys will go for it?" I ask, sitting back on the pillows once again.

"I don't see why not. Remember the boys are looking for a bit more money, and this gig pays more than what we earn in a month so the money's very good. The beauty of it is that the gig doesn't clash at all with what we already do and the same applies with the extra Friday gig Tom wants us to do.

"One thing, however, is that we're going to be pretty tired from playing so many gigs, especially because you have the Classical Cocktails on both Fridays and Saturdays, but the whole thing is on our terms and we'll cover for you so you can take longer rest periods on those days, and if something doesn't work out we're free to stop at any time."

I'm so happy all of a sudden that I can't help but turn to Luke and give him a huge hug. He takes my coffee cup away and sets it on the bedside table and then he returns my hug. "Does this mean you're okay with all this?"

"More than okay. I love it!" I exclaim with excitement.

Luke pulls gently back from the hug and looks into my eyes with desire. "And does this get me laid?" He gives me an impish smile.

I push him back on the pillows and show him just how much he'll get 'laid'.

———————⊙———————

We sleep until early afternoon and when we wake up the room is dark and the snow is still falling, but at least the heating is on and Luke and I are warm under the covers. I sit up and reach for my clothes, which are scattered all over the bed, and I suddenly remember I was meant to ring Dora so I quickly jump into my woollen leggings and pullover and I put on thick socks on my feet.

I get off the bed with the intent of clearing up the coffee things before ringing Dora when a hand reaches out and pulls me gently by the wrist so I fall back into Luke's arms. He kisses me softly. "Hello," he says in a sleepy voice. "I think I'm growing old faster than I thought."

"Why do you say that?"

"Because I got laid big time and I'm still exhausted."

I smile. "Well, you did ask for it after all, and let's not forget that you really are growing old. So I suggest I put you on some vitamin supplements, but in the meantime you should keep away from the babes."

He laughs. "What babes? I can barely handle you and then there's nothing left to go around, so the babes, as you call them, always miss out."

I shake my head at him. "Well, let that be a lesson to you, mister. In the meantime, I need to call Dora."

"Wait a moment." Luke throws on some track pants and an old cable knit turtle neck jumper. "I've been thinking about our discussion of the move, either to Dora's or elsewhere. As you can see, with all the clutter in this studio, we need something a little bigger and with more cupboard space for us both."

I sit on the edge of the bed. "Well, I didn't want to rush you into making a decision after everything that's been going on lately with all the gigs."

"Make your call to Dora," Luke says, "and tell her we accept. We'll go through the details with her and I'll insist we pay her some kind of rent, especially now that we've got two extra gigs coming up so we can afford it."

My heart jumps with joy, but I hide my excitement from Luke. "You realise with the extra money we can pretty much rent anywhere in London, so there's no need to move in with Dora."

"That's not the point. I thought you wanted to live with her and be a family," Luke replies.

"And I still do, but I want you to be absolutely sure about this. I certainly don't want you agreeing to a move simply to please me. If for some reason you feel uncomfortable living at Dora's you should say so now and we can find another rental. I don't want to give her false expectations and then upset her after a short time if you change your mind."

"After the kind of places and people I had to live with during my youth I could live quite comfortably with anyone," Luke remarks, "so if you think I'll be uncomfortable living at Dora's you're wrong; besides, the lady's obviously more 'plugged in' than we are."

We both laugh at this and I say, "Well, I give you that much: she's cool, she's sassy, and she's still after your body—if only she were young, of course."

"In that case, go and make your call, my love, under the condition that I won't be sexually harassed by her," he smiles. "And let's move in before we start the new gigs."

I make for the phone but Luke's voice stops me. "On second thought, don't tell her about our decision just yet; let's surprise her by telling her together at Christmas."

I reach out and hug him. "I know I don't say this enough, but I love you so very much. You are my life."

Chapter 46 - Robert

<u>1961, London, England</u>

Clara arrived safely in Berlin at the beginning of August. She had booked a reservation at a family hotel on Fasanen Strasse, close to all of West Berlin's facilities, and contacted me the moment she checked in. She sounded so happy that my fears were put to rest and although I would have preferred to have gone with her, I was glad she was reunited with her family.

Keeping to her word, she telephoned me every day to let me know how she was doing; she also passed on her parents' congratulations on the baby. Then she went on to describe the many family reunions with her relatives and friends of the Schmidts, and every late afternoon she crossed the border into West Berlin with her UK passport and without a problem. This also went to reassure me that perhaps things were not as dire as what I read in the newspaper clippings.

I asked my boss if I could take some time off to join Clara, but he couldn't spare me as one of our band members took vacation time to get married and he was now on his honeymoon, so I prayed the next four weeks would pass quickly and without any trouble for Clara.

Joey's cousin, Carl, arrived in the UK a week after Clara's departure and he brought with him the latest news from Berlin, which was not so different from what the papers in the UK were reporting. I was still anxious despite the fact that Clara assured me all was fine and I knew I wouldn't relax until her return; even the sound of her voice on the phone was not enough to reassure me completely, not if one read the news.

I tried to get her to return earlier than planned, but Clara insisted things were not as bad as the papers made out, and she wanted to have this long visit with her parents because once she returned home she would be busy with the business plus preparing for the arrival of the baby. I knew I wouldn't be able to convince her to leave Berlin early so I simply sighed and hoped for the best.

I read all I could get my hands on regarding the situation in Berlin, and Carl, who had now joined the 100 Club, told me that to date people kept leaving the East, with nineteen thousand people having left in June, thirty thousand in July, and it looked like another sixteen thousand or so had left during the first ten days of August.

When I heard this, my knees went weak and I had to sit down to take in the situation; which was building up to become a major disaster. Carl even mentioned that from 1958 until present some three million people left for West Germany and other countries. These were young, skilled people such as doctors, teachers, engineers, and anyone with qualifications and experience.

The evening when Carl brought me up to date on the situation was a disaster for me and I kept hitting the wrong notes while trying to play my trumpet, so much so that the boss sent me home, thinking I'd taken ill. The moment I arrived, I called Clara at the hotel, but there was no answer from her room. I asked to speak to the hotel manager and he was able to tell me that Clara was away for a couple of days but she was expected to return on the morning of August 13. She left no message so the manager could not shed any light on where Clara might be.

A cold mantle of fear descended over me and I had to reassure myself that all was well and that Clara had decided to stay at her parents' overnight. Perhaps she lost track of time and it was too late to make the crossing in the late evening; besides, telephone communication from East Berlin was not always reliable and Clara may have decided to ring me the following day.

I went to work as usual that evening and when I returned home I went to bed like a child waiting for Santa Claus to visit during the night, leaving me a Christmas present, which in my case would be news of Clara being safe and sound in West Berlin when I telephoned her in the morning.

I went to sleep thinking I'd be speaking with Clara soon and I woke up super early the next morning and realized it had just gone five, which made it six in Berlin, so I made breakfast and afterwards had a bath and ironed my clothes in readiness for work that evening.

Just before seven o'clock, I was ready to go and buy the newspaper down the road as it was still too early for me to call. I had the radio playing while in the kitchen and I was about to switch it off when the BBC News came on, and then I heard it: *"This is Mark Weston with a special BBC bulletin on the current situation in Berlin. Our latest reports confirm that the construction of the Berlin Wall began during this past night of August 12-13. The East German government, under the control of the Soviet Union, began erecting barriers and barbed wire to separate East Berlin from West Berlin.*

Our correspondents based in West Berlin also confirm several accounts of incidents of violence and clashes between East German border guards and civilians trying to cross the border. Some individuals have been shot and killed while attempting to escape.

As of this report, the exact number of casualties on this specific night is difficult to determine, but this marks the beginning of a tragic period during which many people have already lost their lives while trying to escape from East Germany to the West.

The BBC will cover events as they unfold with analysis and commentary on the political implications of this terrible event."

I switched off the radio and rushed to telephone Clara's hotel, hoping she may have heard something of what was happening and managed to get away. The hotel manager apologized and informed me that Mrs Kelly was not answering the phone.

I was suddenly engulfed by a panic attack so bad that it was worse than what I experienced in the war under fire from the advancing Germans. I was convinced my heart would burst from fear and that I would die alone, right here on the spot; but somehow I managed to pull myself together and picked up the phone, asking operator assistance to connect me through to East Berlin. I gave the number of Clara's parents' home and the UK operator came back on the line and advised they'd had a flurry of calls from the UK to East Berlin and no one has been successful in getting through. She reported all lines had a busy tone and there was no way of knowing when calls to the area would resume.

Chapter 47 - Samantha

1985/86, London, England

Luke and I do the grocery shopping for Dora a couple of days prior to Christmas Eve and this gives us the opportunity to chat with her about the living arrangements.

We come laden with a huge amount of grocery bags to cover the entire week, including the Christmas lunch, and Dora is delighted that we managed to find a large turkey. While we put away all the groceries, Dora makes tea and insists we stay on for dinner, but Luke says something about it being too much trouble.

"Not at all, Luke," Dora replies. "It's been snowing all day and I'm grateful you both took on the crowds at the supermarket so close to Christmas. Usually, I can't get a thing unless I buy well over a week or two ahead. Besides, you both need feeding, you're far too slim."

Luke and I have nothing on for the day and I accept on behalf of both of us. Dora's delighted. "That's great! And it's a good thing I made my famous shepherd's pie."

Luke glances my way and I say, "Dora's a great cook and she never buys frozen stuff unless she feels too tired to make something from scratch."

"Well, I look forward to trying the pie," Luke remarks.

"Now, you young people go and rest in the sitting room and I'll be along with the tea things."

"Can I help with anything?" I say.

"You've done more than enough today, dear. Off you go with Luke and I'll see you in a few minutes."

The sitting room is nice and toasty warm and Luke and I sit on the sofa as we watch the snow falling outside. "Are you warm enough?" Luke puts his arm around me.

"I'm fine. The heating in this place has never let us down," I reply. "So tell me, are we going to tell Dora about the living arrangements today?"

"We may as well. We'll tell her over tea."

236

HEROES

Dora starts to cry when I tell her of our decision and she gets so emotional that I join her while poor Luke doesn't seem to know what to do. "Uhm, ladies, does this mean it's a yes or a no?" He regards us from one to the other while I reach for a box of tissues, grab a bunch for myself and pass the whole box to Dora.

"Oh, my dear, don't look so worried," Dora addresses Luke. "I'm crying because I'm happy. To know that I'm once again part of a family, especially an old dame like me; it's all too much to take in."

Luke smiles. "Dora, you're not a 'dame', you're a lady; and I'm grateful to you because you've been a mother to Sam when she had no one else in her life, so you girls are already family. I just want to make sure you're okay with me being part of the family, too."

Dora takes a moment to dry her eyes and says, "Are you kidding me? I bet Sam's already told you I think you're a hottie, so to have you as family is simply wonderful."

I see Luke's face go red and I smile. This is the man who is pursued by babes of all kinds and he blushes just because an elderly lady pays him a compliment.

"Dora, you must go easy on Luke. He's rather shy with you." We all laugh and later, after dinner, we go through all the points Luke and I discussed between ourselves and Dora agrees with them even though she insists she doesn't want to charge us rent, but Luke tells her it's a condition of our moving in and Dora has no option but to agree. And just before we go back to the studio, I give Luke a quick tour of the areas in the flat that we're going to occupy.

It's past eleven and Luke telephones for a taxi cab and while we wait, Dora and I go through what needs doing for the Christmas lunch.

＊

Luke and I meet up with the boys again and they say yes to both an extra Friday gig and the Odeon gig, which has now been finalised between Tom and the promoter. When Luke tells the boys how much we're going to earn they're speechless and it takes them a while to recover.

"That's more than I thought we'd get," Marcus says.

Luke remarks, "Considering the number of people attending the current Odeon gig, and they've been running at full capacity for months now, this is a gig we can't ignore. The pay's excellent and we have to give them the best of what we do."

We all agree on this point. Luke already has a large number of his own compositions and we make a time to learn and rehearse them until we can play every note without a music score.

"This means going back to rehearsals for some time and I need to have your commitment on this because the Odeon gig's big and we're expected to perform as professionals. Just know that we're not dealing with Tom, who's flexible and lets us run the gigs pretty much as we see fit. The Odeon gig's not going to be like that," Luke is firm when he says this. "We may not be aiming for fame, but whatever we choose to do we'll deliver quality and give the best of ourselves, so if anyone here doesn't agree with what I've said now is the time to tell me."

"I take it we're renting a private place to rehearse?" I ask. "We can't do it here because the pub opens too early plus we might want to rehearse for longer periods of time or even rehearse in the afternoons."

"That's already taken care of," Luke replies. "I know someone who owns a number of studios that he rents out to bands. I'm waiting to hear from him regarding the rate, but I've used this guy's studios before and they're well equipped plus the hire rate's decent. Any other questions?"

No one has anything to add so we pick a day to start rehearsing after the New Year.

On Christmas Eve at Dora's, I help with the preparations for the Christmas lunch while Luke puts up and decorates the tree. It doesn't take him long to do it and he comes looking for us in the kitchen. "All done," he announces. "What else needs doing?"

Dora casts him a smile. "Oh, so good to have a man around!"

Luke meets my eyes and we try not to laugh. Dora's so over the moon about Luke. In her world, it was always the men who did the heavy work and protected the womenfolk; it wasn't like modern times, where women can do pretty much whatever they want.

"Ladies? I'm waiting." Luke speaks and I reply, "I think that's all for you right now. Dora and I have a lot of preparation to do for tomorrow so you can go back to the studio if you like and I'll catch a cab later."

"I brought the music scores for some of my compositions so if you lend me your spare guitar I can work from here and then we'll go back together."

Dora nods and turns to me, "Honestly, Sam, how can you think of going alone in a cab at this time of night? I think Luke's suggestion is the best one." She turns to Luke. "Luke, you can work in the parlour. Just switch on the heating plus feel free to use the piano."

"Thank you." He turns away, but not before he winks at me with a cheeky look on his face.

I turn to Dora when Luke's out of earshot. "Honestly, Dora, stop spoiling him or he'll think he's in control."

"You heard the man, dear. He's working on his music, and he can use the piano any time he wishes."

I raise an eyebrow in wonder. "There was a time you wouldn't let me anywhere near your piano, but I see it's okay for Luke to use it whenever he wants," I complain, but not in a serious way.

Dora moves closer to me in case our voices carry. "My dear, have I taught you nothing? You make the man 'think' he's in charge when in actuality it's the woman who controls him."

This time, I can't help myself and I laugh out loud, so much so that Luke appears at the kitchen door. "Is everything okay in here?"

"Of course," Dora replies while I'm trying to control my laughter. "Off you go, Luke. I'll get Sam to bring you a cuppa in a few minutes."

Luke throws us both a suspicious glance and then turns back towards the parlour.

Christmas lunch looks wonderful and there are six of us at table. After introducing everyone to each other, we sit in the parlour where Dora keeps a folded table that she uses for special dinners and other events. During my time living at Dora's, I never saw her use the table so this must be a new tradition for her or something she did in the past when she and Anne entertained.

The table is covered with a cream coloured embroidered tablecloth with trim and the centrepiece consists of a group of white candles mounted on antique bronze holders and surrounded by pine cones and delicate sprigs of holly and mistletoe.

While Luke is busy serving drinks, I bring in the turkey and set it close to the centrepiece on the table. The fare is traditional and the turkey accompaniments include chipolatas wrapped in bacon, roasted root vegetables, all kinds of potatoes, especially piles of crispy and golden roasted ones plus gravy to go with the turkey. There is mulled wine and mince pies for after the meal in addition to the traditional Christmas pudding, which is soaked in loads of alcohol for when we light it up, accompanied by a choice of brandy butter, poured custard, and whipped cream.

I look around the table and see Luke chatting in German with Mr Adler, the musician. The man looks to be in his late thirties and seems relieved to be able to speak in his own language and delighted that Luke, Dora, and I are all musicians. My German is still limited, but I'm able to pick up some of the conversation and if I'm not mistaken, Mr Adler recently escaped from East Berlin and he now plays the piano with the London Philharmonic Orchestra.

The rest of us chat among ourselves. I'm familiar with both Mrs Bennett and Mr Danvers, but they never met Luke so I talk about the band we're in and the kind of gigs we do, and all present look really interested. I manage to kick Luke under the table with a look in my eyes that tells him to mingle with the other guests. He gets the point and immediately after the pudding he excuses himself from Mr Adler and mingles with the others. Dora's busy chatting with Mrs Bennett and I take the opportunity to talk to Mr Adler so I move to the chair next to his and turn to the man. "Mr Adler, did you enjoy the lunch?"

Mr Adler seems to be a little shy with me, but he understands enough English to reply. "Yes, yes, very much, thank you. And you are Sam Kelly. Luke told me about you and how well you play the piano."

"Probably not as well as you play. I heard you mention the London Philharmonic. Do you play with them?"

"Yes. I was very lucky to be able to find a place with them," he says and changes the subject. "Please forgive me, I didn't introduce myself fully, my first name is Felix, so please call me that."

I smile at him. "Thank you. And I'm Samantha, but call me Sam."

We go on to talk about his music and Dora joins us for a few minutes. "Ah, Felix, did Sam tell you she plays the piano?"

"Yes, yes. I would love to hear her."

I shake my head. "Oh no, no way will I play in front of two concert pianists. I'd rather play my electric guitar, but not today."

"I'm not a concert pianist, Sam," Dora says, "just a humble teacher."

I smile at Felix and tell him Dora is much better than she says. Felix agrees with me and tells me he has already heard Dora at the piano and she's excellent. This makes Dora blush and she goes off on the pretext that someone might want a cup of tea.

Chapter 48 - Robert

<u>1961, London, England</u>

I didn't go to work for a few nights. I just stayed at home, paralyzed with fear, thinking of Clara and the baby. Would she be able to somehow get back into West Berlin? She certainly has the right passport. However, the British Embassy in Germany is located in West Berlin so Clara would have no access to it unless she could somehow manage to communicate with them.

I contacted them from home and spoke to an official who told me they were having similar problems with other British nationals, especially those born in Germany. I informed the official that Clara was born in West Berlin, but this didn't seem to count for much, and the official gave me to understand the East Germans were not honoring their agreement to allow German nationals with a different citizenship to cross into West Germany. Unfortunately, even though this caused an outcry among the international community, the East Germans did not care.

I listened to every BBC update, day and night, hoping to get a better idea of what was happening. One of the BBC's local correspondents discussed the situation in regard to communications between East and West Berlin. I wrote down all updates so I could go over them repeatedly. It was a good thing I learned shorthand during my time in Berlin when working on the demobilization project.

"Telephone lines are among the communication channels that have been greatly affected. The East German authorities, with the support of the Soviet Union, have imposed strict controls on telecommunications between the two parts of the city. Phone calls and other forms of communication are heavily monitored and direct lines between East and West Berlin are often cut off or restricted.

"People living in East Berlin are still allowed to communicate with the outside world, including West Berlin, but only through the tightly controlled channels. In many cases, however, phone calls between East and West are either heavily monitored by the East German government or entirely prohibited."

This latest update was like the last nail in the coffin. No one in East Germany could get through to the West, and even if Clara had been able to contact the British Embassy in West Berlin there was not much they could do unless she was allowed passage to the West with her British passport. The fact that the East German authorities wouldn't honor their arrangement to allow ex-Germans with a different citizenship to go through a checkpoint into West Berlin was to spite the Allies. Therefore, with East Germany heavily monitoring everything that went on in their territory it was enough to take away any hope I had for Clara.

I didn't know what day it was anymore, but one morning someone was knocking at my door and I dragged myself out of bed, thinking by some miracle that Clara had somehow managed to get back. When I opened the door, however, I saw Mike and I broke down in tears.

Mike was shocked to see me in the state I was in and he helped me to dress and then made some breakfast with very strong coffee. He told me our boss had sent him to check on me, although Mike was going to check in with me later today as he was concerned he hadn't heard from me. He knew Clara had gone away, but he was still under the impression that she was Irish and had gone to Ireland to visit her parents.

I soon put Mike straight and told him the whole story about Clara and me, and when I mentioned Germany and the trouble Clara was in now something seemed to light up in his eyes. I couldn't understand why, but Mike soon put me in the picture. I remember our discussion word per word: *"Rob, I understand why you didn't mention Clara was German. This might have been an issue for some back in the forties, but now it no longer matters so much. And I wish you would've told me what Clara was doing because I could've advised you not to let her go."*

I said, *"But I couldn't forbid her. She's pregnant, Mike, and she hasn't seen her parents since the early fifties. She wanted to visit them for a month, before she became busy with the baby and her bakery business."*

"Well, it's a shame the timing was all wrong, but circumstances can't be undone. Rob, we've been good friends for a while and I'm going to trust you with something that's secret. Do you understand?"

"Of course," I said.

"You know Carl, Joey's cousin, right? Anyway, I know you've been reading news articles from Germany that Carl passed on to Joey; Carl's been involved in forming a group of people to help those who wish to escape the Communist regime. Carl and many others saw this coming from a long time ago. In fact, it started to happen just after the war ended, but to get to the point, Carl still has good contacts in West Berlin who can usually get in and out of East Berlin. It's dangerous work, but these people are united in wanting to help others. Do you follow me so far?"

I started to feel a ray of hope inside me and suddenly I wanted to hug Mike and tell him how grateful I was for his help, but I couldn't speak; I still had tears rolling down my face, only this time they were tears of gratitude.

"Rob, the Wall went up about a week ago and we already have at least twenty refugees out of the place. We work with people from free countries and our group's already growing and gathering momentum. So this is what I suggest: I can get through to Clara via someone in the group and we can get her out, but I don't want to raise your hopes and tell you that she'll be back next week. This could take months of monitoring and planning, always looking for different ways of escape and waiting for the right time. If we get caught by the East Germans for helping refugees we get shot, too, so we have to strike when circumstances are right for us.

"What I'm saying is there is a chance to get Clara out, but it may not be any time soon, and we have to take into consideration that she may be heavily pregnant by the time we find the kind of escape that's not too difficult for a pregnant woman to attempt."

I couldn't believe my ears, but here was Mike, extending a helping hand and a way to get to Clara. "I understand and I want to join your group. I'm in your hands."

"*Good man!*" *said Mike.* "*Now, listen to me. I'll get a note to Clara and let you know when she receives it. She may even be able to reply to the note, but I can't promise for sure. Even so, she'll somehow get the message and instructions; the rest is up to our group. And last of all, not a word of this to anyone, except Joey and Carl. Meanwhile, you have to act as if everything's normal. Get back to work or Steve will have to let you go. Keep things as if Clara simply went away on a holiday. Is anyone looking after her bakery?*"

"*Yes, she has a lady she works with.*"

"*So go and see her and tell her Clara's detained in Ireland because her mother's sick. I take it that anyone who knows Clara thinks she's Irish?*"

"*That's correct.*"

"*Okay, I'll see you at work tonight. You get some rest, get cleaned up, and cheer up. We'll get her back somehow and you'll be reunited with Clara.*"

Mike stood, getting ready to go and I hugged the man and thanked him profusely. He reminded me to apologize to the boss and tell him I'd been so ill with the flu that I couldn't even call him and that my wife is away in Ireland.

After Mike left, I felt like a new man. I had help and people with the know-how on the situation in Berlin who would help to rescue Clara—and now I was part of a group of heroes.

Chapter 49 - Samantha

"You know Felix Adler from Berlin, don't you? Were you involved in his escape?" It is late into the night and Luke and I are sitting up in bed talking.

After the lunch at Dora's, we convinced Felix to play the piano and he left us entranced with his skill and talent. He was indeed a brilliant concert pianist and we kept asking for encore after encore until two hours passed by and Dora put an end to the concert so the poor man would not exhaust himself.

The guests departed and we noticed a few Christmas presents under the tree, which they had left for us. Dora, Luke and I had exchanged our gifts earlier, but it was getting late now and we were tired so we left the gift opening for another day and instead we cleaned up and put everything away. Dora was so grateful and happy that she mentioned this was her real Christmas gift from us, meaning all the help with the lunch and socialising with the guests plus our upcoming move to her home; she said she would never forget this Christmas.

It was difficult getting a taxi by the time we left, but we managed to catch one just in time and were lucky because when we arrived at the studio the skies opened up and it started to snow heavily. We left the heating on at the studio when we went to Dora's and it proved a good idea because when we walked in the place was welcoming and toasty warm.

"How do you know about Felix?" Luke asks.

"It was the familiar way in which you both conversed."

"But you don't speak that much German, so how could you tell?"

"Well, it doesn't matter; maybe it was something to do with your body language," my tone held a hint of annoyance.

"Okay," says Luke. "Yes, I know Felix; I was involved in his escape, but I don't understand why you're upset."

"I'm not upset, it's just the fact that you didn't tell me. It's like a secret or something, and why shouldn't I know about Felix? He's not in any danger now."

Luke goes to take my hand but I move it away. "What's got into you, Sam? I didn't know Felix lived in the same complex as Dora. I was surprised to see him there, and he me, so we caught up on what he's been up to since he arrived in the UK. In any case, I wasn't about to tell you that Felix is an escapee from East Berlin in front of everybody else."

"You could've told me later in the cab or when we got home."

Luke sighs. "Yes, I could've, but I had other things on my mind and it wasn't important. I'm not keeping anything from you and I don't understand why you're acting like this."

"Fine!" I say and lie down, facing away from him and drawing up the bedcovers over my head.

Luke's still sitting up but says nothing. He switches off the bedside lamp and after a couple of minutes lies down on his side, facing my back. He wraps his arm around me and I let him turn me towards him. "Why are you acting in this way?" he says softly. "Did I say or do something wrong?"

I shake my head, feeling contrite because I'm acting like a spoilt child. I know there's nothing wrong with Felix and Luke knowing each other, and I'm sure Luke would have told me eventually that he knew Felix. So why am I acting like this? And then it comes to me—Luke's going back to Berlin for another mission. He hasn't said anything yet, but I know it in my heart that he's going and a terrible feeling of fear engulfs me. Tears suddenly spring to my eyes and they roll down my face as I try to sniff them away. Luke switches the lamp back on. When he sees the tears he takes me into his arms and I cling to him, hoping that I'm wrong.

"What is it, my love? Tell me what's going on." He hands me a couple of tissues and brushes my hair back from my face with his fingers.

I dry my tears and blow my nose, and then I say in almost a whisper, "They've called you from Berlin, didn't they? You're going back."

This time Luke sighs in resignation. "I was going to tell you in the morning; I didn't want to spoil Christmas by telling you today. How did you know?"

I shiver and he holds me closer to him. "I didn't. It just came to me as a feeling of distance from you and danger around you."

"Sam, listen to me and please know I'm telling you the truth. Yes, I got a call yesterday, and yes, it's an escape mission, but there's no danger for those of us involved. The escapees are the ones taking all the risks. We're not going into East Berlin this time; the escapees are making their own way through a checkpoint where we have an East German guard that we bribe on a regular basis. He'll stamp their phoney passports and let these people through. Our job is simply to pick them up in a van and take them to MFF headquarters where another group that works with us will immediately take them to sanctuary."

I feel more reassured, but I can never forget the Baltic Sea massacre. It's imprinted in my mind forever and even if Luke helps out with low danger missions there is always a chance that something may happen—all it needs is a stray bullet fired by any of the hundreds of guards around the Wall.

"I'm sorry. I didn't mean to be so horrid. I know we agreed to be lone wolves and you're entitled to do what you want, so I'm not trying to stop you, but I can't help my feelings. I can't lose you; you know that, don't you?" I say all this with my face buried against his chest.

Luke disengages from me gently so he can look into my eyes. "I'll only be gone overnight. Someone couldn't make it at the last minute so they needed a replacement and they called me. The good news is that while I'm there I also have a couple of new escapees to audition for a gig at Ku-dorf and this saves me having to make a second trip later on. I'm leaving the whole of January free so we can move to Dora's and then start getting ready for the Odeon gig. As for the lone wolves, remember I said that wolves hunt in packs? So this time I go alone, but next time I'll take you with me if you want. What do you say?"

I say yes, even if I go on clinging to him.

Luke leaves for Berlin early morning the day after Boxing Day and I go to Dora's to assist her with bathing and to open our presents. The sky clears to a brilliant blue and Dora and I sit in the parlour with its expansive window overlooking a small garden; we soak up the sun while chatting over a cup of tea.

"Thank you for the lovely books," I say. Dora's Christmas gift consists of a couple of coffee table books, one on the history of music and the other on Berlin from its rise to the time the Germans were defeated in 1945.

"I didn't know what to get for you two," Dora explains, "but you both have ties to music and Berlin so I thought you'd enjoy reading the books."

"We will, thank you, and seeing as we're moving in soon I may as well leave the books here. Is that okay with you?"

"Of course, my dear." Dora looks radiantly happy and I'm so glad for her. Luke and I could have easily rented a bigger place elsewhere, especially as we'd have more privacy and this seems to be the thing these days, for people to leave their parents or other family when they get older, and this makes it even worse when the person staying behind is elderly, fragile or ill. The days of families living together, and some with extended families as well, are gone forever, except in many parts of the Continent. Italy's a good example of this; families have a big house and three generations live together under one roof: grandparents, parents, and their young ones. This doesn't always work, however, but it has been the custom for hundreds of years and the beauty of it is that one has a feeling of belonging.

I never experienced this until I lived with Dora for a while and eventually she and I became close. Dora filled the place of a mother for me and now she's going to be mother to Luke, too, seeing as he doesn't have any family that he knows of.

When Luke and I discussed moving in with Dora, I secretly thought he was doing this for me, but he's shown in so many ways how much he's come to care for Dora that I know he genuinely doesn't have a problem sharing the place with an elderly lady.

This is one thing I love about Luke, his consideration and compassion for others, and this is what made me fall in love with him so quickly. In him, I found safety, caring, kindness, and love. Sure, I found him attractive from the moment I met him, but mere attraction usually fades once we get to know the person better and oftentimes we discover they're not the person we thought them to be.

I consider myself very fortunate that Luke loves me. I'm so much younger than he in both years and wisdom, and yet he puts up with me and my moods. He's calm while I can fly off the handle; he's confident when I'm full of doubt and fear. He's my other half.

"The new tea set is gorgeous," Dora's voice interrupts my thoughts. "I've always loved Dresden china. Thank you both for the gift, but you really shouldn't have; the greatest gift you've given me is your and Luke's company plus you introduced me to Helen and now I have the costume store to look forward to as well."

I give Dora a hug and then prepare to leave and get some groceries to refill the empty pantry and fridge at the studio. Luke is supposed to return tomorrow and I can't wait to see him back home safe and sound, so to make time pass quickly I keep myself busy by cleaning the place and tidying up around Luke's boxes.

For dinner, I make a homemade pizza for one. Then, after eating, I grab a couple of Luke's compositions and I play the scores with my guitar. These are two of the songs Luke wants to play at the Odeon gig and I'm sure the audience will like them. One song is a rock ballad and the other speeds up more to a high rock 'n' roll tempo. My role is to play both lead and rhythm guitar plus do backup vocals, while Luke handles the bass and sings. Chris and Marcus will play keyboard and drums respectively.

The rhythm part in the ballad is easy and I master it fairly quickly, but the single notes require a lot of quick finger changes and this'll need quite a bit of practise. Once I get the hang of it, however, I sing and replay both songs over and over and by the time my fingers start to tire, the telephone rings, startling me.

I was truly 'in the zone', as we artists say, and I lost track of time and dimension. I put down the guitar and go to answer the phone. "Hello?" I say in a breathless voice after all the signing I've been doing, and my legs turn to rubber when I hear Luke's voice at the other end. I'm so relieved to hear from him that I can't even think of what to say.

"Hey, are you there? I hope you're not with another man!" he says in jest. "See what I mean? I leave for a few hours and there you are, probably with one of your secret lovers."

This has the desired effect, which brings me back to reality, and I laugh. "Yeah, I wish!" I reply. "Instead, I've been struggling with that cool riff and instrumental in your rock song and my fingers are killing me—but I mastered the beast!"

"Well, if you're too busy to talk now I'll ring you some other time," Luke keeps teasing.

"Oh, stop it and tell me how you are. Is everything okay? Did the mission go well?" My heart is beating rapidly until his reply calms me right down. "Mission accomplished and I'm back at the hotel safe and sound, my love."

I expel a sigh of relief. "That's great! Anyway, I was going through the songs you picked out for the Odeon and I lost track of time and played and sang for hours."

"Good to hear that you're practising. Now, we have to make sure Chris and Marcus catch up. There isn't much time before the debut."

"I know, and there's so much to do in between."

"Well, I'll be back tomorrow evening around eight. I'm auditioning the East German guys in the morning and then I want to catch up with Gianni. He needs a new muso so I'm thinking of placing one of the guys at Gianni's if he's any good. The other guy's already earmarked for Ku-dorf."

"Luke," I say all of a sudden, "I love you so much it hurts." And then I burst into tears.

"Hey, hey! What's this?" Luke exclaims at the other end of the line. "Why are you crying, you crazy, mixed up Irish lass?"

"I don't know; it's just that loving you is the best thing that ever happened to me, but I'm so scared something bad will occur. It happens to so many people, you know? When they finally get their heart's desire, they get killed or die of some wasting disease, and then everything's wiped out."

Luke's voice is serious when he says, "Listen to me, Sam. I realise we can't control what happens in life and horrible things happen all the time, but we have to have faith that we were meant to be together and learn to live in the present. Why waste precious time thinking about negative things that may never happen?"

I dry my tears with a tissue and blow my nose. "I know and I'm sorry. Of course I agree with you; it's just that looking back on my life, things were really tough and I never seemed to get a break until I finally met you."

"And Declan," adds Luke. "I know his tragic suicide affected you to the lowest point in life, but Sam, you have to let Declan go, too. He gave you his best, so be grateful to him for this; in the end we all have the right to choose when we go, no matter what age we are. I think in our souls we know when the time is right to leave and Declan chose his time."

"I know, I know. I'm very grateful to Declan and all he taught me, but I can't help thinking that if he didn't kill himself I might still be with him and then I would never have met you."

"My love, I sense guilt in your voice and you shouldn't feel like that. Declan chose his life and you chose yours. Love him for what you and he had together and be happy that you and I found each other."

"You're right, and I'm sorry. I don't know what came over me, except for the anxiety I felt when you went back to Berlin."

"Well, go to sleep and get your rest, my darling girl. I'll be back tomorrow evening. I love you very much and don't you ever forget it."

We ring off and it is then I notice the time; it's past one in the morning and both Luke and I need our rest. I get ready for sleep and I'm out like a light in a couple of minutes.

Chapter 50 - Robert

1961, London, England

I went back to work and did as Mike instructed. I apologized to Steve and, though he was cool about what happened, he still gave me a warning. He said if I'm ever away again I'm to telephone him or get my wife, a friend, or neighbor to do it. He added that the only reason he didn't fire me was because I was too good a trumpet player, but he couldn't run a club if he didn't know whether his musicians would turn up. I thanked him for understanding and reassured him that the situation would never happen again.

Mike said it was a close shave and that Steve must really like me because he'd sent many a musician packing in the past, so Mike suggested I keep my head down and focus on the job, which I did. I tried not to think about news from Clara and I had to teach myself to be patient.

Mike, Joey, Carl and I took to meeting up for drinks after work at an all night bar around the corner from the club and at other times we'd go to someone's place for coffee. I was part of the group now and I often invited the guys over to my place.

Mike is the leader of the group and he's the eldest, he's thirty-five to my thirty-seven; Joey and Carl are still young, in their twenties. In all, we already have a total of ten members in the London group and they're people of different ages. I haven't met any of the others, but I'm sure I will soon as Mike wants to find a venue for the group to meet regularly and work strategically with Carl's contacts in West Berlin.

The group in Berlin is much bigger than ours, about twenty people or so, and there's also a network of groups that expand outside of West Berlin and we're affiliated with others from Denmark, Sweden, France, and a number of joint UK/US groups based in London, most of which are involved in the music business.

The night we had coffee at my place with the boys was about two weeks after Mike came looking for me when I was ill. We sat around the kitchen table with Carl and Joey, and I made coffee and even had a sponge cake to offer them, which I bought at the market.

Mike waited until we finished devouring the cake before he gave me the news. He said one of the members of the West Berlin group had news of Clara. My heart skipped a beat and I almost spilled hot coffee all over me.

This is what I remember of the conversation: "*One of our members made contact with Clara,*" Mike said. "*He's part of a group of escape attendants, digging a tunnel from a basement in West Berlin that leads to an old building on the East side. The escape attempt is highly dangerous plus we don't know how long it'll take to tunnel. I don't think this is for Clara, especially as she may be heavily pregnant by then. Be assured, however, that we'll keep monitoring this and also try to find other ways to get her out. The good news is that she's safe and she sent a message to you.*"

Mike slipped a folded note to me and I read it immediately while the others waited. The note said: '*My darling, I'm so sorry about what happened. I should have listened to you. I cannot write or telephone, but I'm told by the bearer of this note that there is help. Pray for me, my love. I dream of you always. Yours forever, Clara.*' I folded the note with shaky fingers and put it in my pocket.

Mike continued speaking: "*I know what you're going to say—why can't Clara simply cross into West Berlin because she has a UK passport? You talked to the UK Embassy in West Berlin, right? And what they told you is true; the East Germans are not necessarily co-operating, especially if the passport holder was born in Germany and they don't even care if someone was born in the West, either.*"

I said, "*What if I go there? I'm an American national with UK citizenship, surely...*"

Mike shook his head. "*Surely, nothing. They might let you in, but they most probably won't let you out, especially if you're with Clara.*"

Mike assured me the best way to bring Clara out of East Berlin was for us to bribe an East German guard. Carl took over the conversation and informed me that many of the guards were also looking for a way out, but they would need a lot of money to get papers and passports, all forged, of course. This was an expensive way to escape East Berlin and there was always the risk that the guard in question might be found out, which would mean death to both the guard and the person trying to cross into the West. These guards took a huge risk, too, and they didn't know whom to trust, even their closest friends or a family member could turn them in, plus the Stasi was always watching.

Mike saw me look crestfallen and patted me on the shoulder, telling me to be patient and have faith that somehow we would get Clara out. The other boys agreed and I thanked them all for their help and support.

The guys left my place close to dawn and I fished out Clara's note and read and reread it over and over until I fell asleep.

Chapter 51- Samantha

<u>1985/86, London, England</u>

Luke arrives home just after seven in the evening while I have a chicken roasting in the oven with potatoes and pumpkin. I'm in the middle of preparing a green bean and beetroot salad when his arms suddenly hug me from behind, bringing my body against his chest.

"Mmm.... Something smells delicious," he exclaims and then turns me to him and kisses me deeply and releases me. "As you can see, I'm back in one piece and ready for dinner."

I lower the heat on the vegetables and grab a couple of water bottles. He takes one from me and drinks most of it in one go.

"Good grief! Didn't they give you water on the plane?" I ask.

"These days, you're lucky if they give you anything, especially on cheap flights," he replies and checks out the roast. "Now, this looks and smells appetising. When do we eat?"

"Another ten minutes."

"Okay, I'll go and wash up and get out of these damp clothes. I got caught in the rain coming back from the tube, luckily it wasn't a heavy fall, but I'm still freezing."

"Off you go, then." I set the table, make the gravy, and serve the meal. By the time Luke comes back, wearing track pants and a black pullover, everything's ready and we sit down to eat.

"So it all went well?"

"Yes," Luke replies as he helps himself to chicken and baked vegetables.

"I drizzled the salad with extra virgin olive oil and sea salt."

"I noticed," he responds. "Good thing I fell in love with a good cook."

I laugh. "Good cook? My repertoire's usually brioche or toast. This is special because I'm really happy you're back, safe."

"Oh, and here I was thinking this was a welcome dinner for me."

"Well, it is in a way, you know; I'm happy you're back because I missed you," I reply.

"You can convince me of that when we go to bed tonight."

I laugh. "Is that all you can think about?"

"No. But there's something about you I can't resist. Besides, out of the two of us you're the one who's totally insatiable."

I say nothing because he's right. Luke has incredible control when it comes to making love, but I seem to charge in like an invading army. I blush.

"Hey," Luke pats my hand. "I'm teasing you, okay? You know I love it when you attack me." Before I can come back with a smart remark he says, "But onto other news, I got both the East Berlin guys into gigs."

"That's great!"

"Gianni and Marc are very happy and they each want another muso when I next find more talent."

"Have you had a chance to talk to Tom?" I say. "He wants us to perform on New Year's Eve."

"No, I haven't seen him since I arrived, but I had an idea he'd want us to do that. After all, it's the biggest night of the year for gigs and all kinds of entertainment."

"So we should rehearse with Chris and Marcus," I remark, "plus I already told Tom that Classical Cocktails is on hold until after New Year."

"I guess some people may go to the theatre on New Year's, but they can always drop in to the pub and have a normal drink. It's going to be a really busy night for us, and chances are we'll be playing right through till dawn, so I don't want you doing any other gig except The Eclectics."

"I'm glad you agree and so does Tom."

"Well, Tom's going to make a hell of a lot more money with people drinking all night, dancing, eating, and drinking some more because they'll get really thirsty when dancing and Classical Cocktails doesn't fit into that category."

"That's what Tom said, too," I reply. "And by the way, he wants to know when we're moving so he can reschedule our gigs if need be."

"I say we move on the second of January when everyone goes back to work. It's a Tuesday and we don't have any gigs scheduled for that day."

"That fits in with our plans then." I say. "I told the boys we decided to start rehearsals for the Odeon gig as quickly as possible. We have a lot to cover."

"I already talked to the guy who leases the studios and he's offered a studio at a good rate. I'll take you to see it after we move."

"And do we have a date for the Odeon gig?" Everything's moving so fast that I feel my head spinning.

"Not yet, but Tom mentioned something about mid-January, which means as soon as we move we can start rehearsing at the studio. And in the meantime, Chris and Marcus need to practise like you did while I was away. They need to know those songs back to front."

We finish dinner and I make coffee while Luke clears up and loads the dishwasher. "That was a nice dinner, my love. What else can you make?" He winks at me with a smile.

"I'm going to be very busy with all the gigs; remember I have Classical Cocktails in addition to the other gigs while you guys just sit there and drink cocktails backstage." I reply and add before Luke can say anything, "And don't give me any crap that you're there to support me."

Luke can't help but laugh. "Sheesh! I only asked what else you can cook. I was simply curious; and you should stop spying on us when you're supposed to be playing the piano."

"Yeah, well, I'm onto the lot of you so you can tell the boys to behave, and that includes you, mister! But if you want good home cooking all you need to do is mention it in Dora's presence. She's so excited about having you living with us that she'd arrange a luau if you ask for one."

"Good God, what have I done?" Luke acts out like he's horrified. "You're not going to leave me alone with her, are you?"

"We'll see." I wink at him and go off to get ready for bed.

New Year's Eve is magical even though we're exhausted and still going. Luke's repertoire for the festivities is mainly full of fast and hard rock 'n' roll covers and the crowd is dancing and singing along with us. The pub is jam-packed to full capacity and those who couldn't get in are outside dancing in the streets.

I never took part in something so lively and I'm on a real high, especially when we do the countdown to the New Year and everybody hugs, kisses, and cheers. Those of us in the band take a few minutes from playing and we cheer along with the audience and accept drinks purchased for us by some of our fans. We chat with them, too, and there are more hugs and kisses. And once 1986 is welcomed by all, we go back to the music again and the merry crowd dances and sings along with us.

During one of our breaks Luke draws me into a corner backstage and he doesn't look too happy. "What's wrong with you?" he asks with a serious tone in his voice.

"What are you talking about?"

"Did you take something?"

"What?"

He grabs my upper arm and shakes me. "Did you take drugs?"

I pull back and free my arm. "Where the hell did that come from? I told you I don't do drugs anymore."

"Really? Then why are your pupils dilated?"

I never saw Luke so angry with me, but I have no answer for him short of suggesting that someone might have spiked my drink. After all, most of us have had a number of alcoholic drinks due to the New Year celebrations. "I don't know what's going on with you, but I swear I didn't take any drugs," I reply in an angry tone. "How dare you think I would do something so irresponsible?"

Luke draws me close to him and gazes into my eyes; then he lets me go and walks away. I stand where he left me, wondering what got into him and I check my watch and see that we have five minutes before we're back on.

"Hey, what's up, babe?" Chris pats me on the shoulder, startling me.

"Hey yourself," I reply, suddenly feeling crestfallen.

Chris ruffles my hair and puts an arm around my shoulders. "Are you okay? You look upset. Where's Luke? I thought I'd find him here."

Tears suddenly well in my eyes and roll down my face. I turn to Chris and he hugs me. "Hey! What's going on?" I tell him what Luke said. "Man, he's wrong!" Chris states. "In all the time I've worked with you I never saw you touch anything, except the occasional drink. Luke must be mistaken."

I check my watch again. "We're on in a minute," I say while I dry my tears with a couple of tissues.

"Do you feel okay?" Chris sounds concerned.

"Yes, I'm fine. I'm just so charged up because the atmosphere's so wild tonight. Maybe this is why Luke thinks I took something, but I haven't. I must be high on life then." I can't help the sarcasm in my tone.

"Don't worry about it, he'll get over it," Chris says. "We're back on now, but before we go onstage I want to wish you a 'Happy New Year'!" He grabs me by the waist, pulls me to him and gives me a passionate kiss which is interrupted when Luke suddenly appears out of nowhere. Chris and I break off our hug and he makes himself scarce while Luke gives me a hard look. "What the fuck do you think you're doing?"

And then I lose it. "Me? It's you who lost the plot! I'm not drugged; it's just the atmosphere of the place tonight. And Chris gave me a New Year's kiss, that's all, so if you don't like it, sod off!" I walk straight past him on my way to the stage with a look of thunder on my face.

Luke appears onstage a few moments after me and we immediately launch into the next segment with 'Highway to Hell' by AC/DC.

Tom starts to shut down by four in the morning. He gets his guys to help out those who cannot make it out the door by themselves. Meanwhile, we switch off our equipment and each of us go our own way.

I don't wait for Luke, but simply go to the studio, wash my face, brush my teeth and then get into bed in my pyjamas. The heating is on and all of a sudden I feel totally exhausted and I break into tears, but the moment I hear Luke's footsteps outside the door I quickly lie down with the covers over my head and pretend I'm fast asleep.

Luke doesn't disturb me and while he gets ready for bed I'm close to sleep. I feel the mattress move as he climbs in and turns on his side, but I can't tell which side he's facing because I have my back turned to him. I wait for a moment, in case he wants to talk or even cuddle me, but nothing happens and I feel more tears run down my face. My last thought before I fall asleep is 'so much for lone wolves that hunt in a pack'.

Sometime later, I open my eyes and feel disoriented. The room is dark and the curtains drawn so I can't tell whether it's daylight outside. Luke is still sleeping, but I don't want to turn around in case he thinks I'm spying on him. This also means I can't turn to see the time on the bedside clock, which is on Luke's side of the bed. I therefore slip out from under the covers as quietly as possible and make my way to the bathroom where I quickly glance at the microwave clock in the kitchen, which reads 06:10. No wonder then that the room is still dark, and from the edge of the curtain I can see the sky is dark grey and possibly getting ready to snow again.

I've only slept for about two hours, but it feels as if I haven't slept at all, and I'm exhausted. I drink a few sips of water from the bottle on my side of the bed and then slip back under the covers, but not once do I glance in Luke's direction. All is quiet and he's breathing evenly, so I presume he's asleep.

I close my eyes and begin to relax, hoping to catch a few more hours of sleep, but just when I'm on the verge of unconsciousness I feel Luke's arm go around me and his body spoons me. I pretend I'm asleep even though all my senses come alive at his touch. Luke buries his face against the back of my neck and whispers, "I'm so sorry, so terribly sorry. I was so upset and took it out on you." He sighs, but I say nothing and let him continue. "I know you did nothing wrong and I reacted like a fool and hurt your feelings. I love you so much and I hurt the only person in this world I care about."

I turn around within the circle of his arms, but in the darkness I can't see the expression on his face. However, I'm surprised when I feel tears on his cheeks. I kiss them away and then kiss his mouth like I can't have enough of him. The kiss is so arousing that I can't think or talk, all I want is to have him inside me, but he gently breaks away and while still holding me to him he switches on the bedside lamp.

"Much as I want to make love to you right now," he says, "I need to explain what happened and why I reacted so stupidly."

I reach for my water bottle, have a few more sips and then offer it to Luke, who drinks the rest until the bottle's empty. We sit back against the pillows with him still holding me in his arms. "There's something I didn't tell you when I returned from Berlin."

"What is it?" I exclaim in sudden fear.

"No, I wasn't in danger," he reassures me. "It's more like something from my past that caught up with me as a reminder of how insignificant we all are in this life."

I'm curious as to where the story's going and I ask if he wants me to make coffee first. He agrees and while he goes to the bathroom I quickly put on the coffee, warm up our favourite brioche and I take the lot back to bed along with two fresh bottles of water.

Luke returns looking refreshed and we climb back into bed. I think this has become one of our little traditions, to talk in bed about anything and everything while drinking coffee and eating brioche. I rather like it.

"Remember during our early days I told you about my school friend whose family let me use their campervan to sleep in?"

"Yes," I reply. "This was when you were homeless."

"That's right, but what I never told you was that he came from a German family, and when Max, my friend, finished high school the family moved to East Berlin because his father was offered a really good position by a large engineering company with certain guarantees like special passes to move around from East to West and even travel overseas.

"Max's family was originally from the East Berlin area and they were well placed in high circles prior to the Wall going up. With a father so well connected and with job perks and guarantees of free movement in and out of East Berlin the family accepted the move and Max enrolled at Humboldt University, which was quite prestigious prior to the Wall and is still regarded that way even though it's located in East Berlin.

"Long story short, things didn't turn out very well for them. Perhaps the promises made by the East Germans may have been honoured, but the Soviets also had a say in what went on and I'm guessing things didn't go well. Max's father became ill or was executed by the Stasi, no one knew for sure, but I heard from certain sources that he passed away as a result of all the stress, and I can only imagine the enormity of his mistake, trusting that he and his family would be protected by the East Germans." Luke pauses to finish his brioche and I wonder what this has to do with my dilated eyes.

"Well," Luke continues, "when I went to Berlin to drive those escapees to MFF headquarters, I discovered that one of the men was my old friend, Max. I was given a list of names by MFF plus any details we had on the escapees and I recognised Max's surname. I was so happy to discover that within minutes I'd be able to catch up with him face to face.

"Unfortunately, the moment the escapees made it to the checkpoint our bribed East German guard was shot down and all hell broke loose. The Stasi were onto the guard all along and the whole thing was a set-up. The escapees started running, trying to make it to the West side of the checkpoint, but a whole bunch of East German guards appeared out of nowhere and shot down every one of them.

"I had two guys with me in the van to help in the rescue, but we drove off immediately, not because the German guards knew who we were, because they didn't, but those bullets were flying all over the place and we couldn't afford to sit there and wait to see what happened.

"The last thing I saw through the rearview mirror was a whole bunch of dead bodies, littering the checkpoint area while the East German guards kept shooting bullets into them as if they weren't dead enough yet." Luke pauses for a moment to gather his emotions and I pat his hand, lending him comfort.

"I didn't tell you any of this because of what happened at the Baltic Sea, and you were so worried when I went back to Berlin that I didn't want you to know what had happened; it would only bring back thoughts of the Baltic Sea massacre."

"But how did you know about Max's father passing away? I mean, you weren't corresponding with Max because you didn't know where he was until you saw his name on the list."

"MFF give us as many details as possible. Oftentimes, we manage to rescue an entire family rather than one individual; on this occasion, the list mentioned 'father deceased' but no mention of a mother, so I don't know what happened to her, but Max's father is definitely dead."

"I understand how this must affect you, but where did the anger towards me come from?"

"I don't know where it came from, but I had this rage building up inside me at the needless loss of life, and those bastards, shooting corpses and laughing like it was a game for them! And I knew I couldn't tell you because I didn't want to bring back all the fears about Berlin.

"Anyway, during one of our breaks at the gig I happened to see you at the bar and some guy was giving you a couple of pills, which you took immediately and then, by the next break, I saw your dilated pupils and I put two and two together and somehow all the rage came up and like a fool I took it out on you."

I move closer and give him a hug. "If only you'd let me explain I would've told you what happened, but I was so upset at your reaction and the fact that you believed I was taking drugs. I just got so angry that I let you think whatever you wanted.

"At first, I thought I drank a spiked drink, but later on it came to me—the guy at the bar, Peter, is one of Tom's waiters and he suffers from migraines so he always takes his medication with him. I get migraines sometimes, too, especially when I'm stressed or overly excited, and on this night I was very excited with the New Year festivities and everything that was happening that I started to get pain around my neck and back of the head, plus my eyesight seemed to be playing tricks on me and we still had a long way to go until we'd be finished playing. So I asked Peter for two of the tablets and he told me he also does what I did; he takes the tablets at the first sign of pain and sometimes the medication makes the pain go before it can get started. I wanted to finish the gig and not go off sick; and regarding my eyes, I had spotlights shining over me while on stage and as you know light makes your pupils smaller and this can have an effect on migraines so when I started to feel pain I went backstage for a while and sat in the darkness of the storeroom, which was pretty dark, so when I came back out my eyes were dilated because darkness dilates the eyes. So as far as I know this is what happened and the little trick of sitting in the dark, plus the pills I took, worked well and I was able to finish the gig."

"So am I forgiven?"

"You have to ask?" I reply.

"I guess I never quite lost it like I did with you."

"Well, maybe you also have Irish ancestry."

We smile at each other, but there is seriousness in Luke's gaze. "That's not it though. It takes a lot of anger for me to lose it like I did and I'm not proud of myself."

I squeeze his hand. "Well, I lose it all the time, even with you, and you put up with me. But I have to say that I was surprised because I see us balancing each other. I'm the 'fiery Irish lass' that can sometimes make trouble and you're the calm and rational English gentleman, so if you can put up with me, I guess I can put up with you."

"Deal," Luke shakes hands with me.

"Mind you, don't go getting used to abusing me, mister, because I know how to hit and punch really hard," I warn him, smirking.

With this remark we close the conversation and the exhaustion from the gig catches up with us and we fall asleep.

Chapter 52 - Robert

<u>Oct 1961, London, England</u>

It's been almost three months since Clara left for Berlin. She's now six months pregnant and every day that goes by I wonder whether she'll ever return. I'm so anxious for her and the baby's safety that I can't focus on anything else. I don't eat very much and I can't sleep, either, which means I have to drink something to calm my nerves. I was never a big drinker, but these days I find I need to drink more in order to feel that mantle of numbness that drink can often bring.

While Mike warned me that it could take weeks or months to get Clara out I started to lose faith, and getting through each day is beginning to get harder and harder. I still have my gig, however, and this is the only time I managed to force all thoughts aside so I can focus on the music. I need this job and I can't let the guys down, plus Steve won't hesitate to let me go if I don't perform to his expectations. And then what would I do?

Aside from all this, I'm also keeping an eye on the bakery. Mary was not expecting Clara to be away for so long and she keeps asking when Clara will return. I really don't know what to tell her, except to say Clara's mother is ill and Clara needs to remain in Ireland. Even so, I feel Mary's becoming suspicious of me and she's probably wondering what the hell I did with my wife.

Eventually, I'll have to make a decision: close the bakery and let Clara's business go or hire another person to assist Mary. This would mean giving Mary a little more by way of pay for looking after the business plus paying a part-time person to work under Mary's management.

I did the sums and worked out I can keep the business going, but the biggest problem I haven't considered is who is going to do the baking. Mary's not a baker and Clara's business only started to flourish because her goods became popular with her customers. Not having a baker, therefore, is a real problem and I have no one but Mike to turn to.

I invited Mike over for coffee one night after work and shared my fears regarding Clara, the growing baby, the business, and my own state of mind. Poor Mike, I thought, to have to listen to all my worries, but he and I are such good friends that he genuinely wants to help. Mike also has a high regard for Clara and he told me many times that he would not give up until we get her out of East Berlin.

Over coffee, Mike told me the group in West Berlin was still looking for a way to get Clara out. Earlier on, they considered other more daring rescues that Clara would be able to withstand, but one of the guys in the rescue group got wind that the Stasi were closely monitoring a large number of East Berliners who had businesses. The thing was that with all the escapes from East to West, East Berlin was losing its skilled manpower and this included those who produced food items—and the Schmidts fell into this category.

Mike said our contact in the group could not be one hundred percent sure as to whether the Stasi were watching Clara's parents and assuming that Clara was also part of the bakery business, so he advised to let some time elapse, until we know how things stand, and if the Stasi are not sniffing about after all, we can then smuggle Clara past a checkpoint via a guard accepting bribes. This is just as dangerous in terms of the risk Clara still has to take, but at least she wouldn't be crawling in a tunnel, climbing walls or hiding in vehicles. The fact that she has a legit passport might help a little, especially if the bribe for the guard is large enough, but we have to pick the right time.

Mike assured me the group would keep trying, but it is a matter of being ready for when we find the right guard to bribe and ensure the guard is not being watched by his colleagues or the Stasi.

It was a well known fact by now that a large number of East German guards were escaping into the West and the Stasi kept an even more vigilant eye on all guards. As a result, I would have to keep being patient about Clara, but in the meantime Mike came up with a suggestion for the bakery.

Many escapees had skills they brought to the West and a part of the rescue groups involved in helping these people was to help them find jobs, so Mike said he would look for a baker among the escapees, one that spoke English, and this person would produce the goods under Mary's management. Mary did not need to know anything about the person, except that they were employed to make the bread and pastries which Clara used to bake.

This was an excellent idea, I thought, and while Mary looked after the store, the baker would make the goods and the business could continue trading.

Lastly, Mike gave me a friendly warning. He'd noticed my alcohol intake was increasing and said: *"I know it's none of my business and that you're under a lot of pressure, but be careful with the drinking. You know what it does to musicians when they drink too much, especially trumpet players. You'll lose your lip, Rob, and once that happens, no one will employ you."*

I knew Mike was concerned for me and was telling me the truth. I already started noticing that my lip muscles felt fatigued more easily. If I kept drinking, the muscles would lose their tone more and more over time until I wouldn't be able to play at all.

Chapter 53 - Samantha

<u>1986, London, England</u>

Chris and Marcus help us move to Sloane Square with a small truck we rented and within half a day all our belongings are transferred to Dora's. Tom tells us not to worry about cleaning the studio as he'll assign one of his cleaners to do it. We're grateful for everyone's help, and the boys also offer to drive the hire truck back to the company from which Luke rented it.

Dora is resting in her room after the excitement of the move plus getting to know Chris and Marcus a little better. She only met them once, at my Classical Cocktails debut, so while the boys work with Luke, Dora puts on tea and sandwiches, which are appreciated by the men, and she fusses over them like a mother hen. I help her in the kitchen and then clean up afterwards, when I send her off for a nap.

By the time all is done and the boys leave, Luke and I inspect our hard work. We transferred my bed from the bedroom I used to occupy at Dora's; it's a large Edwardian wrought iron and brass bed that fits a queen size mattress, and this now becomes our bed with the addition of a two-drawer walnut bedside table on either side and antique brass bedside table lamps with square cream coloured shades. Additionally, Anne's room is perfect with its walk-in closet, extra cupboard space wall to wall and ensuite bathroom. What luxury!

"Wow, where did all this come from?" Luke admires the room and its furnishings.

"The furniture belonged to Anne, and Dora insisted I use it when I first moved in. Anne's room was only used as a workshop and showroom for her fashion designs and she used a smaller room for sleeping, which is the room I originally rented. I accepted the bed as I didn't have money to buy any kind of furniture and when I moved in all I did was fork out for a new mattress as Anne's mattress was too old."

"This room alone with the ensuite and cupboards is the size of the studio at the pub," Luke remarks. "And now we have your old bedroom, which we can convert into a sitting room."

"Yes. And Dora has a storage cage in the complex, which she doesn't use, so this might come in handy for us if we need extra space."

"I don't think we'll need it, but we'll see how things pan out." Luke reaches for me and kisses me all of a sudden.

"Mmmm! What was that for?"

"Just telling you I love you, but also making sure that no other man has slept on that mattress with you."

I smile. "Well, I might have to disappoint you there."

Luke seems surprised. "You didn't bring any boyfriends here, did you?"

I let him suffer for a while before I answer. "Well now, let's see... There were Oscar and Vinnie and we made a good threesome if I recall."

Luke regards me with a serious look in his eyes. "What are you talking about? You never told me you brought men here." Then he notices the smirk on my face. "Okay, so what's up?"

"Let's just say the two gentlemen that shared my bed, many times I might add, were furry, had four legs, long tails, pointy ears, whiskers, and they purred very loudly when I brushed their coats."

Luke breaks into laughter and hugs me to him. "You really had me going for a moment."

"They were Dora's old cats, but what would you do if it were true about my having had a threesome with two men?"

"What would I do? Nothing. What you did in the past is your business and I'm not about to judge you."

"Well, you can relax. I already told you Declan was my first and neither he nor I were into threesomes." Despite Luke's devil-may-care attitude about not judging me, I detect relief in his eyes and add, "How about you? Did you ever try it?"

"Not my scene, but I've had my fair share of would-be relationships, as I mentioned to you in the past, and I thought a couple of them may turn out to be long term, but they didn't work out and now I know why."

I feel a tinge of jealousy while picturing Luke with other women, but I don't comment on it. "What do you know?" I say.

He grabs me once again and brings my body close to his. "I know now you're my destiny and that's why nothing worked out in the past. Call me romantic if you will, but I truly believe in this."

"Then, all I can say is 'lucky me.'" I cover his lips with mine and we kiss.

―――――◉―――――

Over the next couple of days, Luke and I finish our unpacking with lots of space left over in our new bedroom, plus we set up my old bedroom as a sitting room. Dora confirms the storage cage was used by Anne and she gives us the keys to it. "I never use it, but it's handy for extra storage."

We're having breakfast before Dora leaves with Helen, who is driving in to collect her, and they're going to be working together most of the day, setting up the store plus interviewing a few young men. Meanwhile, Luke and I are meeting up with Chris and Marcus at the studio in Soho, which Luke's contact is going to be hiring out to us.

We're just finishing our coffee when Luke remarks with a wink in my direction so Dora doesn't see that he's teasing her. "Sam tells me you're into gay men."

"And what's wrong with that, young man? After all, gay males are perfect for an old dame like me—they're usually very handsome, cultured, love refinement, have excellent taste in dress, adore going shopping and travelling, and I don't even have to have sex with them. Oh yes, definitely the perfect males for women young and old."

Luke's lower jaw drops in surprise and I stifle a laugh. Then Helen arrives and the two ladies drive off to the store while Luke and I do the dishes and tidy up. "I can't believe how much Dora's transformed," I remark while drying the breakfast crockery. "When I lived here, before you came into the picture, she was all prim and proper—a true lady—and she still is, don't get me wrong. But since her association with us, Helen, and all the others she's dealing with now, plus this business venture and employing a gay male, the whole thing's changed her into a real hip chick. Don't you agree?"

"I do and I think it's good for her. I can never understand why seniors are cast aside just because they age. I mean, older people are so full of knowledge and wisdom because of the life they lived, and yet we're taught to think that once a person reaches a certain age they should be discarded.

"For someone in her eighties, Dora's more hip than some of the young people I meet, but I tell you yet again, Sam, whatever you do, don't leave me alone with her." Luke's joking of course, and I can't help but tease him in turn.

"Well, if you make sure you don't start batting for the other team, Dora will only stick to the young gay males and leave you alone. Besides, she knows you're taken." We have a good laugh and then get ready to go and view the studio.

Chris and Marcus are waiting for us outside the building and when we arrive, a man hopping out of a dark green MG calls out Luke's name.

"That's Pierre, the owner," Luke says to the rest of us.

Pierre joins us and Luke makes the introductions while Pierre takes the opportunity to kiss the back of my hand in true French fashion. He's a tall man, like Luke, with shoulder length black hair and incredibly light green eyes. I find him attractive and blush at his kiss. Luke notices the blush but disregards it.

"So... this is your band," Pierre addresses Luke with a heavy French accent. "But come on in, let's not hang out here, it's too cold, no?" He leads us past a small office and into a long corridor with six doors, each with a number on it.

"I think number three will suit you, Luke." Pierre takes out a key and opens the door to a rectangular room that's partitioned by thick glass at one end.

"Is that the recording room?" I ask, pointing to it.

"Yes, and it will be very good for you to record yourselves and listen to your playbacks. The room is fully soundproof and equipped."

We take a look around the studio, which has all we need, namely a live room equipped with microphones on stands. Then there's the control room where people can operate professional audio mixing consoles, effects units, and other sound equipment. In one corner of the studio, there is also a bunch of musical instruments in case we don't want to bring our own.

Chris and Marcus go off to check out the various guitars, keyboards, and a set of drums while Luke and Pierre remain engaged in conversation. I slip away into the control room and check out the monitor panels, mixing consoles, and a whole lot of other stuff for which I don't have a name, but just standing here I'm overcome by a sense of excitement and adventure—and suddenly I can't wait to get started.

After leaving the studio and saying farewell to Pierre, the rest of us slip into a nearby café just as it starts to rain heavily and a cold wind picks up. It's almost lunchtime and we're famished; besides, the café's cosy and warm and we take a corner table so we can be more private.

We order single pizzas for each of us, coffee, and mineral water, and while waiting for the food to arrive we chitchat about the studio and the Odeon gig. The consensus is that we love the studio, but can we afford it and how many days per week will we use it?

Luke says, "Tom suggested to the promoter of the Odeon gig, Dave, to cover the cost of the studio hire and the guy agreed.

"That's great!" Marcus exclaims.

"This is in case we end up recording one of our compositions and it starts to sell. Then, Dave gets a cut," Luke explains.

"But I thought we weren't going to go for the big time," Chris remarks.

"We're not," Luke replies. "But most bands still compile their own recordings and some of them do really well by just selling to the public after a gig. It doesn't have to be big, but if you get even ten or twenty per cent of sales on your recordings that's nothing to sniff at."

"True," Marcus says. "I've seen it done lots of times."

"Okay," says Luke, "so how about we start rehearsing once a week on Tuesdays and then we see how we go when we start the gig?"

"Why see how we go?" I ask.

"There's a chance the audience might not like us and we'll get smaller audiences that may not cover all the costs for putting on the gig, paying for roadies to set up, the studio hire, and the hiring of the Odeon venue itself. Unless we fill the place by at least eighty per cent, I can tell you that the gig won't last for long."

"Man, this is making my head spin," Chris exclaims but brightens up as the food arrives.

"So now you know why I chose not 'to go for it' in terms of making it to the top; too much pressure. If I were twenty again I'd probably try, but not now, not at my age."

I pat Luke's hand. "Don't say that. You're not exactly ancient, you know?"

"Well, sometimes it feels that way," Luke winks at me meaningfully and I turn away so he won't see the colour on my face.

Marcus nods while trying to swallow a bite of his pizza. "I can relate," he says once he can talk. "I'm turning thirty-one this year and already I can tell the difference in terms of energy and fitness. No matter how much I work out I just don't feel the same as I did in my twenties."

Chris and I glance at each other. We're the youngest in the group. "This is why you should have more sex, man," Chris addresses Marcus. "Once you reach a certain age it's going to get more difficult to get it up."

I almost spit out the coffee I have in my mouth and I don't dare turn to steal a peek at Luke, seeing as he's the eldest in our group, but I hear him laugh and I'm relieved he doesn't find the comment offensive. Meanwhile, Marcus slaps the back of Chris's head and the poor guy almost chokes on his pizza. I pour some water for him.

"So... so... sorry," Chris manages to apologise after he swallows his food.

"Don't worry, Chris," Luke replies. "We all have to grow up and get older."

I keep eating and look down at my plate. This kind of conversation between guys can sometimes turn into a pissing contest, but I know both Luke and Marcus are mature enough not to get drawn into it.

Luke finishes his meal and signals the waiter for the bill. "Rain's stopped so we better get going. This one's on me, guys," he adds when he sees us all reaching for our wallets. "So we meet at the studio on Tuesday for our first session, say early afternoon at two?"

We agree at once seeing as we all need a sleep-in, plus I want to get home to work out a routine for Dora's personal health needs and I imagine Luke will want to keep working on his compositions. Dora already offered the parlour from where he can work, plus he'll have access to the piano as well.

In the early evening, Luke and I are going through some music scores in the parlour when Dora walks in. "Hi darlings, I'm back," she calls out and goes to the kitchen. I leave Luke working and follow Dora. "How was it?"

Dora fills a glass of water to take some pills. "Exhausting but fun. After we finished for the day we had an early dinner at the pub with Tom, and then he and Helen dropped me off.

"We're going to open in two weeks' time and we've already shortlisted three boys, all gay, all extremely good looking, and even Helen couldn't keep herself from admiring them," Dora smiles. "Oh well, I'm off to bed now, dear. I've done enough for today and while it was great fun I still need my beauty sleep."

"I'll talk to you tomorrow," I say. "Have a good night."

Dora surprises me with a motherly kiss. "Thank you, Sam, for making my life so full again."

I get emotional and try to hold back tears of happiness for Dora. Luckily, she doesn't see me getting weepy because she already left the kitchen.

I'm tired myself due to the move plus all the excitement of today so I tell Luke I'm going to bed. He puts aside the music score he's been working on. "I'll come, too. It's been a long few days with the move and everything else."

Once in bed, we look around our new bedroom and it's like we're in a luxury hotel. There's so much more room and everything looks just right, and I'm back in my home—well, not mine—but what I consider to be the only loving home I ever lived in. Sometimes, I'm afraid I'm going to suddenly wake up under a cold portico somewhere in London, wrapped in my ragged sleeping bag and holding on to my guitar case. I shiver despite the heating in the room and I shift closer into Luke's arms.

"What's wrong, my love?"

"Don't mind me, just ghosts from the past."

His arms tighten around me. "I get those, too, and I try to ignore them. Life can break a person, but if they're fortunate and their luck changes life can be transformed. We happen to be a good example of that."

"I know, but that's the scary part. It's like my luck will change for the worst and I'll be alone and homeless again. I often have vivid nightmares about this."

Luke caresses my hair and his touch is comforting. "You were alone once and then you found Declan, even if it only lasted a short time, but he gave you the strength to carry on and you did. You got on with life and managed to make a living and then you came here to board at Dora's and much later we met. And now you have so many people around who care for you: the boys in the band, Helen and Tom, Dora, all the people who show up to see you play at our gigs, plus we're now moving onto a bigger gig at the Odeon and above all, remember you'll always have me."

"I know, but I'm so happy with my life these days that I think something awful will come along and ruin it. Remember, nature abhors a vacuum."

Luke gently kisses my lips and says, "Nobody knows what's in store for any of us so the best thing we can do is live for the moment. I try to live my life this way and I don't ask for too much out of life, either. I think life's difficult enough without making it more complex. The only thing I hope for is that we can stay together for the rest of our lives."

I feel Luke's love flow into my heart and I relax in the safety of his arms. I have to let the bad thoughts go and live for the moment instead of wasting time thinking about things that may never happen.

Chapter 54 - Robert

<u>1961/62, London, England</u>

It's no good! It all failed! I lost my Clara!

Mike came over after work to tell me the whole thing blew up in our group's face because the guard they bribed was being watched closely by the Stasi and the other guards were ordered to shoot him on the spot while Clara was taken away alive on the account that she was heavily pregnant at seven months and was the holder of a legit UK passport.

It took months of waiting until we could be sure the East German guard agreed to a bribe to let Clara cross the checkpoint into West Berlin. What we didn't know was that somehow one of the other guards found out what was happening, and he reported the whole thing to the Stasi.

When Clara went to the checkpoint along with a small group of other people in order to cross over to the West, all hell broke loose and the shooting started. The guard who was bribed by us was killed with a single bullet to the back of the head while the people in the group, who were all escapees, were machine-gunned, totally riddled with bullet holes.

One of our escape assistants managed to catch sight of Clara, however, and he confirmed she was taken away. It seemed her UK passport saved her life, but not enough that they would let her go. The Stasi made up their minds that Clara was in league with the group of escapees and responsible for bribing the guard. They could have shot her on the spot just for helping out other escapees, but for some reason the fact that she was pregnant seemed to stop the guards from shooting her and the Stasi was heard to say they would take her in for questioning.

Mike told me not to despair and that we may still get Clara out if the UK Embassy put pressure on the East Germans with the fact that they know Clara was illegally held back, but I don't see these devils letting her go. It will be a miracle if Clara and the baby survive in the first place. God knows where she is and what they're doing to her. She'll probably be locked up and left to rot. Oh God! Why Clara? Why? She did nothing wrong!

Now, I can barely write while taking a whole bunch of Librium tablets and washing them down with whiskey as I finish this journal entry. I'm home alone and maybe I'll die when I finish downing all the tablets. I've lost all hope and I'm sure I've lost my Clara.

Mike found me on the floor two days later. He called the ambulance and I spent a night in hospital, even though I vomited before I passed out from the Librium and alcohol, so the tablets didn't kill me nor did the vomit choke me, but I would've been better off if either of them had taken my life.

I lost my gig at the 100 Club and no amount of begging from Mike to Steve saved me from this one. I really don't care. In the past few months, while waiting for Clara's rescue, plus all the anxiety I suffered as a result of Clara's situation, I started to depend more and more on Librium and I never stopped drinking. I knew I was losing my lip, but I didn't care about that, either. All I could think about was Clara, and I held on to the hope that she would make it back to me.

As time went by without any good news, however, I closed the bakery business, gave up our rental home and moved into a cheap boarding house. With only my small savings in the bank this was all I could afford. Besides, I didn't see myself sticking around in this world for long.

Mike still looks in on me and frequently finds me drunk, drugged, or both. He tries to lend me comfort and hope, but I don't listen, I just nod my head and say very little.

Chapter 55 - Samantha

<u>1986, London, England</u>

Dora and Helen open the store the second week after the New Year. The place, which is small but well configured with rows of hanging space, is located in Soho and not too far away from the rehearsal studios where Luke and I meet with the boys on Tuesdays.

"We're a bit early," I say when we arrive. "The boys won't be here for at least a half hour."

"And?" Luke searches for the studio keys in his jeans pocket.

"And I thought we should drop in at the store for a few minutes to check it out, now that all is unpacked, and see how Dora and Helen are settling in. Besides, I want to meet this 'gorgeous creature', as they call their new employee. Dora told me the store's busy already and I wonder whether it's the guy or the costumes that attract the crowd."

Luke laughs. "Look at you, mooning over a guy who's not even interested in women."

"So?" I say defiantly. "I still want to go."

Luke shakes his head with a smile and returns the keys to his pocket. "Okay, let's go; but only for a short while. I can't believe you women, slobbering over a so-called gorgeous creature."

"Oh, shut up!" I tell him, grabbing his hand to hurry his step. Within minutes, we arrive and notice quite a number of customers checking out the merchandise. I head for Dora and Helen and give them both a hug. "Just dropping in for a few minutes to wish you well. We're down the road today, rehearsing at the studio, but I just had to come and see you." Then I lower my voice and Luke shakes his head, trying not to laugh. "So where is he?" I ask the ladies.

Dora points her chin towards a tall, lithe, muscular young man who is currently helping a customer. "Enrique!" she calls out. "When you have a moment I have some people I want you to meet."

Enrique looks like he's from Latino extraction, with dark brown hair in gentle waves that run down his brow and tawny skin with large hazel eyes, plus his perfect body is to die for. When he approaches us I can't help but blush at the rush of sex appeal he exudes. I don't dare glance Luke's way in case he sees the admiration in my eyes.

Dora makes the introductions. "This is my adopted daughter, Sam, and Luke is her partner. Sam and Luke, this is Enrique, but we call him Ricky." Ricky shakes hands with Luke and I steal a quick glance at Luke's reaction, but he remains neutral and I can't read him. Damn!

The young man is as tall as Luke and seems to be in his early twenties. The girls sure picked the right guy! Then, to my surprise, Ricky picks up my hand and kisses the back of it as a gentleman would do. "It is a pleasure, Señorita Sam. Dora told me all about your incredible musical talent and I am honoured to meet you." His sexy Spanish accent lends more allure to his smoothness.

"Oh," I reply humbly, "it's only a band."

"That's not what I hear, Sam. Dora tells me all about your classical music plus your band, and now you will perform at the Odeon? Wow!" He suddenly looks over Luke's shoulder at a customer waiting for service and Ricky excuses himself. "Forgive me, but I must attend to a customer." He throws Luke a quick glance. "I'm sorry we don't have time to talk, but I hear you're very talented, too. Lovely to meet you both." Ricky moves gracefully past us and once he's out of earshot Dora and Helen laugh, especially at Luke's red face.

Dora says, "So you've been treated to the style and finesse of Enrique Reyes from Puerto Rico; and no, he's not related to Ricky Martin."

Luke grabs my hand and starts to pull me out of the store as he addresses Dora and Helen. "Ladies, we're running late for rehearsal. Congratulations on your opening and I'm sure we'll see you soon."

Out in the street Luke lets go of my hand. "So *Señorita Sam with the incredible musical talent*, are you ready to do some work now?"

I burst into laughter. "Oh my God! You're so funny. Don't tell me Ricky got to you and you're jealous? After all, didn't he dismiss you by saying '*I hear you're very talented, too*' as if you were an afterthought? But the way he was checking you out when no one was looking! Well, I think he found you attractive."

Luke doesn't reply, he simply rolls his eyes and grabs my hand again as he hurries his pace towards the studio, and it looks like he's not going to give me the satisfaction of teasing him further.

During rehearsal, Luke puts us through the paces like there's no tomorrow. We play a whole list of new songs, including covers plus two of Luke's compositions, and by six in the evening we're spent. To top things off, it starts to rain heavily just as we lock up at the studio and Luke suggests we go and get something to eat. The nearest place is the café where we had lunch after meeting with Pierre. We sit at the same corner table and order pizza again with much needed coffee and mineral water.

Once the coffees arrive we sit back and top up our caffeine intake with pleasure. "We have a date for the Odeon gig," Luke announces and I'm surprised that he didn't tell me beforehand, but perhaps he forgot because of all the fuss I made about Ricky.

"When?" Marcus says.

"Last Sunday in January. So we have less than a month to get it right."

"Are we really getting roadies?" This from Chris, which earns him a slap at the back of the head from Marcus.

"Ouch!" Chris massages the back of his neck.

"The Odeon provides all the heavy gear like speakers, amplifiers, pianos and keyboards, drum kits, special lighting, and so on," Luke explains, "but the cost of all this comes out from our intake, so we're the ones paying for it."

"I thought Dave, the promoter, paid for it," I remark.

"Well, in a way he does because he gets a percentage of what we make, and if we don't make enough the cost will eat into his cut." Luke finishes his coffee and signals the waiter for another round seeing as we've all finished our drinks. He then turns to Chris. "We're getting a couple of roadies to help us transport our own equipment and to pack up when we're finished and bring all the stuff back to the pub. This is a big gig, and I think we're going to be totally exhausted by the time we're done so I suggest we keep fit, get enough sleep, and if you fancy an alcoholic drink keep it to a minimum."

We're really going to need all our energy for the upcoming gigs, and I have to watch it most of all because I also have the Classical Cocktails gig twice weekly. This reminds me to finalise arrangements for Dora's personal/health care assistance. I've been thinking about it and I know I won't be able to cope with everything, plus Dora will need a regular domestic helper as I won't be around much.

The following day, I telephone the domestic/personal service agency I used to book for Dora on the odd occasion when I was going to be away, but this time I ask for a part-time helper to cover four half days per week. The helper will focus on assistance with bathing and other personal tasks. Luke and I can do the grocery shopping and any errands that come up, but we'll get the helper to do extra hours if Luke and I need to travel. As for medical appointments, these I will deal with personally, but I'll pay extra to the domestic helper if Dora needs to be accompanied to an appointment on occasions when I can't be there.

After I make the booking for the helper, I put a day aside to spend time with the person and take them through the routine that's expected for Dora's care, but the agency manager calls me back a few minutes after we ring off. "Miss Kelly, I've been looking over your mother's records and we have someone on our books who has worked with Miss Brand in the past. You may remember a girl by the name of Diane?"

"I vaguely remember her," I reply. "She's in her twenties, slim, blonde hair?"

"That's the one. Diane's in her last year of completing a nursing degree, but she now intends on completing the last year of it over two years instead. It's a financial thing for her so I thought this would work out really well for Miss Brand, having the same helper for at least two years and for Diane, who enjoyed working with your mother. They got on quite well, according to the feedback I received in the past from Miss Brand and Diane. What do you think?"

"I think that's an excellent idea, in which case may I leave it with you to coordinate between my mother and Diane in terms of days and times? I'll ensure I'm here to meet Diane on her first day and take her through the routine again. As for payment, please send all invoices directly to me."

We chat about some other details for a few moments and then the manager makes an appointment for Diane to meet with me the following week. I feel relieved and happy about the arrangement, knowing Dora will always have someone around the place in addition to Luke and me. Regarding the store, Helen's due to give birth around March or April so Dora will need to make her own arrangements with Helen to cover work hours, but I leave this to them.

The day of our debut at the Hammersmith Odeon dawns with me rushing to the bathroom to throw up, but as there's nothing in my stomach I dry heave instead. I suddenly feel so frightened that I think I'm going to faint or die, and I cry. This is how Luke finds me in the dark, kneeling on the floor with my head in the toilet and hyperventilating.

He switches on the light and immediately throws a bath towel over my shivering body before he scoops me in his arms and takes me back to bed where I sit more comfortably with a bucket he places on my lap in case I vomit.

He then kneels down in front of me and rubs my arms, legs, and parts of my body, trying to warm me up and get the circulation going. "Just take slow breaths, my love," he comforts me in a gentle voice. "Listen to me, Sam: you're okay, this is just nerves and they'll settle. Try to slow down your breathing. I'm here for you, babe. I promise you'll be fine."

The soothing tone of his voice starts to get through to me as is his caring touch. I feel my stomach muscles release some of the fear and the nausea seems to ease a little. Luke sits next to me on the bed while he keeps holding me, his warmth connecting with my body, helping me to relax a little more. He keeps talking in his reassuring way and softly massaging my upper back as we sit in the soft light of the bedside lamp, and after a while I relax fully against his body. The nausea disappears and Luke lies down with me, spooning me and cradling me in his arms. He now speaks almost in a whisper, still reassuring me, and my breathing returns to normal after a while and I feel safely cocooned in the warmth of his being.

I don't know how long we stay like this, but I see daylight starting to seep through the edge of the window blinds and I can see it is dawn. Luke is so still that I think he's asleep, but the moment he feels me move he kisses the nape of my neck and whispers, "How are you, my love?"

I slowly turn around to face him and remain within the circle of his arms. "I'm so sorry," I say. "I don't know what came over me."

"Don't worry about it. You just had an anxiety attack, just like the night I gave you that bit of Valium to calm you down."

"Well, luckily you didn't have to give me any today and at least this time around I have hours to prepare myself until gig time."

"You'll be fine. We're all in this together and nothing will go wrong, just remember that." He kisses me gently. "How about I go and make some chamomile tea and toast and we can have breakfast in bed?"

I nod. "That would be lovely, thank you."

Luke gets out of bed and puts on his dressing robe, but I grab his hand for a moment and he turns to me. "What is it?"

"I just want to say I love you."

———○———

By early evening, I'm anxious again but more in control with the band around me. We are driven on a bus to the Hammersmith Odeon by a couple of roadies sent by Dave. The vehicle has tinted windows and space for storage of equipment and wardrobe. We have our own musical instruments and thankfully all the heavy equipment is provided by the venue.

Tom's travelling with us and so are Helen and Ricky. Helen insists on helping us with dress and make-up, even though we don't necessarily need it, but she says we must dress for the lights to bring out the colours, especially faces and hair. Ricky agrees and tells us about the time he worked wardrobe and make-up for a few bands. We, the band, say nothing as Helen is six months pregnant by now and we don't wish to upset her by refusing her suggestion even though she's not one to get anxious or upset.

"Dora wanted to tag along," Helen says to me during a private moment, "but I didn't think it wise at her age. I hope I did right."

I reassure her. "You did, thank you. Classical Cocktails is one thing, but this is totally different."

Upon arrival at the venue we are greeted by Dave, and he gets one of his assistants to escort us to the dressing rooms, the main one which is full of clothing Helen and Ricky brought over from the store. Meanwhile, Ricky sets up a make-up area. "Okay, who's first?" he calls out when he's ready, but we're all too busy trying to organise ourselves while Tom brings in a whole box of bottled water and some finger food to keep us going during our breaks.

The whole place is like pandemonium with people coming and going, setting things up, checking equipment, and so on. I sometimes feel I'm going to lose it, but each time this happens I glance towards Luke and my sense of calm is restored.

"I'll do you first," Ricky suddenly appears by my side and grabs my hand, leading me to the make-up/wardrobe room. He then stands looking at me, fingers on chin, thinking. "Hmm," he shakes his head. "No, darling, this just won't do. What were you thinking? Blue jeans and an old T-shirt?" He tells me to sit in front of the make-up mirror. "Yes, we'll have to work on this hair and your lovely face, too. I'll just be a moment."

I take a look at my face in the mirror and it's so pale that I start to warm up to the idea of make-up, plus my hair is all over the place. Usually, it falls to my shoulders in natural waves, but this evening I look like I just got out of bed.

Ricky returns holding black jeans, a black satin singlet and a black see-through shirt with long sleeves and silver braiding down the front. "You're a size eight, right?" I nod and he goes on, "And I know you rockers love black, although I would pick something totally different for you. Still, at least the silver braiding will stand out when the lights are shining on you; and darling, I love your leather boots! At least they're cool."

My favourite boots are mid-calf, made with soft leather and held up by thick criss-cross boot laces. I've had them for years and always wear them at gigs. They're my lucky boots. I change into the clothes Ricky chooses for me and I have to agree with him that this is a massive improvement. He then applies make-up to my face, which gets rid of the pale look and he enhances my eyes so they look enormous while my lips are made up to look plump in a sexy, muted wine colour.

When I look in the mirror I'm amazed at the transformation and just at that moment Luke walks in and does a double take when he sees me. "Who is this incredibly gorgeous creature?" He comes over to me and kisses my hand in case he mars my make-up. He then turns to Ricky. "And you, what have you done with my lovely lady?"

Ricky gives me a dreamy look. "I've made her even lovelier. You like?"

I can tell Luke has to hand it to Ricky. He changed my appearance so much with a few strokes of his magic that I can't believe it. "You're an artist," Luke says, and means it. "I never before appreciated what make-up and wardrobe people can do, but from now on I take my hat off to them all."

Ricky's thrilled at Luke's words and he pounces on him. "In that case, you won't mind me touching up a few things here and there for you? I mean, you and Sam are the leading stars of this show and tonight all lights will be on you."

Luke doesn't seem too sure, especially when Ricky says 'touching up a few things'. I feel like laughing, but I stay silent instead; no need to horrify my man even though I'm wearing a secret smile in my eyes. Luke doesn't even see me and instead addresses Ricky, but he doesn't get too far. "Well, I'm dressed already and..."

"No, no," Ricky interrupts. "Your black clothing and boots complement Sam's, but there's too much black between the two of you. So how about you wear a light coloured waistcoat over your black shirt? As for your hair, well... it's divine and if anything I'd like to mess it up so it has that dishevelled look. Lastly, if I may use some make-up to take the shine off your face and slightly enhance your features, you'll look just right. Is that okay?"

I can see Luke is floundering and looking a little worried, but I nod his way and he gives in. "Why not?" he says. "You're right about the lights and I have to agree we all need some powder on our faces because it's going to get hot out there with all those lights on us."

I can tell Ricky has a bit of a crush on Luke, but he knows he's barking up the wrong tree. Despite this, he's genuinely in his element when he says, "Come with me and get your two boys to join us, they'll need a bit of an overhaul, too."

The rest of the night is a blur with excellent music, singing, incredible lighting effects, the venue at full capacity with people dancing and cheering, sometimes singing along with us and at other times whistling and applauding like mad.

I don't feel myself performing; playing and singing come automatically to me so I focus on the crowd and they feel the connection. They get as close as they can to the stage, their hands reaching out to touch ours and we reciprocate while others yell out the name of a song they'd like us to play and we comply where we can. At other times, we play something we like and encourage the crowd to sing and dance.

All in all, the atmosphere is supercharged with incredible energy, emotion, and elation from both the audience and our band. I feel like I'm on top of the world and it looks magic from up here.

Chapter 56 - Robert

1962, London, England

I'm writing in this journal for the first time in about a year. My memory of past events is very hazy, but I do remember some things. I've been in a detox facility for the past ten months or so, ever since the last news of Clara came through from Berlin. She was killed.

One of the rescuers in Mike's group discovered this news via informants on the East Berlin side. It seems the guards took Clara alive the night of the planned escape merely for show. After all, even the East Germans didn't want to be seen killing a pregnant woman in public. It was alleged, however, that once behind closed doors Clara was executed immediately.

This was all Mike learned about the series of events on that terrible night. And though at first we doubted the killing had taken place, we went on thinking the British Embassy would somehow intervene and get Clara out, but it seems we were all far too naïve. I mean, who cares about one pregnant woman being killed in the middle of the Cold War?

Mike was very supportive of me and I couldn't have asked for a better friend, but even he could not stop me from attempting to take my life. Instead, the job fell to the landlady who found my unconscious body halfway up the staircase leading to my room early one winter's morning, so she called the ambulance and the police.

I was told later by Mike that I'd been found sprawled on the stairs with an empty bottle of booze and a few tablets scattered on the floor. Apparently, I was more than half gone, but somehow the ambulance officers revived me and when I finally rejoined the world I found myself at the detox facility.

HEROES

Going through detox was like hell on earth and I lost much of my memory, so much so that at one stage I couldn't even picture what Clara looked like, but I didn't want to think of Clara because thinking of her only brought back the nightmare that culminated in the destruction of our lives; only I'm still occupying space in the land of the living while she's probably off with the angels, if there is such a thing.

I'm in recovery now and I've been told that in a few weeks I can resume my life once again, but I'm horrified at the prospect of leaving this place. Although I don't remember much of what happened to me here, I do remember feeling a sense of safety and peace starting to grow slowly within me, and I believe this is due to the many visits I've had from Mike and, most recently, his sister, Peggy.

I don't know why Peggy comes to visit, but as my senses begin to recover so does my attraction to this woman. Peggy is a singer with a regular gig at a club in Soho and all her talk about music, songs, and the club scene brings to mind my years as a muso from way back in 1945 at the Victory Club in Berlin plus my years in New York, and finally my time at the 100 Club in London. Most of these memories make me feel like there is hope for me to keep on living. I no longer wish to take my life, even though I would give anything to have Clara by my side, but if I choose to live I must build another life, one without my loving Clara.

My mind is still muddled and I realize I will never be a muso again, not when I lost my lip and my dexterity, but there are other things I can focus on while rebuilding my life: a new job, volunteering in Mike's group to rescue people from the East Germans, and perhaps even a life with Peggy, an attractive tall woman with long brown hair and hazel eyes.

Chapter 57 - Samantha

<u>1986, London, England</u>

The Odeon gig finishes at just past midnight and good thing, too, because we started playing at eight and only had a ten minute break after the first two hours. Unlike our gig at the pub, this one runs strictly to the program, but if it goes over the agreed finish time proceeds will come out of our intake in order to pay for the overtime of roadies, sound technicians, etc.

This is a taste of the big business picture Luke sometimes talks about. At the pub, we're fairly free and can have as many breaks as we like and often go overtime just because the audience wants more encores or simply because we get carried away and keep playing a few more songs, and we're also just as free to cut back if we're too tired to continue.

This is the flexibility that comes with the smaller gigs as opposed to the ones that host the big names, and the one thing I learned this evening is the incredible high one gets from performing for a huge crowd. Of course, a capacity of five thousand people is not much when compared to the really big acts that attract a stadium size crowd of up to one hundred thousand, and fully outdoor concerts in public places such as parks, which can attract even larger audiences. I freaked out before the Odeon gig, but just imagining performing before a crowd of up to one hundred thousand or more would totally terrify me.

"What was the largest crowd you ever performed for?" I ask Luke while he's showering and I'm at the bathroom sink washing off my make-up.

"Well, that goes back to when I used to live in Germany in my early twenties. I was with an up and coming band at the time and we played to a crowd of around sixty thousand. Why do you ask?"

"Thinking of my anxiety attack yesterday, before our debut Odeon gig, I was just thinking how scary it would be to perform for so many people, and the crowd we performed for was only five thousand," I remark. "Imagine what kind of drugs you'd have to shove down my throat if we were performing for a really huge crowd. I just don't know how these famous musicians do it."

Luke finishes showering. "You jumping in?"

"Yes, thanks."

He wraps a towel around his waist and while I enter the shower cubicle he goes to the sink to brush his teeth. "You won't have to worry about large crowds, but I can tell you from my limited experience that once you perform for a huge crowd the whole thing's pretty much the same as performing for a smaller one; in the end you still have to please the crowd, whether large or small."

"I guess so," I reply while rinsing off the shampoo out of my hair.

Once in our pyjamas we sit in bed, but it seems neither of us is sleepy despite the amount of energy we spent. "It's almost two in the morning," I say. "How about a cup of chamomile? It might help us sleep."

"I'll get it," Luke says and goes to the kitchen.

Meanwhile, I can't seem to relax and yet the whole gig thing is over. My anxiety is gone and I'm relieved that I didn't make a fool of myself. But what surprises me most is the actual high I got from the crowd, the atmosphere, the music, the lights, everything around me. Is this how it's supposed to feel, I wonder?

Luke returns with a pot of tea and two mugs. "If you're hungry say so now while I'm still out of bed."

"No, thanks."

He gets into bed and fills our mugs with the tea. I hold mine between my hands and warm my fingers.

"Something's the matter," Luke remarks. "I can feel it, so tell me."

"Nothing important. It's just that I can't make sense of why I'm on such a high and I can't seem to come back down."

"That's how it is," Luke replies, "and this is why a lot of famous people turn to drugs; it's the only way they can cope. I never made it to the top, but I was getting close and then I got caught up in the cycle of drugs in order to function. I used drugs like cocaine and barbiturates plus a few others; then, there was alcohol, pot, and so on, until I got to the point where I wasn't coping at all. I was too young to deal with the pressure of going for fame and fortune, and I discovered I didn't even like who I was as a person.

"I told you I was choosy with women and didn't sleep around, so just imagine when all these women, and oftentimes men, wanted to have sex with me; I had to steer around them and find ways not to offend them, especially the ones with all the power. And on top of this, I was performing in concerts with large crowds and I had to please managers, agents, record executives and other VIPs, not to mention the fact that I had to push myself more and more if I was going to make it to the top. I worked hard and played hard, but eventually all this started pushing me to the edge."

I'm shocked by Luke's revelation. "But you said you didn't sleep around, and as for sex with men, what's the deal with that?"

Luke doesn't answer my question, it's like he's in another world, or perhaps he didn't take in what I said. "Luke, are you okay?"

He turns to me as if he suddenly remembers I'm in the same room with him and he regards me for a few moments like he's trying to make up his mind about something.

"Luke?" I say again.

He finishes his tea and sets the mug on the bedside table. "There's something I haven't told you. In fact, this is something I never told anyone."

I sense whatever he didn't tell me is something bad and I suddenly feel my stomach churning with dread. I remain silent and wait for him to speak.

Luke doesn't meet my eyes; instead, he fixes his eyes to a point on the wall opposite our bed and says, "When you asked me earlier about the biggest crowd I ever performed for, all my memories of that time came rushing back. I've never been able to share this with anybody, but we've grown so close now that I know in my heart I can tell you what happened." He takes a moment to gather his thoughts and then continues talking, "Remember when I told you there was a time in my life when I was into drugs but then managed to get myself clean?" I nod. "Then, there was the time I gave you that Valium prior to our Eclectic debut, even though I regretted doing it, and more recently I was so horrible to you when I saw you taking those pills from the waiter and I accused you of being high because your pupils were dilated."

I reply, "I remember, but how does this tie in with you giving up drugs?"

Luke takes a deep breath as if he's trying to find the right words for what he has to say, but in a moment of what seems to be frustration for him because he doesn't seem to know where to start, he suddenly blurts out: "I was raped."

I feel as if someone punched me in the stomach and I almost drop the tea mug I've been holding all this time. I place it on my bedside table and turn around on the bed so I'm sitting facing Luke rather than beside him. "You... you were raped, like sodomy?"

Luke avoids my gaze, his eyes still focusing on the wall opposite the bed, but he throws a quick glance my way and I don't know whether to grasp his hand, throw my arms around him or simply let him be. This is the last thing I expected to hear and I'm not sure how to handle it. In the end, I just give him time and stay as I've been, silent and listening.

"It happened during the time I was doing drugs when I was with the band in Germany and where we performed for that huge crowd I told you about. I was so young, and my dreams of fame and fortune were the only things I cared about. I was so set on making it, no matter what.

"At the time, we played a few cities around Germany and the crowds loved us, and we knew we were on our way up. Our agent was fighting off the offers for cutting an album and he waited for the best offer to present itself. There was also talk of a European tour, which would eventually take us to America. It was my dream come true and we were so close to it that I could literally taste it." Luke pauses for a few moments, still with his focus on the wall. I remain silent, waiting for him to go on, and after a couple of minutes he speaks again.

"When we returned to Berlin from the German tour, we were invited to a huge welcome back party at someone's mansion; supposedly, this was the record producer's place, the one our agent thought would take us to fame—and it was there that it happened." Luke pauses yet again before he says, "The place was full of people: musicians, record executives, managers, agents, media people, VIPs, and groupies looking to cling onto us.

"There were four of us in the band. I was the lead singer and everyone wanted to talk to me that night—I was the up and coming star, their 'golden boy', as they called me. So we're talking and drinking with some record producers and agents, and these guys were the real deal. They had the money, the power, and they liked our style, so our future was pretty much secured.

"I was so excited that I felt sky high that night, especially after having snorted a good amount of cocaine. Meanwhile, the booze kept doing the rounds and we were pretty much toasting to our success with every drink and getting wasted. I can't even remember how much I drank, plus I was still really flying with the effects of the cocaine. I felt like I could do anything; I was young, talented, and I thought I was invincible.

"Everybody was congratulating me on my performance and already talking contracts and stardom for the group, and next thing I know, like in some strange erotic dream, I found myself in a very large semi-lit room, sprawled on a huge bed covered in purple satin sheets—I remember the colour to this day and I cringe every time I see purple—and then, from the corner of my eye, I saw other people sprawled on beds and sofas scattered all over. It was mainly couples having sex: young girls with old men, men with power that could make things happen for them; young men with older men; girls with other girls while men watched them perform like sexual slaves; and then there were some threesomes and orgies with a larger number of people and some filthy acts that I can't talk about and that you can't even begin to imagine.

"I was so out of it that I thought I was watching some kind of horror porno movie or maybe I was trapped in Dante's inferno. I was so confused, and yet I knew I had to get out of there fast. But I couldn't move. It was like I was trapped by some kind of weight and my muscles just wouldn't work. And then I felt a number of hands lifting me slightly and I found myself being flipped face down on the bed. I felt more relaxed, thinking I was here to sleep off the drugs. But then I felt these guys, three or four of them, touching me all over and taking off my clothes. I felt the coolness of the room on my skin and knew I was totally naked and yet, I still had no strength to get up and leave. I felt so weak I may as well have been a kitten."

I feel tears running down my face for the beautiful and naive boy Luke must've been back then, and I let the tears run, I don't wipe them away. I want to share in Luke's pain and feel it along with him. Luke finally turns to me with his own tears pooling in his eyes, looking lost and at the same time terrified. I shift closer and take him in my arms, holding him against me.

His voice is muffled as he holds tightly onto me with his face buried against my neck. "These guys, they held me down. I couldn't escape what was coming, and at that very moment I realised it was my fault for putting myself in a situation where my mind was befuddled by drugs and my body had no strength to fight against them.

"Each of the men took turns at raping me; I don't know how many times, but it was brutal, and each time I was penetrated it felt like I was being torn inside. The pain was horrific, and yet I couldn't even scream for help because someone was holding my face down against the mattress so I was barely able to breathe. And for a moment, I prayed they would put me out of my misery by suffocating me, but they didn't... they just laughed."

My tears are running freely now and even falling on Luke's shoulder as I tighten my embrace around him, wishing I could erase all the memories of the atrocity he suffered. I have no words that can make things any better; all I can do is keep on listening and holding onto him.

"By the time they were done with me, I was a mess of blood and could barely move after they left. I must've passed out because the only thing I remember is being in an ambulance on my way to hospital." And here Luke breaks down like a child, crying with deep sobs for the young boy who lost his soul that night; and then he whispers: "They raped me so savagely that it took two operations and over a year to recover."

I'm still speechless, appalled, aghast, and I feel goose bumps covering me. What does one say to something like this? It breaks my heart that the love of my life had to endure this terrible torture, and yet he blames himself for what happened, just like many rape victims believe they brought it on upon themselves.

I feel a burning hatred for these monsters that took advantage of someone so young, innocent, and promising. I want to scream out in fury and kill those responsible. I want to have the power to erase the horrible hurt and trauma of Luke's experience, but I'm powerless. I can only be here and hope that my love for him can at least start the healing process.

I gently get Luke to lie back on the bed and I lie down with him, my arms wrapped around him, protecting him from the awful memories that he's lived with all this time. I kiss his face softly, like the wings of a butterfly, and my hand caresses his hair back from his face, drying his tears along the way.

So much more becomes clear now when Luke says he doesn't want fame and fortune and that being a lone wolf puts him in charge of his own future. Then, there's his attitude towards drugs, one-night stands with strangers, and so on. These are the things that can land someone in big trouble, especially if they're vulnerable at the hands of evil; and this also explains Luke's involvement in MFF, an organisation where he can do some good to help those who cannot help themselves, just as Luke couldn't help himself in his own youth, and perhaps by doing this rescue work his soul will heal in time.

Thinking back on my own life, the bad foster homes, the abuse, living on the streets in fear of being attacked, the drugs I did, and more, I can relate to some of the pain Luke has had to live with, but I never imagined just how much.

Luke falls asleep in my arms, totally exhausted, but I can't relax after learning about his harrowing experience, so I count my blessings instead. I thank my lucky stars that I had Declan to protect me for a while; then I was with Dora, and now there are Tom and Helen, Chris and Marcus, and even Ricky, who is fast becoming a part of our family. With so many people around me, I feel safe and cherished and I won't have to experience abandonment like I did as a child and teenager—but most importantly, I hope no one will have to go through what Luke did. I am so blessed he came into my life and everything changed forever. Fainting by the Wall on that fateful 4th of July joined our destinies and for this I will always be grateful.

I hear Luke's calm breathing as he sleeps and then sleep finally claims me, still with my arms around my beloved.

Chapter 58 - Robert

<u>1962/65, London, England</u>

Peggy knew of a boarding house that was affordable and she took me to see it. I've been out of detox for almost a month now and have been sleeping on Mike's sofa while looking for a job.

It was tough finding work as my background is mostly musical, but once I added details of what I did in the war and my experience during the years in Berlin, there was more interest in my background from potential employers and eventually I landed a sales job for a company that dealt in homewares.

The position is that of a traveling salesman but I don't need a car, which is a good thing as I would never be able to afford one, at least not at this stage. So I commute from place to place with catalogs full of pictures of the products my company sells. The job pays a low retainer and the commission is fair, so I didn't need to think twice about it. My main goal now is to find a place to live in and start making some money.

The boarding house Peggy took me to inspect was located in my old neighborhood of Covent Garden. At first, I thought I wouldn't be able to bear living there seeing as this was where Clara and I lived happily for a long time, but the room at the boarding house was clean and quaint, and above all affordable. In the end, I decided to give it a go and knew I could always move out if I didn't like it. I started work shortly after my move to the boarding house and I slowly started to heal.

Mike and Peggy have been very supportive of me and somehow, quite without meaning to do so, I fell in love with Peggy and we got married. The whole thing happened in the space of six months or thereabouts and suddenly I found myself doing well at my job; and not long after, baby Samantha (Sam) joined our little fold. Mike found us a small house to rent in the same area and life started to make sense again.

Peggy gave up her singing gig at the club where she worked so she could look after Sam; by this time, my commissions were coming in thick and fast and my boss promoted me to area sales manager, and this job did come with a car!

I feel so blessed that I was given a second chance at life and now I'm part of a family with Mike as my brother-in-law, plus I'm still part of Mike's group of rescuers, which is something I relish doing. Helping others as I've been helped in the past is rewarding. I also have good friends like Joey and Carl, I also got to know some of Peggy's friends, and I have my little daughter.

By Christmas 1963, I felt a new man, full of hope and being able to release the bad memories that still haunt me every so often and have the power to break my heart and soul. As time passes by, however, it is becoming easier for me to deal with the ghosts of the past and I've learned to let them go and now live in the present.

The one thing I did away with is music and, though I miss that part of my life, I know I wouldn't be able to bear it as music tends to conjure up strong memories which never let one go. From time to time, however, I still get out my trumpet and play for fun to entertain little Sam. She seems very curious about the shiny instrument and when she started to talk she asked me to show her how to play. Sam obviously has the musical Kelly blood in her so I decided to teach her about music and I started her on a kid's guitar as a suitable instrument, and whenever I have spare time at home I make sure I put Sam through her lessons. She's turning out to be a fast learner. In fact, in my opinion, she's already showing signs of greatness.

Chapter 59 - Samantha

<u>1986/87, London, England</u>

Little by little I start to notice a change in Luke after revealing his dreadful experience. I'm not yet sure what that change is, but by having kept the awful memories bottled up within him for so long I can't even begin to imagine what this has done to him emotionally.

The morning after his confession he wakes me up with breakfast in bed and seems his usual cheery self after the tempest of emotions from the previous night. I decide not to ever bring up the subject, unless he wants to talk about it, so this morning is like any other morning when we have breakfast in bed and chit chat.

"You haven't told me how things are working out with Diane," Luke says as he hands me my usual coffee and brioche.

"Really well. She's only been on the job for a short time, but it looks like she and Dora are off to a good start," I reply, "and I'm happy I made the decision to engage her; it takes the load off me. Lately, I've been feeling the stress of having so much to do, especially with the Odeon gig, and even with the Classical Cocktails on two of the same nights as The Eclectics gig."

Luke regards me thoughtfully. "Interesting you should bring that up."

"How so?" I wonder if he can read my mind because lately, I've been thinking about this on a number of occasions, but I didn't discuss it with Luke as I wasn't ready to broach the subject."

"I can see you're burning the candle at both ends and this concerns me. Even Dora mentioned it not so long ago. She said you've lost more weight and I can't help thinking how much more you do than we do in the band."

"Yes, but you work just as hard, especially now with the new compositions for the Odeon gig."

"The only difference, though, is that I work in the parlour and I'm not on a deadline, but you're working to a tough schedule with set times and you're not getting enough rest."

I reach out and kiss his lips gently. "You're so sweet to care, but I don't want you to worry. We'll sort things out in time. At least Diane, being here and helping with Dora, makes a huge difference."

"True." Luke refills our coffees. "By the way, I'm sure Dora already told you; Ricky's taking over from Helen while she has the baby."

I nod. "Ricky turned out to be exactly what we needed," I remark. "He's practically taken over, you know? He clucks like a mother hen around Dora and now he's doing the same thing with Helen because it won't be long until the baby arrives." I smile. "Dora tells me she's beginning to feel a little redundant, but I know deep down inside she's relieved to have Ricky with her."

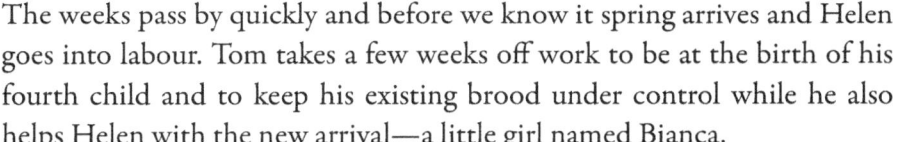

The weeks pass by quickly and before we know it spring arrives and Helen goes into labour. Tom takes a few weeks off work to be at the birth of his fourth child and to keep his existing brood under control while he also helps Helen with the new arrival—a little girl named Bianca.

Dora, Luke and I send Helen a lovely arrangement of spring flowers along with a baby hamper full of creams, lotions, bathing products, bibs, onesies, and a fluffy teddy. We also attach a card signed by us and include the names of the boys in the band, even though they probably forgot we were visiting Helen today, and more likely they were catching up on their sleep. Later, during visiting hours, we briefly visit the hospital to congratulate the proud parents and to meet Bianca, who takes after her mother, but we don't stay long as Helen and Bianca need their rest and Tom is about to take his other children home to give Helen some peace and quiet.

From this point, Ricky and Dora end up fully taking over the store plus Ricky looks after us for wardrobe and make-up, not only for the Odeon gig but now he's doing The Eclectics and Classical Cocktails, too. "That man's a marvel, isn't he?" Dora comments while we're having tea in the kitchen; Luke is in the parlour, working on his latest composition.

I smile. "Which man, Dora? Luke or Ricky?"

"Well, both, dear," Dora replies. "Ricky's practically running things and he's fabulous, but more importantly it's wonderful that Luke's in a creative state of mind again. He seemed a little morose a few weeks back. I hope everything's okay."

I should've known Dora would pick up on Luke's vibes. Even I couldn't work out whether he was happy or if by telling me his story the memories became so real again that he was struggling with them. I suddenly feel like weeping for him and I have to fake a coughing fit to explain the few tears escaping my eyes.

"Oh, are you okay?" Dora hands me a tissue.

"Just went down the wrong way," I lie. "You said morose?"

Dora gets up off her chair, closes the kitchen door and then sits next to me. "I don't want Luke to hear, but I'm a little worried about him. Is everything okay between you two?"

"It couldn't be better," I reassure her. "But why do you say morose? Luke's always cheery."

"I don't know, Sam. It's something about his demeanour. It's like the light in his eyes has dimmed somehow."

Wow! I think to myself, Dora really hit the nail on the head and then some. Why didn't I see this before? Probably because I'm too close to Luke and sometimes it's easy to miss that which is staring at us right in the face.

"I think it's the work," I lie again. "The Odeon gig's quite demanding, especially because he's the one composing all the new stuff and we still have to keep the pub gig going, too."

Dora doesn't seem convinced. "My dear, he's only recently turned thirty-six, that's hardly ancient; he's a fit man in his prime."

I have to end the subject before Dora gets suspicious. "It's just that being a musician, and lead singer at the same time, drains him much more than it does the rest of us. We do such long hours with the gigs and sometimes we even do more than we should, so we're totally exhausted by the time we're done."

Dora finally accepts my excuse. "Well, yes, that's very true, and on top of that he's composing and when he's not doing something musical he's probably playing sexual antics with you. You know, Sam, you should leave the man to come up for air and rest a while.

This sets me laughing out so loudly that the kitchen door suddenly opens and Luke sticks his head in. "Are you two all right or has someone hit the booze?"

Dora hoots with laughter and I feel so relieved that she accepted my reason for Luke's mood.

"Take a break and join us, young man," Dora says when she recovers from her laughter. She gets up and goes to the stove. "Tea or coffee, Luke?" Then she turns to me, "Chop, chop, Sam, ask your man if he wants a slice of that sinful chocolate cake we made earlier."

This brings a smile to Luke's face which reaches his eyes and my heart bursts with love for this man—my man.

"What got into the two of you this afternoon?" Luke says later when we're in our bedroom, reclining back on the pillows after we finish watching a video prior to going to sleep. "I really thought you hit the Baileys or something."

I can't tell Luke what Dora said about him losing the light in his eyes because this will only stir up past memories, so I tell him something similar to what I told Dora. "She's just worried that you're working too hard, and then she accuses us for playing 'sexual antics' and that I should give you a break."

Luke smiles. "You give *me* a break? What about me, shouldn't I give you a break, too?"

"She thinks I'm exhausting you because I'm the youngest out of the two and, therefore, I have more energy."

Now Luke really laughs. "I see. So she thinks I can't handle both my work and my fiery Irish lass."

I love seeing the laughter light up his eyes again, if only for a short while, but this gives me hope that with our deep love for each other, Luke will somehow regain peace of mind and be able to say goodbye to that terrible part of his life.

I cuddle up to him in the soft light of the bedside lamp and his arms cradle me while I run my fingers through his hair, caress his face, and feel the smooth texture of his skin. I regard him with eyes revealing my unconditional love for him and suddenly Luke's mouth swoops down on mine and we share an intimate kiss that unites our souls with the promise of a lifetime together.

———◉———

Today is the last Sunday of the month and we have our gig this evening at the Odeon. I wake just after dawn and catch the early morning sunlight shining through the side of the blinds in our bedroom. I stretch and gaze at Luke, who is still sleeping. His face is peaceful in slumber and he looks like a young boy rather than a man in his thirties, but for some reason I imagine this is how he must have looked when he was brutally attacked. He has the kind of good looks one sees in young male models and handsome boys on the verge of manhood, and this is what I think attracted those monsters to him, a promise of innocence, and not quite yet a mature man.

I shake my head as if to scatter the terrible images that conjure up in my mind at times when I think of what was done to Luke and I shiver at the evil act he was forced to endure.

"Good morning," Luke says suddenly and I jump. "Something wrong?"

I smile reassuringly. "No, it's just that you startled me. It's so early I wasn't expecting you to wake up."

Luke stretches. "Well, I was dreaming about a beautiful Irish girl and then I thought why dream about her when I can have her in real life?"

"You're quite the romantic," I remark.

He smiles with a wicked look in his eyes. "You get ahead of yourself, I'm afraid. I said I was *dreaming* about an Irish girl, but what makes you think I meant you? I knew other Irish girls, too, you know."

I pretend I'm offended. "Oh you! How dare you dream of another woman?" I throw myself on top of his body and tickle him until he begs for mercy.

"Okay, okay!" he tries to pacify me. "Of course I meant you. Please stop, you're killing me with those strong fingers of yours!"

I stop. "They're strong alright. As you know, I play both piano and guitar, and my fingers can be deadly, so watch it, mister!"

We settle down and while I go to make our usual coffee with warm brioche, Luke opens up the blinds to let the sunshine in. It's still cool out there, but we have the heating on at low and the temperature in the room is just right. When I return with our breakfast, we sit back on the pillows and dig in.

"There's something we need to discuss," Luke says after sipping some of his coffee.

I try not to think about the thoughts I had earlier of Luke's attack, and I hope everything is okay with him. "What is it?"

"Tom telephoned me yesterday," Luke says and I breathe a silent sigh of relief.

"He must be missing work rather than changing diapers," I joke.

"No, no. He's enjoying being a father again," Luke replies, "but the reason he called is because Dave contacted him about our gig at the Odeon."

This piques my curiousity. "Oh?"

"As you know, today marks our three month anniversary at the Odeon and Dave's received quite a number of reviews and write-ups about us. There's also been excellent feedback about my compositions. Tom said Dave wants us to cut an album and his sights are set on us becoming a proper group rather than one that plays covers."

I don't know what to say and from the serious tone in Luke's voice I'm guessing he's still struggling with memories of what happened in the past. I take a bite of brioche to buy some time before I respond. "How do you feel about that?"

"I never expected it to go this far. I thought of it only as a gig rather than a career, but if things take off for the band then we would have to give up all the other things we do, including a lot of our freedom."

"Then the answer is simple," I say. "We've already discussed this with Chris and Marcus and we know they're only interested in gigs rather than going in for the big time. It's also a lot of sacrifice for something that may never happen, anyway. I mean, even if we went for it we might turn out to be a flash in the pan."

"I know that."

"Then what's holding you back?"

He shrugs. "I don't know."

"I think you do, but you don't want make the decision on your own."

Luke regards me thoughtfully and after a while he says, "You're right, my love." He reaches out and takes my hand. "After what happened in the past, I promised myself I'd be free for the rest of my life. No pressure to become famous, no managers or agents pushing me into contracts and being nice to the men with the power, and so on. The money's good, of course, but at what cost to our lives?"

I squeeze his hand. "If you want me to speak freely, I will."

Luke nods. "Most definitely."

"Okay, this is what I think: I want to be free to choose what I do. I love our gig at the pub and I actually enjoy myself when we play there despite all the hard work and the long hours we put in, and no one tells us what to do. We do what we want and if we're not happy we can easily move on to some other venue. As for fame and fortune, I think we've all decided on that already—including the boys—this is not what we want. Finally, you're right in what you said some time ago about age; it takes a lot to make it to the big time and it's usually someone who starts on the road to stardom in their teens, and oftentimes they become a commodity to the powers that be rather than a true artist, and this is something I'm not prepared to do."

Luke brings me closer to him so he can hold me in his arms. "I am so thankful I met you, my love. Not many people would agree with what you just said, but you and I are of the same mind, and I'm overwhelmed at your insight and your love for me." He nuzzles me on the side of my neck and I want to melt into him, but I'm not yet finished saying my piece.

"As far as I'm concerned, my home is wherever you are. I want us to have a life together, which will hopefully be a happy one, and the rest means nothing. As long as we can make a decent living, I don't see the point in trying to make it to the top and become some kind of superstars where we can't even walk down the street because our fans will mob us. At least, that's not for me. But if this is a matter of importance to you, I'll go along with it because I love you and I want to do things together with you."

Luke says, "And this brings us back to being two lone wolves who decide to hunt in a pack and we will always hunt together, no matter what."

"Then it's decided. No regrets?"

"None whatsoever." He nuzzles me again and this time I don't hold back.

Chapter 60 - Robert

<u>1966/70, London, England</u>

Peggy and I have been happy for a number of years. Sam started primary school and from the beginning she showed all the signs of precociousness in music and in her school studies.

I still hold the same job and there is talk of a promotion, but this means more travel, plus Peggy was offered her old gig as a singer and she accepted without discussing it with me—and this is when life started to take a turn for the worst.

I had nothing against Peggy working; it wasn't like we needed the money, but she didn't want to stay at home with Sam all the time. Peggy had always been a vibrant people person and she loved working gigs in clubs and socializing.

Unfortunately, because my new job entails extensive travel, it means someone has to be at home to pick up Sam from school and look after her, and this was when the arguments began between us. I begged Peggy to stick it out for another two or three years, until I could save enough money to put down a deposit for a house, and then I would find a local job and be available in the evenings to look after Sam. Peggy wasn't happy, but she agreed when I took her on a vacation to America. While it cost me quite a lot, it was worth seeing Peggy happy again. She fell in love with New York City and its nightlife. It was also a good time for me to touch base with my old buddies from the war, and the trip was an overall success.

Sam was still quite young when we went away so she stayed with her best friend's family, the Evans, who loved Sam almost as much as they loved their own daughter. The girls were thrilled to be together and I was extremely grateful to the Evans, who really enjoyed having Sam over.

Upon our return, I thought things would be smooth sailing for a while, but it turned out Peggy wanted more: the excitement of New York and London, the singing gigs, the hobnobbing with influential people, the glamour of being involved in show business and much more, so our troubles returned and for the next couple of years it was bad between us.

Peggy and I barely spoke to each other and when we did it was to argue. I had fulfilled my end of the bargain by taking her on a very expensive trip, but once back in London she didn't want it to end. This led to us having terrible screaming matches between us, and I remember poor Sam, now six years of age, taking cover under the bed in her room. I couldn't even bring the situation to a compromise; Peggy was not interested. Even Mike offered to talk to his sister, but I asked him not to do so as this would only make her angrier.

By the beginning of 1969, I couldn't handle things any longer. Peggy took a singing gig and I hardly saw her plus I had to make arrangements for Sam to be looked after until I got home from work in the late afternoon and during the times I had to travel for work. It was then that my anxiety caught up with me again and I turned back to the only things that helped me get through—alcohol and drugs.

I don't know how I managed to look after Sam during this time; work was full on to the point where too many mistakes were made and I started to become unreliable, taking days off and missing out on appointments. As a result, the company lost patience with me and it was forced to let me go.

During this time, we lived off the savings I had put aside for the deposit on a home and we moved to a cheaper rental. Peggy was now working four nights a week and I looked after the household and Sam. One thing I managed to do was to hide from Sam how truly bad the situation had become and I made sure I never drank or took drugs in front of her.

Our financial situation grew worse as time went on but just when I thought all would soon be lost, a buddy from my army days contacted me about an opening in the company where he worked. The company, based in Chicago, was looking to open a branch office in the UK, which would give them access to the rest of Europe. They sold homewares and they wanted to know if I'd be interested in working with them on this venture. I would need to work from the US office for a while, in order to see how things worked stateside, and then be instrumental in opening the branch in the UK.

I couldn't believe my luck and I cleaned up my act immediately. Fortunately, I hadn't sunk into a hole of drugs and alcohol, as I had the first time calamity struck in my life, and even Peggy was supportive of the venture and agreed to look after Sam until I came back from America. The money was just too good to turn down and Peggy was never stupid about money; in fact, she was looking to finance a singing tour in New York City and the money my new role would pay was more than enough for her to mount a classy show.

While all this was going on, we still had our screaming matches from time to time and we both knew the marriage was not destined to work. Peggy still agreed to look after Sam until my return from the US as long as I sent her the money to start planning her show business venture. I agreed—what other choice did I have?

At the time, Sam was seven going on eight and her life changed yet again. I told her about the split-up and that Peggy would look after her until I came back from the States. I didn't go into much detail about my job as it was too complicated for a young child to understand plus I didn't want Sam asking questions about the length of time I'd be away, so I simply told her this was a 'gig' that would bring in good money and that once I returned, she and I would live together. Sam was anxious that I should return soon, but I couldn't possibly give her an exact date as I had yet to find out myself how long I was going to be in America.

During our music lessons, I used to tell Sam stories about the Victory Club and talk about the excitement of Berlin after the war, until the Wall went up and people were trapped on the East side. I promised Sam that I would take her to Berlin one day and show her around because I had a special love for that city, and I told her that if we ever became separated in life, no matter where we were in the world, we should meet by the Wall on July 4th, American Independence Day.

In retrospect, I don't know how much of what I said will stay in Sam's memory. She'd only just turned eight when I went off and left her with Peggy. I felt torn up about having to leave my little girl behind, but when I return, hopefully in a few months, I intend to take Sam on vacation to Berlin—just us, father and daughter.

Chapter 61 - Samantha

1986/89, London, England

Luke and I get together with Dave rather than bothering Tom, who is still on leave. We meet at Sunflower Café the day after one of our Odeon gigs. The place is quiet and once we order our coffees, Luke leads the conversation seeing as he has been dealing with both Tom and Dave from the beginning of this venture.

After a few minutes of casual chit chat while we sip our coffees, Luke finally brings up the subject of our meeting. "I haven't had a chance to talk to Tom about our response to your offer, Dave; he's still off on leave."

"It seems becoming a father again is keeping Tom extra busy. How many is it now, four kids?"

"That's right," Luke confirms. "I didn't want to disturb him just now so thank you for meeting with us. As you know, Sam and I are the leads in the band, and we thought of your offer long and hard plus we also ran it by the rest of the band to ensure we're all on the same page." Dave nods and sips more of his coffee while Luke continues, "Dave, your offer is excellent and I'd go as far as to say it's the stuff that dreams are made of. Who wouldn't go for it, right?"

Dave agrees. "True. I have another band right now with the same offer and they snapped it up. Everyone wants to cut a record or album these days, but finding the right band with the right sound is the biggest challenge, and you guys have that sound and talent. I really believe you could go places."

"Thank you, we're flattered by your praise and confidence in us, but after much reflection all members of our band decided this is not what we want."

Dave's face almost blanches in shock and I try not to smile. "You mean you're going to throw this opportunity away?" Dave asks with incredulity in his voice.

Luke motions for the waiter to bring another round of coffees while he gives Dave a chance to recover. I can just imagine what Luke's thinking, which is exactly what I'm thinking—Dave probably never had anyone reject his promise of fame and fortune and he most likely doesn't know how to deal with it, but after a moment he finds his normal voice. "May I ask why?"

"It's quite simple really; each member of the band has their own personal reason for not going ahead with this opportunity. We came together as The Eclectics for the sake of having a regular gig at Tom's pub, but prior to this we were never a band and each of us had their own separate gig, and we also have different plans for our future."

The coffee arrives and we sip in silence for a while, giving Dave a chance to respond, which he does after a few moments. "All I can say is it's a shame, but I understand this isn't for everyone. So what will you do now?"

"Simplify things a little," Luke smiles my way.

"I have a band ready to go on by next fortnight," Dave informs us, "so if you want to finish immediately that's okay with me or you can go through until the end of the month."

"Whatever suits you is fine by us."

We finish our coffees and stand. Dave shakes hands with Luke and me. "I have sufficient time to promote this new band so I'm happy to release you guys immediately."

"Thank you, and please feel free to let us know if this other band should need more time. We'll be happy to fill in."

Dave seems surprised at Luke's accommodating manner. "That's very decent of you; I appreciate it." He then turns to me. "It was a pleasure working with you, too, Sam, plus the other boys in the band." And on this note, we end the meeting.

On the way home, we pick up some groceries and a takeaway roasted chicken for dinner with baked vegetables. Dora's working at the store with Ricky until five and we expect her home at any moment, so we're surprised to see her when we arrive and go through to the kitchen to put away the food. She's sitting at the table with a cup of tea.

"Dora, you're home early," I say.

"No need to worry, Sam," Dora replies. "Ah, I see you brought groceries and dinner. How lucky am I?"

Luke starts putting things away while I pour tea for us all. It's only gone five and it's too early for dinner, but I'm hungry. "Luke, get some biscuits, please."

Luke nods and Dora says, "Not too many or you'll spoil your dinner."

We sit with Dora and I munch into a shortbread biscuit.

"I'm actually glad you're here as I want to talk with you two. This is why I came home early, just in case you had other plans for the evening."

Luke and I glance at each other and he turns to Dora. "Are you feeling okay? You're not coming down with something, I hope."

Dora pats his hand and smiles. "You are so sweet to care, my dear boy, thank you. And I'm just fine, but there is something I wish to tell you both."

Luke and I wait for Dora to continue and she draws out a large envelope from a kitchen cabinet behind her. "It's best if you read it," she says and hands it to me. I draw out a document with the logo of a legal firm and my heart stops. I look up at Dora and she says, "Well, don't gawp, dear, just read it and then pass it on to Luke."

It takes me a couple of minutes to read what turns out to be Dora's Will and I feel tears run down my face that I can't control. Dora gazes my way while Luke has concern written all over his face. When I'm done reading, I pass on the document to Luke while Dora gives me a box of tissues so I can dry my face. I turn to Luke and see the surprise on his face, but at least he doesn't cry. In fact, he seems stunned more than anything else.

Dora takes the document off him when he's finished reading and puts it back in the envelope. For a moment no one talks, but after a while Dora says, "Well? Have you two lost your tongue? Sam, I've never known you to be speechless; and Luke, please don't look so stunned, dear."

I still can't control my voice in case I break into tears again, but I do manage to get some words out of my mouth. "You're sick? We can't lose you!"

Dora bursts into laughter and both Luke and I gaze at her as if she's lost her mind. "Oh, you young people, haven't you ever been taught to make a Will in case something happens to you?"

I breathe a sigh of relief and my normal voice comes back. "I'm so glad you're not ill, Dora, you gave us quite a shock!"

Luke agrees. "You're one for surprises, but I'm happy you're okay. As for what's in this document, I have no right to be here. This is between you and Sam."

"Not so, dear. Your name's also in my Will and I want to know what you and Sam think."

"But Dora," Luke argues, "this is more about Sam than anything else; I don't count."

"You stay here, Luke, and let Sam speak first," Dora admonishes him with laughter in her eyes.

I'm fully recovered from the shock by now and thankfully my tears have stopped falling. "Dora, I don't know what to say. No one has ever cared this much for me and I've never owned anything of value, which explains why I never made a Will. But, surely, you must have other extended family. But to will your possessions, including your home, to me is crazy. I don't mean to be ungrateful; I'm simply shocked, surprised, and most of all touched, but if I go on talking, I'll cry again."

"Very well, dear, so let me do the talking," Dora says. "After Anne died, not one single relative came to visit. I had some cousins, but I was never close to my Uncle, my father's brother, who didn't get on with my father and always looked down his nose at us because shortly before my father died he was impoverished after losing his investments. As you may remember, Anne and I inherited this apartment from a wealthy aunt on my mother's side.

"She was a dear lady and never married, but she loved us very much and we were like her daughters. And this is one thing I learned from Aunty Nell, she believed that a woman should always remain independent as far as financial issues are concerned. Many were the women of that time that lost all their possessions when they married, and heaven forbid if the man turned out to be a cad, beat his wife and took her fortune! But in those days, once you married a man all your possessions automatically became his.

"In any case, I don't have any family left. I believe my cousins died out, too, but we never kept in touch and good riddance to them in any case. Sam, you're the only person in this world who looked after me so I didn't have to go into aged care when Anne passed on. I would have lost my cosy home and my freedom. You're the daughter I never had and you built a family around me with Luke, Helen and Tom, and now Ricky. You changed my life in so many ways that there is no way I could ever repay you."

I start to cry again, but Dora ignores my tears and keeps talking. "I intend living at least into my nineties, if that's my destiny, so you won't be rid of me just yet," she says with determination, making us laugh and lightening the atmosphere in the kitchen. "Sam, you're the sole heir to all my possessions and everything will be in your name, but I want to include Luke in the Will because I love him and he has become like the son I never had. And because I'm so sure you two will stay together for the rest of your lives, as long as Luke lives with you, protects you, and loves you, he can live here for the rest of his life, too. But if for some reason, and I really doubt this, you two decide to split up then Luke will have to leave this home, which will always remain in Sam's name.

"Having said this, I want to provide Luke with a few of my investments because he should have something, too." Dora then smiles wickedly and says, "Of course, if you beat up on my darling Sam, you get nothing, Luke, and Sam has the right to smash a guitar over your head." This makes us all laugh.

"Lastly, I'd like to say that I'm positive you two will live and love together until the end of your lives. I say this because I know about Sam's background and the life she was forced to lead; and I know you also came from a broken home, Luke." Dora stops for a moment as if she's trying to find the right words, then she continues, "I hope you don't mind my saying this, my dear boy, but since I've met you I caught a kind of haunted look in your eyes now and then. I don't know what happened to you in your youth and it's not my business to pry, either, but as someone who has many years over you and much life experience I can tell when a soul has been broken."

I turn to Luke and see no emotion on his face, but when I look closer I can see the threat of tears, which he's holding back with all his might.

Dora distracts him by patting his hand again. "I said I spotted a broken soul, but recently I detected a change in you, my dear; and I can see the love between you and Sam is so strong that you are both healing within, even as I speak. I no longer see a broken soul in you, Luke, nor do I see one in Sam, and if you like to humour an old lady, please believe me when I say that when you two met, your souls came together like two pieces of a puzzle that fit with each other perfectly."

I don't know about Luke, but I know I'm stunned. How could Dora have picked up on all this? If Luke hadn't told me about that awful attack I would never have known his soul was broken. I guess I'm still too young to pick up on these things, but I hope as I grow older I will develop more wisdom.

Luke doesn't say a word, he simply gets up from the table and goes to Dora, where he takes hold of both her hands and kisses them.

Chapter 62 - Robert

<u>1970, London, England</u>

Just as I was preparing to depart for the States, one of Mike's rescuers came down with the flu and had to be replaced at the last minute for a mission that couldn't be rescheduled.

This particular mission consists of an escape via the Baltic Sea and the rescue group is made up of guys from the UK, West Germany and Denmark. The plan is for the refugees to make their way to a small fishing town outside of Rostock, which is around 150 miles from Berlin. Here, we pick them up by sea on a fishing boat from Falster, which is on the southern tip of Denmark, approximately 137 miles from the German border.

There are fifty refugees meeting us near Rostock comprising of men, women and a small number of children. We'll take them to safety where a Danish team from Copenhagen will travel to our meeting point at Falster and transport them to sanctuary.

When I heard about this mission from one of the rescuers in Mike's group, I volunteered to replace the guy who couldn't make it. The mission captured my imagination and it reminded me of the war, especially when our troops were transported by sea in the Battle of Italy back in 1943.

How ironic that we were once again facing the same enemy, but this time with a different demographic. A portion of the enemies we fought against back in WWII were now trying to escape from their own motherland, East Germany, while the other portion in West Germany were working with us.

Chapter 63 - Samantha

1988/89, London, England/Berlin, Germany

It seems as if life has come full circle and I am happier for it. Giving up the Odeon gig was the best thing we ever did. The band that took over from us made it big, but they lasted a short time and soon became a '1980s has-been' minus the lead singer, who tragically committed suicide. This occurred at the beginning of 1988 by which time The Eclectics had a popular gig four nights a week at The Treble and Bass with the original members of the band.

Chris finally got tired of different 'chicks' every night and it was then he met a lovely girl called Laura; she transformed him to the point where he became a one-woman man and to everyone's surprise he and Laura got married. Marcus still remains single, but he loves his freedom and he's never short of female company and good friends.

Helen and Dora's store is still running and has introduced expanded services for wardrobe and make-up by its resident artist, Ricky. The whole venture turned into a success story, especially when Helen returned to work fulltime after little Bianca was old enough to feel comfortable with a nanny.

The light in Luke's eyes these days is pretty much fully restored. Once we made changes in our lives, Dora went on to pronounce Luke's soul as pretty much healed. She tells me that along with the good, there will always be some of the bad, but if the good outbalances the bad, then all is well. Dora also goes as far as to predict that I will have a child by Luke, but not just yet. I'm twenty-six now and as far as she's concerned, Dora says I won't be ready until age thirty or thereabouts.

I'm not planning on a family, and only the future will tell. Of course, I never take any of this seriously, but I do make a quick calculation in my head that Luke will be forty-two if I have a child at thirty; this seems the perfect age for a man to become a father. After all, men usually take longer to mature than women—at least that's what Dora says.

Another gig I recently gave up is Classical Cocktails. This enables me to spend more time with Dora, even though Diane's still employed by us, but having Diane around enables me to travel with Luke, who remains involved with the MFF group, although the part he plays in it mainly involves finding gigs for refugee musicians. We travel to Berlin at least twice a month and Luke acquaints me with his muso agent business and I help out where I can while at the same time I'm learning to speak German and becoming quite fluent.

————◉————

Luke and I are in Berlin for a couple of days when he gets a phone call at six in the morning. He's on the phone for a few minutes and then rings off.

"What's going on?" I stretch and sit up in bed.

"My MFF leader's in Berlin," Luke replies. "He wants to meet this morning, hoping I can babysit a few refugees while he goes to the Berlin MFF headquarters to make arrangements for these people."

I look confused. "Shouldn't he have done this before? And didn't you say your MFF leader is based with the London group?"

"Yes, and this is who called just now. He had to travel at the last minute to take over for this latest group of refugee arrivals because the Berlin MFF leader is on an urgent rescue that came up at the last minute so someone has to go with the Berlin group and look after them."

"And your MFF leader, the London guy, what will he do with these people and how come he needs you?" I get out of bed and put on the jug to boil for coffee.

"Mike doesn't speak German, so he can't do much unless one of us can translate. The group's already at the Berlin headquarters and we need to send these people to their respective asylum locations."

I can only make instant coffee seeing as waiting for room service breakfast will make us run late, so I return to bed with our coffees and some biscuits. "Okay, now I understand. And is there anything I can help with?"

Luke replies, "I don't see why not. This'll be like an orientation type of session in order to prepare the refugees for life in the West; answer any questions they might have, and so on."

320

"What time do we need to be there?"

"Nine. Enough time for a quick shower and something more solid to eat on the way," Luke replies and once we finish our coffees we spring into action.

The Berlin MFF headquarters is located in the basement of an old five-storey office building in a dead end street that runs off the Ku-damm and which is within walking distance of our hotel. Luke and I walk past Fasanen Strasse, where I used to stay on my trips to Berlin, and I wonder if Herr Groth is still running his quaint hotel.

After two blocks north of this intersection, Luke and I turn right into a narrow lane and we enter a grey stone building that has seen better days. The foyer is small and there's a stairwell to the left leading down to the basement.

"This looks a little spooky, don't you think?" I whisper in Luke's ear.

Luke responds in his normal tone of voice. "The building only has a few offices running businesses because the rent's cheap, but in a couple of years developers are converting the place into flats and then all the occupants here will have to move out."

We descend the stairway and find ourselves in front of a solid timber door, but before we can ring the bell the door opens suddenly and a tall man in his late fifties or early sixties, with curly graying hair and unusual amber eyes, ushers us in and leads us to a small room that offers a view of a large office across the hallway where about fifteen people, mainly males, are sitting around a couple of large wooden tables.

The man invites us to sit at a small desk while he takes a seat opposite us. "Thank you so very much, Luke, for helping out. You really got me out of a jam; otherwise, the whole thing would've been delayed," says the MFF leader when we're all sitting around the desk. Then he turns to me with a questioning gaze. "But where are my manners? Luke, please introduce me to your companion."

"Mike Jobson, meet Samantha Kelly, my partner in crime," Luke replies with a smile and one of my hands in his.

I extend my right hand to shake Mike's, but his gaze is still on me, staring, and I suddenly think I must have snot coming out of my nose or something. "What's wrong?" I say, but get no reply. I retrieve my hand and shoot a glance in Luke's direction; he also seems to be wondering what's going on.

"Mike, are you okay?" Luke's voice seems to break the trancelike gaze Mike has been giving me, but his eyes keep returning to me and I begin to feel uncomfortable.

"What's going on here?" I address Mike with a glare.

He suddenly snaps out of it and smiles. "My God! You're Sam Kelly! Rob's daughter. Don't you remember me, Sam?"

I stare at him with my mouth half open, and I feel Luke squeezing my hand, which he hasn't yet released from his grasp so I feel a sense of reassurance. "I'm sorry," I say, "but do I know you?"

Mike breaks into laughter. "Sam! My little Sam! I've been looking for you for as long as I can remember."

I turn to Luke with concern in my eyes and practically sit on his lap, especially as Mike stands up and looks as if he's going to try and hug me.

"Mike, care to explain what's going on?" Luke stands up with me, still holding onto my hand, and I hold onto his arm tightly with my other hand.

Mike suddenly seems to come to his senses and he bids us to sit back down. "I'm so very sorry. I didn't mean to frighten anyone, but there's so much I have to tell Sam." Then he turns to me, "Sam, I held you in my arms when you were born, and you lived in my home for a couple of years until Rob recovered from detox."

I feel my head beginning to spin, as if I'm going to faint, but Luke holds my body against his and helps me to sit down. "Got some water?" Luke asks Mike.

Mike nods and exits the office. Meanwhile, Luke cradles me, trying to reassure me, and I'm in a kind of daze where I think I'm in someone else's life.

When Mike returns, he brings some bottled water and a bottle of scotch with three glasses. Luke opens the water for me and also pours a bit of scotch in a glass. "Drink up," he says, "and try to relax. You've had a shock."

"I apologise for throwing this at you without warning, Sam. It's just that once Luke said your name, I suddenly recognised you even though I haven't seen you since you were a little girl. In fact, I didn't see much of you because I was travelling with gigs and for MFF, but I did see you from time to time, and the last time was when you were around seven years old. Remember? I used to call you 'Kinky Sammy', after The Kinks, your favourite rock group at the time. And you called me your 'Uncle Trumpet' because I used to play in a jazz band with your father."

I swallow the entire contents of the scotch and ask Luke to give me another and while I drink the second shot it's like something opens up in my mind and it all comes back like an asteroid smashing into earth and opening up a huge hole with all kinds of memory debris spewing out of it.

"Oh my God!" I clutch at Luke's shirtsleeve but he sees the smile on my face and relaxes. I then cross over to Mike and throw my arms around the man and he hugs me back, tears rolling down his face. "Uncle Trumpet! Where have you been all this time? I've been looking for Dad, but for some reason I have no memory of you."

Luke takes me back into his arms and says to Mike, "Why don't we get through this session with your refugees and then I'll take Sam to the hotel for a rest? Are you free for dinner tonight? We can go somewhere quiet and talk."

Mike agrees immediately. "That's a good idea."

Luke glances at me. "And you, my love?"

I nod and tighten my arms around him.

"Okay," says Luke. "You stay here with Mike and chat if you like. We have all night to talk and I'd like to be with you when Mike reveals the whole story. Is that all right with you?" I agree and assure him that we'll wait for him so he can also hear what Mike has to say.

"I'll be a couple of hours at most and then we'll go back to rest at the hotel." Luke kisses me and exits the office.

When we're alone, Mike offers to make coffee and I accept. He returns with freshly brewed coffee and Danish pastries. "I just popped down the road to get these," he says, holding up the bag of pastries, "they go down well with the coffee."

While he sets the coffee and pastries on the desk, I keep getting memory fragments of my childhood coming back to me. "I remember Dad giving me a children's guitar," I remark while trying to stop myself from asking the thousand questions I have inside my head. I don't want to wait until this evening; I want to know everything now.

"It's best to wait for Luke," Mike suggests as if he can read my mind.

"You're right. Even so, before I can even move on from this very moment I have to confirm one thing," I reply, "despite the fact that I already know the answer—I've known it in my heart for many years now. My father's dead, isn't he?"

Mike doesn't speak, but merely nods his head.

I sigh and speak with both a tinge of sadness and relief in my voice, "It's okay, Mike. I think I've known it all along but I just didn't want to believe it."

Mike reaches out and pats my hand in sympathy.

"You know, I've been coming to Berlin since I was sixteen—every year on the 4th of July. Dad told me if we ever became separated by circumstances we should meet by the Wall in Berlin on American Independence Day."

"And you actually came here every year?"

"Yes, only when I was old enough to travel, but about eight years later I stopped coming. I felt something had happened to him; I never believed he'd abandon me; so the only thing that could prevent him from meeting me had to be his death."

Mike regards me with compassion. "There's so much I have to tell you, plus Rob entrusted a journal to me that he'd been keeping since 1943, and there's also a letter he left for you. He gave me these things the last time I saw him. I'll bring them with me this evening and once you read everything you'll know how life unfolded for all of us."

My hand shakes a little and I lift my coffee cup with both hands and take a few sips. "Good coffee," I say while I keep my emotions in check, but there is only one more question that cannot wait until this evening and before I vocalise it, Mike reaches out again and puts his hand over mine.

"He died painlessly, Sam. He volunteered to go on a mission for MFF and was shot along with a group of rescuers."

I help myself to a pastry and take a bite while holding back tears as I tell myself I'll have plenty of time to mourn my father, but right now I choose to be proud of him for the courage he's shown in helping others who couldn't help themselves.

Mike gives me a few moments to myself and then says, "Rob was killed in 1970."

A few traitorous tears escape from my eyes and Mike passes me a box of tissues. "My God! He was already dead all that time when I went to Berlin. I was only eight when he left us for the States, but he didn't go, did he? He lied to me and went to Berlin instead."

"Rob was on his way to the States for a big job opportunity but just before he went, the mission came up and he really wanted to be a part of it."

"Well, at least he told me the truth," I remark. "I was too young to understand at the time and I thought he was off to the US for a music gig and that he'd be back within a few months; and that's when he told me he'd send for me, but if we somehow couldn't find each other we should meet by the Wall."

Mike refills my coffee and I take a few sips while I compose myself. I quickly look through the office window to find Luke glancing my way and I paste a smile on my face to reassure him; he smiles back before he turns to the refugees in the group.

"We'd best wait for Luke or he'll get upset with me," Mike remarks.

I reassure him, "Luke and I are of one mind and soul. Out of all that's gone wrong in my life, and his, we managed to find each other and only death will separate us. Luke simply wants to be present when you tell me everything because he wants to protect me and give me emotional support. In any case, I won't pester you with more questions now; I have enough to digest until this evening, but tell me how you and Luke know each other and why you never made the connection that you both knew me."

Mike relaxes, knowing Luke won't get upset with him. "Well, that's a simple enough story. I was elected leader of MFF in London since the Wall went up. I was thirty five at the time and I had some connections with musicians in Berlin who also started a group, and this is how the network spread. We help anybody—they don't necessarily have to be musos—having said this, our focus is mainly on musicians.

"I met Luke when he joined our group in 1975. He was a young punk in his twenties with a huge heart. Not only this, but he spoke fluent German and that was something we needed desperately at the time. He used to be in some band that was going places, but apparently he decided to change from that path and became our liaison between the UK and Germany, plus he was heavily involved in finding gigs for refugee musos."

The first thought in my head was that Luke went straight to MFF pretty much after that horrible incident—I should say his rape, but I still can't bring myself to think of what the love of my life had to endure so I banish the thought and focus on my discussion with Mike. "I met Luke in '85 and in all that time until now he never mentioned me?"

"No. Luke keeps his personal life to himself and having lost track of you since Rob left, there was no reason why I should mention your name to him."

"Life's crazy sometimes, isn't it? Things might have turned out so differently if somehow you'd found me back then."

"I know," Mike agrees, "but I believe in destiny. Had I found you back then, things might have been a lot more different than they are now. Perhaps you just had to meet Luke first to help get you through whatever obstacles you faced in your life to date." Mike glances towards the room where Luke seems to be wrapping things up. "It looks like we've been talking for two hours, but it seems like it's been only ten minutes. Luke's almost finished and so I'll see you guys this evening, but let me tell you this: the love Luke has for you is the real thing. I saw it in his eyes the moment he introduced you to me."

I go over to Mike and hug him. "Thank you, Uncle Trumpet. I'm so happy we reconnected. I finally found a family member who cared for me when I was little and I love you; and my love for Luke is the real thing, too."

I kiss Mike's cheek just as Luke makes his entry to the office. "Hey!" he calls out with feigned bravado, "stay away from my woman." We laugh.

Chapter 64 - Samantha

Luke and I grab a quick bite of lunch at a nearby café on the Ku-damm and on arrival to our hotel the front desk clerk gives us a package addressed to me. I know immediately what it is, but I wait until we get to our room to unwrap it. The package has an attached note from Mike, which reads:

Dear Sam,

I thought you may want to read through this before we meet for dinner.

See you both this evening,

Uncle Mike.

I pass the note to Luke and he says, "Do you want to read this alone? I can make myself scarce if you like."

I hug him. "No. I want us both to read this together. I don't keep any secrets from you; you're my family." I bring his mouth to mine and we share a long kiss that overcomes the sexual impulse but amplifies the feelings of love we have for each other; so we make ourselves comfortable, sitting back on a bunch of pillows in bed with the journal.

We read silently and wait for the other to finish a page before we turn to the next one. There are times when I want to say something, but I force myself to continue reading; questions and remarks will be addressed when we see Mike this evening.

Reading about my father's relationship with this woman, Clara, mystifies me because he never mentioned her to me, but of course he wouldn't mention this to a child. What would my mother have said if I'd let out by chance that my father's first wife was killed? As a child, I wouldn't have had an adult's filtering system; therefore, my dad obviously decided to omit mentioning Clara altogether.

I go on reading about my father's time during the war, the move to the US afterwards, his marriage to Clara, the rejection of his parents because Clara was German, the move to the UK, the happiness he found in life with Clara, and finally the tragedy of Clara: pregnant after so many years of trying and being caught on the East side of the Wall, divided from my father and killed by the East Germans.

My father's meltdown at this tragedy was understandable and after his time in detox he managed to move on, and this was when he met my mother. I realise now that my mother wasn't ready to have a child; she merely wanted to follow her musical career, so I don't understand why she bothered to have a baby. I guess it could've been an accident; I may never know why she had me, but whatever the reason I can never forgive her for giving me up after my father left us. It is good to know, however, that my father had every intention of returning for me, and he was even going to take me on holidays to Berlin.

Regarding Uncle Mike, I can only say the man tried everything to help my father, especially when Clara was trapped in East Berlin. As for my mother, Mike never mentioned during my childhood that Peggy was his sister, but then I don't seem to have many memories of my childhood. Could it be that I blocked them out during the years of going from foster home to foster home and finally to the streets?

When we finish reading the journal I remark, "Mike mentioned something about a letter from my father, but it doesn't seem to be here."

"He'll probably bring it this evening," Luke replies and takes my hand. "How do you feel after reading all this, my love?"

I shrug. "I don't know. I think there's more to this story and, hopefully, Mike will be able to answer my questions."

"What about your dad's death?"

I shiver. "Actually, I had goose bumps about his passing. It brought back the time you were injured during the Baltic Sea rescue. What are the chances of that? The two men I love; both shot at the Baltic Sea. And now I finally understand why Dad's name never appeared in a German death register—the East Germans didn't register those they massacred outright, it may be that they only recorded the names of the victims for their own secret documents, right?" I pause and shake my head at the horrid thought of how my father was executed.

"Regarding my father's death, though, at least he didn't suffer and for all it's worth he got to go on that mission. It's tragic, of course, plus the decision he made led to the path my life took. Had he lived, he would've come back home and taken me to Berlin with him. I know he and my mother were ready to split up, but at least I would have lived with my father and my life would've been very different.

"I don't mean to sound ungrateful; I love my father, but at the same time there's a kind of resentment in me because he just didn't think of his daughter when he went on that rescue mission. Anyway, I've mourned him for a long time, never knowing why he left, but I will find a way to forgive him for abandoning me—I know now this was never his intention."

Evening arrives all too quickly and I start to feel anxious. There are still questions that only Mike will be able to answer and I have a feeling that something just doesn't click with the story of my father's life. Something's missing, but what?

We arranged to meet at a quiet upmarket restaurant just off the Ku-damm. Luke booked a corner table and upon arrival we find Mike already seated, drinking a glass of red.

"Are we late?" I ask.

"Not at all," Mike replies, smiling, "the taxi driver just drove too fast."

A waiter appears with menus. "Would you like to order any drinks before dinner?"

Luke glances at us. "Wine all around?"

I nod immediately and Mike comments, "You should try this pinot noir, it's really smooth."

Luke orders a bottle of the wine and the waiter fills our water glasses on the table from a carafe. "I'll be back with the wine and to take your food order." He walks away.

We chat once we make our selection from the menu. "Did you get the refugees settled?" Luke asks.

"Yes, thanks. After you left, a couple of our local rescuers returned and took charge of them."

"And the rescue mission?"

"All went well," Mike responds, "which means I'm flying back home tomorrow morning." Then, he turns to me. "And when you guys get back to London we must get together socially."

"In that case, you'll have to come to one of our gigs at The Treble and Bass," I say.

"That's a great idea! Imagine living so close to Covent Garden and never having bumped into you."

The waiter arrives with the wine, which he pours for us, and then he takes our order. Mike draws a small envelope out of his jacket pocket and when the waiter goes off he hands it to me. "I expect you already read Rob's journal; this is the note he left for you. It's best if you read it before I explain the rest."

I feel my hand shake a little as I take the envelope, but after a few sips of wine I tear it open and pull out a piece of paper. This is the last communication I receive from my father and it's kind of unnerving to read it in front of the others, but I don't want to wait until later so I unfold the piece of paper and read it.

My dearest Sam,

If you're reading this note it means I'm no longer alive and for this I am so sorry. I know I should have thought of you before I decided to go on one more rescue mission to Berlin, and I hope you will forgive me for this.

Your Uncle Mike promised me he would look after you if anything happened to me, so I am relieved that at least you will have family around you. Peggy will also be back in London after her singing tour in New York and between her and Mike, I'm sure you will be cared for. Whatever savings I had I gave to Peggy for her tour, but I also left money with her for your safekeeping plus this will go toward your living expenses and education.

Sam, there's also something I never told you, and I regret this. At the time, I was battling ill health and spent time in detox and when I got out, I married Peggy and we became a family, so there seemed to be no point in making matters more complicated for you. I realize now, however, that I should have been truthful with you and so I hope once you learn this you won't think too badly of me and that you will remember how much I love you.

Uncle Mike will explain the details, but I want to be the one to tell you that Peggy is not your biological mother. Your mother was my beautiful Clara, who as far as I know was killed by the East Germans, but not before you were born prematurely and survived.

I gave a photo of Clara to Mike so he can pass it onto you. You have so much of your mother in you, especially her big brown eyes with such a magic light in them that people always wanted to be close to her. My dear Sam, you have inherited my hair color, but your eyes are Clara's, as is the spirit of strength that you both share.

Dearest daughter, I know I could have been a better father to you, and I wish I had, but now it's too late for regrets. All I can say is that both your mother and I love you very much. Of course, it's a tragedy that Clara did not live to see you grow up, but she was so happy to know she would have a baby—and that baby was you.

Forgive me, my dear Sam, for all the pain I have caused you without meaning to do so, and please remember that no matter where I am, I will always love you and so will Clara.

Your loving father forever,
Robert Kelly

Luke is the first person to see the tears rolling down my face so he passes me a handkerchief; good thing he had the foresight to carry one. Mike looks on with sympathy in his eyes as he draws a rectangular piece of semi-matt paper out of his jacket pocket and hands it to me. And it is then that I see the face of my real mother for the first time in the 1961 photo, which was taken just before she went to East Berlin with me, hiding in her tummy and not yet showing.

My eyes are still shedding tears and I feel too choked up to speak. I pass on my father's note and Clara's photo to Luke and excuse myself from the table by going to the ladies room. Fortunately, there is no one in the ladies and I can give way to my tears and then take the time to put cool water over my eyes with paper towels. It takes some time to make myself look presentable again, but I achieve this with a little make-up I'm carrying in my handbag.

When I regain my composure, I rejoin the men and notice the meals have arrived. My stomach turns at the sight of food and I know I can't eat a single morsel. All I can manage is a cappuccino.

"Perhaps it wasn't such a good idea to come to a restaurant," I remark when I reach the table. "You guys eat while I order myself a coffee."

Luke takes my hand in his and gives it a squeeze. "Do you want to go back to the hotel?"

"No. You guys finish dinner and then I have some questions for you, Mike. Right now, I just want to have a cappuccino."

Luke immediately signals the waiter and tells him to take away my meal and then he orders the coffee along with some little cakes on the side. The waiter removes my plate and goes to fill the new order.

"You're right, Sam," Mike says. "We should've gone to the hotel."

I smile at him. "Please, don't worry. You guys need to eat something, and then we can talk."

After dinner, we go back to the hotel for a nightcap in our room. We sit at a round table by the window and Luke grabs glasses and a number of small liquor bottles from the minibar fridge; the men go for scotch and I'm lucky the hotel stocks my favourite drink, Baileys Irish Cream.

"What happened to Peggy?" I ask.

"She returned to New York," Mike states, sounding rather terse. "Soon after we got the news of Robert's passing, Peggy packed her bags and was never seen again by any of us. She took all the money your father entrusted to her for your upbringing and used it for her new life in America."

"Lovely," I reply with sarcasm in my voice.

Mike says with a tone of disapproval. "She was meant to come back and look after you until Robert returned, but once she knew he wouldn't be coming back she turned you over to welfare. I almost killed her when I found out. Then, while I spent years following you from foster home to foster home, but I could never find you because you'd run away from each of them and, as far as the authorities knew, you lived on the streets so in the end even the system lost you. I blamed myself for what happened because I trusted Peggy and she let us down, especially you. I even tried to find her through contacts in New York, but she proved to be so elusive that no one could find her. In the end, I was told she most likely changed her name and appearance, and probably headed to California. Apparently, many people disappeared that way in those days."

"Well," I say after my second drink of Baileys, "at least she's not my biological mother and for this I'm grateful." I feel Luke take hold of my hand and I glance his way, my love for him shining in my eyes. "I'm so glad you're here," I say in a low voice and he squeezes my hand in response.

"There is something that doesn't gel though," I address Mike. "If Clara was my mother, why is Peggy's name on my birth certificate?"

Mike finishes his scotch and Luke replenishes our drinks. "We smuggled you out of East Berlin and brought you back to the UK, where we registered your birth under Rob and Peggy's name because by this time the tragedy of Clara, a UK citizen killed in East Berlin, became public, there was much pressure from above not to start an international incident. The East German government went as far as claiming responsibility for Clara's death, which they referred to as an 'unfortunate incident' but they denied anything about a baby.

"We tried to appeal to the UK Embassy to clarify this and get the truth. Unfortunately, their hands were tied behind their backs with all the Cold War stuff going on and by this time Clara had already been executed and the East German side got away with it, plus we had no real proof that Clara was actually killed.

"A witness, from MFF, came forward and declared he saw something that night, but this was dismissed as unreliable, especially because it was a dark, snowy night and he could have seen anything. Unfortunately, we didn't even have photo evidence to show Clara being apprehended while heavily pregnant, so the East Germans claimed this was all an invention by the witness," Mike pauses here and I look down at my drink, hiding the new light of tears in my eyes.

"So how did you get to Sam?" Luke asks and surprises me because I hadn't even thought of this.

Mike says, "This is quite upsetting." He gazes my way, "Do you really want to know the details?"

I look up, fortified by my drink. "I have a right to know."

"You do," Mike agrees, "but it's ugly."

"I still want to hear it," I insist.

"Very well." Mike nods. "After the East German guards shot all the refugees and most of the rescuers, Clara went into labour and the guards didn't seem to know what to do. One of our rescuers, the actual witness that came forward in the first place, was in hiding and managed to see what happened. Basically, Clara delivered the baby by herself and afterwards the guards dragged her away, leaving the baby behind, which someone wrapped up in a soldier's coat. After this, we're not sure what happened with Clara, but the rescuer who witnessed your birth had seconds to make a decision, which was to sneak up to the checkpoint, take the baby, and run like hell or leave it there to die. He chose to take you and luckily was not seen by the guards because everyone was too busy dealing with Clara's situation." Mike's voice is on the point of breaking and Luke refills his glass; Mike swallows the shot in full.

I close my eyes, trying not to shed tears, and I feel Luke's arms around me as he sits on the armrest of my chair, holding me close.

"In the end," Mike continues, "the rescuer left you at the UK Embassy, but he didn't want to become further involved, especially after he was not believed the first time around and the fact that he still had no evidence; after all, showing up with a baby meant it could be anybody's baby and not necessarily Clara's. Therefore, we, representing this witness as part of MFF, requested the issue of a birth certificate under Rob's and Peggy's name. Rob was not in a state to function at the time with the intense grief of Clara's death and I had to make the decision as to what to do. Peggy suggested we put down her name as your mother rather than 'mother deceased or mother unknown.'"

"What a crazy mess," I remark. "But why didn't my father tell me about Clara when I was older?"

"He married Peggy shortly after he came out of detox and things were going well for them at the time, so he didn't see a reason to burden you with the truth. After all, you were still his daughter and this is what counted most to him."

It's past three in the morning by the time we finish our talk and we're exhausted. Mike returns to London in a few hours and he prepares to leave; he gives me a hug and says, "I'll catch you in London now that I know where to find you." He shakes hands with Luke and then we're alone. "Are you okay?" Luke gathers me in his arms.

I put my arms around his neck. "I need time to process all this, especially the ugliness of the events that led to my real mother dying, the death of my father, and the life I led thanks to Peggy's actions. But I don't want to think about the ugly things right now, all I want is to be with you."

We kiss with a passion that leaves no doubt that we will always be two lone wolves hunting in a pack.

Chapter 65 - Samantha

<u>Nov, 1989, Berlin, Germany</u>

Luke and I have been together for almost four and a half years and we truly have become lone wolves hunting in a pack. The irony is that we're not alone at all, and this is by choice. We love each other's company and spend most of our time together composing music, performing at gigs; and yes, we still play at The Treble and Bass. I also gave up Classical Cocktails and turned to teaching classical piano to young people, just as Declan taught me when we were together.

Luke and I may be together most of the time, but we also have a wonderful circle of family and friends. Our family includes Dora and Uncle Mike, and our friends are many, including Tom and Helen, Ricky, Chris and his wife, Laura, plus Marcus and a whole bunch of people from MFF. Luke and I have been involved in helping refugees settle in the West and Luke still finds gigs for East German musos.

I feel Luke and I have been blessed in life—a life that started rough and ugly, but one that changed into music, laughter, and love. We never take this for granted and we make every day count because as some say 'life can change at the snap of two fingers' and this is so true. Life can change for the better or for the worse, but in our situation life has changed for many people—and for the better!

In early November, 1989, Luke and I took one of our short trips to Berlin in order to audition some refugee musos, and overnight, like a miracle from heaven, the Wall came down. And on the 9th of November, Berlin became a crowded city full of elation, freedom, and hope for the future. The Cold War was over and the Wall that changed so many lives for the worse was no more, giving way to the most incredible reunion of East and West.

Life in Berlin really did change at the snap of two fingers and Luke and I celebrated with millions of people. We hugged, we kissed, we cried with joy, we took pieces of the Wall and watched it get smaller and smaller by the hour.

Seeing this incredible spectacle brought to mind a snippet of the lyrics written by one of my favourite musicians: *'We can be heroes, just for one day'*

THE END

HEROES

Note from The Berlin Wall: "The Fall of the Wall"

On November 9, 1989, as the Cold War began to thaw across Eastern Europe, an East German Communist Party spokesman announced a series of new policies regarding border crossings. When pressed on when the changes would take place, he said "As far as I know... effective immediately, without delay." East Berliners flocked to border checkpoints, some chanting "Tor auf!" ("Open the gate!"). Within hours, the guards were letting the crowds through where West Berliners greeted them with flowers and champagne.

More than two million people from East Berlin visited West Berlin that weekend to participate in a celebration that was, one journalist wrote, 'the greatest street party in the history of the world'. People used hammers and picks to knock away chunks of the wall—they became known as 'mauerspechte', or 'wall woodpeckers'—while cranes and bulldozers pulled down section after section. Soon the wall was gone and Berlin was united for the first time since 1945. 'Only today,' one Berliner spray-painted on a piece of the wall, 'The war is really over.'

The reunification of East and West Germany was made official on October 3, 1990, almost one year after the fall of the Berlin Wall.

Source: History.com.editors – Berlin Wall

About the author

Sylvia Massara is a multi-genre author based in Sydney, Australia. She loves to dabble in wacky love affairs, drama, thrillers, sci-fi and anything else that takes her fancy over good coffee.

Born in Argentina from Italian descent and with a fusion of Spanish, Swiss and Scandinavian lineage, plus transplanted to Australia at age ten, Sylvia describes herself as a bit of a moggie cat by way of mixed pedigree. She is also a citizen of the world as she has travelled widely throughout most of her life and she is the proud owner of three passports.

As with most authors, Sylvia draws on her varied experience from the often puzzling tapestry of life and she tends to live vicariously through the many characters inside her head. Sylvia loves nature and communing with the animal kingdom (as her pampered kitty, Mia, will attest). Occasionally, however, Sylvia ventures into the world of humans, albeit for a limited time as she prefers the unconditional and genuine company that animals bring to our planet.

Sylvia has recently published her eighth novel plus she has a number of other projects on the go, which have been approved by her eternal muse—the great David Bowie.

www.ingramcontent.com/pod-product-compliance
Lightning Source LLC
Chambersburg PA
CBHW022247020726
47496CB00004B/1107